T0196923

LACKING IN
SUBSTANCE

A NOVEL

LAURA OTIS

LACKING IN SUBSTANCE
A NOVEL

iUniverse books may be ordered through booksellers or by contacting:

iUniverse
1663 Liberty Drive
Bloomington, IN 47403
www.iuniverse.com
1-800-Authors (1-800-288-4677)

ISBN: 978-1-5320-8716-5 (sc)
ISBN: 978-1-5320-8715-8 (e)

Library of Congress Control Number: 2019919772

Print information available on the last page.

iUniverse rev. date: 12/09/2019

CHAPTER 1

ATLANTA

A man calls you a whore when you don't want to touch him; a woman, when he'd rather touch you than her. I've been called a puta so many times, that word circles my blood. It must have pierced me like a virus that bursts out, since everyone can see it on me. Men say I'm a whore when I send them away because I want to sleep with someone else. Women hurl that word when their men prefer me to their melting, marshmallow bodies. Puta, malísima, maleducada, the words pelt me like heavy drops. That's what they call a woman who won't be told how to love.

Me, I've always liked buffets more than restaurants. Why order a whole plate of one thing when you can take what you want of each one? A husband sits like an antagonist on a receptor, blocking molecules that could set off wonders. Why keep a guy in your apartment telling you you're defective when you can meet one for a day who will say you're wonderful, and then go back home to his wife? I guess I should feel sorry for the wives, those poor, fat, scrub-headed things. Instead, I think of the guys, their souls melting in their wives' acidic guilt. Having sex with a married man is like giving a care package to a soldier in a prison camp. I suppose we need marriage for humans to survive, but being bound to one person in a world of seven billion seems as unworthy as suicide.

I mean, let's face it, who wouldn't rather have sex with me? Why settle for some short-haired fat chick telling you to pick up your kid at soccer when you can come inside a hundred pounds of pure energy? Why talk about refurbishing the deck when you can hear about what character you'll be in someone's novel?

"Díme, Mala," asks my friend Gonzalo. "¿Qué tal la novela? How is that novel coming along?"

For years now, that's what everyone's been asking. I wrote *The Rainbow Bar* like I was taking dictation, but Teresa's story is popping out in miserable, constipated pebbles. Without a full draft and a publisher, I won't get tenure, and this summer is my last chance. You can only teach creative writing so long before you have to prove you can write.

But there isn't any novel yet, and there won't be until Teresa starts talking. You can't tell someone's story until you can hear her voice. I can see Teresa, but I still can't hear her, no matter how hard I try. She has brown wrists twice the width of mine, thick bronze arms, a watchful face. Short legs, a rectangular body, and solid, marzipan breasts. A body used to lift, carry, and pull, but topped with shining black hair. A body that does the world's work but is hard to see, hidden under a blue hoodie and jeans.

Maybe Teresa hurts too much to talk, with Raúl pounding her all the time. Not knowing when the next pain-bomb will explode—that will tighten your throat. Maybe Teresa has too much to do, running after a demented lady all day. Teresa grips the trembling arms of Sandy Marshall, who is refusing to wash her hands. Mrs. Marshall has crescents of brown shit under her nails because she's been trying to dig it out again. Teresa strains to pull her toward the faucet since crazy people are so strong—they never hold any of their forces back. Teresa is gaining, her brown wrists nearing the white sink, but Mrs. Marshall clenches her teeth and balks. A few years ago, my mother used to fight me just like that.

It's been a while now since I visited her in her nursing home in Pennsylvania. For the past six years, she's been wasting there, unable to speak, move, or see. When I can stand it, I fly up and talk to her, tell her stories and wheel her outside. Maybe she knows me, so I try to feed her, this thing that can only swallow and shit. I heap pureed turkey on a spoon and shove it between her rotted teeth. Like porridge, it bubbles back out again. Seeing the mixture of brown paste and hanging drool, my stomach heaves once—twice—will I throw up? No. I wipe her mouth on a towel stiff with food and try a spoonful of pureed peas. It still has to eat, this shriveled, greasy thing that used to be my mom.

The image of my mother crushes my thoughts like a relentless hand. I need to get out into the air, where the wind will dissolve her ghost in puffs. If I'm going to write, I need to move, like an old car that won't start unless it rolls. I was going to stay in Atlanta all summer, but why not drive off? There's no partner to be called like a parole officer, no demanding kids, no sulking cat. My mother is safe with her nurses and Louise, who watches her with carping eyes. My car, Wilma, is longing to break the seal between her tires and the gummy asphalt.

I poke my computer, and Google takes me to a San Francisco lab. I press a few buttons, and a soft voice brushes me, quick, husky, professional.

"John Turner here."

"John Turner, this is Carrie McFadden."

Johnny laughs in a quick rhythm. "Carrie McFadden? Are you kiddin' me?"

I'm lucky to have caught him. Nowadays he's always traveling, or protected by secretaries. But at seven thirty in the morning, Johnny Turner is alone in his lab.

"Carrie McFadden." Johnny's mind stalks around me, trying to view me from all sides. "How have you been? What have you been doin'? It's got to be what—five, ten years?"

"I'm going to be driving to San Francisco." I push forward. "I'd like to see you. Should take me about two weeks. Are you going to be there in two weeks?"

"You're still crazy, aren't you?" He chuckles. "You're completely nuts. How'd you ever survive for this long? Listen, I've got a lot goin' on. What do you want to see me about?"

"May thirty-first," I breathe. "What are you doing May thirty-first?"

May 31 twenty years ago is a night I'll never forget.

I met Johnny Turner my very first day in Marty Cohen's lab. I wanted to make myself useful, so I volunteered to help Connie take out the radioactive waste. It was an ugly job and a scary one, emptying the toxic buckets of two groups. To save money, we pooled our trash with that of Wilson's lab, and we were pushing our cart down the long, central alley of his space. I was wearing a white coat and plastic safety goggles, and I had my hair clipped up in back. Unused to all that peripheral vision, I was scanning the benches to see what kind of work Wilson's group did. A batch of blue sequence gels grinned, their toothy smiles halfway down to the electrified fluid.

"We-hell. Hello there!"

Next to the gels stood a tall, thin guy. Six three? Six four? I tilted my head. He had black eyes; light, shiny brown hair; and the biggest hands I ever saw.

"You new here?" he asked.

"Yeah, just started today. Second-year grad student," Connie explained for me.

"Well, welcome!" He smiled. Near the corner of his jaw, a muscle twitched. He loped back toward the far end of the lab, his legs carrying him with a musing glide.

Connie and I continued our round until all the yellow cans had been emptied into the shielded bin. In the freight elevator, I asked, "Who was that southern guy?"

I figured anyone that friendly had to be southern.

Connie looked confused. "Southern? You mean Johnny? I hear he's from West Texas."

She told me Johnny was always in the lab and his cheerful energy never waned. Seven days a week from nine until midnight, he'd be there, solving crises, ordering equipment, frowning at autoradiographs. Johnny ran Wilson's lab, a group of forty people, while Wilson lectured and brought in the grants.

"I couldn't live like that." Connie laughed. "But he seems to like it. There's nothing else he'd rather do."

That spring, I saw Johnny each day. I was purifying vesicles from nerve terminals, updating a procedure from the 1960s. If I could isolate the little sacs of membrane, I might find a marker that would light up young neurons like Christmas trees. It seemed like an exciting project, and I should have loved it, but I knew I didn't belong. I felt like an impostor in another actor's role, and I knew I'd be caught at any moment.

The night of May 31, I stood, pipette in hand, ready to add radioactive antibody to a paper of proteins. I've always loved proteins, the sticky substance of life. Johnny worked on the enzymes that chop them up, altering the enzymes' DNA sequences to learn how they cut. For a second, I paused and leaned to one side. At the far end of Wilson's alley, Johnny sat alone at his desk. I added the antibody and set the timer. Then I took off my gloves.

Johnny was so absorbed in the twisted shape on his screen that he didn't move until the air stirred. He started, his dark eyes warming as he turned.

"What're you doin' here so late?" he asked.

"I'm putting antibody on a Western blot," I said. "What's your excuse?"

"Oh, I'm trying to figure out this enzyme." Johnny rubbed his forehead with his finger and thumb. Across the top of his screen marched amino acids, their three-letter codes announcing them like banners. Underneath them lay a rolling web, his working model of the enzyme.

"Looks like two cats fighting under a quilt."

"That's what my dad would say." Johnny pinched the skin over his nose. He said nothing more, and I feared I'd offended him.

"Are you okay?" I asked. "You have a headache?" Like a butterfly, my hand floated toward his shoulder.

"Yeah." He sighed and looked back at the screen. "I knew I shouldn't have called him. I don't know why I do. Sometimes I just wonder what's goin' on back there."

"Back where?" I stepped in closer until I was inches from his chair. A sweet smell was rising from his hair, which looked warm and shiny under the lamp.

"Oh, West Texas. Out near Amarillo. That's where I'm from. We live on a ranch out there." With his eyes on his web, Johnny released his breath. "My dad's still back there," he said. "He doesn't want me here."

"But he must respect what you're doing. I mean—"

Johnny stared at his enzyme and laughed bitterly. "You know what he calls this? What he said just"—he glanced at his watch—"three, four hours ago?"

"No, what?"

"Jerkin' off. 'You're just jerkin' off out there,' he says."

My hand settled onto Johnny's shoulder. Under his gray shirt, I felt bone and very little warm flesh.

"He doesn't understand what you're doing?"

Johnny spoke as though he were talking to himself. "'Just jerkin' off,' he says. I tell him what I'm doin' here could save people's lives, but he won't buy it. 'When you were little, you used to like playin' with Tinkertoys,' he says. 'I know you, I know what you're like. Well, that's what you're still doin', only now it's on the government's dime. Quit jerkin' off! Grow up!'"

"That's horrible!" I said. "What about your mom?"

Johnny laughed. "Oh, yeah, her. She's proud of me. But she'd be just as proud if I were sellin' cheese graters."

"Gee," I said. "My mom always wanted me to be a scientist. If I hadn't, I think she would have—I don't know—wished I were never born."

For the first time, Johnny seemed to hear me. My hand slipped from his shoulder as he turned.

"You're lucky," he said. "To have someone who cares. To have someone who appreciates what you're doin'."

His eyes fixed me with black intensity.

"Y'know, people—" My voice wavered, and Johnny frowned. "People call you immature when you're different. When you don't want what they want. Makes them feel better about what they do."

"Yeah." Johnny sighed and glanced down at his desk. Under the fresh snow of paper related to tonight's work, its scratched gray surface was bare.

With a quick twist, Johnny turned to face me. "Let's get out of here. Let's go home. I'm sick of this place."

"Home?" I asked.

"Oh—yeah ..." Johnny reddened. "My place. Up on postdoc hill. It's just ten minutes from here. We could talk some more."

I faltered. "I ... just put antibody on my blot."

Johnny grinned and shook his head. "Science. Okay, how long do you need? When have you gotta take it down?"

I looked at my watch. "Forty-five minutes. Then I can leave it in buffer."

"You sure? 'Cause I don't want to ruin your experiment."

Johnny's words sounded strange, and I realized I had never thought of my Westerns as experiments, just as something I had to do.

"No, no, it's okay. I'm sure."

"Okay, then pull up a chair. Here, take that one." He pointed to a stained wooden chair with a stack of journals on it.

I put the heavy stack on the floor and pulled the chair next to his. Johnny draped his arm across my shoulders.

"Here's the sequence," he murmured. He jerked his chin toward the screen. "Somehow it's formin' a pocket, and the protein slips in. Once it's in there, the enzyme grabs it, and— snip!" Two long fingers sliced the air. "These enzymes do all kinds of stuff—they control things we never even thought about. With these restriction enzymes, I can cut chunks out of the gene and know exactly where they are. Past three months, I've been snippin' pieces outa this puppy, but the thing's still cuttin' protein. Wilson says to try here." Johnny scrolled back through the sequence. "But I don't think so. What do you think? Where should I cut next?"

I squinted at the enzyme and cocked my head. "Here." I pointed.

"Why?"

"Hell, I don't know. Why not?"

Johnny doubled over with laughter, which he welcomed with an eager appetite. An hour later, he and I were walking through the murky streets, breathing eucalyptus and listening to distant foghorns.

A few days later when I developed my film, its dim ladders mocked me. None of the antibodies I had made stuck to a protein on the Western blot. My feeling of being in the wrong place sharpened, as though I had usurped a role I couldn't play. Science lay on me like a heavy husband, with the terrible weight of "should." I could leave and start writing, I thought. Get a job, any job, and just write. But what about my mother? She had given up her life to make me a scientist. Only being with Johnny made me feel better.

Trouble was, Johnny avoided me in daylight. Late at night, when his work allowed, he'd take me up the hill, and we'd drink orange juice and watch the dust of lights. He'd come into me so fast that it burned, then fall asleep in minutes. In the morning there'd be more orange juice, and he would hustle me out. Any time outside the lab was time wasted. The more I wanted to be with him, the less he wanted to be with me. If I was looking for a boyfriend, he said, I should find someone else. He couldn't do that now. He had to work.

But I didn't want *a* guy. I wanted him. Johnny Turner.

"You're crazy," he said, and he stopped seeing me.

Sometimes in the hallway our eyes would meet, and his thin lips would spread in a smile. I'd persuade him to take me home, and then he would get angry afterward. Long after I left science, I felt bound to him, and he gave *The Rainbow Bar* much of its life. He stayed hard and solid in the silt after Penn College, while I floundered in academia's branched, muddy bed. Men wanted me in Pennsylvania the way local universities did, all those years—eagerly, for temporary hires. When I moved to Atlanta, only Gonzalo remained like a fond moon pulling at my life. Over twenty men's faces, Johnny's still looks out, his black eyes troubled until they warm with laughter.

"Carrie," says Johnny through the phone. "Carrie—you still there? Listen, I don't think I can do this. I'm booked solid. Meeting with folks in Berkeley that morning. Thesis defense at two ... Why do you want to see me, anyway?"

"I— It's a surprise," I stammer. "It—it'd mean a lot to me. Knowing you—you've inspired me in all kinds of ways. I have this feeling I need to check in with you—to hear about your work, to tell you—"

"Well, you always were good at surprises." Johnny's breathing slows, and I sense his grin. "I could see you late that afternoon, maybe ... around four? But why are you driving to San Francisco?"

Johnny Turner always asks the hardest questions. I pity the guy defending his thesis.

"I want to work on a novel. I write better when I'm moving."

"Oh, yeah—you write novels now. That's right."

I feel Johnny looking at his watch.

"Okay, so the thirty-first—at four—since I'm going to be in the neighborhood—"

"Yup. Thirty-first at four. You take care, now. You have a safe trip."

As Johnny hangs up, he is still laughing. I wonder what he wrote in his calendar.

I dig in the drawer for my address book, thinking maybe I can see Connie too. It's been so long I've almost lost track of her, but Oklahoma City is on my way. After Cohen's lab, she got a postdoc in Boulder, where she met this guy Bruce who works on the cytoskeleton. When he got a job in Oklahoma, she moved down with him, but she never found a faculty position.

"Research assistant," they call her. Then, in her Christmas letter a few years ago, she wrote that she'd had a kid.

"Came in under the wire," she said. "A normal kid at forty-three—ten toes, ten fingers, an overactive brain, and the voice of a Wagnerian soprano."

It's hard to imagine Connie with a kid. In the lab, she used to pipette to Elvis, and her blue leggings revealed the sculpted curves of a dancer. I know I wrote her number somewhere …

"Hello?" Connie's voice is still a low, musical alto.

"Connie?"

"Yeah. Who's this?" Not so friendly this time.

"It's Carrie."

"Carrie?" She sounds suspicious.

"Yeah, Carrie McFadden. Connie, it's me! From Marty Cohen's lab!"

"Carrie? My God, is that you? It's been …" Her voice trails off as she calculates. From somewhere near her comes a high-pitched shriek.

"Is that your kid?"

"Yeah, the Germinator. That's what Bruce calls her. You have any kids?"

"No, no!" My God, what a thought!

"Oh … well … how's it going? What's going on?"

"Well, I'm driving cross-country. You're still in Oklahoma City, right?"

"No, Norman. But it's not that far. Wow, that'd be great! You could stay with us—"

"Oh, no, I don't want to put you out. I have to get up early. I can stay at the Run-Rite Inn."

"Well, sure, if you want, but you're always welcome—hey, wait—wait just a second—honey, be careful—"

Some muffled thuds squash her voice.

"Sorry, Carrie. Wow, that's … I can't believe … So when do you think you'll be coming?"

"Oh, pretty soon." I count on my fingers. The pinkie for Memphis, that's the first night. Then—no, nothing in between. I could make Oklahoma City in two days.

"How about Friday night, the twentieth?"

"What, this Friday?" She laughs.

"Oh—uh—sorry. Is that too soon?"

"Gosh, I'm sorry. Bruce's brother is coming up this weekend, and they have three kids. They always take over the house."

"Oh." I imagine a cascade of small heads tumbling downstairs and screaming. "Well …"

"Is there any way you could put it off? I dunno, just drive a little slower? Suppose you came Monday night. They'll be gone by then. Could you do that? We could go out for dinner."

"Yeah, sure … Yeah, I think so."

Let's see … That would give me eight days to reach San Francisco. I bet even the guys in *The Grapes of Wrath* could do that.

"Wow, so tell me how you're doing. Tell me—oh. Oh, no. Oh, shit. Carrie, I'm sorry. I'm going to have to go. So, Monday?"

"Yeah. Yeah, Monday. It'll be great to see you—and meet …"

"Bedelia! Oh, yeah, and Bruce. You'll like him. I think the two of you will hit it off. Shit! Bye, Carrie!"

"Bye."

I stand with the phone in my hand, staring out at leaves wobbling like plates of sunlight. If I take off tomorrow, I could spend three nights in Memphis, then maybe one in Arkansas ... That way I would have to start writing.

I decide to leave tomorrow morning after rush hour, and I start packing right away. From the bed, Joey watches mistrustfully, his dark eyes following me from dresser to suitcase. I've had Joey for nineteen years now, ever since my last days in California. As a kid, I hardly had any stuffed animals. I hungered for them later, in those last painful months in the lab.

A week before I moved east, I went to this store in the Mission, the cheapest place I knew to buy boxes and tape. In a bin near the front lay a heap of animals who all looked pretty beat up. A long, stiff crocodile was missing one eye, and the legs of a blue unicorn flopped crazily. I couldn't resist touching them, and when I pulled a lone brown paw, up came a chocolate bear. He hung there in my hand, and I brushed back his fur to find deep, hopeful brown eyes. When I rested him on my hip, his nose tickled my nipple.

This is stupid, I thought. *You can't buy this bear. You're supposed to be getting rid of stuff.*

I carried him on my hip to the boxes and tape, and then I couldn't put him down.

What'll happen? I wondered. *What'll happen if I leave him?*

Fierce boys might yank out his eyes. At the checkout counter, he rode anxiously forward until the cashier stopped him and stroked his head.

"Suavecito," she murmured. Her long black hair fell forward as she looked for his price tag.

I've had Joey with me ever since, through the move to Penn College and then down to Georgia. When I'm sad, I still sleep curled around him, my breasts against his back and my chin tucked over his head.

"Okay," I tell him. "Okay, you're coming." I bounce him on my hip, and he nuzzles my neck. I can't leave Joey alone in this blank apartment, and something tells me that on this trip, I'm going to need him.

CHAPTER 2

BIRMINGHAM

Wilma roars to life with groggy joy, like a man awakened by his climax. Her tires crunch hickory leaves and then relax as they taste the hot, dry road. Under scaly oaks, ramshackle houses float past, moldy chairs festering on their porches. A black-haired boy swings around a street sign, his fingers raking the air. Wilma quivers as she waits for a light. "No trespassing!" warns a pink house with lacy black gates. A gigantic oak with roots like lava has turned the sidewalk to a heaving mosaic. As I pull away, the dark little boy twirls, his small brown hand reaching out.

Wilma pushes into the crawl of I-20 West, and my breath flows in shallow rills. No doubt about which way to go. West toward science, San Francisco, the lab, fluorescent prison under dancing eucalyptus trees. West toward Johnny Turner with his gigantic hands, his restless eyes, his slamming truths.

Wilma streaks across the Alabama border. Morning photons pock her fleeing backside. The bleached interstate rests uneasily in its bed of pulsing green. In the median, cheerful daisies thrive in tall grass, which hides hungry blue police cars. Rippling curtains of woods on both sides darken the road as the sun's angle shifts.

Birmingham opens the dense cloak of woods, and with relief I glide off I-20. I want to visit the Civil Rights Institute, but the drone of hunger overpowers my thoughts. No life is stirring these wide, shaded streets—no stores, no restaurants, no cafés. Wilma floats past sealed glass buildings surrounded by gleaming lots. Where is everybody? Where do all these people eat? I'm so hungry the flesh of my upper arm is inviting my teeth. The Civil Rights Institute has no food, so I search in a nearby tower. In a rushing food court under smoky glass, I create a mandala of salad. Whirling ceiling fans whip the chilled air. I wish I had a fluffy red blanket.

"Scuse me, ma'am, is that chair free?"

I hate when people call me that.

Before me stands a smiling blond man with a bulging belly and wiener fingers. His eyes are brown, and I wonder how they'd look if my lips closed tight around him. Shocked, probably, and enormously grateful. Just look at those mountains of food he's eating. Brown runoff from his hills of potatoes floods soggy chicken and soft lima beans. Something sad in his tone reminds me of Sandy Marshall's son, who looks longingly at Teresa in my novel.

"That chair—may I take it?" The fat man falters, probably wondering if I'm crazy. A warmth in his voice tells me that, for all his bumbling, his soul is kind.

"Yeah, sure, there's nobody there."

"You're not from around here, are you?"

A scrub-head waiting at a nearby table fixes me with a laser gaze. Probably a coworker who was hoping that, for an hour, this man's chocolate voice would flow toward her.

"Well," I say, "I was going to the Civil Rights Institute, but there's no food there, so I came in here." The fat man looks at my leafy masterpiece and smiles, hiding his teeth. "You don't eat very much, do you?"

"Oh, I eat what I want, when I want."

He keeps standing there, unsure what to do. With two hands on that loaded tray, how is he going to haul off the chair? I guess he hadn't thought about that. Two tables away, the waiting woman folds her arms.

"I—I'd like to hear what you think of the Civil Rights Institute," he says. "Maybe we could talk—later on."

My lips twitch. "Well, I'm really just stopping to see the institute. I've got to be in Memphis tonight."

"Oh. Oh, well ... I hope you enjoy Birmingham. But— maybe—I could call you ..."

For no reason, I write my cell phone number on a napkin. His broad fingers tremble as he sets down his tray. He stuffs the napkin deep in his pocket. Good. That crop-headed marshmallow waiting for him looks like she's capable of anything.

I spend an hour inside the institute, although I worry about Joey. In this sun, Wilma will turn hot enough to ignite his parched brown fur. Inside the building it's dark and cool, a tunnel from slave ships to freedom rides. Courageous black kids clutch their books while a white girl jeers, her cobra mouth gaping. Police with hoses blast a line of people whose upraised hands break the water's stream. I lift up my arms to meet theirs and try to feel the explosive force.

The story ends with a show on Mexicans, apparently all from one place. Two of them are working right outside, cyborgs wrapped in leaf blower tubes. Their shaded eyes follow me as I rush to Wilma, and one of them steps forward. Raúl! He's shorter than I am, but his shielded eyes scare me. I flee with his image in pursuit.

To reach Highway 78, I could take the interstate, but I want to see the town. A tall black woman says that if I stay on Seventeenth, it will feed into 78 … eventually. After a few blocks, I start to sweat as I roll past shotgun shacks with barred windows. In front of them, kids are playing in clusters, hovering in groups that tighten and burst. I don't realize how much breath I've held until I climb back onto the highway. I wouldn't have thought I could hold that much air, but you never know what you've got inside you.

Route 78 is a schizophrenic road, unsure of who or what it is. It winds through dark woods as a single lane, then grooves hills as a superhighway. To stay with the road as it flips identities, I follow trucks hauling shaggy pines. Why do they stack the logs bottom forward, so that the wind resistance is high? Probably so they won't fly off and lance me like gigantic spears. "REPENT NOW!" commands a red-and-white billboard. Inches behind Wilma's tail, a gray truck bares its steely teeth. I wonder what the fat guy is doing at work. Maybe scanning his cubicle's burlap walls, looking for a gap in the pattern.

When I spot the blue Run-Rite Inn sign, the day has gone murky and dim. In the back seat, Joey looks wilted and limp. Next door, a check-cashing place glows, and a bodega offers to wire money to Puebla. I slip my credit card to a shy Indian girl who is reading behind bulletproof glass.

"Boop!" sings Wilma's alarm as I bounce Joey on my hip. There he goes again, rubbing my nipple. The metal stairs ring under my feet.

When I run my card, the door flashes green, and I step into a dark, droning space. Cool air laps me in a mildewy wave, but once the light is on, the room pleases me. A spread of blue and lilac squares covers the bed, and the fake wooden dresser offers a smooth expanse. I set Joey down in the middle of the bed, where he hangs his head and droops. With growing pleasure, I lay my clothes in the drawers and settle in for the night.

Brrrp. Brrrp. Brrrp. Doo-doo-doo-DEE-doo.

What?

Brrrp. Brrr—

"H'lo?"

"Hey. It's Clifton," says a breathy voice. "You know—we met in the food court today."

I fall back on the bed and hold the phone away so that he can't hear me laugh. Clifton? The guy's name is *Clifton*? Like Clifton, New Jersey?

"I just wanted to say hey," he says, "and make sure you got to Memphis all right."

With my left hand I grab my breast and squeeze it.

"Why, did I look like I was sick or something?"

"No—no—you just looked—you had that long drive all by yourself."

I try to imagine having someone with me, wanting to stop and eat all the time. I can't stand it when people hold me back.

"Oh, I like to drive," I say. "I wouldn't want to do this with anyone else."

Clifton doesn't answer, but drumrolls of air mark his breaths.

"H'lo? Clifton?"

"Oh, sorry," he says. "I was thinking how much fun it would be to take that drive."

"You don't get to travel? Do you work a lot?"

"Oh yeah." He laughs. "Mobile South. I lead a group studying how to make billing easier. You know that summary you get at the beginning of your bill? Well, that's me—that was my idea."

"Wow. That was you, huh?"

"Yeah, only—" A quick chuckle scatters his voice. "You're different, aren't you? Where are you from?"

"Well, I'm from Atlanta. But I grew up near Scranton."

"Scranton—what is that, Pennsylvania?"

"Yeah, old mining country. Lot of hills."

"Hm. Hm." He falls silent, his breath damped to faint static.

"So what brought you to Birmingham—work?"

"Yeah, kind of. I'm trying to write something. I teach writing, but I also write my own stuff."

"Wow," he breathes. "Oh, my. Do you have any books out? Any books I might know?"

"*The Rainbow Bar.*"

On its cover, seven pastel ice-cream balls balance on a pale sugar cone. That delectable totem pole lured three hundred thousand people to buy it.

"Oh … so what's it about?" he asks.

"This woman who moves to San Francisco when her mother dies and works in an ice-cream store. All these crazy people who hang out there."

"Wow. That sounds like fun. I'd like to try that."

His round belly must be pushing against his pants. What sound would he make if I kissed it?

"Well, maybe I should go now," he murmurs. "It's late."

"Sure, if you want."

He doesn't say anything, but he won't hang up. "I just wanted to call you because you looked ... so lonely sitting there today."

I laugh and rub my nose against Joey. "Nah. Just wanted to get some food."

"And you're so thin. You eat so little—"

"What are you, worried?"

"No—no—I—"

"Well, I'm fine. I'm lying here with my teddy bear, and we're about to start watching *Law and Order.*"

Clifton chuckles. "Well, I mustn't keep you. That sounds important."

Still he won't hang up. "What kind of bear?"

"Oh, chocolate brown. About half as big as I am."

"Mm," he murmurs. "Not very big."

"Listen, I've got to get unpacked here."

"Okay—sorry—but . . . tell me your name. I don't know your name."

A lot of breath. A lot of static.

"Theresa."

"Theresa. That's pretty. I like that."

"Well, g'night, Clifton."

"Okay—good night . . . Theresa. You have a safe trip now. Bye."

CHAPTER 3

MEMPHIS

On the floor of Johnny's office, I wrestle with a rubbery black bra. If I used it as a slingshot, could it shoot two rocks at once? Some purple pants lie next to me, a crumpled top. Almost—I almost have it hooked. Oh no, it's on upside down!

Johnny stalks in, his long arms taut. "You know," he says, "I take what goes on in this office very seriously."

Oh. Where ...? Memphis, I think. Yeah, Memphis. There's Joey, all fuzzy ... What part of him is that against my cheek?

Johnny.

I shove Joey back and roll onto my belly.

Slowly I circle my hips, and the mattress squeaks its approval. Johnny. Johnny's eyes, so dark it hurts. Round and round. Press into it. Hand under. Johnny smiles when he sees my unclothed body.

Ready? Yeah, ready.

I roll onto my back.

With my legs apart, I stick my middle finger in my mouth. I wince as a string of spit tickles my chin. Irritated, I push my fur out of the way. What's it all doing down there, anyway? My knees form a tent, a cathedral of air. The sheet flops in my face, but I brush it back. Test pass. Am I wet? Yeah, very. Mm. Up and down, yeah, there's the spot. My finger glides softly, and my back arches.

Johnny grins as he kneels down beside me. "Lemme help you with that." He laughs. "Gimme that thing."

I'm so open my finger slips right in. My back curves, and my hips rise. A little worm starts nibbling at the wall between chambers of matter and antimatter. Which way will he bite next? When he gets through—

One hook is still stuck. Johnny is laughing, pulling. "Damn!"

Could happen any second now. No more time to wet my finger. Got to catch the wave right. Johnny laughs. My legs shoot up. The last hook comes free—

Brrrp. Brrrp. Brrrp. Doo-doo-doo-DEE-doo.

Oh, fuck.

Brrrp. Brrrp. Brrrp. Doo-doo-doo-DEE-doo!

Where did I leave that—

Brrrp!

"H'lo?"

"Hello, Carrie? This is Louise. I hope I didn't wake you." Her words sprinkle me like cold drops.

"No, no. I was up." I switch the phone to my left hand and wipe my fingers on my thigh.

"It's eight thirty, so I was sure you'd be up."

"It's seven thirty here—but no, I'm up."

"Oh … where are you?"

Shivering, I claw at the covers and pull them closer around me. "Memphis. I'm driving cross-country. I left you a message."

"Oh, a message? I didn't get it, honey. When did you leave it?"

If this scrub-head doesn't stop calling me honey—

"Yesterday. On your voice mail."

"Oh, that's strange …" Louise hesitates. "I check it every day, and I didn't get it."

"Well, anyway, I'm driving cross-country. But you should be able to get me anywhere on this phone, so it doesn't matter. How's my mom doing? Is she okay?"

"Well, that's what I wanted to talk to you about, dear."

I take hold of Joey, who is lying rump up, hiding his face in the sheet.

"Oh." Joey settles between my hips, and I bounce him playfully.

"You know how I wrote you about those gloves?"

"Yeah, those long ones, so she can't chew her fingers."

Before the gloves, my mother's hands were raw purple figs that she gnawed with determined hunger.

"Right. Well, I came in this morning, and the gloves were gone. Those nurse's aides must have thrown them in the laundry again, and now we'll never find them. I always take them home to wash."

"Wow, that's too bad." I press Joey against me so that his fur prickles my chest. His chin curves gently over my shoulder.

"She had her thumb in her mouth, and she chewed it open. All bloody. I had to call the RN, and she let them have it. These young girls, all they think of is their next paycheck. If it weren't for me—"

"I'm glad you caught that," I say quickly. "So did they bandage her thumb?"

"Yeah, just like last time. They wanted to tie her hands to the bed, but I wouldn't let them. Can you imagine? Like some wild animal..."

"Wow, so do you want me to talk to them?"

"No, I think I have it under control. She's going to need some new gloves, though."

Something in the flow of her words tells me this isn't why she called, but I match her pace and wait for the trouble to emerge.

"Yeah, sure," I mutter. "Is there enough in her account to cover it?"

"Well, I buy them myself." She sighs. "At this medical supply store in Scranton. I get a much better deal there than at Hillcrest."

"Oh, yeah? Well, that's great. You'd better get them there, then. Tell me how much they are, and I'll send a check."

"Thanks, honey. That's good of you."

This time her word slaps me like a wet rag.

"Louise? Could you please stop calling me honey? I'm forty-three."

"All right, dear. Listen, that's not the only reason I'm calling. Your mom, she's not doing so well."

"Not doing well? What do you mean?"

Under the rubber-lined curtain, the fringe of morning light is tantalizing.

"Well, she's just kind of ... drooping. I see her more than anyone else, and this past week, she hasn't been herself. I think you should come up and see her."

"Well, I'm on this trip now. I can't just fly off and leave my car."

I picture the police impounding Wilma, with Joey strapped in back. One of the cops gives him to his kid, who throws up on him. Chunky brown lava runs down his furry forehead.

"Just for a day or two, to see for yourself. She is your mom, honey."

I squirm. "Louise, I can't come right now. She's a tough woman. I'm sure whatever it is, she'll pull through."

Louise's voice focuses into a beam. "Well, if you can manage, I think you should come up."

"I will, but just not right now. I have to meet someone in San Francisco."

"Oh ... I see. Well, try and think of your mom, dear. I'll pray for you both."

"Okay. Thanks. Bye, Louise." I blow out my breath.

"Goodbye, honey."

I press the red button to end the call and raise my eyes to the bare dresser. Johnny has vanished, and I feel embarrassed that I ever thought of fumbling with him on his office floor. I shiver as I stand before the mirror, pale and naked under loose black hair.

I'm so hungry I could eat almost anything. As an experiment, I close my jaws on my upper arm and leave a red bracelet of tooth marks. As I untangle my hair, the comb clatters to the floor, and its blue spines bite my foot. Somewhere out there, I've got to get food, no matter what it is.

With Joey bobbing on my hip, I float down to Wilma. "We're going to see Elvis!" I say as I strap him in.

I'm going to have to spend the day in Memphis, since I can't see Connie until Monday. Ever since the days she and I pipetted to Elvis, I've wanted to see that supple man's home. As we sucked up yellow liquid and squirted cherry-red medium, his fast beat set our pulse. Our hungry cells in their round, flat dishes seemed to need him as much as we did.

By the time I start Wilma, I'm feeling so faint the world is pulsing in and out. I plan to stop at the first restaurant I see, but black bars guard all the windows. On both sides of the road crouch redbrick buildings with grass worn to dust around the doors. In between them lurk pawnshops, liquor stores, check-cashing places, title-loan joints, and hybrids that combine all four. If I stop, they'll steal Wilma, they'll get Joey, I think. But a friendly fast-food sign rises over the mess. What am I so worried about? People who steal bears are asleep at nine in the morning.

I stop with a jolt, and I park near the street so that no one can jump me out back. Inside, some dark, grizzled men sip coffee. They glance me over and look away, bored. A round-faced girl presses her palms into the counter, as though she were pushing it back. I ask for a big breakfast and a hot tea, and she says, "We ain' got no tea, ma'am."

There's that word again. What am I, sixty? The food comes quickly, and I retreat to a window. Under a rusted canopy outside, sausage-legged women are squinting down the boulevard, trying to conjure a bus. I stare at the food in my Styrofoam clam: scrambled eggs, a lopsided biscuit, a greasy round of meat, and a crispy, rancid wedge of hash browns. My plastic fork trembles over the glistening yellow mound. The sausage and potatoes are too risky, and I vow not to touch them, but I want that biscuit and those eggs. Their warm saltiness is so good I could cry. I savor them in small, slow bites.

"*What are you doing?*"

My eyes scan the dingy space.

"*What are you guys doing?*"

Those tough alto tones are Teresa's!

I jiggle the table to test it and pull out a sheet of blue-lined paper. I've got to be careful. One nudge of my foot, and Teresa will drown in a lake of coffee. With quick, determined steps, she's approaching a chilly bus stop at six in the morning. Two short, flat-faced men huddle in hoodies. One of them is kicking a dead dog.

"*¿'Tá muerto, el perro ése?*"

"*Yeah, he's dead. But look, man, he's a she.*"

In the cold darkness, the man nudges the stiff brown dog with his sneaker.

"*He must have got hit by a car or something.*"

"*I'm telling you, man, es una hembra. Just look at her face.*"

"*It's not the FACE that—*"

Gingerly his companion reaches for the rigid hind leg, catches hold of it, and pulls up sharply.

"*I told you, man. Si es un macho, alguien le ha robado algo.*"

"*Hey, what are you guys doing?*"

A small, sturdy woman in a blue sweatshirt approaches them from behind.

"What are you guys doing to that dog?"

"Mira, guapa, she's dead. Nobody can't do nothing to her no more."

"So why don't you leave her alone?"

She faces the hooded men in their boots and jeans, her long black hair gleaming in the electric light.

"¡Pero mírala! Princesa, you got any more orders for us today?"

"What you doing tonight, baby?"

"Stop it. I'm married. Estoy casada."

The man who pulled the dog's leg begins to laugh. His face looms out at her, a dark, flat face with broad, black eyes.

"¿Casada? You hear that? She's married! Ca-sa-da. ¿Y qué? ¿En qué tipo de casa vives, tú y tu dizque marido?"

"Shut up." *Her face hardens.*

"The only nice house you ever seen, you clean it."

"Yeah, and I watch you guys cut the grass."

His friend nudges him. "Ooo, she got you, man. Es una culebra, ésta."

Out of the darkness, the bus approaches like a vengeful ghost. They climb aboard, and as it pulls away, three brown plastic bags rise in a mournful dance.

I swish the last of my coffee and wince at its cool, sour taste. This isn't working. Teresa looks right, she sounds right, but she's not in charge. A woman like her doesn't float through life like a mat of seaweed on a wave. No matter how painful, life is something she does, not something that happens to her. Teresa needs to tell this story.

By the opposite window, three girls titter and stare, the sequins flashing on their red tops. Old guys are one thing, but girls attack for fun. I force my Styrofoam clamshell into the trash, and something sticky defiles my fingers. Outside Wilma looks relieved to see me, though she growls when I start her. I turn south onto Elvis Presley Boulevard, then into an enormous lot where a rectangular patch costs six bucks.

"See you got a passenger there." The bald attendant grins. His yellow teeth form a broken range.

Can I take Joey with me? On the pilgrimage to Elvis, people must have carried stranger things. But fearing unknown hands, I leave Joey in the shadows. I'll have to tell him about it later.

Smiling uniformed women send me through Graceland like a nut in a chocolate factory. I am inspected, shuttled, and pushed. When I cross the threshold into the white living room, I try to swallow a laugh. It's like going to church: the whole business is ludicrous, but if you giggle, someone might smack you. In the gaudy living room, every surface reflects light—white leather, glittering pictures, gold studs. Orange-and-green counters glow in the kitchen, and the playroom has tiger stripes. The sealed basement is a breeding ground for psychedelic nightmares. Out of all of it, only the back lawn has grace.

Dizzy with hunger, I wander back to Joey and recall a Chinese buffet down the street. How long has it been since I ate breakfast? Can I really be hungry again? Reaching the buffet is no easy matter: left onto the huge boulevard, then left off it again. Why are my fingers sticking to the wheel? It clings to my hands as I park, unwilling to be released.

"Iced tea, unsweetened!" I gasp.

From colorful bins, I help myself to broccoli and shiny morsels of meat. I settle down, but a wet spot blossoms at the corner of my page. Oh, no! All I have with me are three sheets. Although my plate is half-full, I push it away and rub down the table with my napkin. Teresa is trudging up the driveway of a magnificent brick house. Justin is looking out the window, because she's late. The door swings open ...

You always know how tall a guy is by how you tilt your head to see him. This one is not so tall. Bigger than Raúl, maybe, but short for a gringo. Blond, with eyes like black coffee. Raúl is hard all over, but this one is soft, like la masa de tortilla. If I poked him with my finger, I don't know if his belly would spring back.

"Can I get you something to drink?" he asks. "Maybe some water?"

Poor guy. He thinks I'm his guest. Bueno, si es tan güey—

"Yes," I say. "Some water, please."

On the wine-colored carpet, his feet make no sound as he hurries off to the kitchen. His broad hand trembles as he gives me the glass.

"Did it take you long to get here?" he asks. "You were going to be here at seven thirty."

Now he sounds like a gringo boss.

"*I'm sorry, Mr. Marshall,*" I say. "*I had to take two buses. I didn't know how long it would take. Tomorrow I'll be on time, I promise.*"

"*Oh, yes, Atlanta traffic ...*"

Probably he's never been on a bus in his life. When he smiles, you can't see his teeth.

"*Well, Fred Chase said you took good care of his mother, until ...*"

"*Oh, yes, a nice lady. I took good care of her.*"

He doesn't like what I just said. He's looking at me like I can't speak English. What didn't he like?

"*Well, in some ways my mother will be easier to deal with than Mrs. Chase, and in some ways harder.*"

Under his pink shirt, his trapped belly is straining against his pants. I want to stick my finger in to see what will happen.

"*Can she go to the bathroom by herself?*"

"*Yes ... but it's hard for her. You'll have to go in with her and show her—*"

Poor guy. Until now, probably he had to take her.

"*She can still do everything,*" he explains. "*But she does it all wrong—and ... and then she gets angry.*" He looks down at the wine velvet carpet.

"*I understand,*" I say. *Está confundida. Hay que tener paciencia.* How do you say this? "*You must ... respect her.*"

"*Yes!*" He raises his eyes to meet mine. So dark, with that golden hair of his.

"*Yes,*" he says again. "*I try, but it's hard, when she ... Well, you'll see.*"

His arms are thicker than Raúl's, but he doesn't use them. They could be very strong, but he won't work with them.

"I have to go to work now," he says. "Are you ready to meet her?" He makes it sound like a wrestling match.

"Yes."

He hurries off to an adjacent room. How dark this house is, and how quiet! If I were an old lady, I'd go crazy in here. It needs children's crashing waves of sound. Why isn't this guy married? Un poco gordo, un poco soso, pero no es tan malo.

"Please, Mom, she's here." His low voice tightens.

"I don't want anyone. Tell her to go home!"

"No, Mom. She's only here to help if you need it. Otherwise she'll leave you alone. A nice, quiet lady with long black hair. Mexican, I think."

"Mexican!"

"Come meet her, Mom. I promise if you don't like her in a week, we'll find someone else."

"But I don't WANT anyone."

"I can't just leave you here alone all day. What about the stove? Remember what happened with the stove last week?"

The voices approach. Que la chingada. He didn't tell me that part about if she doesn't like me. We need that money to get out of el pinche garaje. Six dollars an hour, forty hours a week—we could buy a car—

"Hi, Mrs. Marshall." I smile.

La vieja, she stands straighter than her son—taller than he is—strange. Her eyes are blue spears, her hair only half gray. What's wrong with her? She doesn't look that old.

"I don't need anyone," she says.

How thin she is! She must have been beautiful when she was young. She turns to her son, who grips his briefcase and keys.

"*Make her go away!*" *She stamps her foot, and her face contorts. Poor thing.*

"*It's okay, Mrs. Marshall,*" *I say.* "*I promise I won't bother you. I'll only help you if you need it.*"

She glances at me sharply.

"*Justin, who is this? How did she get in here?*"

"*This is Teresa, Mom. Teresa Ramírez. She'll be here all day in case you need anything.*"

The door closes behind him, and his car vrooms. La vieja looks down at me.

"*I had long hair like that once,*" *she says.*

I smile at her, but my eyes are already exploring the dim space. What a house! Mrs. Chase's was big, but nothing like this. This one goes on forever, with passages like dark fingers reaching out. If this place were mine, I'd open up all the windows. Then I'd rip up the carpet and lay clean tiles. You never know what kind of crud is hiding in a carpet. It rises up like a dusty ghost anytime someone's feet disturb it.

A picture. That must be her husband—heavy, this silver frame—I guess her son looks like him, that round, sad face, but the husband has green eyes, close together like a fish.

"*Don't touch that! Don't you touch that!*"

¡Ay! ¡Pinche vieja, qué sustote me pegó!

"*Sorry, Mrs. Marshall. I just wanted to see … Is this your husband?*"

The bald man with green eyes smiles through closed lips. His neck bulges over his collar. His eyes tell me he can do things and he isn't mean, but still there's something wrong with him.

"*Yes, that's Bill. He's dead.*"

Poor thing. She really is crazy.

"Oh, I'm sorry. A long time ago?"

"Yes. No. A long time …"

"He looks like a nice man. What did he do?"

"He was dean."

¿El dín? Must be something like a college president, to live in a place like this.

"Your son—he looks like his father."

La vieja smiles, and her bitter eyes clear. She even begins to laugh.

"Yes, like his father."

"You have any more children?"

Her laugh collapses. Her light dims. "No, just Justin. Just Justin."

And such a big house! But gringos are like that. They always want so much space.

"Well, he's nice too. You must be happy to have such a nice son who takes care of you."

La vieja frowns, and her eyes shoot a blue arc. "He's always at work," she says.

"Yes, he has to work. What does he do?"

"Count … Count … Money! Count …"

The poor thing strains like she's on the toilet trying to squeeze something out. I'm also groping for the word.

"In a bank?"

"A bank … yes … Count!"

"An accountant?"

"Yes, an accountant." How can blue eyes be so dark? Black fear is eating their color.

"You have such a beautiful house," I say. "Maybe you can show me. I promise not to hurt anything."

La vieja wanders off without saying a word and leads me to a bright, tiny room. With three glass walls, it juts out from the house into the calm, green world outside. Orange-brown tiles cover the floor, and long straw chairs with pink cushions lie as though just abandoned by millionaires.

"The sunporch," she says.

"It's so warm," I murmur. "Maybe we could just stay here."

But she's off again, and I have to follow. She moves fast for an old woman, gliding over that wine-red sea. This time she leads me to the kitchen. Under my feet, the stone floor glints with colored specks. A steel refrigerator hums to its partner, an oven big enough to roast four chickens.

"Do you have a lot of parties here?" I ask. "A lot of friends for dinner?"

La vieja's eyes stretch wide, and her dry mouth opens.

"I have to—I need—" she says, looking from side to side.

"Do you have to go to the bathroom, Mrs. Marshall?"

The tall, thin woman nods her head.

"Where is it? Tell me—show me where it is, and I'll help you."

She rushes out of the kitchen, and I run after her. She flits first one way, then the other, like a trapped fly.

"I have to—I have to—where's Justin?"

"It's okay, Mrs. Marshall. I'll find it for you."

I try the hallway leading toward the sunporch. One door opens into a dark room full of books, but the second reveals a small white bathroom. When I find la vieja, she's panting like a dog. I take her rigid, bony hand.

"I found it, Mrs. Marshall," I say. "Let me show you."

She tries to pull away, but I hold on hard. Wildly, she yanks at me.

"Justin!" she screams.

I keep my voice quiet. "I know where a bathroom is. I found one."

Her desperate eyes dig me, wondering whether to trust. "You know where one is?" she whispers.

"Yes," I murmur. "It's right back here."

I let go of her hand, and she follows. When she sees the white tiles, she looks so grateful.

"Here it is," I say. "I'll wait outside."

Without closing the door, she pulls down her pants to reveal a dead, gray bush. I swing the door shut and study a painting of a strong-armed woman pouring milk from a heavy brown pitcher. With her face soft, her full breasts covered, the woman smiles into the waiting bowl. From behind the door come ragged pants, broken by a deep breath and a gasp. Poor thing. Estreñimiento.

I wander across to the room full of books. It smells so dank I wonder if the hidden pages are spotted with black. I never saw so many books in one house. The shelves start on the floor and go up over my head, and they take up three whole walls. The smooth, dark books stand jammed together like teeth. Only some loose notebooks near the bottom offer themselves to exploring hands.

"Help! Justin! Help!"

I run to the bathroom door.

"Help, help!"

I push it open and try not to laugh. She's unrolled all the paper and is clutching great handfuls, with billowy loops falling from her clenched fingers. As she reaches out to me, cotton spirals twirl. It looks like she's throwing a one-woman fiesta to celebrate what just came out.

"There's no paper!" she cries. "There's never any clean paper!"

"I'll try to find you some," I say. *I pick up a piece and tear off a few sheets, more than she needs with estreñimiento like that.*

"That's dirty!" she exclaims. "That was on the floor! You get me clean paper!"

Next to the bathroom I find a small closet filled with stacked white rolls. I tear off a few sheets while her eyes sear my hands, and when I give them to her, she looks triumphant. La vieja wipes herself and pulls up her pants, but no brown pebbles have settled in the white pool.

"Mrs. Marshall, did you . . ." I ask.

"No," she says. "It wouldn't come out."

Brrrp. Brrrp. Brrrp. Doo-doo-doo-DEE-doo.

Oh, no. Now what?

Brrrp. Brrrp. Brrrp. Doo-doo-doo—

"H'lo?"

"Hello—Theresa?"

"Sorry, wro—Clifton?" My whole body smiles. Under the table, I lift my legs and point my toes.

"Theresa? You sound different." Clifton laughs softly.

"Well, I'm eating some Chinese food."

"Oh—well, sorry to bother you while you're eating. I won't keep you." He falls silent.

I finish chewing and swallow, then try to free a string caught between my teeth.

"Theresa? I'm on the Barnes and Noble website."

I picture a bookstore and wish that websites had that papery smell. What's Clifton doing surfing? What time is it, anyway?

"You calling from work?" I ask.

"Well, yeah, but on my cell. It's okay. I'm on lunch."

"Oh. What's for lunch?"

"Well, let's see ... finished a while ago ... Roast beef sandwich, chips, carrot cake ... ate too much again."

I imagine him eating that carrot cake, sour-sweet cream cheese gliding over his tongue.

"So anyway, I was looking for your book, and I ran the title since I don't know your last name. *The Rainbow Bar*, right?"

"Yeah, that's it."

A drop of water emerges from the heavy dew on my glass. It trembles and bulges like a nervous amoeba, dreading the long slide down.

"Well, they have it, but they say it's by Carrie McFadden."

The amoeba drops with a sudden jerk.

"Oh, that's just—"

"That's you?"

"Well, it's—"

"Oh, a pen name! I didn't know people still did that."

Clifton gurgles. He must still be eating.

"Sometimes we do," I say, eyeing the steaming bins nearby. I poke at a shiny piece of chicken flecked with pepper.

"Well, I'm really looking forward to reading it," says Clifton. "The branch near our mall has it, so I'm going to stop there on the way home."

"Hey, that's great. I hope you like it."

"Oh, I'm sure I will. You seem like such an interesting person."

The phone crackles, then offers soft waves of breath. He must have moved it closer to his mouth.

"What makes you say that?" I ask. "I mean, you don't even know me. How do you know that I'm interesting?"

"Well, the writing." He sighs. "I never knew anyone who wrote novels. And traveling alone . . ."

"Maybe I travel alone because I'm so boring no one can stand me."

The freckled piece of chicken glistens, and I pop it in my mouth.

"Oh, I doubt that," he chuckles. "I bet you're trouble."

"Mmmph."

"Theresa?"

"Muffing. Juss chewing."

"Oh—I was worried there for a second that I'd offended you."

"Mope. Juss chewing."

Clifton stays perfectly still. Either he's waiting for me to chew or deciding what to say next.

"Theresa? Can I ask you something?"

My stomach clenches.

"What's it like writing? I mean, how do you know what happens in your books?"

"Well, you think of people. Pairs of people who love and hate each other. Then you hear them talking, and you write down what they say."

"That sounds kind of crazy. Like hearing voices?"

Why do people always have to ask me that? I inhale deeply and release the air in a slow, fine stream.

"No. You start with a model. Someone you know, so you're pretty sure what he'd say."

"Wow. But don't people recognize themselves? Don't they get mad?"

The phone spits in my ear.

"No. Because as soon as you're writing, they become someone else. Not the model anymore."

"Wow. That's interesting."

"It is when it works."

I blow some air back into the phone.

"Now I really want to read your book."

"Sure, if you want."

I raise my eyes from my plate to see a congregation of empty chairs. At the buffet, a somber Chinese girl is loading bins onto a silver cart. What time is it? Where did everybody go?

"Well, I should let you finish your lunch," says Clifton.

"Mm-hmm."

That peppery chicken has left my mouth burning. I reach for my tea, and the ice clunks.

"But it sure was nice talking to you."

"You too, Clifton."

The grave Chinese girl pushes her cart, her long brown arms extended. It shudders as it catches on the carpet.

"Clifton." He laughs. "I like how you say my name."

"Why, how am I supposed to say it?"

"Oh, I don't know. Just in less of a hurry."

"Clifff-ton." My lips harden to a kiss.

Clifton laughs delightedly. "No—no—"

"Clifff-tonnn."

"No!" He gasps, sounding as though he's about to fall off his chair.

"Well, what do you want? It's a friggin' town in New Jersey!"

Clifton's voice emerges through his laughter. "New Jersey?"

"Yeah, google it."

"Listen, you, I've got to go, or I won't be able to do any more work today. I'm going to start laughing in the middle of a meeting."

"Hope you do."

The Chinese girl turns her head. I must be laughing too loud.

"Oh, no, not this one."

"Hope you do."

"I'm hanging up now."

"Hope you do!"

"Bye, Theresa."

He's gone. With my fork, I roll over a greasy string bean. I want to write more, but Teresa and Sandy have withdrawn into dark rooms. If I'm going to spend a day here, I guess I should see something. A round-faced blonde woman brings me my check with a wrapped fortune cookie on a tiny tray. Inside the crisp shell, a dry scroll says, "Listen to your elders, for they have traveled the path you think is new." These old people who want to squash you to death hide their propaganda even in crunchy cookies.

When I ask the pale hostess how to drive downtown, she tells me to take the interstate. I won't see Memphis that way, and on my map, Elvis Presley Boulevard leads north in a slim red line. What's out there? What do these people not want me to see? From the back seat, Joey goads me, so I pull out of the lot and head north.

Between me and downtown lie miles of rubble— junkyards, used-furniture shops, and faded shacks. After twenty minutes, I turn west onto a broad boulevard and spot the pale brown skyline. The Mississippi! To reach the river, I creep across a district where I bet bullets are as common as flies. Joey looks anxiously in the mirror although Wilma's doors are power-locked.

At first, the city center seems safe and solid, heavy white buildings and broad one-way streets. A lacy skyscraper flanks a cool, green square, and a jazz band serenades a shaved-ice vendor offering thirty brilliant flavors of syrup. I follow the trolley line south, paralleling the river, along what looks to be the main drag. As I burn past dollar stores, thin-faced men beg me for money. I loop through a street of famous blues clubs, but the people trying to look happy unsettle me. I round the corner, seeking a mall I've seen advertised, and inside its heavy glass doors, my shoulders relax.

Hungry again, I discover white plastic tables under a Victorian glass dome. I can write in here, with all that space overhead and no one to bother me. I order a grilled-steak soft taco and try to picture Teresa. I haven't seen her in hours. As I try to conjure her, my eyes roam the crescent of restaurants pushing warm, spicy food. All I see is an Italian chain advertising a personal pan pizza. Suddenly I hear Raúl.

"This pinche garaje's like a pizza," he says. "You can walk around as much as you want, but you always end up in the same place."

"Ten times? You had to take her ten times?" Raúl laughs, his face deep red. His dark eyes warm me as he pictures la vieja in the bathroom, the loops of white hanging from her hands.

"Yeah, ten, twenty times, I don't know. I was in there with her all day. Poor thing. Once she tried to dig it out with her fingers, and it got under her nails. I had to hold her hands under the water to wash them. She kept pulling away—she's strong."

"¡Qué asco!" Raúl shudders. "You shouldn't have to do that. That woman needs a nurse."

"That's pretty much what I am," I say.

"Yeah—for six dollars an hour."

Raúl has stopped laughing. He throws his jacket on the scuffed green chair and turns on the TV. He's been angry lately, since he's been working at this place with a big dog. The family wants their whole yard redone, and every five minutes he steps in shit. He seems better today, but as he fingers a shaggy rip on the chair, his round face hardens with disgust.

When he's happy, Raúl calls our place la pizza caprichosa. One corner forms the living room, with a scratchy plaid couch and that battered armchair where he broods. In the next lie our bed and a fake wood wardrobe whose doors will never close. We wash in the shower cabin wedged against it, next to the graying toilet and sink. The last corner makes up the kitchen, with a little gas stove, refrigerator, and grooved metal counter. Four parts, four different flavors, all on one small pizza. You can go round and round, but you're still in the same room. Mostly we call it el pinche garaje.

Once, I tried to explain to them back in Puebla that Raúl and I live in a garage. It's not bad, really. Lots of people do it, and sometimes you get more space than in a real apartment. But back home they didn't get it.

"¡Un garaje! ¡Qué barbaridad! In there with the cars? Does it smell like gas?"

I told them it's okay the way Mr. Brady fixed it, round lights on the ceiling, brown carpet on the floor. He has lots of houses, and he's divided them all up. You can make real money that way if you know a good contractor.

When Raúl heard me telling them, he turned dark red. He grabbed the phone and pushed me so hard that I fell.

"She doesn't know what she's talking about," he told his brother Martín. "Yeah, a long time ago it used to be a garage, in one of those big houses where the gringos live, but now it's a nice apartment with clean carpet and a brand-new kitchen."

When he hung up, I was still lying there on the rug. His face twitched, as though something behind it broke. He drew back his leg and kicked me hard. I saw his foot coming and tried to twist away, but it slammed my side with a thwack.

"¡Pendeja!" he yelled, his eyes black on his flat face. "Don't ever tell anyone we live in a garage! What will they think of us? Have you thought about that?"

My side was burning, and it hurt to suck in air, so I didn't tell him I thought it was okay. If we lived in a real apartment, como Dios manda, we couldn't send money to Martín, and we might not have enough to eat. Four hundred dollars a month we pay

Mr. Brady, and in a good month, when Raúl has lots of work, two hundred to Martín and a hundred to my mother.

The trouble with el pinche garaje is that there's no color. It's as brown as a cave, and with just one window, it feels like one. Dirt-colored carpet, brown plaid couch, green armchair covered with scars. Even the quilt on the bed looks like spilled coffee. The only light in here comes from the rays around the Virgin. Real apartments have windows with flowering plants. Someday I want an apartment like the sunporch of Mrs. Marshall, with light shining in from every side.

"What do you have in that bag?" asks Raúl. "Did they give you something?"

I was having so much fun talking about la vieja, I forgot. My hand shakes as I pull out some red cloth.

"No," I say. "I bought it at the fabric store—to make curtains."

Raúl reaches out to rub the stiff red cotton with yellow flowers like kernels of corn. His nails come nowhere near the ends of his thick brown fingers, sliced by crusty cuts. He rolls the cloth twice between his thumb and forefinger, then drops it and raises his eyes.

"What did I tell you, eh? ¿Qué te he dicho? How much money did you spend this time?"

"Almost nothing—it was on sale," I say. "I had to wait half an hour for the bus, and Amparo was going to the fabric store, so I went too. I found it in back on the remnant table. Two yards for 2.99."

"¿Tres pesos? ¡Que la chingada! You know how many branches I have to cut for three dollars? You know how long I have to drag a fucking rake? Half an hour! You call that nothing?"

I stuff the cloth in the bag so he won't see it, but the crackling makes him madder.

"Give me that!"

"No!" I yell. My fingers dig into the white plastic.

"¡Puta!"

He grabs the bag and pulls, but I hold on, and it rips open. The red cloth with yellow flowers falls softly onto the brown carpet. Raúl pushes me back.

"No!" I yell. "¡Deja eso! ¡Es mío!"

But his two strong hands have seized the cloth. He tears it right down the middle, fffffffffffffffffffffffffft!

"What did I tell you?" he shouts. "¿Qué te he dicho? Every peso you spend, you ask me! You're all the same. Fucking women, parásitas! I sweat half an hour throwing branches in a machine, and you throw it away on something that pleases your eye. What goes on in your head? We need that money—for a car, for an apartment, for Martín. You buy nothing, you hear? If I can't eat it, I don't want it in this house!"

I reach out with my foot to retrieve the cloth, trying not to get near enough to hit.

"You buy beer," I say. "Beer costs that much. And when you drink it, it's gone. The curtains will last."

"That's right—I DRINK it," he says.

Raúl steps forward until I breathe his hot fumes. His face turns flat and white when he's mad, with eyes like two round, black stones. "Beer is food, groceries! We need food. We don't need curtains."

Raúl goes back to his TV, mutters about parásitas, and settles into his green chair. He flips the channels until he finds the Univisión sports, and I gather the cloth and fold it. The two pieces are almost the same size, and the tear is almost straight. If I turn more under than I was going to, it might still work. Maybe he did me a favor. I push up on the wardrobe door so that it won't squeak, swing it open, and stuff the cloth in back. Raúl's body looks softer now, his eyes fixed on the glowing screen.

I step over to the kitchen and open the refrigerator. The bottles in the door chatter nervously. As I thought, there's still enough hamburger, but I sniff to make sure it's okay. In my hand it feels wet and cool, rancid-smelling like all the meat here, but once I cook it, it'll be all right. I smile as it falls into the pan with a plop, and I think of poor Mrs. Marshall. I put most of the refrigerator's contents on the table—a bag of tortillas, some salsa, an onion, a bowl of beans, and two tomatoes. Everything waits its turn to be cut or heated, since there's so little space. In half an hour the bags and bottles have become dinner.

Raúl doesn't need to be called, and we sit at the enamel-topped table. He pokes it with his finger and watches it wobble. Some twitch in my face makes him laugh.

"Maybe next time you wait for the bus, you should look at tables."

He reaches for a tortilla, piles it with beans and hamburger, and folds it neatly. As he takes a huge bite, an eyetooth flashes. I take a spoonful of meat, a spoonful of salsa, and hold the food in my mouth until the flavors have mixed. I want to tell him more about la vieja and her strange, dark house, but I wait until he's had a chance to eat. After five tortillas, he starts to slow down. He doesn't complain when the meat is gone, a good sign.

"Tell me more about vieja," he says. "Is she as crazy as Mrs. Chase?"

"Oh, much crazier." I laugh. "She can't do anything. She gets lost in her big house. It's so sad. I can't believe her son left her there alone."

Raúl blinks. "What's he like? He lives there alone with his mother?"

"I think so," I say. "I don't think he's married."

Raúl tears off a piece of tortilla and scoops up two beans clinging to the yellow bowl.

"Marica," he says with his mouth full.

"I can't tell. Could be. He seems so nice."

Raúl shakes his head. "What a loser, living there with his mother. How old is this guy?"

"Oh, about forty," I say. "Much older than us. Gordo. Panzón. You should see his fat belly."

Raúl laughs, fast and deep. "You better watch out for this guy. I don't want him putting any moves on you."

"Why would he put moves on me if he's a marica?"

"You never know. Maybe he never saw a good-looking woman before."

His eyes warm me like good, black coffee.

"Me?"

Raúl reaches for my hand and squeezes. "No eres tan mala. Probably the best he's ever seen. So what does he do?"

"He's an accountant."

"Oh."

Raúl turns quiet, probably wondering how much Justin makes in an hour. Maybe ten, twenty times what Raúl does.

"I can't understand why he's not married," I say.

Raúl stiffens and draws in his breath.

"You like this guy," he says.

"No! He's just a fat old gringo."

"A fat old gringo with no woman and a lot of money."

Raúl leans back, folds his arms, and looks me up and down.

"I think it's nice he takes care of his mother," I say. "Not many gringos do that. They put them in a home and wait for them to die."

"You've got that right, chingados gringos de mierda. But he's not taking care of her. You are."

"He has to work."

"You like this guy. I can tell."

"Why would I like a fat, gay gabacho who lives with his mother?"

"You tell me," he says. "You women are all crazy. Now bring me a coffee—and some of those cookies. What are they called? Náter Báter."

I pick up empty dishes from the table, and I smile, then start to laugh. Raúl catches me around the waist and pulls me onto his lap. He wiggles his nose into my hair and growls.

"If he tries anything," he says, "he's going to be a dead fat, gay gabacho."

CHAPTER 4

LITTLE ROCK

"Hey, Joey, we're crossing the Mississippi!" I cry as we spin up a ramp over chocolate water.

Joey nods, unimpressed. Poor guy, he probably can't even see out the window, strapped down in the back seat like that. I'm off to an early start today, gliding over the river with orange haze at my back. Arkansas lures me across into an unknown world of white dust. Until I see Connie tomorrow, I want to peer into crop rows and study the tales in Clinton's library. Teresa keeps talking, but I can't write all the time. My mind is eating itself in its quest for words.

On the far shore, the land flattens out as though it's been steamrolled. Memphis launches FedEx trucks in concentric waves, and I dodge the westbound fleet. Wilma shoots through dim fields, where farmhouses lie like lost dice. Instead of dust, I find rice paddies where pale green stalks rise from murky brown puddles. On a billboard, a freckled girl with pigtails grins. "Rice! Awesome!"

The moist heat and huge, palpitating sky make me feel faint, so I pull into a waffle place for oatmeal and whole wheat toast. When I emerge, Joey is sweltering.

"Poor bear," I murmur. "You need to go to the mountains. This is no place for you."

Though it's overcast, I lower the sunshades, because there's way too much sky. I race west through soft Arkansas green, wondering what happens where brown mud meets gray haze. With my left hand on the wheel, I jump through the stations in search of an intelligent voice.

The religious chants lure me, but I wonder how anyone could let them colonize her mind. One preacher's resonance seizes me, so that my finger can't stifle his voice. He's telling me why I have to stay married. No matter what my husband is doing, my divorce would wound the world like a hatchet chop.

"Now, you say, what does this one marriage matter? Don't I have a right to be happy? But you see, each marriage is a pillar. And society is a wharf—a structure built on those pillars. Each time you take one of 'em away, you destabilize the structure, and eventually, it'll come crashing down."

Each sentence holds as firmly to the next as links in a steel chain. I sit paralyzed with my finger poised, unable to break the flow.

"Now, people say, I don't love this man anymore. I don't love this woman. I don't care that I made a sacred vow to God to spend the rest of my life with this person. I want out! Now, what do you suppose God thinks when he hears that? Well, it makes him mad. And he lets those selfish people do what they want, but he makes 'em pay. He makes us all pay."

Embarrassed, Joey tries to pretend that he's watching a faded white house. The clapboard home cowers in its circle of protective trees, whose magic can't avert passing eyes.

"Now, some of you out there, you may have served in the army. You may have a son or daughter in the armed forces. So you know that in the army, one foolish, careless soldier can endanger his whole unit. Just one mistake—and poof. Now, when they train those soldiers, they make sure that if one person is careless, or selfish, or lazy, they punish the whole group. 'Cause in a real war, that's what would happen. When a whole team has to suffer for one person's mistake, those other soldiers, they get riled up. That's not fair, they say. He did it! Not us! We didn't do anything! But those officers, they're smart. 'Cause the other soldiers, they're gonna go to that selfish person and tell him to straighten up. Tell him like he won't ever forget it, if you know what I mean. They shouldn't have to suffer for his selfishness. And they let him know that, loud and clear."

The preacher's voice intensifies into a red, searing beam.

"Now, you, as a good Christian—as a faithful, honest servant of God—you've got to do two things. First off, if you're that wavering soldier—that sleepy man on guard, thinking, *Well, I'll just close my eyes for a minute. Just a minute. Who'll know? Who'll care?*—you don't do that, you hear? 'Cause in that one second, when your eyelids start to droop and you're starting to nod off—you've gotta think of all those other people you're gonna hurt. Your whole family—your whole unit wiped out, just like that, because of the incoming rocket you didn't see. You violate your vows to God, you betray your whole family—you betray your whole society. They suffer for your sins! And they'll let you know that they aren't gonna suffer that gladly."

I start to picture it, a crowd of avenging scrub-heads advancing on me, broom handles raised. I am a lone martial artist in a closing circle of fat, gray-haired attackers.

"Now, the second thing you've gotta do, as a faithful Christian, is to *be* those other soldiers. If you know someone who's contemplatin' breakin' her vows, be it through adultery, or separation, or divorce—well, you've got to say to that person, you can't do that. That kind of selfish behavior undermines our whole society. That kind of behavior puts all our lives at risk. Like those officers, God knows what he's doing. Like those officers, he knows that faithful Christians will make sure God's will is enforced."

Joey looks frightened. His eyes are downcast, but he's begging me to hit "scan." That burning voice still has me paralyzed, unable to move.

"Now, I know it's not easy. Maybe the person contemplating divorce is your big brother. Maybe it's your boss. Maybe it's someone you love. But think about your love of God. How much do you love him? Think about three hundred million Americans. How much do you love them? Think about that beautiful pier, that magnificent structure, groaning and cracking, splitting and splintering, all because—"

Brrrp. Brrrp. Brrrp. Doo-doo-doo-DEE-doo.

What? Who could be calling me? Where is that thing? Oh, yeah, down in the cup holder.

Brrrp. Brr—

"H'lo?"

"¡Mala!"

"¡Gonzalo! ¿Qué tal?" My face spreads in a broad grin.

"Mala, you have been bad!"

"Bad, what—me, bad? Even badder than usual?"

A grove of pale trees quivers in a freshly awakened wind.

"¡Más mala que nunca! You have not answered my calls. Where have you been?"

"Well, let's see—Birmingham, Memphis ... now Arkansas."

"Arkansas!"

I laugh delightedly at his tone of amazement. "Yeah, Arkansas. I'm driving to San Francisco. I'm driving cross-country."

"Cross-country! ¡Pero, qué maravilla!"

Suddenly I feel proud. "Yeah, it's amazing. I'm driving through all these rice paddies. I think I'm about an hour east of Little Rock."

"Little Rock!" Gonzalo laughs. "Can you imagine? The capital of a state—Little Rock!"

"Yeah, I would have gone for Big Rock, definitely."

"Big Rock!" Gonzalo savors his laugh. "Pero Mala—Malísima—why are you doing this? I mean, it is a nice idea, but what about your book? Don't you have to write your book this summer?" As his professorial tone emerges, some of the warmth fades.

"I am writing it—I mean, not right now. Right now, I'm passing a FedEx truck. But I'm writing every day. It's finally coming out. It's like a constipated person—I had to move around to get it out of me."

"Your novel is like shit?"

He sounds so serious I have to laugh. "No—no—I mean—it's pretty good, but getting it out is like—"

Gonzalo ignores me. "Mala, this is not good. Your novel is not shit. I am glad it is coming out, though. You were so worried. It took so long."

"Yeah, this one took a long time. Plus I was grading all these goddamn short stories. There ought to be a law. They shouldn't let some people write."

"Allí tienes toda la razón, tienes toda la razón, Mala. It is good that you are writing your novel. So how is it going? Are you writing about that crazy old lady, like you said?"

I wish he didn't sound like he was my father.

"Well, sort of," I say. "More about the woman taking—shit!"

"Mala? Are you okay?"

"Yeah. Blown-out tire in the road."

The sooty tire lies like a crow torn by a cubist painter, its shredded black wings pointing six ways.

"Oh. So you are driving a lot. Do you have time to write, with all this driving? You are by yourself, right?"

"Yeah, except for Joey."

"Joey?"

Gonzalo's earnest brows must be drawing together, giving his round face even more charm.

"Yeah, Joey, my bear."

"Oh no—not that bear."

Gonzalo never did like Joey. Anytime he came over, he used to look at him funny.

"Yeah—well, I've got to talk to somebody."

"So you are driving and writing—and talking to a bear."

Now he sounds like a philosopher, pressing toward the conclusion.

"Well, right now I'm talking to you."

"¿Y no hay ningún hombre—ningún macho por allí?" he asks. "I know you, Mala. Somewhere in this there is a man."

"Well, I did just meet a guy in Birmingham."

I imagine Clifton face-to-face with Gonzalo, who prevails with his radiance and taut posture. Gonzalo has never liked any of my men.

"¡Lo sabía!" he cries. "¡Qué mala eres! Pobre tío. ¿Cómo se llama?"

"Clifton."

"Clifton?" He snorts. "This is a name?"

"It is in Alabama."

"And you have broken his heart already?"

Our conversation has turned to a familiar melody, but still it brings a laugh.

"Nah," I say. "He's just reading my book. He seems kind of nice. Anyway, I need him. He's just like Sandy's son, and I have to listen to what he says."

"Who is Sandy?" asks Gonzalo patiently.

"The old woman with dementia in my book. Clifton—Justin—hires Teresa to take care of her."

"But how can you study him when you are driving alone with a bear, in Arkansas, and he is—where? Alabama?" His voice tightens.

"Birmingham. Cell phone. Great invention. He even works for the phone company."

"¡Qué mala eres! So now you seduce innocent phone-company workers? Mala, you are a national security risk!"

I smile at another rice billboard, a bright-eyed black boy offering a bowl of white grains.

"So what about that last one of yours, didn't she work for the State Department?"

"Yes, but she was single—I bet this Clinton is married." I try to picture Clifton's wife but see only a gray blur.

"If he is, he hasn't said so."

"Mala, they never say so. I bet he lives in a big house with a fat wife and three kids."

Mrs. Clifton emerges from the outside in. Square gold earrings glint in flabby lobes.

"So what? It's going to hurt him to talk to me?"

"Mala, this guy wants to do more than talk. Te lo prometo. You are probably the best-looking woman he has ever seen. What did you do, camp outside his building and wait for him to come out?"

"No! I was friggin' starving to death, and I sat down to eat! He came to *me*!" I explode. "I'm not taking this trip to hook up with fat men from Alabama!"

"I think maybe you are taking it to hook up with thin men from California."

"No!"

My cry surprises me, and Joey looks up, startled.

"Mala, this is not good for you. Remember what happened the last time you saw him?"

"Yeah, he took me down a basement and—"

"No, no, after that—three, four years ago?"

I wish Gonzalo didn't have such a good memory.

"That was different. He was busy. He couldn't—"

"It is over, Mala. He has been trying to tell you that, but he can't. Maybe he doesn't want to hurt you, but he is hurting you more this way. Don't you remember how you cried last time? I have never heard you cry like that. It is bad for you to see him. Maybe this time he will not be so nice."

My hands tighten. "What—Johnny Turner?" I choke. "They don't come any nicer than him."

"Mala—he is a guy. He has a wife—two kids, you said?"

"He had a wife and kid when he took me down the basement."

Three waxy calla lilies point toward a blue cellar door.

"As I said, he's a guy," lectures Gonzalo. "You are a beautiful woman, Mala. You are hard to resist. But guys don't want to keep seeing the women they had sex with twenty years ago. Mala, he doesn't love you."

"I know he doesn't!" I burst out. "I want to see him anyway!"

"Why?"

"Because—because I care about him!"

"Even if he doesn't care about you?"

"He does! He just—" My voice dissolves.

"Mala, Mala, lo siento, I didn't mean to make you cry."

"You didn't. I was thinking of Johnny. He knows I'm coming. I called him. I have an appointment."

I still wonder what Johnny wrote in his calendar.

"Oh—you have an appointment."

Why does he have to sound so damned ironic?

"Yeah, and he can't cancel it either. He doesn't have my number."

"Eres una mala muy lista."

I sense that Gonzalo is satisfied—at least for now.

"Más lista que este flaco en San Francisco."

"¡Qué mala eres! ¡Un gordo y un flaco!"

"Yeah, fat or thin, I take 'em either way."

"So you are driving cross-country, talking to a bear, from a fat lover in Alabama to a thin one in California."

"And writing a novel about a crazy woman." I smile.

"Mala, you sound very busy. I had better let you go."

"Yeah. And stay away from the State Department."

"All right, Mala. Sé buena. Drive carefully. I will call again soon."

"¿Aun soy la chica más mala que conoces?" My voice wavers.

"Aun eres la chica más mala que conozco. ¡Ciao, Mala!"

"¡Adios, Gonzalo!"

I blink. If only eyelids worked as well as windshield wipers. Arkansas has gone faint and dim. Against the pale green fields shimmers Johnny Turner. His chin rests on his hand as he frowns, his other long arm draped over his chair. His eyes are black against his fair skin. His low voice warms the lab.

"Keep on pourin', Gina."

A few days after Johnny took me up the hill, a first-year student's sequence gel was leaking. Poor Gina was about to lose a whole day's work. Stewart, who was training her, was nearly screaming, and Johnny strode over to investigate. The spreading spot on the white bench paper said it all.

"Fuck!" yelled Stewart.

"Nope. Don't give up yet," said Johnny.

I had been passing the alley, and his low voice drew me in. With a blue rack of pipette tips in my hand, I hovered to watch.

Johnny noted the size of the spot and the volume in Gina's Erlenmeyer, and he did some quick calculus.

"Just keep on pourin', Gina. It's gonna gel."

I looked at Gina, a round-faced girl with short, even blonde hair. The lip of her flask chattered against the glass plate, but she kept the sticky stream coming.

"You just keep on pourin', Gina," said Johnny. His voice held perfectly steady.

The spot grew from a half-dollar to a small pancake. At a glance from Johnny, Stewart shut up.

"Just keep on pourin' ..."

The spot stopped growing. Just before Gina ran out of solution, the leak plugged itself and the fluid gelled. She looked up at Johnny with reddened eyes, and her lips parted in a radiant smile.

Gina's face breaks apart and darkens to form a group of brown cows. The rice paddies have congealed to damp pastures.

"Hey, Joey, cows!" I call and glance behind me.

Joey feigns interest and looks up loyally, but he wants to know when we'll be in Little Rock. I follow signs through an industrial strip sapping a narrow, dark-brown river. Clinton's Presidential Library stands like a cake in a gravelly, abandoned lot. Enormous people float in, so fat that they look as though someone stuck hoses in their mouths and blew. Curious about Bill's childhood, I breathe the satisfying tale: heroic mother, drinking stepfather, Rhodes Scholarship. Bill's achievements impress me even more—balancing the budget, raising the minimum wage. But most intriguing are his daily schedules. Let's see ... what was he doing in spring 1998?

What these gigantic people and I have come to see is missing from this museum. I know—I heard them sniggering about it around the Oval Office. The upright displays mention Bill's impeachment but never the reason why. In all this glory, the name Monica appears nowhere. How could they edit her out of the story like that? To me, Bill and Monica made perfect sense. A guy wants a competent partner, but no one with any gumption settles just for that. That girl radiated desire, and she adored him. Who wants to go through life with just one person? It would be like going through life with just one book.

Although I'm about to collapse with hunger, I ask at the information desk how to reach Central High. Once again, they tell me to take the interstate. What is it with these people? Doesn't anyone in the South want me to see their town? I choose a road that takes me straight through downtown, a small world of clean white blocks. Then come the title-loan and package stores and red brick with black iron bars. I park at the visitors' center, a 1950s-style Mobile station, and drift through the exhibit, which is turning fuzzy. That same screaming girl I saw in Alabama is cursing a black woman on her way to school. In the white girl's pink snake mouth, the half-formed words lie frozen: "Go home, bitch!" Instead of heading home, I press west.

Since I want to make Fort Smith by nightfall, I curve up into dark hills. In the sky, the morning haze has crystallized to brilliant blue. Along the steep slopes, the dense trees are nearly black. I stop at the first restaurant I see and hope that with an iced tea and a fruit salad, my head will clear. Teresa wants to explore that room full of books and tell Justin to buy cheaper toilet paper.

I like to go to work. At the Marta stop, I shiver in the dark, but in the house of Mrs. Marshall, I float through warm space. Sometimes Justin talks to me before he leaves for the office. Yesterday he even offered me a cup of coffee. He tells me things to do for la vieja, and I'm glad he does, since watching her is hard. She can get upset so fast and then start to pant and wring her hands.

Unlike a little kid, she won't watch TV. If you turn it on, she jumps up two minutes later and says it's stupid.

"Yeah, she never did like to watch TV," says Justin. "She never could sit still."

"What did she like to do?" I ask. It makes me sad to watch her flit around all day.

"Well, she liked to read—she used to read a lot."

"Yeah, all those books," I murmur.

"But—but—" Justin squints at chips of color on the floor. "I don't think—I'm not sure she can read anymore."

¡Qué pena! The poor old lady. "But she looks at the books," I say.

"Yeah, she still loves her books." Justin swirls his last bit of coffee and swallows it like a shot of tequila. "I have to go." He smiles a little, but his puffy lips hide his teeth. "I think she likes you. She wanted to know when you were coming today."

I smile into his dark brown eyes. The wrinkles around them show me how he'll look when he's old.

"Bye, Teresa," he says. "Hope she has a good day. Try the magazines. See you tonight."

But Mrs. Marshall isn't having a good day. Usually she likes her magazines. I've thought for a while that she can't read the writing, but she still loves to turn the pages. I think it feels like work to her, and she's someone who needs to work. Like Raúl—he complains about all those branches, but if he couldn't work, he'd go crazy.

Today Mrs. Marshall whips through the pages like she wants to kill someone.

"Stupid! Stupid!" she hisses.

I wonder what kind of work she used to do. I doubt she spent her life cleaning this house and watching Justin. Instead of looking at the pictures, she stares at me, her blue eyes narrow as a cat's.

"Where's my book?" she demands.

"What book?"

"You took it, didn't you?" She rises.

"No, no, but maybe I can help you find it."

"You hid it, didn't you?"

"No," I say. "What did it look like? What kind of book?"

She looks at me disgustedly, as if wondering how I can think she can't see through me.

"Is it in the room with all the books?" I ask.

I start to move that way, and she follows, sure I'll lead her to where I hid it. The book room is brighter today, the rays of sun piercing the window like daggers. The golden knives blaze like the rays around the virgin, pointing down toward the notebooks below.

Mrs. Marshall pulls a red book from the shelf and settles onto a stiff brown chair. Maybe she wanted that book, but probably *she forgot. Since she's quiet, I choose one of the notebooks. "Nov. 1963–June 1965," says the cover in faded black ink. I flip it open, and a woman's writing appears, so clear that even I can read it.*

*"**I hate to go to the dead room,**" it says.*

I raise my eyes to Mrs. Marshall, but she's staring so hard at her red book she's forgotten I'm even here. I return to the notebook.

The bag of dead rats warms my hand, hairy white bodies floating in tomato soup. I'm always afraid it will leak in the elevator. And that smell. Sticky, heavy, rotten. I hold my breath, pull the steel door open, and raise the heavy lid. In the metal can hangs a blue plastic bag, thick as a glove. I toss in my soup and hold my breath until I'm halfway down the hall. Still that smell defiles my nose. It must seep right through my skin.

Yesterday I blew out and out, trying to rid myself of that stench, and when the elevator doors opened, the world turned fuzzy. Someone got in, but all I saw was a dark shape.

"Are you okay?" asked a distant voice.

I smiled and nodded, but the elevator tilted, and my right cheek and ear smashed the wall.

"I've got you!" said the voice. Something gripped me hard around the waist, but I couldn't tell what it was.

"Keep your head down. That's it," I heard.

I couldn't breathe the way it was pressing me, but I couldn't tell it to let go.

A pterodactyl wing stroked my head. "Aw gee," said the low voice. "Your nice long hair's draggin' on the floor."

"Bing!" went the elevator.

"Hey, help!" called the voice. "Who's a doctor down here?"

Someone lowered me to the cold, hard floor, and when I was lying, I began to breathe again. Sneakered feet came pounding up.

"What happened? What's wrong?" asked a tight voice.

A big hand lifted my head and slid something soft under it. Leather. The sweet smell reassured me.

"Here, take this. Your hair's gettin' all dirty," said the first voice.

"I know her. That's Bill Marshall's wife. Somebody call Bill Marshall," said the second.

I felt so cold and ashamed, like I had gone to the bathroom in my pants. I wanted to hide, but there was no place to go. I tried not to cry.

Soft breath brushed my face, and a shadow screened the light. Over me hovered a white face with two worried black eyes.

"You gave us a scare," it said, the thin lips spreading.

"Here! I've got some water!" Thudding footsteps approached, and something cool splashed my leg.

"Can you sit up?" asked the pale man.

"Yeah," I said. "I'm sorry. This is so embarrassing."

"Well, you didn't plan it, did you?" His smile settled.

Bill rushed up, panting. "Jimmy—what happened?"

"I got in the elevator, and she just fell," said Jimmy. He spoke with a slow, chewy accent, but I couldn't tell what kind.

"Are you okay, Sandy?" asked Bill. His warm, fleshy fingers rubbed my hand.

"Yeah, I'm okay."

I leaned against the wall and sipped the water, wondering if they were going to kick me out. I'm married to a professor, but there's no fainting allowed in science.

"You want to try standin' up now?" asked Jimmy.

He reached for my hands, but Bill caught one of his long arms.

"No! We've got to get her checked out."

And would you believe it—two men wheeled me down to the ER on a gurney. As they raised me, I watched Jimmy's tense legs. Bill was squeezing my hand.

"You be good. Don't give 'em too much trouble down there," called Jimmy.

They held me in the hospital all afternoon. They took blood, but I didn't faint again. I hate myself so much. How are they ever going to take me seriously now?

My head itches as though a fly has landed on it, and I look up to find Mrs. Marshall staring. Her red book has fallen, but on the thick carpet, I didn't hear it.

"What's that?" she asks. "What are you reading?"

"Just a book," I say. "It's pretty good. How's yours?"

"Stupid."

I shove the notebook back in the gap where I found it and realize that the sun's rays have withdrawn.

The road winds up between dark hills, seeking the lost, hazy sky. How fiercely those black trees grip the slopes! I am longing for movement, any sign of life, but these dense firs occlude it.

The trees grow almost to the edge of the road, and if deer slip among them, they walk unseen.

In San Francisco, it's four in the afternoon. Maybe Johnny's gaze has escaped his screen to feast on the white city. Nowadays he spends more time in his office than his lab. Probably he's reviving some depressed student, telling her new experiments to try. In New York, it's seven at night. Gonzalo must be between women, or he wouldn't have called. Right now, he'll be cooking dinner, thinking of a clove-scented woman as he swirls oil into a black pan. Probably he's right that Clifton is married, but who cares? Didn't Clifton come to me? I peer into the dark between the dense trees and wonder what he's doing tonight.

I scoop up my phone, which has swallowed his number, and hold the silver shell over the rising road. I scan back—nope, that's Gonzalo—yeah, there it is, the one with the weird area code. I glance back at Joey, who raises his nose. These black hills have lightened his mood. Steering with my left hand, I hold the phone to my ear. The FedEx trucks have all gone somewhere else.

Boop.

My heart beats faster. Why? He's just some fat guy from Birmingham.

Boop.

Probably he's out. I'll try again la—

"H'lo?"

"Hello, Clifton?"

"Yeah—who's this?" His voice sounds tight, almost angry.

"Clifton? It's—"

"Theresa? Hey! How'd you—" His voice retains an edge of alarm.

"Get this number? I didn't. My phone learned it. They're getting smarter."

"Yeah, kind of scary, isn't it?" Finally he sounds like the man in the food court.

The road gleams as I rise around a curve.

"Yeah, I like cell phones."

Clifton exhales in a puff. "Funny you should call—I was just thinking about you. I just didn't think ..." His voice trails off.

"Are you busy? I can call again later."

The top of the rise disappoints me, nothing but firs on heartless hills.

"Oh, no, no." Clifton returns from his mental blink. "I'm just sitting out in my backyard, drinking a beer."

"Hey, that's great. Do you have a nice yard?"

I try to envision it. All I can see is the garden my mother once dug in a dingy patch between clapboard houses.

"Oh, yeah." He breathes. "There are flowers all around me. My— A lot of flowers. The roses are blooming."

"Hey, that's wonderful." I picture his round, pink body surrounded by fragrant petals.

Clifton pauses, and I hear a sucking sound, then a sigh.

"Clifton?"

"Just finishing my beer. You know, I was going to call you, 'cause I've really gotten into your book. I've got it out here with me now."

A warm wave spreads down my legs. "Yeah, I wanted to ask if you found a copy."

"Yup, right after I talked to you about it that night. I was up half of last night reading it. It's strange, but—I like it. I've never read anything like it before."

I picture him balancing my book on his stomach, his stare igniting the crisp pages.

"What's so strange about it?"

"Well—the woman's so crazy. I never know what she's going to do next. The beginning about her mother dying is horrible—the sound of her breathing—that steamy smell in the hospital. It made me think—" Clifton's voice rises and tightens. "Did your mother …?"

"No, she's alive. She's in a nursing home. She had early-onset dementia."

It's gotten so easy to say that now. Used to be, I couldn't say it without crying.

"Oh, I'm sorry." He sighs. "That's awful. That's almost worse than—"

"No, no, not really," I cut in. "I've gotten used to it. It was only bad at first, when she was doing crazy things all the time."

Once, she cut off her pants, because she said they were tripping her. I found her with the scissors in her hand, their blades snipping the air.

"I'm sorry," says Clifton. "Do you have any brothers or sisters to help?"

"No, just me," I answer. "My father died a long time ago. But there's a lady who comes in twice a week to check on her."

"Isn't she in a nursing home?"

"Yeah—but this woman reads to her, and massages her, and checks to make sure they're doing their jobs."

"That sounds like a good idea. You must really care about her. How often do you see her?"

Clifton's core of concern loosens, probably as he thinks of his own mother.

"Oh, a couple of times a year," I say.

Silence spreads in a black wave.

"She's in Pennsylvania," I add.

"Pennsylvania—but aren't you …?" Clifton sounds more confused than reproachful.

"Well, she always lived there," I explain. "So when she needed it, I put her in a local home. It's a good place, and it would be hard to move her, so when I got this job, I left her there."

Hillcrest stands among dark wooded hills, proud of its red brick and white trim. It looks respectable, but I picked it for the smell. In most of them, the urine stench tightens your nose, but Hillcrest just smells of bland food.

"Oh. I guess that makes sense," says Clifton.

"She can't recognize me," I murmur. "She doesn't even know I'm there. She can't walk or talk or see me—just swallow and …"

"Wow, that's sad. That's really sad."

Clifton breathes out in a long sigh, followed by a puff of static.

"Clifton?"

"Yeah, I'm here. Just going in for another beer."

I see silver appliances shimmering in his kitchen. He approaches a daunting steel refrigerator.

"So when was the last time you saw her?" he asks.

A scruffy fir clings valiantly to a gray cliff.

"Theresa? Are you still there?"

"Yeah. I was just thinking."

Clifton lets me dream while he opens his beer.

"You know who I really like in your book?" he asks.

"Who?"

"That big, tall skinny guy. He's so funny. I hope she ends up with him."

"You do?" I laugh.

Clifton has such an odd way of talking about my book, as though it were something that hadn't happened yet.

"Yeah, he's funny. I love what he did with those fish. I think he'd be nice to her. I get the feeling she's this way because nobody—"

"Yeah?"

I fly past the cliff. I love it when people talk about my characters as if they were real.

"She's changing, though." Clifton hesitates. "I can't tell— Anyway, I like your book." He laughs. "This is terrible, but you know what my favorite thing was?"

"What?"

"The ice cream. All those descriptions of ice cream. Chocolate marshmallow, maple walnut, black cherry …"

The cover of *The Rainbow Bar* drips sweetness. I still wonder if that's what sold my book.

"Pistachio!" I laugh. "Chocolate fudge ripple. Mint almond chip."

"I think it was the hot fudge that did it," says Clifton. "The night she and Leila got into the fudge. When that big, tall guy came in— It was the middle of the night, and I had to get up and raid the freezer."

"What did you find in there?"

"Rum raisin. You forgot that one."

My mind's tongue savors cold, bittersweet chews.

Clifton breathes softly. "Theresa?"

"Yeah. I was just picturing you alone in your kitchen in the middle of the night."

Clifton laughs. "I like the way you think—but there's something scary about it."

"Why? What's scary? No one's ever said that before."

"Your mind just breaks in and sees things. I feel like you're in my house right now."

"Nope. I'm in the Ozarks heading for Fort Smith."

These black hills crouch like waiting monsters. Whoever called them "Ozarks" had the right idea.

"The Ozarks! Wow! I wish I were there with you."

A pop pricks my ear. Why did he wait so long to open his beer?

"So why don't you drive cross-country?"

"My job!" he exclaims. "I'm lucky if I can get two days. And—" Some static tells me he's on the move.

"Yeah. Yeah, I guess I'm lucky to have a job that lets me do this." I sigh.

"You are. And the writing—you have such freedom. I wish—"

There's a sucking sound, and then silence.

"Anyway, I liked the ice cream. How did you ever come up with that?"

"I like ice cream," I say quickly.

Mint almond chip. The joy of realizing you have something big in your mouth, nudging it into position to bite.

"Yeah, me too, but—oh. Oh, I get it."

"What?"

"Well, you're so nice and slim. So tiny. You like ice cream, but you won't eat it, so you write about it."

"Sometimes I eat it." I try to remember the last time I had mint almond chip.

"Not too often, I bet, with a figure like that."

"Like what?" A smile warms my legs.

"Slim. Graceful. Pretty. You're very pretty," he says softly.

"Thanks. That's nice."

"Very pretty."

His whisper brushes my ear. My lips tingle in the silence.

"So Fort Smith, huh?" he asks.

"Yeah, that's the plan. Oklahoma City tomorrow." Now I'm not so sure I want to see Connie.

"But where are you headed eventually?" he asks. "San Francisco?"

"Eventually back to Atlanta. Big circle. But yeah, I'm going to San Francisco."

"I loved your descriptions of that city," he says. "The fog, the white flowers, the eucalyptus smell."

"Yeah, the eucalyptus. I miss the eucalyptus ..."

At night those shaggy trees shook off their scent. Johnny and I glided through living clouds of it.

"Did you live there?" asks Clifton.

"Yeah. For three years. Funny. I hated it so much, but now I want to go back."

"I'd like to see it," he says quietly. "I wish—"

Thuds and scrapes bury his voice. A distant shout crowns the heap of noise.

"I've got to go, Theresa," he says quickly. "Sorry, I've got to go."

The phone reverts to lifeless metal. I rub my ear and glance at Joey, but he has withdrawn to a world of salmon and rushing streams. Poor bear. I should let him out to explore these hills. But night is coming, and they are seeping darkness.

All day long she drags me from the bathroom to the book, and then back to the bathroom. Every day a different book becomes "my book," marked as "it" in a game of tag. Her question, "When is Justin coming home?" chops the time more finely than the clock's tunes. The tall wooden timekeeper cuts up the minutes like an angry cook.

"Not long," I say. "Just two more hours."

Two minutes later she asks me again. Poor Justin. No wonder he's not married. Anytime he's not at work, he's soothing her.

When I go to the bathroom, she scratches at the door.

"Where's Justin?" she demands.

"Don't worry—he'll be home soon." I find that I'm clutching a bouquet of toilet paper just like she does.

When Justin's car scrapes the driveway, I'm as relieved as Mrs. Marshall. The front door swings open, and he smiles at us both as though we were his family.

"Hi," he says. "Did you have a good day?"

His playful grin says that he knows what kind of day we had. For the first time, his lips reveal shy white teeth. He seems cheerful—maybe because a woman he likes finally spoke to him at work.

Mrs. Marshall and I follow him to the kitchen, although it's time for me to go. Like the sunporch, the kitchen is a room you can live in, with creamy cabinets and a speckled floor. Justin pops open a beer, just like Raúl does when he comes home.

"Do you want something to drink, Mom?" he asks.

"White wine," she says.

Justin pours it silently into a tulip-shaped glass. He shakes his head and looks at me, embarrassed.

"Sorry—sorry—Teresa, would you like anything?"

"No, thanks."

Mrs. Marshall sips her wine and looks at him from the corner of her eye.

"What did you and Teresa do today, Mom?" he asks.

"She took my book. She won't say where it is."

Justin rubs her shoulder affectionately. "Come on, Mom, I bet she wouldn't do that."

"We tried to find it," I say. "But I don't know which one it is."

"It's okay." He smiles. "We'll find it tonight."

His eyes move downward instead of meeting mine. Mrs. Marshall finishes her wine with a gurgle.

"Hey, I have an idea!" says Justin. "Want to go for a ride, Mom? Why don't we drive Teresa home?"

"Oh, no," I say.

Raúl would kill me if he knew I rode with el gringo panzón. The round, white clock says ten after six. In this house, there's a clock in every room. We might get home before Raúl. He might not find out. And I'm so sick of those guys at the bus stop.

"It could be fun," says Justin. "She needs to go out. Wouldn't you like that, Mom?"

"No."

"Oh, come on, Mom. We could go for ice cream afterward—or before. Teresa could have some too."

"Oh, no, I need to go home."

Justin heads for the hall, and we guide his mother's arms into her blue coat. As soon as we get one arm in and start the other, she pulls the first one out again. Finally, I hold her hand while Justin coaxes her second arm until both are sheathed in blue wool.

I loop my arm through hers and lead her down to the car, heavy, glossy, and black. I don't know cars the way Raúl does, but this one looks expensive. The door opens with a soft click of parts. The doors of Raúl's friends' cars creak and groan, like prisoners fighting their bonds. And Justin's car smells so nice—new, classy, and clean. A big, solid car, probably Swedish or German.

We try to strap Mrs. Marshall into the back seat, but her arms fly up.

"Stop! Why are you putting me back here? I want to sit in front!"

Justin loops the belt over her, and the buckle clicks.

"Teresa needs to sit in front," he says, "so she can tell me where to go. She has to tell me where to turn."

Justin smiles faintly as he starts the motor. His back softens against the fragrant leather. On the gearshift, his fingers look broad and strong. He takes us very fast down the driveway.

"What kind of car is this?" I ask. I can't tell Raúl, but I want to know.

"A BMW 520i," he says. "So how do I go? Where do you live?"

"You have to go to the Buford Highway."

He nods as though he expected this and seems to trace the route in his head.

How black it is out here at night, with so much space between the houses! Justin's headlights form two ghostly cones revealing the pitted street. The world comes back when we reach a road packed solid with slow-moving cars. At six fifteen, everyone in Atlanta is driving. Maybe Raúl will beat us home, and I worry about what to tell him. He might say that I can't go back. I'd miss crazy old Mrs. Marshall with her books and Justin with his half-hidden smiles.

As we creep along, I feel sorry for the car. It vibrates with a panther's soft power. Justin's fingers twitch on the gearshift.

"Don't worry—we'll be out of this soon. It'll open up when we reach Clifton Road."

He turns left onto a narrow street that twists its way through dense woods. Mrs. Marshall seems to like peering out as we rush around the curves. Justin sighs. The road divides, and without hesitation, he veers left. A few dimly lit wooden houses glow like haunted islands in the night.

"So you looked for the book all day?" *asks Justin.*

"Well, not just that. We also read."

"It's hard to find something she likes to do," *he murmurs.* "She's always so restless."

I glance back at Mrs. Marshall, but she's staring out at the houses, a memory shaping her soft smile.

"It's okay," *says Justin.* "She can't hear us back there."

We stop at a light guarding a rushing road, and Mrs. Marshall tracks the swift cars. I've never seen her so quiet. The street opens out ahead of us, with huge glowing buildings on each side.

"That's Edgewood University," *says Justin.* "That's the hospital—the medical buildings."

"Is that where your father used to work?"

"*Yeah, he ran a lab there for years. Then he was dean of the medical school.*"

Justin's steady voice doesn't sound like he's proud. He dislikes something about this place.

"*Did your mother work in a science lab too?*"

"*Yeah, she was a research assistant until I came along. Then she stopped and stayed home with me.*"

"*Did she miss it—the lab?*"

"*I can't really tell. My dad kept trying to make her go back, and she did, but she didn't like it. She said everything had changed—and she wanted to be there for me, so she gave up science. I'm not sure how much she liked it anyway.*"

"*It must be hard work. A lot to know.*"

"*Yeah, but my dad loved it. He lived it and breathed it twenty-four hours a day—at least, until he became dean. But she was different. It's hard to know how she felt about science.*"

Justin turns from the bright alley back into empty, dark woods. The trees rule here, and even in the hospital-palaces, their shadowy branches are never more than a street away. We shoot down a road so steep that I grab the padded seat. I feel as though I'm falling down but my insides are falling up.

Justin pats my hand and laughs. "*Don't worry. I'm a good driver. Isn't that right, Mom?*"

His hand is warm, but he withdraws it quickly. Mrs. Marshall squints into the woods.

"*How about you?*" asks Justin. "*What did you do before Mrs. Chase?*"

"*Oh, a lot of things. Cleaning. Publicidad.*"

"*Publicidad, what's that?*"

We rush down another hill, but this time I like the feeling.

"Giving out papers," I say. "You know. On cars. In mailboxes. On the street."

We speed up a steep slope. All the crawling cars keep to the big roads, but these crazy streets through the woods are empty.

"Here's La Vista," he says. "Wasn't that a great shortcut?"

"Justin, I want to go home," calls Mrs. Marshall.

"Very soon, Mom. We have to take Teresa first."

The blue clock on the dashboard says 6:37, and as we creep like a beetle, I doubt we'll make it. Raúl stops working as soon as it gets dark, and the truck drops him at the bus stop, unless he rides with friends. My only hope is if they stopped for a beer, and for the first time, I wish they did.

"What are you thinking?"

The heavy black car trembles.

"Oh, nothing." I blink at a brilliant sign that says "Tara."

"I'm going to go up Lenox, then onto the Buford Highway. You'll have to tell me where to go from there."

"Okay."

The bright light blasts Justin's profile and welds his small features away. Over his collar bulges skin as smooth as a child's.

"Did your parents want you to be a scientist too?"

Justin stares at the red lights marking our trail. "Oh, yeah. But I was never much good at it. I was good in math—good with numbers—but not with my hands. And the lab—have you ever been in one of those places? They smell so bad."

"No, never." I laugh. "But accounting—that's good."

"Not good enough for my father," murmurs Justin.

"Can we go home now?" calls Mrs. Marshall.

"As soon as we take Teresa, Mom. Very soon now," he promises.

We climb up the ramp onto the Buford Highway and shoot past the fabric store.

"Lots of good restaurants up here," says Justin. "Haven't been up this way in a while. Didn't know anyone lived along here."

"Oh, yes. On the other side. A lot of people."

All the gringos who drive here see nothing but their favorite restaurants.

"You live by yourself?"

"With Raúl."

"Oh." Justin draws in his breath. "Your husband?"

"Yes."

His fingers grip the wheel. "That's nice. Have you been together long?"

"Yes."

"From before you came here?"

"No. No, we met here."

"Oh," Justin breathes.

Raúl watched me as I moved from car to car and slipped pink papers under gummy wiper blades. All their eyes followed me, but only he approached.

"Oye, guapa, ¿qué tal tu vida?" he asked.

"Justin, I want to get out of here!" Mrs. Marshall fumbles with her belt.

"Oh, shit. Don't do that, Mom!" Justin checks the power lock.

"See that red-and-blue Dixie Buffet sign?" I ask. "You have to turn left there."

"Okay." Justin checks on his mother. Luckily, she can't figure out how to undo her belt.

He cuts left and turns off the Buford Highway. In case Raúl is home, I direct him to Carlos's place. Even if Raúl's not back, I don't want Justin to know where we live. Already he's breathing faster as he eyes the brick buildings and dirt yards. One thing different from the gringo neighborhood, out here there are people everywhere. Even in this cold, some guys are out drinking beer, and boys are kicking a ball in a pool of light. Justin glances from side to side and brakes to a slow roll.

"Is this the street?"

"Yes."

I lead him to Carlos's place, since Carlos lives with some guys in a real house. To Justin it won't look so bad. Oh, no. The lights are on.

"Right here."

"Oh. This is nice."

In the dark, the pale house looks almost like a gringo home, with patchy grass and tall bushes in front.

"Thanks very much." I stab at buttons to open the door.

"Here, let me help." Justin leans across me, strong, heavy, and warm.

"Thanks."

"Let me out!" cries Mrs. Marshall.

"Okay, Mom." Justin cuts the motor. "You want to get in front? We're going to go back home now."

I open the door and free her from her belt, and she leaps up and runs toward the house. For an old lady, she moves very fast. I rush after her and seize her bony hand just before she reaches the porch.

"Let me go!" she cries.

She wrenches my arm, but I hold tight as Justin pants up.

"Where am I? What is this place?" she screams.

Carlos's porch light flashes, and he and another guy explode from the house. I hold Mrs. Marshall's hand, and Justin grips the other while she screams and screams. Desperate with his mother, Justin doesn't even notice the men a few steps behind him. Carlos has his knife out, and his housemate holds a screwdriver ready to pierce with a downward stroke.

"¡Suéltala, gordo de mierda!" he yells.

Justin turns, astonished, just before the housemate wraps his free arm around his fat neck. Justin is bigger, but he has never fought. He tries to pull the arm away instead of hitting where it could hurt.

Mrs. Marshall shrieks as the first man holds his screwdriver against Justin's ear. Carlos raises his knifepoint to Justin's eye.

"¡Para, para!" I shout. "¡Es mi jefe! ¡No nos hizo nada!"

Carlos hesitates. "¿Teresa?"

"Sí, soy yo. Estos son mi jefe y su madre."

Carlos's housemate is not convinced. He rams his screwdriver into Justin's ear. "Aquí no se vende mujeres, gringo de mierda. Si quieres una, ve con los negros."

"Oye, yo conozco a esta chava," says Carlos. "Creo que realmente es su jefe. Mira la vieja. Mira el coche que tiene."

I've wrapped myself around Mrs. Marshall the way my mother held me when my father roared. She quivers in my arms, but she has stopped screaming. The housemate glances from me to the blue-black car and kicks Justin loose.

"Me trajo a casa. Sólo me trajo a casa," I say.

"¿Por qué te trajo aquí?" asks Carlos.

"La madre salió. Está mal de la cabeza. Abrió la puerta y salió. Estábamos intentando regresarla."

Carlos looks scared. "*Díle que lo sentimos,*" he says. "*Pensamos que—tú sabes—que quiso hacerte daño, a tí y a la pobre señora.*"

Justin breathes hard and fast, his face so white it scares me.

"He says they're sorry," I tell him. "They thought you were hurting us."

Justin tries to breathe, and I rub Mrs. Marshall's back. She is trembling like a whipped dog.

"I want to go home," she whispers.

"Here, Mrs. Marshall. Let's get you back in the car. In your favorite seat, okay?"

I'll miss her, I think, as we cross the lawn. I really liked this job. I hope that Justin doesn't call the police. Mrs. Marshall stays still as I strap her in, thin and rigid in the dark. Justin's warmth stirs the air behind me.

"Are you okay?" I ask.

"It looked worse than it was." His voice sounds odd, and there's blood on his ear.

"They thought you were—"

"Yeah. I know."

"Are you going to call the police?"

"I don't know." He walks to the driver's side as though I weren't there.

"Goodbye," I say, but Justin doesn't answer.

He pulls away without looking at me, but Mrs. Marshall raises a claw and stares.

"*¡Que la chingada!*" says Carlos. "*¿Viste el coche que trae?*"

"*Sí, un BMW 520i.*"

"*Teresa, ¿tú trabajas para ellos? ¿Cuánto te pagan?*"

CHAPTER 5

OKLAHOMA

As I cross the border into Oklahoma, I feel less free, even with all this sky.

"Yeehaw!" I yell and stab my fist in the air, although I don't know what I'm celebrating.

Tonight I see Connie, and I told her that I'd reach Norman around six. Having to be somewhere at a set time makes me feel like I'm tethered to a post.

A truck with lattice sides flaps up beside me. What's it carrying? I turn my head to see. Suddenly I'm staring into sad, red eyes. Ugh! Poor cow, I know where you're headed. I have left the South and entered the West.

After the black hills of Arkansas, the Oklahoma sky is immense. Light rays extend from billowy clouds like divine fingers trying to pluck me up. As I race past gray lakes, God's fingers dissolve, but the sky continues to grow. Signs welcome me to the Cherokee Nation, then to the Seminole and Creek. The land around me is rich, green, and rolling, nothing like I thought it would be. It flattens as I approach Oklahoma City, and when I turn south toward Norman, strip malls sprout. Following Connie's directions, I exit toward red-and-gray stores, then turn onto tree-lined streets with wooden houses.

"You'll know our place from the tree down in front," said Connie, and sure enough, a gray trunk bifurcates the lawn of number 27. I cut Wilma's motor, and the silence startles me. My watch says it's only five thirty. Uneasy, I glance back at Joey. Should I bring him in? Nah, he'll be safer out here. I push aside branches and breathe the sharp scent of beech. Inside, footsteps trip and thump. The door swings open, and there stands Connie, warm and radiant in a beet-colored sweatshirt.

"Carrie! My God! You haven't changed at all!"

Connie's face has faded and stretched, and her breasts hang loosely. Gray threads have colonized her wavy black hair, but her mischievous eyes still glint with energy. Her voice strikes me with its old assertiveness.

"C'mon in! Lemme show you our place. Sorry about the tree. The Wood-Chuckers wanted five hundred bucks to make it go away, so we're looking for someone else."

A tiny girl clings to Connie's thigh, black-haired and blue-eyed like her mother. She lets out a shriek that cuts like a razor. I jump and cover my ears, and she points at me and laughs.

"Oh, she got you." Connie chuckles. "C'mon, Bedelia. That's Mommy's friend. No screaming at Mommy's friend, okay?"

Bedelia trots into the living room, whose floor hosts a ramshackle fortress of blocks. The colored city spans the valley from one bookcase to another, but the girl has worn a path around the side.

"Here. Lemme clear some space for you." Connie gathers thin, battered books from the plaid couch. I sit down and study Connie's broadened silhouette against the picture window. Bedelia gallops back, waving a red cup. "Mommy, maw juice!"

"Can I get you anything?" asks Connie.

"Yeah, maybe some water."

Bedelia seizes Connie's leg, so that she has to drag her down the path to the kitchen. When they return, the girl is sucking vigorously on a straw mounted in a tomato-shaped cup. Connie settles down beside me.

"Wow," she says. "It's so good to see you. You look wonderful! It's been so long—I just can't believe ..."

"It doesn't seem like that long," I say. "I feel like I just walked out of the lab. Are you still working on vesicle transport?"

Connie raises her dark brows and laughs. "Man, are you kidding me? That was twenty years ago. No, I work mostly with Bruce now, on microtubule assembly."

"Oh, wow. That sounds interesting."

"Yeah." Connie looks at her daughter, who is staring at me with relentless blue eyes. "Right now I'm part-time, so I can hang out with Bedelia. It's so amazing to watch her grow—all the changes from day to day. Nothing in the lab was ever this interesting."

The little girl grins so that a dimple pecks her cheek. Fixing me with her gaze, she moves my way. She pats Connie's and my legs one by one, then shoves them back and forth like clothes on a discount rack. "Bing!" She punches my thigh. "Bing!" She punches Connie, then alternates between us as though playing a xylophone.

"Ow! Stop that!" cries her mother.

Bedelia scowls and clambers back onto the couch.

"Those were crazy times." Connie smiles. "Did you know Marty retired?"

"No way."

I can't imagine Marty Cohen retired. What would he do? All he ever talked about was vesicle transport.

"And Julie—she got this amazing job in Madison. Her sorting stuff really took off. Are you still in touch with anyone?"

"Not really. Just Johnny Turner."

"Johnny Turner!" Connie's face brightens.

"Yeah, we still email each other sometimes. Not too often. I've been working on this science novel, and I ask him stuff about viruses."

Bedelia squirms and nudges me with her hip.

"Johnny Turner!" Connie laughs. "Man, I haven't heard that name in a while. Who did he marry?"

Bedelia rises to her feet, supporting herself on Connie's shoulder. "Mommy, maw juice!" she demands.

The phone's high-pitched ring drills the room.

Connie jumps up. "Oh, I'd better get that. That might be Bruce."

While she looks for the phone, her daughter creeps closer, and her small fingers nest in my hair.

"Yaw pretty," she says.

"Thanks."

She shifts her weight and stares up at me, so close I can feel her tiny breaths.

"Yeah. Okay. So we'll meet you there," says Connie. "Yeah. No, that's okay. You can find us. Yeah. In our usual corner. Love you too. G'bye."

Her breasts jounce under the warm purple sweatshirt.

"Mommy, maw juice!" Bedelia waves her cup.

"Sorry about that." Connie laughs. "Adult conversations are the first thing to go. I think my brain has adjusted to kidspeak. Anyway, Bruce says he's gonna meet us there. He's going over a paper with his new postdoc, Meredith, and she can drop him off. Is the Oh Boy Buffet okay? We like to go there, 'cause it's good for kids."

"Mommy, jooooooooooos!" wails Bedelia.

"No, no more juice, or you won't be able to eat your dinner. We're taking Carrie to the Oh Boy Buffet. You like the Oh Boy Buffet, right?"

"No!" Bedelia's face crumples, and she bangs her cup against the wall.

"Sorry," mutters Connie. "You're meeting her at the worst time of day. She gets tired around now—hungry. In the morning she's so sweet. Hey, did you see a blue coat for a miniature human being around here anywhere?"

Bedelia helps Connie search while I scan the room. In the fortress of blocks, a red central chamber encloses a stuffed stegosaurus. Connie locates Bedelia's coat and maneuvers her daughter into it. With a grunt, she hoists her onto her hip to carry her around the fallen beech. As she passes my car, Bedelia spots Joey, still strapped in the back seat.

"Bear!" she cries.

Leather hailstones strike the window as she kicks to free herself.

"Wow, look at Carrie's bear! That sure is a nice bear. Maybe he wants to come to dinner. Do you mind? She really loves bears."

Bedelia is battering Wilma so hard I'm worried her alarm will go off. I disarm it with a "boop!" and Connie opens the door.

"Bear! Bear!"

Connie sets Bedelia down to undo the seatbelt, and soon Joey is in her daughter's arms. It's an odd sight, the rapturous girl squeezing a furry brown creature bigger than she is. I'm glad I can't see Joey's eyes.

As we glide past tan strip malls, Bedelia digs her fingers into Joey's fur and nuzzles him, openmouthed. Is she drooling? My stomach heaves when I think of how his fur is going to look.

"Bearrrrrr," she gurgles lovingly.

Although it's just past six, the lot is nearly full.

"Oh, boy." Connie guides the SUV into a far corner. "This place is gonna be a madhouse."

We have a tough time freeing Bedelia from her seat since she won't let go of Joey.

"I don't think we should take him in there," I say. "He might get food all over him."

"He's hungry!" insists Bedelia, trying to pry open his mouth.

When Connie tries to take him, Bedelia shrieks so shrilly that two men stride over.

"Everything all right, ladies?"

"Yeah, she's okay." Connie laughs. "She just wants to take the bear in to dinner."

The two sunburned blond men relax and let their full bellies roll.

One of them grins. "Oh, I think you should give that bear his dinner. Bears need to eat a lot. They have to build up that fat to get through the winter."

"It's May," I say.

The meaty man looks me up and down. His brows are shades lighter than his round, pink face. "So after that long hibernation, he needs to get his strength back. Looks like you could use some nourishment too."

Bedelia beams and clutches Joey around the neck. As we inch through the line, she bounces him on the railing. Other kids join the dance and reach up to stroke his fur. Ugh—I can almost feel their pasty fingers in my own hair. When we reach the register, a cheerful girl with a brown ponytail greets us.

"Two adults, one child, and—hey, today's your lucky day, ladies. Bears eat free. Would you like an extra chair for your friend?"

Connie leads us to a far corner, which she says is best.

"It's near the desserts, so you can see right away when they bring out something new."

Strapped in his chair, Joey hunches forward, his downcast nose almost touching the tray.

"Should we wait for Bruce?" I ask.

"Nah. Bedelia's hungry. She gets loud like this when she needs to eat. I'll take her through first, and then you can go. Bruce will get here when he gets here. That okay with you?"

Connie merges with the enormous people crowding the buffet. With Brownian motion, they drift like Thanksgiving Day floats, inflated, hovering, menacing. Fascinated, I stare at their enormous bodies. The men hold their thick necks back and bellies forward, like chickens; the women rock from side to side, barely able to bend their legs. Only the children look human to me, running, pushing, and grabbing.

Connie returns with a smiling Bedelia, carrying a plate of chicken fingers, mashed potatoes, and red Jell-O.

"Okay, you're up!" She grins. "Knock yourself out! This place will do you good."

I take a thin white plate and start with the salads, amazed by the spectacle that meets my eyes. In brown plastic buckets lies a quantized cornucopia: pale lettuce, deep-green spinach, crumbled egg, slippery peaches, black olives, bacon bits, glinting Jell-O. I count calories on the cash register in my head, reaching for protein and vitamins and shunning fat. I have a harder time surveying the hot food, since I can see so little of it at once. An old woman blocks my view of the shrimp, and I hover until a boy thrusts me aside.

"Hey, Raymond! I saw that! Is that any way to treat another person? You apologize to that lady!"

Raymond turns and glowers, fingering his metal tongs.

"Sorry," he mutters.

"I'm sorry about that, ma'am," rumbles his father.

His bulk is warming the small of my back. Before me lie fried shrimp, fried okra, and tater tots in delectable golden rounds. I shake my head at the father, who has seized some shrimp and is about to toss them onto my plate. The taco stand tempts me more with its crisp tortillas, crumbly hamburger, shredded lettuce, tomato cubes, sour cream, guacamole, and orange cheese. Then I spot a baked-potato stand with potatoes as big as a baby's head.

I don't partake until I reach the dinner area, with stringy turkey, brown gravy, mashed potatoes, and dressing. Glazed with sugar, the sweet potatoes collapse when I touch them, as do the soft trees of broccoli. There's meat loaf with red sauce; spicy, glistening roast chicken; and ham with pineapple and melted sugar. Choosing morsels like a Japanese florist, I create a pungent work of art out of green vegetables and lean meat.

"Oh, Carrie, no!" Connie moans. "Is that all you're gonna eat? Well, maybe you can make up for it later. You should see the desserts in this place." Her eyes turn toward the buffet of sweets, and she rises up in search of food.

From the table, I have a lurid view of carrot cake with cream cheese frosting and German chocolate cake with coconut. Beside them stand pineapple upside-down cake, white cake with chocolate frosting, and apple, peach, and cherry pie. I spot two kinds of brownies, solid cubes and deep chocolate sludge topped with goo. The prime attraction is soft ice cream with chocolate, butterscotch, and strawberry syrup. Tired of waiting, Raymond drizzles butterscotch onto the silky red hair of the girl next to him. She punches his shoulder, and their shouts rip the air.

"Carrie?"

A tall man with taut posture is gazing down at me. His dark eyes beam intelligence.

"You're Carrie, right? Not some stranger who's kidnapped my kid?"

"Daaaaaaaaa!" Bedelia bangs her tray.

"Bruce?"

"Yeah. Sorry I got held up," he says. "It's this dynamic instability paper. This group at Hopkins swears they can stop disassembly, but—"

Bruce breaks off, embarrassed. Probably he thinks I can't follow him. My mind has gone into orbit around his first phrase, and it can't break free.

"Dynamic instability?"

Bruce smiles, grateful that I'm listening.

"Yeah—microtubules. The strings of protein that give cells their shape—and let them move things around, like the tracks on a cog railway—"

"Yeah, I know microtubules." I hate it when people talk down to me.

Bedelia thrashes and tries to rise in her chair, but Bruce seems not to notice. He ignores her kicks and sits down opposite me.

"You do?" He smiles. "Yeah—yeah—that's right. Connie said she knew you from Marty Cohen's lab."

"So what's going on?" I ask. "They can block depolymerization?"

"Maybe." Bruce frowns. "They had a *Cell* paper on it last fall. They claim they can reduce disassembly to almost zero. But we've tried it six times, and the things are still shrinking."

I squirm to adjust my back. "Are you doing everything the same as them?"

Bruce's gaze settles on my lips. Piece by piece, he runs through each element: the cell line, the proteins, the buffers. It sounds like a prayer he's been reciting for months. As he's describing his culture medium, Connie walks up.

"Hey, honey!" She kisses his brown hair, and Bruce smiles up at her.

Connie settles beside him and fondles Bedelia.

Bruce turns back to me. "We've got to get this article out before the cell bio meeting. Then we can slug it out face-to-face."

Connie must be hungrier than I am. On her plate, a taco borders turkey with dressing, surrounded by peas, carrots, meat loaf, and mashed potatoes.

"How'd it go today?" she asks Bruce. "Has Meredith learned to write?"

When Bruce laughs, his eyes shoot dark energy. "Don't hold your breath. I think it's a requirement for grad school. No one gets in who can write a decent sentence."

"Carrie's a writer. Maybe she can help," says Connie.

"Oh, yeah?"

"Yeah. I write novels. But I'd be glad to take a look."

"Novels?" Bruce shakes his head. "Wow. Well, what the hell. I guess it can't hurt. When do you need to head out? We could do it tonight."

Connie pauses with her mouth full. "Mmm."

"That any good?" asks Bruce without looking.

"Mm. No. Bedelia, honey, what are you doing?"

Twisted ninety degrees, Bedelia is tugging at Joey's nose, trying to pull it apart.

"He wants dessert!"

"Dessert! He hasn't even had any dinner!" Lights dance in Connie's blue eyes.

"I don't think he's hungry," I say.

"Yes, he is!"

For the first time, Bruce notices the bear in the high chair next to his daughter. "Where did he come from?"

"Oh, that's Carrie's bear."

Bruce's dark brown eyes pulse.

"He's hungry!"

"Well, what does he want to eat?" Bruce sounds genuinely curious.

"A brownie. A *big* brownie. With ice cream."

"He told you all that?" Connie laughs.

"A *big* brownie!"

"Well, why don't you let Mom and Carrie finish eating, and then they can get you and Joey some dessert."

On my milky-white plate, the brown and green morsels seem to have crystallized.

"Don't you want anything?" asks Connie.

"Nah." Bruce shakes his head. "Meredith and I had some ramen at five."

As Connie crunches her taco, a big, curly-haired girl brings a fresh tub of brownies. She scoops the sludge of the old ones on top and bangs the clinging tar from her spoon.

"Ooo!" Bedelia points and bounces.

Bruce's eyes flicker. "Connie said you used to work together. You've written science papers too, right?"

"Yeah, sure." I nod. How boring that used to be, shuffling formulaic blocks of words.

Connie pushes her plate to the side. "I'd better get that brownie before the vultures descend. Anyone else want some?"

"Nah." Bruce waves a long-fingered hand. "So what do you do with a student who can't write a sentence?"

"Send her to med school?"

"Man, I could use you in the lab."

Connie returns with three bowls of brownies, soft ice cream, and chocolate sauce. The warm fudge sinks into the gently grooved spirals, creating creamy rivulets. Connie hands one yellow bowl to Bedelia, keeps one for herself, and offers the third one to me.

"I thought you might want it. You had so little to eat."

"Give it to the bear," says Bruce. He turns back to me. "I don't know what to do about Meredith. You won't believe what she came up with today: 'Despite chronic efforts to disenhance dynamic instability, we can detect no salient diminution of depolymerization.'"

"No way!" I can't stop laughing at Meredith's phrases. Like her microtubules, they seem to have grown in a medium unique to labs.

"Oh, *shit!*"

Bruce and I unlock our eyes at a shout from Connie. With both hands on Joey's head, Bedelia is pushing his nose into the ice cream. Chocolate sauce and white foam bubble from the yellow bowl.

"Fuck!" I cry.

Connie pulls Bedelia off of Joey, and the girl shrieks as though she's been stabbed. All around us, people are turning to watch.

Connie grabs a napkin. "Maybe we can clean him up."

"He was hungry! He wanted to eat!"

Joey's fuzzy brown face is plastered with white.

"Fuck!" I gasp.

Bruce lays his hand on my arm. Connie struggles to guide Bedelia into her jacket.

"The language of some people," murmurs a silver-haired woman, regarding me with narrowed eyes.

"Why didn't you watch her?" asks Bruce.

"I did—but she moves so fast."

With the napkin, I try to scrub Joey's sticky nose, but it clings to him in pieces.

"Fuck."

"Oh, Carrie, I'm so sorry."

"Fuck!" cries Bedelia.

"God damn it! Let's get out of here!" Bruce's lips tighten with rage.

None too gently, he buckles Bedelia into her car seat and slides into the back seat beside her. Connie and I sit side by side in the darkness, she gripping the wheel and me clutching brown fuzz. Joey's matted fur has begun to harden and is scratching my chin with each breath.

"I'm sorry you had to see her like this," murmurs Connie. "She's so creative—so bright. You should see the things she builds with those blocks. I wish you could stay longer. Where are you headed tomorrow?"

"Santa Fe."

"Santa Fe! My God, it's been a while since I was there. What is that, eight, ten hours?"

"Yeah, but I'm staying at a Run-Rite Inn west of Oklahoma City. I'm hoping to get an early start."

Connie guides the SUV into the driveway until black leaves block the windshield. She climbs out and calls to me as I grope for the door release.

"You're welcome to stay with us, you know. We'd love to have you. And we wouldn't hold you up in the morning. We're early risers."

Blue longing in Connie's eyes says this isn't a performance, but fear squeezes my rising breath. Tendrils are emerging from the fallen beech, reaching toward me with deadly curls.

"Oh, I'm sorry. It's too late to cancel— I don't want to put you out—"

"Hey," calls Bruce from the back seat. "Don't you want to—"

Connie shushes him with a nudge.

"That's okay." She smiles. "It's been wonderful to see you." She opens her purple arms.

Surrounded by her softness, I feel a sob rise, and something hot stings my lids. In the shadows, Bedelia's cheek curves softly against the seat where she's fallen asleep. I unlock Wilma and toss Joey in back.

"Drive safely!" calls Connie.

My wheels start to turn. By the time I merge onto I-35, I'm doing close to eighty.

When Carlos and Luis brought me home, they made Raúl laugh so hard he forgot to get mad.

"You should have seen him—¡se estaba cagando!"

Carlos imitates Justin, panting and paralyzed, until even I have to laugh.

"¡Y la vieja!"

This I don't like so much, Luis screaming and waving his arms.

"She's sick," I say. "She's just a poor old lady."

But it's wonderful to see Raúl laugh, his eyes warm and his face all red. It is pretty funny, the thought of some gringo driving up here on the prowl for women. Anyone who's been here would know there are hardly any, just a bunch of guys working to send money home. A few lucky ones have brought along their families, but unmarried women are scarce.

"Teresa, you better get used to the bus." Carlos laughs. "'Cause el Panzón ain't gonna drive you home no more."

"No," says Raúl. "He's not." But his jaw doesn't tighten. He knows something. And it has nothing to do with the gringo.

The next night, Raúl is so late that I worry. If he got hurt, I wouldn't know where to call. What if he got his hand caught in a tree chopper? I heard of a guy who did that once, and they had to cut off most of his arm. I circle from the Virgin to the TV to the stove, but still I can't start cooking. Over the bed, the red curtains bulge in the draft. The night after our fight, Raúl brought home a curtain rod from Mercado del Mundo.

"Mira," he said. "Quizás no fue tan mala idea."

Light pushes through the cracks around the garage door, and tires scrape the dry asphalt. A great big car has pulled into the driveway. The guys must have gone out, and they're bringing him home. I hope Raúl is okay. A horn jabs the night, and I run outside. In the driveway stands a square white station wagon. Its motor sounds a lot like a tree chopper, but in the driver's seat, Raúl is grinning.

"¡Teresa! ¡Ven! Check it out! ¡Mira, Teresa, tenemos un coche!"

I run to the window to kiss Raúl. Luis and Carlos are sprawled out in back.

"¡Hola, Teresa! ¡Mira qué coche!"

The seats are deep red, almost the color of Mrs. Marshall's carpet.

"¡Al otro lado, tonta!" cries Raúl.

I run through the headlight beams, which sear my legs. Raúl has reserved the front seat for me.

"¡Tengo que cerrar la puerta!" I call and rush to the house for my key.

While I'm inside, Raúl honks the horn again.

"¡Que la chingada! ¡Las mujeres! You spend your whole life waiting for them!"

I yank open the door and jump onto the dark-red seat.

"¡Vamos! ¿'Onde vamos?"

"¡A todas partes!" cries Raúl.

We roar down the driveway. In back, Carlos and Luis keep shouting, Carlos praising the car, Luis running it down.

"With a car this big, you could move people. Make lots of money."

"Si jala ... es un milagro que aun camine. Cuatro cilindros, y con el peso ..."

The car accelerates so slowly that I worry.

"Let's take it out on 85! Let's see how fast it can go!" yells Carlos.

When the Buford Highway ends, we zoom up the ramp onto the interstate. By now, most of the evening traffic has cleared. Raúl takes us straight toward downtown, onto the biggest road I've ever seen. I try to count the lanes, but there are too many. Ten, maybe twelve each way, all full of rushing cars. And the lights! We seem to be driving into heaven, with brilliance on every side. Ahead of us magic towers twinkle, and shining walls of light flank our path.

"¡Qué maravilla!" I whisper.

Two years I have lived in this city, and I never knew that it looked like this. As long as the light glows, we all stay quiet, each of us swimming in our own thoughts. When the darkness settles, Luis wants to try the radio, and Raúl blasts 95.6, "tan latino como tú." It crackles a little, but it sounds pretty good. A thumping song matches the traffic's pulse.

Huge green signs warn that the road is splitting, and we all start yelling at once.

"¡A la izquierda! ¡No, no, a la derecha!"

"¡Que la chingada!" shouts Raúl. "¡Inútiles! ¡Los bajo aquí, se los juro!"

On 285 there are fewer cars, and Raúl takes Carlos up on his dare. Seventy miles an hour. Eighty. Ninety. We shoot past cars like they're standing still. When we hit one hundred, Raúl howls like a wolf, and even Luis looks impressed. We roar past a truck, whose driver yells something I can't hear. One hundred ten. One hundred fifteen. One hundred twenty. At 123, the car rattles and shakes, and the engine gives a high-pitched shriek. Raúl slows, and we all applaud—123 no está mal para una morra d'esta edad.

When we reach the far end of the Buford Highway, Raúl turns off. He treats us to food at a taco drive-through but yells at Carlos for dropping his chalupa on the seat.

"¡Limpia eso! ¡Que's bueno, ese!"

He drops Carlos and Luis off at their house, then eases into our driveway. In the sudden quiet, he fondles my hair.

"Nobody's going to drive you home no more," he says. "Tomorrow I take you to work."

CHAPTER 6

WEST TEXAS

Well, so much for my early start. I must have lost two hours at that pancake place. It was worth it, though, to get that scene out. Raúl and Teresa needed to move. I'm so groggy it's a wonder I can write. Washing Joey kept me up until midnight. My volumizing shampoo soothed his stiff fur, but he's still wet, and I worry about mildew. Now his hair doesn't catch the light the way it used to—it chisels the sun into Cezanne strips. Poor bear. He looks as though someone's been wiping her feet on his face. I've got to do a better job of protecting him.

As I shoot west, the sky opens out, deep blue with thin cirrus clouds. The land and sky fade until they're bleached and dirty. Trees shrink into shrubs, and herds of black cows lower. In a few spots the soil glows brilliant orange, and the road begins to rise. Black pumps bob like metal horses drinking. By the time I cross the Texas border, the land offers nothing but sage and scrub.

For the first time since Georgia, the world looks strange. Brown grass and pale sky form a perfect line. Drowsily, I breathe the stinging scent of cows, although there's not a single one in sight. A flash cuts my eyes, reflected from a silver sign swinging between two posts: "J. M. Turner Ranch."

I hit the brakes, and Wilma skids sideways, grinding noisily onto the shoulder. Luckily there's no one behind me, not another car on the road. I step out into perfect silence until my ear catches the wind in the grass. The searing stench makes my eyes water, and I breathe it gingerly as I watch the sign. The silver bar frames a road headed straight for the horizon, an unbroken line where the land and sky meet. So this is it. Johnny said his ranch was near Amarillo, but I never pictured it as a real place.

"Where're you from, Johnny?"

Johnny rests his chin on his hand and looks down at me, amused. In a Japanese restaurant we called the black-and-brown place, golden-framed prints brighten chocolate walls.

"Oh, no place special."

"C'mon. What are you, a military kid? I never heard anybody talk like you do."

I bite a crisp, chewy blob of tempura and realize I've crammed too much in my mouth.

Johnny sucks in his cheeks. "Man, I sure do love to watch you eat that tempura."

Johnny's gaze burns my lips. "C'mon. Where're you from?"

"I'm from West Texas."

"West Texas—what is that? Cattle? Oil?"

Johnny smiles wanly. "Oh, a lot of cows. Lot of grass. Lot of sky. I grew up on a ranch."

I chortle, and Johnny grimaces. He must be sick of people laughing when he says that. Hooves mark the beat of *Bonanza* music as I imagine him bouncing on a horse.

"A ranch?"

"Yeah. Great big ranch. But not like you're thinkin'. This ranch has three towns on it. It's a business, like growin' up on a Ford plant."

Points of anger spark in his eyes.

"I went to Texas A&M. Studied chemistry. I was supposed to go into ranching, but I got too interested in what I was studyin'."

I shift my leg until it touches Johnny's. His long leg warms me as he slides it forward.

"Somebody didn't like that?"

His lower lip twitches. "Nope. Somebody didn't like it at all."

Johnny studies my face until it burns.

"So what'd you find?" he asks. "You said you saw a peak of activity for that antibody right where the vesicle concentration was highest."

A clank of the sign brings back the dull, open sky. Johnny ... Johnny Turner ... The horizon blurs. I shake my head and take a few steps toward Wilma, but I'm transfixed by that sign. Damn! Where are all the cows creating that smell? It's doing such a number on my eyes—

Brrrp. Brrrp. Brrp. Doo-doo-doo-DEE-doo!

In the silence of this place, my phone's cry is obscene. I thrust my hand into my purse to still it.

"H'lo?"

"Hey, Theresa!"

"Oh." My voice wobbles.

"Hey, Theresa, are you okay?"

Clifton comes through so clearly today.

"Yeah, yeah, I'm okay."

"You sound strange. Where are you?"

I sniff. For some reason, Clifton's voice is comforting.

"O-oh, nowhere. God knows. Somebody's ranch out in West Texas."

"Oh, no! Did your car break down?"

I blink and smile at the swaying sign. "No-o, no. Just stopped. I like to do that sometimes. Just to listen to the silence." I take a big snuff.

"You sound upset. Are you sure you're all right?"

I wonder if this is what a father sounds like. "Yeah," I say. "I just like the quiet."

A car swirls past, a voice half emerging from its roar: "… it, baby!"

"What was that?"

"Well, it's not as quiet as I said. But between cars … it's almost holy … All you hear is the wind in the grass. You don't realize how noisy life is until you're in a place like this. Sometimes I just pull over …" The sign mesmerizes me with its flashes.

"Theresa, what happened? Did someone hurt you? Is anybody with you now?"

"No, no, I'm fine. I just pulled over. I'll start driving again if it'll make you feel better."

"Would you? I hate to think of you out there all alone like that. Go on. I'll hang on. You'll be safe in your car."

One-handed, I unlock Wilma and start her. The sign recedes into dim brown haze.

"Okay. I'm back on I-40 West."

"That's better. You sound better now." I picture Clifton's neck wrinkling as he nods.

"Yeah. It was partly the air. It's the craziest thing. It smells like the whole universe has been marinated in cow piss, but there's not a single one in sight."

"Wow!" He laughs.

"You ever been to West Texas?"

"No. Just Houston and Dallas." A tightening of his voice suggests distaste. I try to imagine those spilled-out cities and see only a swirl of lights.

"Hey, a cow!"

I can feel Clifton smile. "What kind?"

"Brown. Whole bunch of 'em. Must belong to the Tur ..." As I scan the herd, my voice crumples.

"Theresa? Theresa, you've got to tell me what's wrong. Please ..."

"Okay. Okay."

I snuff. You can start a car while holding a phone but not drive and blow your nose.

"Nothing's wrong. I'm just remembering something."

"Something sad?" Clifton's low tone settles.

"No, no, someone ..."

"Oh, Theresa, I wish I were there with you. I wish ... But tell me. A guy?"

"Yeah. A guy." I feel so dirty, telling Clifton about Johnny, but somehow I can't stop talking.

"A guy who hurt you?"

"No! Why do you keep saying that? The most wonderful guy I ever knew."

"Oh."

Clifton breathes quietly, and my eyes drift to the horizon.

"How long— Are you still— Are you with him now?" His voice quivers.

"No."

"Do you have a boyfriend?"

"No." I squint to the side. How can light be so dim but so oppressive?

"Wow—no boyfriend—that's hard to believe. And you're not married—I saw you weren't wearing a ring."

"No. Are you?"

Some black cows stir the horizon like restless ants. With only dirt and sky, I can't judge the scale of things. The phone has gone silent.

"Clifton?"

"Yeah." A whisper. "Yeah."

I let out my breath and glance back at Joey. He's hanging his head, as though watching a bug on the floor.

"That's all right," I say. "I mean, if you like it. You sound like you're confessing a crime."

"No—no—I mean—of course I like it. I'm sorry. I should have told you sooner." I sense Clifton straightening.

"That's okay," I say. "I already knew."

"Oh." His voice is harmonized breath.

"So what's your wife's name?"

"Karen."

Karen. I try to picture her. "You been together long?"

"Yeah ... wow, it's fifteen—no, sixteen years now. Twenty if you count the time before we got married."

"Wow. You guys have kids?"

"Yeah. Jason, he's ten, and Emily, she's eight. She's great—she's always drawing things. She has a real talent for drawing."

Once, I drew a fire engine on our living room rug. My mother scrubbed furiously, but she could never exorcise its red ghost. That cool beige rug was begging for the heat of a red crayon. I wonder where Clifton's daughter draws.

"That sounds nice," I say. "So tell me about Karen. What does she do?"

"She's a kindergarten teacher."

"Wow, that's brave." I imagine a kaleidoscope of screaming faces, tiny, fine-haired, and red.

"Yeah, she's a pretty strong woman." Clifton inhales to say something more, but he doesn't.

"So how did you guys meet?"

"In college ... It's funny—I can't think of a time when I didn't know her."

"What does she look like?"

"Oh, I don't know—different from you. Curly hair, blue eyes ..." Clifton hesitates.

"Big?"

"Yeah ... But look at me. Who am I to talk?"

"You look okay," I say quickly.

Clifton's voice brightens. "Oh. So you really don't have a—partner, I guess people say nowadays."

"No."

"But you're so—"

"What?"

A frayed black heap lies in the road ahead of me. A blown-out tire, or a dead animal? One-handed, I steer around it. Just another splayed-out tire, another tortured crow's wing.

"You're so beautiful!" Clifton breathes. "Exciting, alluring—I just want to—"

His words arouse me, but their logic rankles.

"You're kidding, right?" I snap. "What do you think, only ugly women don't have partners?"

"No! No! I just—"

"I don't want one. I've had them before, and I don't want one."

"It's that guy, isn't it?" Clifton asks slowly.

"No. What guy?"

"The one you're remembering. You still want him."

"No!" God damn it! Why do guys always have to think that if you don't want them, you must want someone else?

"Tell me about him," Clifton insists.

"No!" I cry.

The shredded tire shrinks in the rearview mirror.

"Why do I have to live my life locked in a cage with just one other animal? It's like—there's no one right way to live. You have to find the way that works best for you. For some people, it's a one-on-one lifetime partnership. For some, it's smorgasbord, a little of everyone. And for some, a partnership with the chance to know other people. Seven billion people in the world, and you can only talk to one about anything that matters? It's obscene! It's a crime against humanity!"

"But you can talk to other people when you're married."

I sense Clifton smiling. Shit! This is funny? Why can't anyone ever take me seriously?

"Yeah," I say. "About home equity loans."

Clifton chuckles. "So what do you want to talk about?"

I scowl at the dingy sky ahead of me. "Like—like—are you spending your life the right way, and how did people come up with the idea of God, and what shape was your shit this morning!"

Clifton chokes. "What shape was my— I don't think I've ever had that conversation."

"But you know what I mean. Talking about things that matter. Not holding back. Saying everything that you feel."

"Yeah ..." Clifton's voice dwindles. I bet he and his wife haven't talked in years.

"So which kind are you?" he asks finally.

"What?"

"You said there were three kinds of people."

"No, I didn't."

"Well, you said some people ..."

"Oh. Oh, yeah."

Joey is dozing.

"I like a little of everyone," I say. "I like guys. Lots of guys. And I want to come home to my bear at night, with nobody telling me how I can be improved, or what I can do for him, or how selfish I am for not doing what he wants."

"Whoa—whoa—" Clifton laughs. "It's not always like that. Sometimes you come home and he tells you how nice you are."

"Not me. Never happened yet."

"But don't you get lonely?" he asks.

"No."

"That's right. You have all those guys." Clifton's smile laps at my feet. I wish that I could see his eyes.

"Trouble is," I say, "the system's rigged so that if you don't want to be trapped with one person all your life, you can't talk to anyone, because everyone's locked in a cage with someone else."

"That's loneliness."

Clifton's confidence irks me. "No! Don't stick that label on me! It just explains me away!"

"Okay—okay—" He falters. "I guess I see. But I still think it's that guy. What if *he* wanted to marry you? Wouldn't you climb in a cage with him?"

Johnny winks and swings one long leg over a chain-link fence. The metal rattles from the shift of his weight. Johnny jerks his head, daring me to follow.

"No. He's married."

"Well, what if he weren't?"

"He didn't want me before either."

It's hard to tell where the land and sky cleave, since both are such a fuzzy, dull brown. Dusty ghosts arise in the nearby fields, as though disturbed by Clifton's short breaths.

"Theresa? Don't take this the wrong way or anything, but I think he's nuts. He's got to be crazy not to want you."

"That's nice."

The horizon dims.

"A real fool." Clifton's voice gains momentum. "Me—I think I'm that third kind of guy. I guess I'd like to be married but also know other women."

"Other people, I said."

"Oh." He chuckles. "I guess I don't listen too well."

A red-and-gray strip mall spreads its wings. Amarillo can't be far off.

"Theresa?" asks Clifton. "What's your last name?"

"Ramírez."

"Ramírez? Are you …"

"My mother," I say. "I took her name when my parents divorced."

"Oh. All that beautiful, long, black hair."

"Yeah. It's from south of the border," I laugh. "What about you?"

"Oh, me, I'm just English."

"No. Your name."

"Bowles."

"No way! Like bowls of ice cream?" That's the silliest name I ever heard.

"Please. I had such a hard time in school. Now my own kids are getting it."

I think of all the things I would call a kid named Bowles. Salad bowls, sugar bowls—

"You're thinking of something bad, aren't you?"

"Who, me?"

"Yeah, you've got a wicked mind." I sense laughter spinning in Clifton's chocolate eyes.

"Ty-D-Bowles!"

"Oh, no! It's been years since I heard that one!"

"Toilet Bowles!"

"Oh, you are bad—bad! This isn't going to be one of those conversations you were talking about earlier, is it?"

"No. Not unless you want it to be."

"No." Clifton suppresses his laugh. "Theresa—know what I want to do?"

"No, what?"

"I want to touch your hair, real gently, just over your forehead, and run my hands all the way down, all the way down …"

Warm hands glide over my hair, slipping softly downward. "That's nice," I whisper. "That's really nice."

"I'd better stop thinking," he murmurs. "I'm—"

"Yeah, me too. I'm coming into Amarillo, and the Texas cops won't take well to a chick with Georgia plates and a phone stuck to her ear."

"Yeah. You'd better go. But I'll be thinking of you," says Clifton. "I'm reading your book. I'm thinking of you all the time."

"I'll be thinking about you too, Clifton."

"Yeah? Really?" he whispers.

"Yeah. You're nice."

"You're nice too. You take care, now. Bye."

I shoot through Amarillo at seventy miles an hour, but I never see the city. Giant billboards blast so many cheerful messages that my only impression is a yellow blur.

Twenty miles before the New Mexico border, the first mesas arise. The land thrusts itself up, and the perfect, clean horizon tears. In the distance, soft purple mountains emerge. The road rises and dips, and I gasp at the vistas. It's easy to see why someone drew a state line here: the colors, smell, and sky are all new. I urge Wilma onward, and we fly past rocky slopes mottled with soft green sage. Overhead, the puffy white clouds look close enough to hug.

As the sun slips toward the broken horizon, I count the miles to 285. They tell you the miles to junctions out here instead of the distance to towns. At six thirty I reach the 285 turnoff and must decide whether to feed Wilma or push on to Santa Fe. The gas station, which sells Navajo blankets, looks like a lure that could hold you for hours. Joey urges me to keep going, so I curve north onto the most beautiful road I've ever seen.

The boulder-strewn slopes are soft, pinkish tan, in some places brown; in others, white. Pale green brush grows between the rocks, showing its joy in red and yellow flowers. In the evening light, the silent hills glow gold, but the weary red needle holds my eyes. Wilma's gas gauge has sunk below a quarter of a tank, and Santa Fe is fifty miles off. I have never been on a road like this: no gas stations, no bars, no stores. The radio offers only a long, sad hiss, so no signal will reach my phone. What will I do if I run out of gas? After sundown I'll be swimming in blackness. Each reflected flash brings a stab of hope. That glint must have come from a metal sign. But every man-made structure out here has been abandoned—the gas stations have dried up and died.

At seven thirty, with the needle near empty, green grass divides the gray road. Grass! Someone must have planted that! A white gas station beams at me, and Wilma drinks her fill. Trembling, I ease Wilma down the strip. Joey sniffs the air with his matted nose. A blue Run-Rite Inn sign glows on its post, and in a minute we're safe on a purple bedspread. Normally I don't write at night, but I can't settle in my humming room. I conjure Teresa, who won't usually emerge in a closed space. Her voice cuts through the crunch of Wheat Snacks.

How did Raúl know that Justin wouldn't fire me? If I were Justin, I think that I would. But when I come in the next morning, he only smiles.

"She's been asking for you," he says.

"I'm sorry. Is she upset?"

"No. She doesn't remember a thing."

"What about you?" I ask.

Justin's ear looks okay, and he smiles when he sees me scanning it.

"Oh, I'm fine. Raúl must really love you."

"Yes—where we live, we have to take care of each other."

"I know." Justin's smile quivers with sadness.

He swirls his coffee and gulps the last swallow. As he looks down at me, he hesitates. Mrs. Marshall slips up behind him and rubs him like a cat.

"Hey, Mom! Look who's here."

"Hi, Mrs. Marshall."

Justin hands me his empty cup and heads off to work.

Since it's a bright morning, I take our books to the sunporch: a bird book with bright pictures for her; a spiral-bound notebook from the bottom shelf for me. I can't imagine her writing such neat, tiny letters when I can barely pry her fingers apart. But forty years ago, she must have been a different person. I wonder what I'll be like in forty years.

I glance through the dry, forgotten pages, looking for the part that I was reading last week. There's a lot about a mother-in-law she can't stand. Toward the back, I find something interesting.

I don't know if it was such a good idea for me to work here. I guess I should be glad Bill wants me in the lab. He has always respected my interest in science, and most husbands won't let their wives work at all. What's weird is the transition. When we walk in each day, we have to pretend I'm not his wife. And it never works either. People won't tell me things. When I talk to them, it's like we're on those phones in prison. I sit behind glass because they're scared of me, and they can't say what they mean, because someone's listening. I can only relax when Bill is gone. Then people treat me as if I were almost human, knowing that I won't be home in bed with him that night.

Yesterday when I was working at the sink, Jimmy wandered in.

"Glad to see you on your feet," he said.

He glanced down at my silver guillotine and six white, headless rats smeared with blood.

"Geez, you must have a strong stomach!"

"I just want them for their vesicles." I frowned.

Jimmy smiled at me ironically. "Listen," he said. "You want to have dinner tonight?"

I looked at the crystal wart under my bloody glove and told him that I couldn't.

"Oh, I don't want to steal you." Jimmy grinned. "I just want to borrow you. Anybody in here can tell you that you're in safe hands with me."

It was true. After that day in the elevator, I had asked about Jimmy, and everyone said he worked all the time.

Unleashed, he drove his convertible at breakneck speed all the way to a restaurant in Decatur. For the first time ever since I got married, someone from the lab talked to me like a real person. Mainly he wanted to know about my prep.

"We're trying to purify synaptosomes," I said. "Sealed-off sacs of membrane from nerve terminals. Maybe that way, someday, people can figure out what's in 'em."

"Pure research." He gazed at me steadily. "That's not always much fun. No quick rewards, no easy answers. You've got to be optimistic to do that—and have a big enough grant."

"Yeah, Bill says that with the money from the pharmaceutical companies, he can finally study what he wants to learn."

"And he's lettin' you do it—he must respect you a lot."

But a black flicker showed me he had guessed the truth. As a research assistant, I didn't have to publish or give talks, and as long as I did the prep, Bill could keep things quiet. When I told Jimmy how I hated the thrashing bodies, he took my hands and gazed into my eyes.

"They're just rats," he said. "You're not doin' anything wrong. It's not like they're an endangered species. Hell, some people kill 'em for a living."

We sat there with our fingers interlocked and drew synchronized breaths. Then he pulled my right hand to his lips and kissed it. I shivered at the soft, wet tickle.

"You cold?"

"No, no, I—"

Jimmy brought my left hand to his mouth. "You're turnin' red," he whispered.

He looked at me as though he knew something about me that I didn't know. I think I was supposed to speak, and when I didn't, he squeezed my hands and released them. As he lowered his eyes and withdrew, I thought I caught a ray of pity.

Jimmy told me all about his work on proteins, and the tricks he knew for learning how they fold. He molded protein structures in the air, his long, thin body taut with energy. Cracking the genetic code had changed biology, since once you knew a protein's sequence, you could imagine how it worked. With puppetlike hands, he showed me three possible conformations of a cryptic molecule he was studying.

"Your synaptosome prep is going to give us a crucial part of the picture." He beamed.

Bill never said anything that inspired me like that.

By the time Jimmy brought me home, the heavy night was pulsing with crickets. We pulled up at our house, and he leaned over and whispered, "I'd like to borrow you again sometime." His lip brushed my ear, and every neuron in my body fired. The place where he touched it hasn't stopped tingling. Today I—

Is that the doorbell? Mrs. Marshall leaps from her chair. To beat her to the door, I have to run. Who could it be at eleven thirty? When I look through the peephole, I can't believe it.

There stands Raúl, scowling down at his boots. He kicks a toe against the mat to knock mud from his cleats.

I whip open the door. "¿Qué pasó? ¿Te corrieron?"

"No, no, se tronó la máquina. It just broke, the machine that grinds up the branches. They told us all to go home."

Mrs. Marshall's breath warms my shoulder. "Who are you?" she quavers.

"Hi, Mrs. Marshall. My name is Raúl. I've come to take you to lunch."

I gasp. "No, no, no puedes. ¿'Stás loco?"

"No, it's okay. We can both take care of her." Raúl smiles past me at the skinny lady hovering behind my back.

"No—we can't. What if Justin calls? What is he going to think?"

"He calls you during the day?" Raúl glares at me, black-eyed.

"No, no, he never has."

"So why would he call you today? He knows that you take good care of her. You've got to come with me. Luis, he works at the Dixie Buffet, and he says he can get us in for free."

"No. We can't."

"So why don't you ask her?"

I turn to find Mrs. Marshall beaming. She looks taller, prouder than I've ever seen. No doubt about it, she wants to go.

"You see? It'll be fun. Go get her coat."

I shake my head, but I grope for her wool wrap. Mrs. Marshall stands smugly with her arm through Raúl's. They make the craziest couple you ever saw, her smooth gray hair shining a head above his Braves cap.

"Come on, Mrs. Marshall. Let me take you to your car."

Raúl struggles with the creaking rear door. Grit invades my nails as I claw for the belt under the cold seat. I find twenty-five cents and a stick of gum, stiff and dry as a sliver of wood.

"Here, Mrs. Marshall. Isn't this nice?"

"I want to sit in front!" she cries.

She smirks triumphantly as Raúl straps her into the broad wine-red front seat. He starts the engine with a roar that shakes the neighborhood, and we scour through the quiet streets. Raúl takes a different route from Justin and never asks me where to turn. He favors the larger roads and gets us there in half the time. Maybe Justin didn't want to go the fastest way that night.

At the restaurant, the lunchtime wave is breaking, old gringo couples, black people, and families from across the highway. Like Raúl, I love the Dixie Buffet. They have gringo food and our food side by side, and you can eat well here without wasting money. Looped together, Raúl and Mrs. Marshall advance slowly through the line. At the register, he leans forward and whispers, "Somos amigos de Luis." The slick-haired girl looks dubiously at Mrs. Marshall but punches some buttons and hands us three red cards.

Under our feet, the brown carpet draws the light and sound, creating the kind of hush you feel in church. Raúl leads Mrs. Marshall toward the back, where soft voices are lapping like waves.

"Come bien," a grim woman tells her boy, "porque no sé cuando vas a cenar."

"I hope they have that okra again," says a tall black lady to her husband.

Raúl pulls out a padded chair for Mrs. Marshall, who sits down, soldier-straight. She looks in wonder at the huge brown room, busy as a grainy hill of ants.

"Take her up, go get her some food," orders Raúl. "I'll wait here and save the seats."

"Come on, Mrs. Marshall," I say. "At this restaurant you get your own food. That's the fun of it. You'll see."

I take her cool, bony hand and lead her to the salads. I choose two yellow plates, but then I have a hard time. To grab food,

I have to set both plates down, and I nudge her along with my hips. Mrs. Marshall moves slowly, fascinated by the colors: green lettuce, orange carrots, purple beets. Red Jell-O cubes quiver at white cottage cheese, brown pinto beans, and red tomatoes. I can't blame her for staring at this fiesta of color. She points to glistening peaches, and I slide one onto her plate. Her eyes brighten with amusement when she discovers that anything she points to, I'll serve.

When we reach the breads, her breathing quickens, and I give her a plate to hold. Before us lie fresh rolls, steaming yellow cornbread, and spicy buns whose glaze has invaded their spirals. I cut Mrs. Marshall a cube of cornbread, but her eyes shift to my pale-moon plate.

"What's that? I want that!" she exclaims.

With silver tongs, I peel off a tortilla.

I have a harder time serving her hot food, since so many people have clustered around the meat. A full-hipped girl whose bottom strains her tan pants bumps Mrs. Marshall, and the peach slides downward.

"¡Ay, perdón! ¡Perdón, señora!" She smiles apologetically, patting her round belly. "Con el hambre que tengo … Oye, ¿necesitas ayuda con la señora? Te ayudo. Te traigo otro durazno."

She runs to fetch us another peach, and Mrs. Marshall turns to watch her brown hair bounce.

"Look at all this good food!" I say. "Just tell me what you want. What's your favorite thing to eat?"

To tell the truth, I've never seen Mrs. Marshall eat much. Every day I make her a sandwich, sometimes with tomato soup, but she swallows it listlessly. I think she'd rather be let loose amid a crazy, steaming feast like this.

Heat rises from vegetables in silver bins: corn, carrots, string beans, spinach, and slimy green rounds. Chicken, steak, and stringy carnitas wait to be piled into crispy taco shells. Meat loaf, fish, and crisp brown potatoes trade salty whiffs with macaroni and cheese. Balancing three peaches on a plastic plate, the friendly girl returns. Creamy flesh bulges below her pink top.

"Gracias," I say.

She spoons up carnitas but then hesitates, intrigued by Mrs. Marshall. "¡Pero qué preciosa, la señora, qué ojos azules más lindos!"

Laughing with delight, she seizes silver spoons as Mrs. Marshall points to what she wants. Onto la vieja's tortilla go steak, carnitas, corn, and mashed potatoes. Between the peaches fall rice, beans, fish, meat loaf, and gobs of sticky macaroni. When I take a tamal, the girl seizes three, one for Mrs. Marshall and two for herself. Raúl bursts out laughing when he sees us approach, me, the bouncing brown girl, and the old lady with two plates of food.

Raúl grins at the hungry girl. "La señora tiene hambre. Yo también—yo también tengo muchas ganas."

"¡Uuii!" She purses her lips and touches his cheek. "No lo dudo. Pero tengo que regresar con mi novio."

Mrs. Marshall frowns as Raúl's eyes dance after the girl. He heads purposefully for the drinks, and I hand Mrs. Marshall her fork. Amazed, she looks from one plate to the other, uncertain where to start.

"Where's Justin?" she asks.

"Oh, he's still at work. But he'll be back tonight."

Raúl is helping the pretty girl with her drinks, since she has a glass in each hand and can't raise the basket to fetch a third. Everything about her is round and full, her bottom, her belly, even her pink fingertips. Laughing, she retreats with four brimming glasses balanced skillfully between her fingers. Two of them must be for her and the other two for her novio.

Raúl appears with three foaming cokes.

"Oh, I'm not sure she should drink that," I say. "She'll get crazy."

"Más loca no puede estar." He stalks off to look for his food. I unwrap Mrs. Marshall's tamal, pungent and pasty in its husk of leaves.

La vieja sucks long and hard at her coke as Raúl settles down to eat. On his plate are two tacos, two tamales, rice, beans, and a sticky cluster of macaroni. Raúl likes to eat as much as he can, then sleep it off like a lion. I try to eat less, since he doesn't want me fat, but the food is so good I can't stop. Raúl grins at me, then jerks his head to show that I should help Mrs. Marshall. Gingerly, she has speared a peach on her fork and is holding it to her mouth, unsure where to bite.

"Here, Mrs. Marshall."

I slice the peach into clean, slippery cubes while Raúl devours a taco. Saying little, he quickly clears his plate, and Mrs. Marshall flattens the hills the girl dished out for her. With his lids drooping, Raúl leans back in his chair and spreads his fingers over his round belly.

"You take good care of la vieja." He smiles. "I like to see how you care for her. Eres una buena mujer."

I smile at the husk of my tamal, whose broken wings are reaching upward.

"Y muy guapa. Yo te voy a comprar un bilet y unos pantalones como los de ésa."

Raúl swings his shoulders like the brown-haired girl.

"I don't know if I could walk like that."

"Sure you could. Tienes un buen culito."

He reaches under the table to pinch my thigh. Mrs. Marshall looks on dreamily, very full.

"Oye, reina, bring me a coffee and some dessert. You know what I like."

"Can you watch her?"

"Sure. Don't worry. We get along well, la vieja and I. And go get yourself something too, to feed that nice little ass of yours."

First I bring Raúl his coffee. He leans toward Mrs. Marshall, and her widened eyes shine. At the dessert stand, I choose a small blue plate for myself and a full-size one for Raúl. I cut the moistest, neatest pieces of apple pie, bread pudding, peanut butter bars, and fudge cake. In the middle I form a giant volcano of ice cream with warm chocolate lava and a cherry crater.

"¡Qué maravilla!" he cries when he sees it. "¡Qué mujer! ¡Esto es una obra de arte!"

Mrs. Marshall's bright eyes burn holes in the mountain. Spoon in hand, she extends her arm toward Raúl's plate.

"Mírala, qué maleducada!" He laughs. "Go get her some before she eats mine."

I smile to myself and fill a bowl with soft, sweet things: hot apple crisp, gooey brownie, ice cream, and chocolate pudding. Next to me, the girl's novio is twisting threads of sauce onto her ice cream while she squeals and begs for more. He catches her around the waist and nips her neck.

"¡Pero qué golosa eres!"

When I get back, Raúl is spooning up the last of his ice cream, his eyes fixed on the girl's pink top.

"That guy's gonna have a good time tonight."

"Her too."

"And you too."

Raúl grins at me, drunk with good food.

Of everything in her bowl, Mrs. Marshall likes the pudding best. She swallows it solemnly in big spoonfuls. Raúl adjusts his pants and leans back lazily. He studies my hair, my eyes, and my lips, then my neck and my breasts.

"Things are not going so bad for us," he says. "I like that you care for la vieja. Now we have a car—pretty soon, a nice house— you'll see—with all the curtains you want. Then we'll get married, como Dios manda, you in a beautiful white dress, y yo te hago mamá. We'll have lots of kids. We'll go at it day and night, until we have lots of kids."

I don't ask him how I'm going to care for la vieja if we have lots of kids, or how we're going to feed the kids if I don't care for la vieja. I just smile back at him, my eyes hot and wet.

"Eres una mujer muy buena," he whispers. His eyes burn in his flushed face. I wish we were home instead of here.

I glance over at Mrs. Marshall and find her chair empty. How could— Where—

Alarmed, Raúl and I scan the restaurant. We don't have far to look. Spoon in hand, she has advanced on the desserts and is scooping pudding directly from the bin.

"Scuse me, ma'am, you can't do that!" squawks a dark, pimply worker.

She looks up, startled, clutching her spoon.

"¡Que la chingada! ¿Por qué no te fijaste?" shouts Raúl.

The young man grabs her arm, and she thrashes in panic.

"Justin!" she screams. "Justin! Jimmy!"

Raúl and I rush up, apologizing in two languages at once.

"*Lo siento—está enferma—está muy confundida—*"

"She's old, confused—we'll take her home—we're sorry—"

The bathroom smells of heartless disinfectant. Mrs. Marshall winces against the cold water as I wash her face. She begs for Justin and Jimmy, Jimmy and Justin. Where are they? Why don't they come?

I tell her Justin will be here very soon and lead her trembling out to the car. Raúl is kicking the pavement with his boot.

"Who's Jimmy?" he asks as he starts the motor. "Does she have another kid?"

CHAPTER 7

SANTA FE

wake up with my mouth full of fur, my body curved behind Joey's. The roar of the air conditioner flattens my thoughts, but fringes of light tickle the curtains' edges. With my tongue, I explore the roof of my mouth.

7:34 a.m. Santa Fe.

Although I wrote until three, I want to get up. The city's hard edges are drawing me. At breakfast, I find that two parallel universes are conducting their business in the same space. In one live black-haired families and heavyset men with moist ponytails. They order in Spanish, speaking with soft *l*'s and *r*'s. In the other live gringos, big-bellied men and wrinkled red women who have rediscovered themselves as artists. The waitress switches from Spanish to English, knowing at a glance which to use. With me, she hesitates. Straight black hair, blue-green eyes? She pauses, then speaks to me in English.

Joey wants to see the town, so I strap him in, but he rides only as far as the garage. After a day of driving, I'm tired of

Wilma, and I want to explore Santa Fe on foot. At nine in the morning, the air is so hot and dry that when I inhale, my cells tighten. Adobe buildings cut the sky in sharp, clean lines. At both ends, Francisco Street trails off into orange soil, soft green brush, and purple mountains. In the plaza, black-haired men are stringing cables for a fiesta. Since the museums won't open for an hour, I circle slowly. Under an arcade, fat Indian women arrange chunky jewelry on a long string of gray sheets.

Seeking shade, I explore the streets beyond the plaza and find a store full of brilliant ceramics. Though it's May, they sell figures for the Day of the Dead, chalky skeletons playing guitars, drums, and trumpets. Bride and groom skeletons grin at ghastly doctors and nurses, while other muertos sell miniature versions of themselves. One vain female thrusts out her breasts, proud of her sparkly green dress and orange parasol. On the darkest shelves, red devils leer. Waving their pitchforks, they dare me to pick them up. Others cavort around the bedposts of reclining women who seem eager for their approach. Arms slack, legs wide apart, the fleshy beauties await their fate. If you let a woman sleep alone, she'll invite evil to bed. We're all in cahoots with the devil.

By noon, the sun is searing, and I creep through the shadows like a roach. I wander into the Governor's House, where I learn how adobe is made and how the gringos never invented anything as good. Uninspired by mud, I turn the corner and find myself in a familiar place. On a wooden rack hang all sorts of tools: hammers, saws, hand drills, and clamps. The smell of fresh wood arouses me as my eyes flit from one tool to the next. Attracted by their smooth, solid weight, I move in closer and risk my finger against a handsaw's jagged teeth. In the center stands a rotating device with a husky wax figure bent over it. I've wandered into a nineteenth-century woodshop, but I sense that I've been here before.

Fascinated, I move systematically down the wall, trying to picture what each tool does and who used it. One clamp begs me to pick it up. How heavy it is, and how well made! I press my finger into the screws' sharp threads, then try the fly nuts, which have been jammed for years. Next to the clamp hangs a more complex device, with adjustable rods that meet at right angles. I replace the clamp and follow the rods until they join. I wonder what—oh.

Eight years ago, I went to a workshop in San Francisco, a bunch of writers critiquing each other's stories. *The Rainbow Bar* existed only on loose-leaf pages then, and I was teaching creative writing in Pennsylvania. Funny—I set that novel in San Francisco, but I wrote it in cafés so cold the sentences had to chew their way out through my coat.

I called Johnny the day that the workshop accepted my draft.

"Carrie McFadden!" He laughed. "Damn! What have you been up to?"

Johnny told me he didn't have much time but I could come by the last afternoon.

As I walked into his building, I was breathing so fast the world became a grainy copy of itself. I had to think about how many breaths to take in a minute. Fifteen, I remembered, and I tried to count them, but I lost track each time I asked for the Turner lab. I was wearing black high-heeled boots, black leggings, and an indigo blouse, standard fare for the Northeast. But among these white coats, I might as well have been wearing a Brazilian carnival outfit. I feared that I would embarrass Johnny. In a tight voice, a girl directed me down the hall. After that I asked only men.

"You seen Johnny?"

"He's not in his office. Try his lab."

Breathing once a second, I entered a doorway. I hesitated as I scanned the white benches. Three heads rose to look at me, two Asian guys and a red-haired girl.

"Is Johnny here?"

The freckled girl pointed left, then looked back at what she was writing.

"Yup. Okay. You keep workin' on that."

Johnny's low voice wafted from behind a bench. I turned the corner to see his long, straight back.

"Yeah, just do it again. You're gonna get it eventually. Do it fifteen times if you have to."

As though my gaze had pricked his neck, Johnny spun around.

"Carrie!"

He reached me in three long steps. I wrapped my arms around his waist, and he squashed my nose into his sweet-smelling shirt. The curly-haired girl to whom he'd been talking parted her lips in a half smile.

"Carrie used to work in Marty Cohen's lab. Synaptic vesicle proteins." Johnny jerked his chin my way, trying to explain me.

"Oh." The girl next to him nodded respectfully.

"C'mon, let's go to my office where we can talk," said Johnny. "I've got a few minutes; then I've gotta go do some stuff."

I followed Johnny to an office so small he could touch both walls with his hands. The packed space reminded me of a van Eyck chamber whose window looks out on an infinite universe. Far below, the Golden Gate Bridge hung like a coral necklace between the bleached city and the green mounds of Marin. In twelve years, Johnny still hadn't found a chair he could fit into, so his long legs framed the stool where I sat.

"So tell me what you've been doin'." He looked so deep into me I trembled.

"Well, I got an MFA," I muttered.

"An MFA—what is that? Master of—"

"Fine arts. It lets you teach creative writing."

"Oh. So that's what you're doin' now?" Johnny nodded in acknowledgment.

"Yeah. But I'm writing a novel. That's what I really want to do."

"Wow. A novel. That's great."

Johnny ruffled his hair. "So that's really what you want to do, huh? I could never—"

"Excuse me—sorry." The curly-haired student appeared in the doorway. "Johnny—do you want me to do it exactly the same way or try what Saito's been doing?"

Johnny smiled patiently. "No—no—do it exactly the same way—exactly the same. Don't worry about Saito. Saito doesn't exist. Do it like you're the only one doin' it."

Behind his shoulder, a silver frame encircled an image of Johnny with a tall blonde woman. She stood resting her hand lightly on the shoulder of a towheaded boy.

A sharp ring pierced the air.

"John Turner here. Yup. Yup." Johnny reached across his ordered desk for his calendar. "Nope. Not Tuesday. Thursday at four I could do." He smiled at me mischievously as a high-pitched voice spilled from the receiver. "Yup. We can talk about that on Thursday, okay? I've got someone here." With his eyes on mine, Johnny hung up while the man was still talking.

"So a novel, huh? What's it about?" His eyes dimmed as he filed the man's complaint.

"Ice cream. San Francisco," I said.

"So you're sittin' in Pennsylvania writin' a novel about San Francisco?" Johnny's jaw twitched.

Half the redhead's sprigged face appeared in the doorway.

"Johnny—that guy from Charles River is here. You said I should tell you next time he came."

"Oh, yeah, right. Look, can you tell him to call me in my office tomorrow? Around ten? I've got some stuff I've gotta do."

Johnny swung to his feet. "C'mon. Let's get out of here. You wanna go do some stuff with me?"

I could hardly believe it. My minutes with Johnny had turned into hours. Ecstatic, I followed him out to this car.

"So what are we going to do?"

Johnny opened the door for me, eying the silk of my blouse. "Nothing too exciting. Gotta drop off a key for Patrick—my tenant. Gotta go buy some fish food. My kid, Tommy—he likes fish."

"Wow, that's great—I think I saw his picture. He's going to be tall like you, right?" I can easily imagine a boy with Johnny's face, which shines with a three-year-old's eagerness.

Johnny blushes and nods. "Yeah. Like his mom too."

"Sounds great," I pronounce. "So how long you been married?" My heart is thudding.

"Five years—no, six. Yeah, it's good."

"Is your wife in science too?" I draw a long, slow breath.

"God, no! I could never take that. No, she's a lawyer. Keeps you sane, you know, hearin' about things from a different point of view."

Johnny's smile fades as we glide down a hill. "So what about you?" he asks. "You with anybody?"

"No, not me."

"Yeah, I can't picture you married."

We rush past pale houses with twisted Van Gogh bushes.

"Why not?" I frown.

"Oh, I dunno. You've just got this way about you. Like you don't need anyone else."

In two moves, Johnny backs us into a parking space so tight, synapses could form front and back. The afternoon sun enlivens pink and blue houses, and the air smells of licorice and eucalyptus. Elephantine leaves brush us as we push toward the basement door.

"This is Patrick's workshop," he explains. "Biker. Cool guy. Sabine and I, we own some houses, and I let him use this basement, 'cause he does some work for us. Just gotta leave him this key, here—"

I inhale the sweet, burnt smell of fresh wood. Johnny switches on the light.

"Wow!" Dazzled, I admire the tools on the walls, hung carefully according to function.

Johnny closes the door and locks it.

"What is all this stuff?"

"Amazing, isn't it?" Johnny tilts a level, tracking its slippery bubble with dark eyes.

Unable to resist, I finger the tools. I weigh hammers, turn recalcitrant screws, and play lobster with the pliers.

Johnny lays the key on Patrick's workbench and drifts toward me.

"What's that you've got there?"

I have taken down a frame with cold metal arms and am squinting along its guiding lines.

"I think it's for joining the edges of cabinets—something in three dimensions."

"You're good." He grins. "You learn that from your dad?"

"No. Not my dad." I grip the frame until its edges bite.

Together we move down the wall, and Johnny is impressed that I can guess what things do. He stops and looks at me, hesitating. His mind seems to have disconnected, as though he's processing an inner quandary.

"Johnny?"

Gazing down at me, he cups my face in his hands, then bends over and kisses me. He pulls me against him, retreats to the wall, and switches off the light.

"Mmm …"

The kiss is so delicious I squirm for another. I clasp him so that my body is tight against his. Johnny's hands glide down to the ends of my hair, and he rocks me back and forth against him.

"Oh … Oh, God …"

Openmouthed, I sink down along his body. He's so tall I don't have to bend my legs far. Hesitating, I look up at him. Tiny, penetrating points of light reveal his dark face. Johnny nods. One tooth at a time, I pull down his zipper, so taut that it doesn't want to budge. Johnny's eyes close. I pull down his jeans, then some kind of soft underwear. Keeping my lips tight, I swallow him with a fierce, driving hunger.

Scratch. Click.

With both hands, Johnny thrusts me back. The workbench slams my shoulder blades, and I seize it to keep from falling. Johnny zips himself up and snaps on the light. When the door swings open, we're studying the joining device on the table.

"Hey, Patrick!"

"Oh, hi, Johnny."

A rough, long-haired man surveys me quickly, then looks back at his boss.

"I was just bringin' you that key to the place on Frederick. This is Carrie. She's visiting from Pennsylvania."

"Hey, Carrie." Patrick extends a calloused hand.

"Well, we better—where did I say we were goin' next?" Johnny's voice holds steady, but his eyes are wild.

"Fish food."

"Oh, yeah." Johnny grins. Patrick's eyes shift from my blouse to his tool on the table.

"So you'll call me to let me know how much those supplies are?"

Patrick grips the frame. "Yeah. Nice meeting you, Carrie. Enjoy San Francisco."

The door shuts behind us, and Johnny looks down at me. "You okay?" he asks.

"Yeah. That was pretty funny."

The enormous leaves settle. Waxy lilies lean toward us, frozen in their slow, twisting dance.

"Not really. You hit that table pretty hard. I didn't mean to—"

"No, I'm okay."

Johnny rests his hands on my shoulders. "Carrie, I'm sorry. I really am. I don't know what it is. You just do somethin' to me. Anytime I see you, I just—I just start doin' things I wouldn't normally do. I start doin' crazy things."

"I like when you do crazy things."

Johnny's fingers tighten. His eyes seek my lips.

"You do, huh?" His face softens.

We're standing on a cement walk in full view of the street, but for the first time all day, I breathe easily. I shift my weight so that my hips invite him.

"Damn!" Johnny pulls my head against his chest. Under my cheek, his heart beats a violent rhythm. "Damn, that sure felt nice."

He holds me back so he can read my eyes. "I don't want to hurt you," he says. "I don't want to hurt anybody. I've got a kid now. It's just— You make me— I can't control myself around you."

"So don't."

I move my hips slightly.

"Oh, shit ... Look. We can't do this. If this is gonna happen every time I see you— I can't believe this. After what, ten, twelve years? Nobody's ever—"

Johnny's fingers clutch me. Sadness flows from his black eyes.

"Not even ...?"

"No." He sighs. "That's different. Look, I don't wanna do this. I mean, I do—I really do—but I can't." His fingers tremble inches from my hair. "You okay? You gonna be okay?"

"Yeah. As long as I can see you again."

"Oh, you will." Johnny smiles at me ironically. "Somehow I know you will."

He shakes his head to clear it, then takes a step back. The pulse of his heart has slowed.

"Okay? Yeah? So … fish food. You still wanna come?"

"Oh, yeah!"

Johnny swats me playfully, and we push past reaching leaves and lilies onto the street. The afternoon sun warms gingerbread houses with brilliant blue and purple trim. Johnny's long legs carry him so fast I rush to compensate for my shorter wavelength. He turns quiet, mentally returning to his lab. A bell tinkles as we enter a pet shop where the damp, rancid air smells like a guinea pig cage. Behind the counter, a brown-haired girl's eyes snap.

"May I help you?"

"Yeah, we're lookin' for some fish food." Johnny greets her with a troublemaking grin.

"What kind of fish?"

"Gosh. Gee. I dunno. Fish."

The girl's guarded face brightens. "Well, are they tropical? Freshwater? What do they look like?"

"Well, they've got this—" Johnny sticks his thumbs in his ears and rhythmically waves his long fingers. Opening and closing his mouth, he acts out the fish. The pet-store girl and I double over with laughter.

"So what color are they?"

"Bright blue—with this sort of black mask thing." Johnny rotates his fingers inward.

"Tropical. Sort of like what she's wearing."

"Yeah. Hey, you should be doin' this, not me." Johnny nudges my arm.

The girl dissolves. A strange warmth breaches my wrist.

"Ma'am? Uh … ma'am? Are you all right?"

Next to me stands a worried guard in a khaki uniform. I am laughing alone in a museum workshop with both hands wrapped around a joiner's clamp.

"I'm sorry, ma'am, but we can't let our visitors touch the exhibits."

"Oh. I'm sorry." My hands drop to my sides.

"Ma'am, would you like to sit down for a minute? You look kind of pale. Can I get you a glass of water or something?"

On his fleshy nose, the pores beg to be squeezed. It's so satisfying when those little brown worms pop out.

"No, no, I'm okay."

The husky guard gazes at me, unsatisfied. "This heat—it can do funny things to you if you're not used to it. Have you had enough to eat today?"

"Oh, yeah, sure, I had some oatmeal …"

"But it's twelve thirty now—time for lunch."

"Oh. Is it?"

He leads me out to a courtyard bench with a grimy wagon wheel leaning against its side. I settle down and gratefully accept his waxy cup of warm water. The guard smiles at me, a little less worried.

"You know, there's a great Mexican buffet at the corner of Francisco and Main. I eat over there all the time. I hope you don't mind my saying this—but you look like you could use a good meal."

At eye level, the belly pushing against his brown belt looks a lot like Clifton's.

"Why don't you rest here awhile? You can call me if you need anything. My name is John—easy to remember."

"Okay, John," I say. "Thanks. My name is Theresa."

My eyes sweep the courtyard, craving color, but after one round they've had enough. Walls, dirt, and junked equipment share the same dull brown, brightened only by lichens of rust. I have never been one for resting, and the static wheel disturbs my inner gyroscope. Reaching into my purse, I grope for smooth metal. What time is it in New York?

"Hola. Aquí habla tu pésima pesadilla."

"¡Mala! ¡Más mala que nunca!" Gonzalo's voice flows. "¿Qué tal? Where are you today?"

"Santa Fe."

"¡Santa Fe!" He pauses, as though picturing me on a map. "You are moving fast. ¡Qué chica más vagabunda! Oye, ¿qué tal la zarzuela del gordo y el flaco?"

I finger the wagon wheel and scowl at the dark smudge it leaves. "Well, the fat guy's reading my book, and he can't understand why I have no boyfriend."

"Tan tonto no es." He chuckles. "And he thinks he is the right man for the job?"

"Yup. It's starting to look like it." I grind my heels into the grit, first one and then the other.

"I told you!" he exclaims. "And by now he has confessed that he has a fat wife and three kids?"

"Only two."

"Mala—deja eso." His voice contracts. "What is the point of this pollastrería?"

Good question. What's the point of my passion for guys? What's the point of my circuit through the world? Does Gonzalo think about the point of his women?

"Well, he's pretty nice," I say, imagining Clifton's plump warmth. "I like to talk to him."

"Mala, every man is nice when he wants to sleep with you. You should find someone like you, who can do things with you."

Clifton presses me against him in a slow, throbbing dance. As he steps back, he lengthens until he has assumed Johnny's proportions.

"El flaco—he's like me."

"Maybe in body mass index, but from what you tell me, he works on science fifteen hours a day and never uses words of more than one syllable."

"That's not true!"

"Mala," reproves Gonzalo, "all I know is what you tell me. I have not met this man. You have said this yourself."

"I was mad at him that day. He blew me off."

"So if he doesn't respect you, why do you want to see him?"

That adobe roof slices the sky so cleanly. Why can't roofs do that back east?

"He does!" I cry. "I know he does! I have this feeling of connection with him, like there's a secret only we understand."

"A secret—only you understand," echoes Gonzalo. "This can be good. I know this feeling. But Mala—he has married another woman."

"Yeah. A friggin' German. Sabine." I snort.

"Oh, German women can be very nice ..." He chuckles.

"Yeah, if you're six foot four and like sausages."

"Didn't you say he was—"

"Yeah, he's six four." I remember that picture, Johnny smiling next to the tall woman with fluffy blonde hair. Gonzalo turns silent, and I grind my heels.

"Mala," he says finally, "this feeling of connection—it is not a reason to get married."

"How do you know? You've never been married."

"No, but I have been with enough married people to know."

Across the courtyard, a broken-toothed harrow is trying to bite the ground. Why couldn't they plant some red flowers out here? Maybe around that dead fountain.

"Why do people get married, anyway?" I ask. "Why would anyone do it? It's like voluntarily walking into a jail cell."

The expert on marriage doesn't hesitate. "Oh, there are lots of reasons. Some people want to have kids. Peer pressure— sometimes their friends make them, or their families. Some people feel like failures if they're not married. But the people I know—most of them like it. They want to go through life with someone else."

My free fingers are burning for contact, and I push them into a splintery gap. Someone has carved letters into this wooden bench.

"If all these married women are so happy," I ask, "what are they doing with you? Why are these married men coming to me?"

What does it say down there? A-s- When I tune back in, I have missed a few words.

"—a wife, a man looks for a woman he can talk to, someone who wants to have kids and will give things up to build a life together. But this is not enough. He has other parts of him that his wife can't understand. This feeling of connection you're talking about—I believe you. Probably you do share something that his wife can't. But whatever it is, other things are more important to him. He has married the woman who shares what is important."

What is that third letter down there? It could be an *h*.

"Okay," I say. "So she can have him most of the time—I just want him sometimes, when he wants the thing that he can share with me."

"Mala ..." Gonzalo's voice warms with irony. "What if this thing—what if it is just sex? This feeling of connection, this secret, it is the feeling I get just before—"

"It's not just sex." I kick my heel into the dirt. "It's some kind of understanding—some deep understanding of life."

"Mala," says Gonzalo, "didn't you say that he took you down a basement? And before that ...?"

"Oh, he likes sex," I admit. "But sex is just the catalyst—it's what we do to reinforce the bond."

"Ashley"—that's what the bench says. Geez, if that were my name, I'd be too embarrassed to carve it. I wonder what else they've written down here ...

"Pero este deseo," insists Gonzalo, "this urge to have sex—it can disguise itself as anything—sobre todo en un hombre. Créeme, Mala. You are a beautiful woman. Any man who wouldn't want to take you down a basement would have to be gay."

"But only some try it." I laugh.

My eyes dance over a dull chain coiled like a snake.

Two thousand miles away, Gonzalo laughs with me. "Right. I have to admit, Mala, I like this man—a famous scientist, you said—with a family—and still he gets you down the basement. Éste tiene cojones."

I feel the demand of Johnny against me. "Yeah," I murmur. "He's smart. I just wish—"

Letters trail across my bench like the tracks of staggering birds.

"Mala, I know what you're going to say. Let's say he dumps Brunhilde. Let's say she takes the kids. Let's say he calls you up and asks you to move in with him. Would you do it?"

"Yes."

"You would leave your job—"

"Yes."

"You would have a child with him?"

"Yes."

"You would stop writing novels to nurse his baby and shop for his favorite foods?"

What does it say down there? E-s- The phone is awaiting my reply.

"Well, she's a lawyer," I say. "She must have figured out some way to have a life."

"That is just it, Mala, that is just it!" he cries. "For you and me, the life is not the marriage and the baby."

"It's just an expression!"

"I know. Do not insult me. It is an expression that says what you think."

"España está cabrón," says the bench. Spain sucks. I couldn't have put it better myself.

"You haven't seen him," I protest. "You haven't seen how he looks at me—I know that he wants me!"

Gonzalo remains frustratingly calm. "Mala, please don't get angry. Don't get upset. Maybe you are right. Maybe he does love you. How can I know? What I am saying is, what matters is you. You need to take care of yourself. What is happening with your book?"

My eyes plant flowers around the chipped fountain, a burst of red every two feet.

"It's going pretty well," I say. "I was up half the night writing."

"¡Qué bien! Now, this is what I want to hear!"

"Yeah—it's getting so I hear them talking, and I just write down what they say."

"That is good, Mala. That is very good." I can see Gonzalo's round chin bob with satisfaction. "So why don't you just stay there and write? If it is flowing like you say … Santa Fe is beautiful. Go to some cafés, look at some jewelry. Why don't you just stay there?"

"Well, I have to be in San Francisco on the thirty-first."

"Blow him off!" He laughs. "He deserves it!"

"That's not exactly what I had in mind."

"¡Qué mala eres!" he scolds. "So you must have your scientist?"

"Yeah." I smile. "This time it's going to happen. I just hope I don't injure his brain."

Gonzalo's voice narrows like a river. "Listen, Mala. What I have been saying, I have only been thinking of you. I want you to be happy. Write your book. Your book is what matters."

"Yeah … you're right."

I wonder what words are carved under where I'm sitting.

"If el flaco depresses you, try el gordo. At least he is nice to you."

No radiant messages are screened by my bottom. I must have sat in a barren place.

"This Sabine," asks Gonzalo, "you say she's good looking?"

"Yeah, very." I grimace.

"How good looking? Does she have long legs? Does she have blonde hair?"

For someone so smart, Gonzalo has boring taste.

"I couldn't tell from the picture—but they must be long if her head's up near his. Why?"

"Well, it has been a long time since I was with a German woman. I like them—very strong, very set in their ways."

"You mean ..." I need to eat something. My wheeling thoughts won't settle into words.

"If it doesn't work out, maybe I will pay her a visit. I have all these frequent-flier miles."

"Y tú me llamas mala ..."

"No, no, this would be an act of charity," he protests. "You say he is fifteen hours a day in the lab?"

"Yeah." I grin. "Now you're starting to cheer me up."

"Sabine and I will find a connection," he vows. "We will find a deep understanding of life."

"¡Pero qué malo eres!"

"Oh, I think she will like me, don't you?"

I envision the disrobing. Her silk blouse drops like a petal on a windless day.

"Yeah." I smile. "She's going to like you. So you'll be plan B."

"I am plan B?"

"Yeah." I finger the bench. The brown courtyard is starting to shimmer.

"Okay, Mala," says Gonzalo. "Te dejo con tu arte y tus amores."

"Sí, mi amor. Brindo por el arte del amor y el amor del arte."

"Ciao, Mala."

"Adios, Gonzalo."

Spurred by hunger, I venture down the searing street to find the restaurant John recommended. The Mexican buffet pleases me, dark wood and waiters in tight black vests. The iron pots bubble enticingly, their crusty overflow promising spicy riches. I scoop up small piles of red beans, rice, and faded vegetables trailing strings of cheese. From my purse, I pull out two sheets of paper. My mouth explodes. No matter which pile of paste I poke, my lips and tongue are attacked by a flamethrower. A sweet-faced waiter pours me some more iced tea, the only thing I can swallow. I go back for more rice, which looks safe enough, but even that is tinctured with fire. Taking tiny bites and great sucks of tea, I try not to cry. I am not leaving. I have paid ten bucks for this seat, and I'm staying until I've finished this scene.

After that day, I asked Justin if I could try some other things for lunch. He gave me money, and I made Raúl stop for tortillas, beans, salsa, and pudding.

"Esta vieja está comiendo mejor que yo," he growled.

Now lunch is more fun. The radio spices the air as we cook, and Mrs. Marshall smiles over her food.

I never used to like reading, but now I look forward to the quiet hours on the sunporch. Every day I let Mrs. Marshall choose a book, which takes a long time. What goes on in her head as she pretends to read? She stares at the words like she's deciphering code and turns the pages so I'll think she understands. I grab my favorite notebook from the bottom shelf. Strange that since that first day in the library, she's never asked me what I'm reading. Today the sun is bright, and the air smells of fresh mud. I pull two chairs into shining squares of light.

I feel like a whore, and I haven't even done anything. How did I get to be this bad? I majored in biochemistry, something women couldn't study a generation ago—hell, most women can't study it now! I found a man who encouraged me from the start, one who wants a wife with a mind. Bill is never mean or sarcastic, and he tries to keep me from getting hurt. I've got to be the luckiest woman alive, but how do I repay him? This privileged mind can't think of proteins for a minute—all I can think about is Jimmy.

Three years ago, I thought Bill was as good as they come—competent, reliable, a man you can trust. Being with him made me feel so much better about myself—if he wanted me, I must be a good scientist, since he wouldn't marry a loser. Bill is round, soft, and warm, like a teddy bear that hugs you back. But last week when he was inside me, I saw Jimmy's face in a flash. Dark eyes, pale skin, that ghost face! In a sudden spasm, I tightened around him.

"Oooh," he whispered. "What was that? I like that!"

Bill was all sweaty by then, so just as an experiment, I tried to do it again. I couldn't. Then I let myself think of Jimmy's lips on my ear, and my insides just wrenched. Bill came with a roar I haven't heard in a while, and now he's been wanting it each night. I have stopped holding back, and I think of Jimmy all the time—black eyes, taut lips, long legs. I love the way his jaw twitches when he sees me, like he knows something funny about me he can't tell. When I remember the feel of his lips, bubbles of energy shoot through me. If I'm with Bill, my insides grab hold of him, and he likes it better each time. In the lab now, he gives me proud, secret looks. I'm just wondering when Jimmy will be back. They said he had to go to New York.

I look up at Mrs. Marshall. I don't know why, but I like that mentally, she was putting horns on her sweaty husband. She glares at her book, her blue eyes blasting the page. Her thick gray hair is carefully pinned up—Justin must have done that. Imagine, a forty-year-old man combing his mother's hair! ¡Qué pena! She needs a daughter.

The next entry is dated a few weeks later.

Now I really am a whore. Next time I saw Jimmy, he looked at me like he had decided something. I read it in his eyelids' droop.

"How's that prep goin'?" he asked, and I said fine, Bill thought we had the synaptosomes almost pure. Jimmy frowned slightly, then said he had to catch up on some things and hurried off to his desk.

When Bill had to go to that meeting in Augusta, Jimmy seemed to know it before I did. Late in the day as I was soaping the glassware, he wandered in, chuckling.

"What's so funny?" I asked.

"I dunno." He grinned. "There's just somethin' so funny about you."

He said they were seeing all kinds of things in nerve terminals with this new electron microscope at the Rockefeller Institute.

"Why don't you come over?" he asked. "I can cook us dinner. I'll show you the EM pictures they gave me."

Since Bill had his talk that night, I knew he wouldn't call, and I wanted to see the marvels in that gray grit. I was having my period, so I felt safe. Even if Jimmy were planning something, that sticky redness should hold him back.

Jimmy turned out to be a good cook. We cut up beans and potatoes, and he concocted spicy sauce for the chicken. To set the table, I bulldozed inches of journals. He said it was the first time the table had had a meal on it for as long as he could remember. As we ate, he paused to watch me chew, his thin face warming with amusement.

"What's so funny?" I asked, worrying that I had food wedged between my teeth.

"You've got an interesting mouth," he murmured. "I like to watch you eat."

I figured if Jimmy could say things about my mouth, I could ask him about his eyes. Genetically, how could someone with skin that light have eyes that were almost black?

"Somebody was part Cherokee—or Comanche. I've heard it both ways. I'm Scotch Irish. Happens a lot in my part of the country."

He started to tell me stories of West Texas dust storms that blasted the paint off cars. We studied the EM pictures on his living room rug, our legs dividing it into soft triangles. The detail of those images astounded me. I saw the curves of single vesicles and the thick, fuzzy membrane that would receive them.

"Someday soon," said Jimmy, "they're gonna have pictures of vesicles halfway in and halfway out, so we can watch the membranes fuse."

I wondered why the Rockefeller people trusted him with these pictures and why he was showing them to me. He must have known how much I cared about them.

Two warm fingers stroked my arm.

"It's two thirty," he said. "You want me to drive you home?"

"No," I whispered.

He pulled me close to him and smoothed my hair. "That's what I hoped you'd say."

I got to know that beige rug well, since Jimmy wasn't one to waste time. His touch felt so different than Bill's—sure, insistent, demanding. He took charge of me as though he were entitled—as if he had the right. He explored every pore and whispered things in my ear, things no other guy has ever said. That he wanted me from the first time he ever saw me, that if I hadn't been sick, he would have hit the stop button in the elevator that day. That I had the silkiest hair, the most brilliant blue eyes, and the sexiest lips he had ever seen, that he couldn't sleep nights, he was hard all the time, and he just couldn't take it anymore.

"How did Bill Marshall ever get you?" he asked. "How did he do it? He's gonna make a great department chair, but he doesn't know what the hell to do with you, does he?"

I shook my head, and he crushed my mouth with an affirming kiss. I had to stop him when he pulled down my panties. I bleed pretty hard, and that was such a nice rug.

"That's okay." He smiled. "There are other things we can do."

First, he wanted to come in my mouth. That seemed kind of sick, kind of crazy. I tasted dirt and even pee. But I loved the feel of him growing against my tongue while he gripped me with shaking fingers. That hot spurt in my mouth had a strange, bitter taste, like nothing I've ever known. It amazed him that I swallowed it—most girls wouldn't, he said. I wondered what they did with it. I didn't want to spit it out.

Five minutes later he wanted to try something else. He spread some cool jelly on a part of me I don't pay much attention to. He angled himself behind me and pushed with a sudden stab.

"Ow!" I cried.

It hurt in a way that was worse than burning—like an insult, belittling, crushing. I cried and fought, but his arm held me like a steel bar, the way it did in the elevator that day.

"Relax," he murmured. "It's going to stop hurting."

He was right. Pretty soon, I opened in ways I never knew I could, and I accepted the strange feel of him sliding in and out. I liked that he gasped my name when he came, and afterward, he didn't fall asleep.

"Let's stay up," he whispered. "Let's stay up and fuck all night. Hey, you wanna take a bath with me? I've got this great bathtub."

Jimmy turned on the water, and we climbed right in, settling knee to knee like some four-legged monster. As the water rose, it tickled my breasts.

"Damn, you've got a great body!" he said. "It's a crime to cover it up with water. It's a crime to cover it up with clothes."

A period doesn't stop when you want it to, and there in the water, I let out a viscous red blob. We watched it pulse and turn like a jellyfish, until Jimmy snagged it on one finger and rubbed it on my nose. I laughed so hard I filled the tub with red seaweed. I felt as though I had seen life from the inside out.

We rested close together until the light came, and Jimmy washed the dishes and made us breakfast. With sweet-smelling shampoo, I scrubbed the rug until its fuzz bit my knees. I tried to rub away every wine-red spot. Jimmy drove me home in that crazy car of his, and I slept all through the next day. Jimmy worked in the lab, same as always, and Bill didn't call until the next day. He never suspected a thing.

Since then, Jimmy and I have seen each other each day—nothing elegant—no candlelit dinners. There was once in the darkroom, once in his car, and once in his office, against the wall with the blinds down. He's incredibly smart and the best actor I've seen, talking to Bill the same as before. I only hope that I'm as good, since so much depends on it. Bill feels so fleshy now, so clammy and soft, that touching him turns my stomach. He's going to find out. I know he is. Why can't he just read it in my body?

A creak cuts the air. Mrs. Marshall has risen.

"Is it time for lunch?" she asks.

Sure enough, it's exactly twelve o'clock.

"Is there pudding?" she demands.

Once I have conjured Jimmy, I can't get rid of him. He follows me out into the sunlight. As I squint at turquoise jewelry, his thin finger jabs me. Most of these clunky necklaces would weigh me down with aqua chunks as big as a baby's eyes. A coyote trickster up on two legs ogles a shimmering blue-green band.

"I like that one," says Jimmy, and vanishes.

Next door at the Cyber Cactus, networked neon splits the window into panes. Through the green spiderweb, I spot a free terminal. All the others have fused with people typing. Unable to resist, I go in and bring up Google, since Jimmy has me fully charged. With my heart pounding, I slip stealthily into the Turner lab.

Anytime I do this, I feel as if I'm stalking, and I glance uneasily at the people near me. A sunburned blonde girl is crying as she types, and a greasy guy is squeezing his mouse. No one cares how hard I'm staring at Johnny, surrounded by sixteen smiling people who work for him. With his shiny brown hair and boyish grin, he hasn't changed at all; he's just won a lot of grants. I should be checking out his publications—otherwise I have no business here. I quit Firefox and savor the blue screen, hoping that cyber sand will cover my tracks.

To clear the system, I run Carrie McFadden, and listings for *The Rainbow Bar* arise. Interspersed with them are links to a Trinity University student, a magazine editor, and a professor of embryology. I guess there are a lot of us out there.

Intrigued, I type in "Clifton Bowles." Nothing. I don't think I've ever googled anyone and found nothing at all. The list of close matches has none with both names, although it includes the Clifton, New Jersey, Chamber of Commerce and a serial killer named Gary Ray Bowles. I wonder if Clifton is Clifton Bowles like I'm Theresa Ramírez, so I search the Birmingham telephone directory. According to this guide, Clifton and Karen Bowles live at 33 Richmond Drive. He may not be networked, but he's real. I jot down the number of his landline.

Just for the heck of it, I google Teresa Ramírez and set off a three-million-hit avalanche. By now, I am laughing at the screen, and the sticky guy next to me frowns nervously. I type "J-i-m-" and then realize that Jimmy has no last name. I replace the last two letters with "o-h-n" and google Johnny once again. This time I look past his lab entry. What do you know? Besides being a scientist, Johnny Turner was a singing cowboy actor in the 1960s. The red-faced blonde next to me winces as I burst out laughing. I think it's time to go.

Out in the brilliant sunlight I hesitate, forgetting which way I was headed. Next door, the coyote leers at the thin turquoise necklace, a row of blue-and-green stones rimmed with silver wire. In the afternoon sun, it glows enticingly.

"That's pretty," says Jimmy.

Around my throat, it hangs with a cool, solid weight. Blue-green bursts from the stones flash at sparks from my eyes to create a coruscating symphony of light.

"Damn!"

That wasn't Jimmy's voice. That was Johnny's.

My nipples tighten under my turquoise top, and my hair tickles the backs of my thighs. I am going to wear this necklace when I see Johnny. It costs seventy-five dollars, as much as two nights at a Run-Rite Inn, but I flash my credit card and make it mine.

Next morning, I drive out to see some museums in the desert—Native American, Spanish Colonial, and folk art. I try the folk art first because it sounds like fun, but it's silly. I wander past cases of bright-colored kitsch that look as though they were gathered by a magpie. Outside on the terrace, a light wind stirs the air. Past the buildings lie golden sand, pale green brush, and soft, snowcapped purple mountains. Nothing in the museums compares to this view, so I order huevos rancheros in the restaurant. This feels like the right spot to commune with Teresa, and she comes to me before my eggs do.

Tonight I ride home on the bus, since Raúl said he has to work late. At nine o'clock he still isn't home, and I start to worry. If he goes out drinking and the cops catch him driving, they could take away his license or worse. Like me, Raúl has a work permit, but they can take it back anytime they want.

If you hold the pan at just the right height, you can make tostadas on the stove. Two inches, maybe three, and the cheese melts before the tortilla burns. At Mercado del Mundo I bought some fresh beef and peppers since I think Raúl is planning a surprise. Why doesn't he come? With my green cubes chopped, I test the circle of flames. The pointy blue jets burn like the Virgin's rays, and I ask her to help guide him home. I open and shut the wardrobe a few times to see if I can make it close.

Tires crunch the driveway, and the room fills with light. Raúl pushes open the door. I throw my arms around him, and my hair spills into his face.

"Así, sí," he growls. "This is the way to come home. A beautiful woman, a nice dinner—yes?"

I hurry to the stove and turn on the blue flame, not as a test this time.

"Oye, reina," he calls from his chair.

The cheese softens over the green pepper cubes, like a blanket drawing them close.

"I have good news and bad news. Which do you want first?"

"¡Las buenas!"

"¡Ésa es mi niña! Okay. I have found another job. Tomás, he started working at this country club. You should see it—a pool like a silver lake! They need more people to clean at night—the golf carts, the clubhouse, the pool. They're paying seven dollars an hour. Tomás, he's got it all figured out. When we get done landscaping, I'll drive us down there, and we can work for three more hours. That's good money—so we can save for an apartment."

I slide the tostada from the pan to his plate just as the cheese oozes between the pepper cubes.

"¡Qué bueno!" I murmur, setting the plate down before him.

Raúl is too excited to admire the tostada, but I hear his knife tear it as I start another.

"What did you say the security deposit was for Briarwood?" Food muffles Raúl's voice.

"Fifteen hundred dollars. Two months' rent."

"We can save that. Traime una Bic."

I set the pan down on the unlit burner and run to my purse for a pen. Raúl writes numbers down on a napkin. He sounds like our car at 123 miles an hour, vibrating as he runs at top speed. I'm not sure I like this, but the news is good. An apartment! I didn't think we could ever afford one.

"*Oye, we each make about a thousand a month, menos los impuestos que nos chingan … This would be maybe another four hundred. That's twenty-four hundred, minus five hundred for rent, three hundred for Martín y tu mamá, la comida, el seguro …*" He writes some more numbers. "I think that we can do it in two months. *¡Adios, pinche garaje! ¡Hasta la vista, baby! Oye, traime otra, ¿no?*"

I bring Raúl the next tostada, which is not as pretty as the first. This time he notices.

"*¡Pero qué rica! ¡Qué buena mujer tengo!*" His strong hand catches my behind. "Hey, I think it's growing! *Vas a estar más gordita que Miss Dixie Buffet.*"

We still joke about the girl at the buffet, Raúl boasting that he'll take over when her novio is exhausted. No man could keep up with her appetites.

The bad thing about tostadas is you can only make one at once, at least in a kitchen like ours. If I had an oven like Mrs. Marshall, I would do them all together, en bola. Raúl hasn't eaten since noon, and he's devouring them faster than I can make them, so I chew some stray pieces of beef. I hope all the food will calm him down. He's so wound up I'm getting worried.

As Raúl eats, he describes the great apartment we'll have.

"With a beautiful couch! And a flat-screen TV! *¡Satélite—con todos los canales que hay!*"

After his fifth tostada, his usual limit, he calls for one more. I bring it, and he tells me to sit.

"What's the bad news?" I ask.

Raúl waves his hand. "Oh—eso, nada. Since I'll be working, I can't pick you up. You'll have to take the bus again. But no more rides with el Panzón."

"Oh, I don't think he'll try that again." I poke at a shiny green cube, its edges softened to slime.

"He better not."

The warmth has left his voice, and fearfully, I raise my eyes. "No—he's not like that," I say. "He thinks we're married."

"We are married." Raúl's eyes darken.

"But not in a church—not according to the law—not like I told my mother."

Raúl grips his fork. "We are married. You know it, and I know it. That's all that counts. Oye, traime un café."

I boil some water for Raúl's coffee and form a necklace of Oreos on a blue plate. While the water simmers, I eat some dark, crusty meat and crunch on one of the cookies.

Still frowning, Raúl has gone back to his numbers. "Hey, why don't you ask el Panzón for a raise?" He brightens when he sees the Oreos and coffee. "¡Qué bueno! You could work more hours—stay with her longer. Why don't you ask him about that?"

"Okay," I say, "but usually he gets home around six. He can take care of her after that."

Raúl bites off half an Oreo and chews it thoughtfully. "¿Cómo 'stá la ruca? I like her—how is she doing?"

"Oh, the same. We read a lot. I cook her lunch. She has an easier time in the bathroom now that I'm feeding her all these beans."

Raúl splutters, his mouth full of cookie. "I wouldn't want to trade jobs with you. At least the only shit I clean up is from dogs."

Raúl's face has reddened from the coffee and food, and his eyes are soft, deep black.

"Oye—I've been wondering something—about la vieja," I say.

Raúl squints at me, his eyes full of fun.

"Her eyes are blue, right?"

"Sí, como violetas."

"And in the picture, her husband's are green."

"¿Sí?"

"So how come el Panzón's are dark brown, like these Oreos?"

Raúl lets out a whoop and laughs like crazy, his face turning redder and redder. "¡No me digas! ¿Ésta le puso los cuernos a su marido, el gran dín?"

"I don't know. I've heard that people with green eyes are a mix. Maybe it could still happen."

"El marido—¿cómo es?"

"Well, you can't tell much from the picture—pero gordo, soso—soft and round like el Panzón."

"I bet she did—I bet she did it!" He laughs. "Brown eyes— seguro que encontró a algún bato que sabía tratar a una mujer."

With our mouths full of Oreos, we laugh at la vieja's lovers. The mailman. The landscapers. We decide there must have been hundreds, all of them Mexican.

"So when el Panzón drove you home that night, he was coming home himself."

Raúl studies my face as I laugh, and I realize I'm the only one laughing.

"You think it's funny—a woman putting horns on her husband?"

"No, no! Only her—only because it's her!"

"You ever think of doing that? You think it might be fun?"

"No!"

"'Cause when I got through with you, it wouldn't be fun—te lo juro." Raúl grips the table, his thick brown fingers spread. They curl as his knuckles rise.

"No—no," I cry. "I never think about it!"

"Maybe you were thinking about it in the BMW that night," he shoots. "Maybe you'll be thinking of it when the gringo comes home from work and your own husband is still working?" His hand closes on my arm, his fingers pressing to the bone.

"No! No! He's old—fat!"

"Oh, so this gringo is not good enough—maybe you want one better looking?"

"No! No!"

"¿Sabes cuál es tu problema?" Without releasing me, Raúl pushes back his chair. "Your problem is, nobody knows who you belong to. Sometimes I don't think even you know."

His eyes are flat, black stones.

"Yes, I do! I do! I just wish we could get married. If I had a ring—"

"No, not a ring."

With one snap of his arm, Raúl yanks me toward him. His other hand twists into my hair.

"Ven." He drags me to the bed. "You have put me off long enough. Te voy a hacer mamá. No more protection, no more missed days. I am going to make you a baby. Then you'll know who you belong to, tú y tu chingado Panzón."

He rips off my T-shirt, smashing my nose, then pulls down his jeans and mine.

"No!" I cry. "No, not like this!"

He slaps my face. "Oh, so you don't like how I do it?"

Raúl is already hard, but when he pushes into me, he sticks.

"¡Puta inútil!" He hits me again, this time on the other side. "¿Sólo estás mojada por tu gringo?"

I spit on my fingers and wipe it all over. If he thinks I don't like it, he can get really wild. I wince at the burn as he rams into me, but it feels good to him now, and he won't get madder.

A few qu—

Brrrp. Brrrp. Brrrp. Doo-doo-doo-DEE-doo.

Whuh?

Brrrp. Brrrp. Brrrp. Doo-doo-doo-DEE-doo!

Oh, fuck. Now what? Where—

Brrrp. Brr—

"H'lo?"

"Carrie?"

"Yeah?"

"Oh, I'm so glad I got you, honey. It's Louise. It's about your mom."

Gazing at the dim mountains, I release my breath. Louise. The hills shimmer into the waves of her smooth gray hair.

"Oh—how is she? Is she doing better with those new gloves?"

In the bucking bed, Raúl is panting, and Teresa is crying.

"No. I'm afraid they had to take her to the hospital."

My breath catches. "Oh, wow. Why?"

"Well, she's got this fluid in her lungs. You know how she's been having trouble breathing." Louise's voice lacks her accusing tone. Today she sounds worried.

"Yeah, that gurgling noise—she's been like that for a while."

I can still hear her loose, phlegmy rattle. Last time I saw her at Hillcrest, a lay preacher was ranting at his captive audience of old ladies. The preacher told about his wicked sister-in-law, who had locked herself in a bathroom so she wouldn't have to hear him. My mother's breathing grew louder and louder, a heavy, ominous growl.

"And that poor, stubborn woman denied herself the word of God!"

"Grrrr! Rrrrrr! Rrrrrr!"

"Carrie?"

"Yeah?" My lips are warm from smiling.

"Oh, good. I thought I lost you there for a minute."

"No, no, I'm here. So when did they move her?" I squirm in my chair, whose metal lattice has stamped my thighs.

"Just now. I called as soon as I could."

"So what do they think?"

"Well, I'm afraid it's serious. They think it's pneumonia."

I frown at the mountains' soft blue curves. "But they know she's been like this for a while, right?"

"Yes, of course. But this is different. She's struggling to breathe."

In my throat, I feel the invasive squirt of cool liquid vitamins. When I was little, I couldn't swallow pills, so my mother bought vitamins that I could drink. She had to drop them in my mouth with a pipette, and one day she squirted them straight down my windpipe. I still remember the terror, the heaving gasps. My mother thumped me until I could breathe again, but I've always thought she did it on purpose.

"Carrie." Louise's flat voice brings me back. "I know you're on this trip, but you need to come and see her. It's serious. She's really struggling."

I peer out at the sand and sage. Teresa has stopped crying.

"Carrie?" A little louder.

"Yeah, I'm sorry. I can't leave right now. I'm in the middle of something, and there's someone I have to see."

"Carrie, it's your mom!" Louise's voice tightens. "Just for a few days. You could see this person another time, when you get back."

I won't let her push me. "No. I can't. I can't do that."

"Carrie—I didn't want to have to tell you this, but we could lose her. We could—"

Louise's voice quivers and breaks. My eyes sweep my determined black letters. Lose her. She hasn't known me for six years. I remember that first foggy day of oblivion, her fearful, questioning gaze. Her eyes have turned so much bluer now that she's forgotten who I am.

"I'm sorry—" Louise falters. "She's such a sweet lady. I can't understand. I'm sure you had your differences, dear, but she loved you. It's your mom, honey. Don't you want to see your mom again? What could be more important? This vacation—"

"It's not a vacation!" I cry. "I'm writing! If I don't get this written, I could lose my job. She's going to get through this. She always does."

Louise's drilling tone doesn't waver. "You can get another job, dear. You can't get another mom. Honey, think of all that she's done for you."

"Don't call me that!" I shout.

"What?"

My voice is melting, but viscous words emerge. "Honey! It's degrading! I'm not a child!"

Even this doesn't faze her. If anything, she seems more in her element. "Oh—well, I didn't mean it that way. I see you're upset—"

"Just don't call me that!"

A round-faced woman with glasses looks at me like a ruffled owl.

"Sorry," murmurs Louise. "I didn't mean to upset you. I just don't understand your values. This is your mom."

"I value doing something with my life," I say.

"Well, we all do, dear, but we can't just think of ourselves."

How does she think of her answers so fast? "I don't just think of myself," I say. "I've got my students, my friends— I don't see how it's going to help for me to fly up there. She won't even know I'm there."

"But you'll know," she says quietly. "God will know."

I wish I could wrap my arms around those solid clouds, hovering so temptingly close. "I don't believe that," I say.

"You know," Louise tells me, her voice soft and tight, "it wasn't my idea to call you today. It was the doctor's. 'Get the daughter up here,' he said. He's the one who thinks it's serious."

"Well, I appreciate that," I say, "but I don't think it's going to help."

"It would," she insists. "I know you don't see it, but it would. Your mom may be dying, hon— If you don't come now, you may always regret it."

An odd release of tension tells me I've won. "I'm sorry, I just don't believe that," I say.

"Well—I hope you change your mind." Grim and heavyset, Louise starts to recede.

"I'm sorry—I just can't come right now," I repeat.

"I'll be praying for you and your mom, dear. My whole congregation, we'll be praying for her."

"That's nice." I sigh and imagine what Louise is telling her congregation.

"Carrie?"

"Mm?"

"Oh—I thought I lost you again. Where are you now?"

"Santa Fe." I smile at the faded purple mountains.

"Santa Fe! Imagine that! But you could still get here in a few hours if you had to, right?"

"Yeah—probably from Albuquerque." I picture the sunny, sealed airport.

"Well, will you look into it?" she asks. "Just look and see how you might get here?"

"Okay. But I'm right in the middle of something," I repeat. "I can't just leave."

"Well, I hope you're making the right decision."

"I am." For once I like the sound of my voice, low and steady like Johnny's.

"Okay. Well, you know where to reach me."

"Yeah. Bye, Louise." My voice wobbles.

"Bye, Carrie."

I run my hands through my hair and gaze at the blurred tufts of sage. I have lost Teresa, and my bladder aches. In short, dim sentences, I finish the scene, but I'll have to run through it again.

A few quick shoves, and it's over. Raúl's hands relax in my hair, and the anger runs out of him like water. Sensing me crying beneath him, he kisses my neck.

"¿Ves? ¿Ves? No es tan malo. We are going to have a beautiful baby. I'm going to buy you a beautiful white dress—and we'll get married in a church, like you told your mother."

When he falls asleep, I get up and wash the dishes. I crunch through the crescent of Oreos on the plate. If I have a baby, how will I work? I don't want to leave Mrs. Marshall and her fat son.

CHAPTER 8

THE GRAND CANYON

In the back seat, Joey scowls. I can't blame him for hating Santa Fe, trapped down in that dark garage. He's glad to be moving, but he won't forgive me. Why did I bring him if I'm just going to keep him bound and stifled in the car?

For days now, mountains have been hovering in the distance, watching me with a soft purple stare. In the morning sun, the peaks smile knowingly and hold their wisdom close. I never seem to reach them, no matter how long I drive. The radio tells me of fierce brown floods. Somewhere in those mountains, hardpacked snow is melting, then rushing down to die in the desert.

After two runs through the stations, I abandon the radio, and the bleached sage and sand dim to haze. The searing gray road gapes at me, a shimmering runway empty of cars. I wonder what Clifton is up to this morning. With Wilma shooting straight ahead, I dig in my purse for my phone. A mechanical female voice greets me, but I hesitate to leave him a message. Now, where did I write down his landline number? On the steering wheel, I open my memo pad, and Clifton's number pops up like a seed in a cleft fruit.

"Hello?" A woman's voice.

"Hello," I rasp. I clear my throat. "May I speak to Clifton, please?"

"Who may I say is calling?"

Geez, is this really his home? This woman sounds like a secretary.

"Theresa—" I falter. "Theresa Ramírez."

"And it concerns ..."

A mirage ripples into mush. "His new design for the Mobile South bill. I'm a freelance designer, and I'm working with his team."

"And he gave you this number? Excuse me, Miss Ramírez ... This is Mrs. Bowles. This is his private residence."

The secretary's tones have condensed into the kindergarten teacher's. "Oh, well ... sorry to bother you. He gave me this number. He told me to call anytime." I struggle to hold my voice steady. I wonder what I sound like to her.

"Oh ..." Her low tones convey solid weight. "Usually he handles his work-related calls on his cell."

"Well, if it's inconvenient ..." I waver. "Is he there?"

"He's having breakfast with his children now. Why don't you leave him a message on his cell, and he'll call you back when he can."

I picture Clifton's thick arm reaching for a jar of red jam.

"All right," I murmur. "Sorry to bother you."

"That's all right. We're just trying to preserve our family time."

"I understand. Sorry to interrupt."

Ahead of me another mirage shines, this one wider than the last. The pool of silver has the saddest beauty as it coalesces into solid road.

"That's all right. You have a nice day, now."

"You too. Goodbye."

The road dissolves again into silver ripples. I know the configuration of Gonzalo's number so well I don't need to see the phone.

"How come every time I find a guy who treats me halfway decently, there's always some bitch in the way?"

"Mala? Is this you?" Gonzalo greets me with a muffled voice.

"Yeah. Who else would it be?"

"Oh, I don't know." His voice stretches and warms. "I know so many women who hate women."

"Don't laugh!"

"Bueno, Mala, bueno. I will not laugh. Just tell me what happened. Were you caught in the act?"

"No! I just called his house—el gordo—and his wife answered."

"Bizcochitos and fry bread, next exit!" cries a giant yellow billboard. Against its buttercup background, the cookies form pale roses of dough.

"Yes?" Gonzalo seems wide-awake now.

"Well—and I even thought of a good story—a really good one, thinking on my feet—but she made me feel like I was five years old." I still hear that tone of self-righteous ownership.

"So she put you in your place, eh?"

"Place? What place?" Why isn't there any pattern in these clumps of sage?

"Just far away," he says. "Some married women are like that. If this pollo is all she has, she has to keep other women away."

"God, I hate women. I *hate* them!" I seethe. "Fat, scrub-headed, parasitic, palpitating bitches! Why do they always have to humiliate me? If I won the Nobel Prize in Literature, some bitch would laugh at me for what I'm wearing!"

Gonzalo chokes with laughter.

"Stop laughing!"

"Bueno, Mala, but with you it is hard. Have you not noticed you are also a woman?"

There's something about this desert I love, so open, no dividing lines anywhere.

"Yeah, but I'm not like that," I say. "I do things with my life—travel, write books. I don't have to go around humiliating women, because I don't base my identity on the exclusive ownership of some man."

"I don't know, Mala. I don't know," Gonzalo says slowly. "I think that most women are pretty nice."

What's wrong with him? Why doesn't he get this? "Of course they are—to you," I say. "You're a great-looking Spanish professor from Manhattan."

"So you are saying that all these nice women I have known—to me they are Dr. Jekyll, but to you they are Mr. Hyde?"

"Yeah." Now he's getting it. "Because I'm a good-looking woman. They only treat me like shit when you don't see."

"Well …" Amusement still dances in his voice. "I guess it could be true. How could I know, if I don't see? But—"

Ahead on the right, a dazzling, psychedelic palace shimmers.

"Women are bitches, I'm telling you!" I explode. "They're all bitches. They're Nazi jailers holding men prisoner, exploiting them, starving them, stripping them of their dignity. It's like—marriage is the Holocaust, and I'm Oscar Schindler. I want to save as many as I can … Stop it! Stop laughing!"

This time it takes Gonzalo longer to stop.

"Eres la chica más mala que conozco—la pesadilla de cada mujer."

"Blood-sucking bitches!"

As I whip past, the brilliant palace becomes a casino, its pink signs blasting the desert light.

"Tranquila, Mala, tranquila," he soothes. "Why are you so upset that this fat woman wants to keep you away from her fat man? Do you want him so badly?"

"No—" I falter. "I just can't stand being treated like that— it's so humiliating!"

I'm still goaded by that triumphant blonde smirk.

"She's defending her family," says Gonzalo. "Her kids. If she loses el gordo, she loses everything."

"So he can't even talk to anybody?" I ask. "Nobody but her?"

"Not to you, Mala," he says patiently. "Anyone can see that you're dangerous."

"What, on the phone? I could weigh three hundred pounds. I could have leprosy. How would she know?"

"Mala—" Some thuds hit my ears as though a cat were biffing the phone. "Mala, you have called him—what time is it there? At ten thirty in the morning."

Another daffodil billboard promises bizcochitos. Do those pale roses taste as sweet as they look?

"And you called his house?" persists Gonzalo. "Not his cell phone?"

"Yeah. He didn't answer."

Two miles to the exit. Must be just past those brown crags.

"But, Mala—how did you get his home number?"

"Internet."

"¡Pero qué mala eres! ¡Estás stalking al pobre gordo!"

"No!"

"Well, what would you call it, then?"

"Liberating him. No—not even that. He's nice. I just want to talk to him."

One and a half miles to the exit. Should I turn? They say they have turquoise jewelry too.

"Mala—" Gonzalo is laughing. Through furry static, a female voice penetrates. "Oye, Mala, I have to go."

"Is someone there?" I ask.

"Yes—Silke."

"Silke?"

"Yes—I could not help it, Mala. The power of suggestion." His voice expands with pleasure.

"A German woman." I smile.

"Yes, very nice. We have just had brunch, and now we're going to a museum."

"Well, I won't hold you up," I mutter. "Knock yourself out."

On both sides, reddish-brown rocks are glowing, and I wish I could feel their warmth. I would press my palms to the stone with my fingers spread and drink their heat like a lizard.

"Knock?"

"Yeah, it's just an expression."

One mile to the exit.

"I know. Do not—"

"It just means have fun."

"Take care of yourself, Mala. Do something nice for yourself. Find a new guy, one with no women attached. Forget about el gordo y el flaco."

"Okay. I'll do my best."

"Bueno, Mala. Sé buena."

"I'll try. Adios, Gonzalo."

I flash past the exit and scowl at the empty desert ahead.

I climb up to Gallup, then sink to the Petrified Forest. Joey broods silently, accusing.

"What can I do?" I ask. "If I carry you around, they'll take me away in a net."

Hunger doesn't invade my thoughts until two, so I hold out for Winslow, Arizona. At a fast-food place, I order a broccoli-and-cheese potato. I wipe viscous brown spots from my table, then switch to another when my napkin sticks. The new table wobbles, but that's not as bad as having Teresa glued to its surface. Once my fingers clear it with one smooth glide, I pull out a piece of loose-leaf paper. Under the sticky cheese, my potato cools quickly, and after a few bites, I ignore it.

I wake up with purple marks on my face. The right one is round, so I could almost be blushing, but the left one has ghostly red streaks. It looks like Raúl wiped his hand on my face with purple-red jam on his fingers. He tilts up my chin, frowns, and shakes his head.

"Lo siento," he says softly. "Lo siento."

He wraps his arms around me and holds me close while I listen to the thump of his heart.

Before I go to work, I smear on makeup, which costs so much I use it only on special days. Under the brown cream, the right mark almost disappears, but the left one won't stay out of sight. No matter how much I use, my face looks wrong, flat brown with that ghost hand pushing out.

In the murkiness of the Marshalls' front hall, Justin doesn't notice my face. With his mind already in the office, he talks breathlessly about a big mistake.

Mrs. Marshall is having a friendly day. Sometimes she almost screams if I touch her, but on these days, she rubs me like a cat. It's no use trying to read by myself, since she gets angry as soon as I release her. Instead I read out loud to her and stroke her clinging arm. She leans against me and glares at the page, her breath warming me in sickly puffs. With her skinny hand, she reaches for my face and lightly fingers the red splotch.

At lunch she wants only one tostada, so I store the meat and cheese in the refrigerator. Even after eating, she's restless. She wants to move but never to be more than a few inches away from me. Her roving hands seek my hair, and I let her run her fingers through it. Her hands almost remember how to make a braid, clutching three strands and intertwining them.

We follow the afternoon sun to the kitchen, the last bright room in the house. I have spent hours there, rearranging the cabinets so that the creamy cups we drink from are down low and the odd-shaped dishes up high. The stacks of flowered plates wait patiently behind jewellike glass doors. With the last rays of sun streaming in, I turn on the radio and change from Justin's droning news to La Mega.

Instantly the kitchen comes alive, the china cups trembling on their hooks. Mrs. Marshall tenses, and her blue eyes snap.

"What? What?" she asks.

Late in the day, La Mega revives the world with hot spirals of salsa. It's not Mexican, but it helps you work through those last few dragging hours. The drums spur your heart, the brass jolts your bones, and a voice cries out about lost love. No matter where you are or what you're doing, you simply have to move.

"¡Sí, sí, sí, este amor es tan profundo, que tú eres mi consentida y que lo sepa todo el mundo!"

"What? What?" demands Mrs. Marshall, rocking from side to side.

"It's a song about a man who loves a woman so much he wants the whole world to know."

Mrs. Marshall frowns, and she shifts her feet and swings her hard, dry hips.

"Would you like to dance, Mrs. Marshall?"

She shakes her head vigorously.

With the beat still thumping, the traffic report bursts, then melts back into another song.

"Tú volverás, lo sé, tú volverás a mí," cries the singer.

"A woman is leaving a man," I say, "and he tells her she'll be sorry and she'll come back."

Mrs. Marshall turns with her wings outstretched and chants half-formed words.

"Would you like to dance?" I ask, but she doesn't seem to hear. I take her bony hand and guide her sharp hip. La vieja stiffens.

"Like this," I say. "First one foot, then the other."

She giggles as though we were doing something dirty.

"Tú volverás, lo sé, tú volverás a mí …"

Mrs. Marshall wants to spin, so I free her hip and extend my arm.

"¡Qué bien!" I cry as she whirls.

Sometime in her life, this woman has danced. Her stiff movements hack up the salsa, but her body loves its rhythm. Every time a new tune starts, she makes me tell her the story. Her favorite is "Juliana, qué mala eres," about a very bad woman—at least according to the guy singing. We're dancing to "Abajo las suegras," waving our hands over our heads, when a low voice folds into our laughter. Justin is leaning in the doorway.

"Well, this is nice to come home to." He smiles. "My very own dance club."

Mrs. Marshall scurries over to him, and he wraps her in a hug. "You and Teresa are looking good, Mom!"

She burrows her head into his shoulder, and he laughs and strokes her hair. I start to turn down the music, but Justin tells me to leave it.

"No, no—it's happy. I could use it after the day I've had."

"Would you like something to eat?" I ask. "I have all this food for tostadas. Your mom wasn't hungry today."

"Oh, yeah?" He looks down at her, concerned. "Why was that, Mom?"

She presses deeper into his shoulder.

"What happened at work?" I ask. "You're home early today."

A new song begins. Mrs. Marshall raises her head and shifts her hips slightly.

"What's this, Mom?" asks Justin. "Do you want to dance?"

He tries to appease her, but he's awful. I swallow giggles as I pull out the chicken, clammy lettuce, and cheese. Justin sways around the beat and tells me about a woman named Cathy. This Cathy made a $10,000 mistake, and he's in charge. Somehow, he has to make sure that she won't botch up any more accounts.

Sure enough, in this oven you can make eight tostadas at once. Laughing, Justin gives up trying to dance.

"Would you like something to drink, Mom? Teresa?"

I shake my head and clutch soft handfuls of grated cheese. Mrs. Marshall wants some white wine, and Justin gets himself a beer. His eyes tickle me as the cheese snows from my fingers.

"Have you worked with Cathy for long?" I ask.

"No, no—I've known her a while, but we've never been on the same account before."

Justin reddens and turns to his mother. "I didn't know you like to dance, Mom."

She glances at him sideways and swallows a gulp of wine.

"Yes, she's very good," I say. "She really likes it."

"You're full of surprises, Mom." Justin smiles.

Mrs. Marshall shoots him another look, not so friendly this time.

Admiringly, he peers through the glass as the cheese starts to melt in the oven. Pale yellow curls collapse and fuse, softening the edges of ragged chunks.

"Boy, those look good. I'm glad you can stay longer now—but it must be a very long day for you."

"Oh, no, I like it here," I murmur.

"I'm glad." He smiles. "We like having you."

I choose three plates with rings of violets dancing around the rims. With two huge blue mittens, I pull out the sheets of tostadas just as the cheese starts to glisten.

"Ah … oh my …" Justin sighs after his first bite.

Whatever he's done today, it's given him an appetite as big as Raúl's. Slowly, he munches his way through five tostadas and drinks almost as many beers. Mrs. Marshall and I swallow just a little and watch him enjoy his food. As he eats, Justin turns pink and swells with pleasure. He asks me about what we did today.

"Your mom really seems to like dancing," I say. "Did she use to dance a lot?"

Justin shakes his head, his mouth full. "No—no." He swallows. "Not dancing. It's sad—I can't remember that she ever really liked to do anything."

I glance quickly at Mrs. Marshall, but she is twirling her wineglass dreamily.

Justin sighs and reaches for another tostada. "These are so good. You'll have to tell me how to make them."

I meet his eyes, and his gaze suddenly focuses. "What happened to your face? Is that an allergy?"

"Yes—an allergy—I'm not sure to what." I raise my hand to the spot, and it burns.

"Wow, that looks pretty bad." He frowns. "You should have a doctor look at that."

"Yeah … maybe."

"Oh—sorry—didn't mean to—" Justin takes a long swallow of beer.

Mrs. Marshall sets down her wineglass and rises.

"What's wrong, Mom? You done eating?"

"No," I say, "the music—"

The dim salsa barely stirs the air, but I recognize "Juliana, qué mala eres." Mrs. Marshall wants to dance.

"Go ahead, Mom," Justin says with a smile, and she begins a private shuffle near the oven.

Justin is eating and drinking more slowly, but he doesn't want to stop. Suddenly he laughs and shakes his head.

"This Cathy," he says. "She really is something. 'Can't we just fix it?' she asks. You know, they—I shouldn't—oh, what the hell. They put me together with her on purpose. They laugh at me— say I need practice. This Cathy, she's really good looking. Little miniskirts, silky blouses."

I nod.

"So they assigned her to me—some of them even made bets. And then this happens ..."

Half smiling, Justin stares at the black-and-silver stove.

"People can be really mean," I say. "Probably she's not right for you."

Justin laughs. "Thing is, she looks so great I probably would have—but now ..."

"It's okay," I tell him. "You should wait for someone who's right for you."

"Yeah ..." Justin stares at his greasy plate.

"Justin!" calls Mrs. Marshall.

"Oh, no," he moans.

Laughing, I turn up the music, then start to put away the food.

"Justin!" she cries again.

He downs his beer with a swirl and a gulp. "I really should stop," he murmurs.

Angry now, his mother scuffles over and tries to pull him to his feet.

"Estoy aquí, pero mi mente 'stá 'llá," sings a voice.

She takes one hand, and I take the other, and we drag him up. While I stack the greasy plates in the dishwasher, she twists his hand and tries to make him twirl her.

"I don't know what you want, Mom," he protests.

I wipe my hands on a blue-and-white towel. "Here. Let me show you."

I take Justin's hand, and my fingers slip easily between his. He wraps his other arm around my waist, and his body relaxes into mine. Touching him is so different than I thought it would be— he's warm and solid, not soft like a fat old woman. Justin pulls me to him, and our bodies fit together.

"What's this song? I like it," he murmurs.

"Oh, it's very sad. A man is working here, and he says he's here, but his mind is back there, where he came from."

"Funny. It doesn't sound sad to me." Justin draws me closer, and his breathing quickens.

Behind his shoulder, Mrs. Marshall glares.

"Mmm …" He presses his face into my hair. I pull back, but he holds me tightly.

He's not as bad a dancer as I thought, swaying slightly in time to the music. His big belly feels nice and warm against me, and his hand gently circles my back. Justin raises my chin and looks down at my face. His eyes darken.

"That's not an allergy, is it?" he whispers.

"No."

"Oh, Teresa. What can I do? Can I do anything?"

I shake my head. Slowly he brings his face closer to mine. He touches his lips to the bruise and blows on it softly.

"Mmm …" He wants more. And more.

With a violent push, I thrust him back. "No! Mira!" I point to his mother, who stands silently raging.

I race to the hallway for my jacket and purse.

"Teresa! I'm so sorry! I won't— Please, you'll come back, won't you? It's so late. Why don't you let me drive you?"

"No!"

The streets are black, but I know them well. I run all the way to the bus stop.

By the time I leave Winslow, it's well after four. The canyon is still two hours away. I sprint through the last stretch of I-40 to Flagstaff, then streak up 180 into the hills. Joey sniffs hopefully as we enter a pine forest with rough black mountains behind it. When the road splits a meadow, a peak draws my eyes, dark at the base, then lighter green, then gray at its delicate point.

"Look at that! How'd you like to climb that?" I ask Joey.

From his upward gaze, I know that he'd love to. But determined to reach the canyon by sunset, I shoot onward. Yellow signs warn me to watch for fat deer, which haunt the darkening woods. When I reach Tusayan with its brown motels, I press on into the park. Entering costs me twenty bucks, but the pass will last me a week. Where is this canyon? I want to see it. I wind through sparse piney woods. If I keep heading north, I'll have to hit it, but a puffy white car blocks my way. A crescent of curled gray hair suggests the prudent scrub-head driving it. Finally, she stops altogether, and a bony hand points into the woods. A gray dog is slinking among the pines. No—two, three of them, all with grizzled snouts.

"Hey, Joey, coyotes!" I cry.

Joey straightens and strains to see.

I take the first turnoff, and at last the road ends in dense, dusky sky. Dry air brushes my parted lips. Before me lies a great, gaping emptiness, bounded by distant glowing cliffs. Below me, red stone crumbles into flaky candy layers. The land spreads its skirts to the chocolate river, a muddy trickle far below. Black crows caw, but their jeers dissolve into the restful silence. I close my eyes and spread my arms, absorbing the spirit of the place. My feet hover millimeters above dusty ground.

Clunk. A car door slams.

"Cool!" A lively boy scampers out.

I open my eyes. A tall, tanned couple are regarding me suspiciously. In the back seat, Joey looks longingly out the window, so I free him from his oppressive strap. In one glide I mount the gray stone wall and point his eyes into the hazy mystery.

"Mira, Joey," I whisper. "¿Qué maravilla, eh?" I rub my chin against his fuzzy brown head.

"Hey, Mom, she's got a bear!"

I glance at the family, and the boy's father nods nervously.

"Hey, Mom, can I climb up on there like she's doin'?"

I extend my arms until the fresh air fills Joey's fur. He's been cooped up so long he needs to inhale through every stitch of his weave. Elated, I hoist him up and down and watch him relish the open space. He's so grateful he wants to turn and rub noses. As I shift my grip, he slips from my hands, tumbles in the dust, and disappears.

I scream.

"Hey, Mom! Hey, Mom! She dropped her bear! The lady dropped her bear!"

I jump from the fence.

"Hey, Mom! She jumped! I think she's goin' after it!"

Footsteps pound overhead. "Where did she jump from, Bobby?"

"Now, don't you go after her, Fred! She may be crazy."

The voices fade as I slide downward. Joey. I've got to get Joey. Stabs of murderous guilt spur me on. I angle myself like a surfer, pointing my hip to the hazy north rim. The canyon here is not a sheer drop, but the rock-strewn slope is treacherous. Crisp yucca and juniper cling to the soil, and I slide from tuft to tuft. On a rock that promises solid substance, my feet shoot out from under me. I scream as I fall, clawing the air. I catch myself with my arms and legs splayed on a patch that's almost level. Beyond my burning right cheek, the brittle ground drops away.

I roll over on the rock. Bees are zooming in a nearby bush. The twisted branches of a dead tree have sliced the sky into puzzle pieces. When I dare to look down, I notice a brown lump against some yucca far below. Dark and round, it contrasts with the pale leaves that surround it like a spiky halo.

I sit up on my rock. If I pick my way down to the left, I can slide from plant to plant. The right side looks hopeless, a red-rock avalanche in freeze-frame. Sharp stones shred my leggings and rake my skin. In the brush, the crash of my feet is deafening. Below me, the brown spot has grown. Its compact shape is bulging, and I can almost make out a furry head.

The next bush below me lies to the right, so I have to aim myself carefully. I slide faster this time, my legs on fire, and I almost shoot past it. Its green swords slice my hands as I seize them. My feet are dangling, just a few spikes holding me in place. Fuck! I can't remember where the next bush was. I let go.

This time I tumble as I fall, grit and stone battering me from all sides. No solid substance answers my questioning hands. The ground tosses me, slams me. In the brown whirl, Johnny smiles, and my mother purses her tired lips. Colors blossom in a rising pastel totem pole of ice cream.

I have stopped. Under me, the rock is hot and wet. My legs are burning, and I inhale a sharp scent. Beside me lies a fuzzy brown bear. Crying, I pull him to me. The yucca rattles as I draw him from its snagging spikes.

"Joey," I murmur and burrow my face into his neck. My bear. My bear. My bear.

One by one, I test my arms and legs. They sting, and bending them salts the burns. At least I can feel them. At least they still work. I open my eyes. Up above stands a stack of reddish-brown cogs. Dark and jagged, they form a shaft I'll have to ascend. I came down *that*?

"Don't worry, Joey," I say. "I'm going to get you out of here."

I'll never make it if I have to carry him, but I can't leave him down here to desiccate. I untie my sneakers so that I can strip off my shredded purple leggings. I drape the crotch around Joey's back, loop the legs under his arms, and tie them securely under my breasts.

Seeking anything solid, I begin the climb with bare legs and a fuzzy papoose. Even this late, the heat is searing. Streams of sweat slide down my back and tickle the cleft of my behind. I test each foothold in the crumbly rock. I'm not going to gamble as I did on the way down. Pressing my hips into the warm stone, I grip with all ten fingers and both thighs. To hold myself in place, I even ram my face into the burning wall. My foot slips, and I rocket down, clawing until I can stop.

"Hello!" A metal voice cuts the air. "Hello! Ma'am, please answer if you can hear us!"

"Yes!" I scream. Oh, fuck. This is going to be so embarrassing.

"Ma'am, this is the Park Service. We're coming down to you. Are you hurt?"

"No!"

"Are you somewhere safe?"

"Sort of!" My lips are coated with grit.

"Stay where you are. We're coming down."

One foot has found a one-inch wedge of rock; the other, a tuft of something dead. My fingers have burrowed into loose stone, and I'm ramming my hips into the cliff. The knot in my leggings gouges me.

"I see her!"

A shower of dirt baptizes my head.

"I've got her! Fifty more yards!"

A dark man in khaki dangles next to me, suspended by a blue nylon rope. His arms are bronzed and strong, his hair thick and black. He smiles at my papoose, but only for an instant.

"You gave us quite a scare, ma'am."

Oh, no. Not that word again.

"My bear fell," I say. "I was trying to get him back."

"Well, you probably should have left him. Right now, let's just concentrate on getting you out of here."

His flat eyes offer no flicker of sympathy.

"That foothold doesn't look too good to me. I'm going to put this line around you. It may feel funny at first. Don't make any sudden moves."

He works his hand between my hips and the rock until I'm tethered to a rope on a metal clip.

"Okay, I got her!" he yells to someone above. "You ever do any serious rock climbing?"

"No."

"Well, you're about to. It's not hard. My buddy up there will crank us up. Use your legs to keep you away from the rock, and go slow and steady. Think you can do that?"

I test the knot at my waist. Joey is still fastened to my back.

"Don't worry. Looks like you got your friend tied on real good there."

For a second, I glimpse a spark, but I'm not sure what's making him laugh. Bracing ourselves, crunching loose rock, we creep slowly up the cliff face.

When our feet hit the solid stone wall, I hear mottled applause. Everyone who came to see the sunset has stayed to watch the show. In front of the crowd, Bobby's father rubs the restless boy's shoulder as he grins, open-eyed. Parked behind Wilma stands a real live ambulance, and once my ranger and his blond buddy have unhooked me, he brings me a navy-blue blanket. I'm grateful, since everyone's eyes are raking me. Only Bobby looks glad that I found my bear.

Once I'm covered, people wander back to their cars, except for Fred and his wife. They withdraw to the wall, and against darkening haze, they talk earnestly with the blond ranger.

"Ma'am, if you would just come with me, we're gonna check you out," says my rescuer in a deadpan voice. "You look okay, but you never know."

I follow him to the ambulance. His unrevealing black eyes could be harboring amusement, disgust, or damped rage. My stomach tightens with that sick clench set off by other people's anger. My insides form a fist when people hate something I did without understanding why I did it.

Inside the ambulance, I untie Joey from my back and set him on a silver chest. I've always wanted to ride in an ambulance, and even this low-service one is impressive. It's a whole doctor's office on wheels, with probing tools bolted to the walls. With my heart thudding, I lie down on a gurney and let my ranger do his work. If he's angry, I wish he would just tell me. His silence reminds me of my mother. Her nauseous contempt used to brew for days before it erupted in an accusation.

The ranger finds that my pulse and blood pressure are high, but that's normal for someone who just climbed out of the Grand Canyon. He asks me to follow his fingers in order to test me for a concussion. From forehead to ankles, he checks my cuts and bruises, and he wipes and bandages the worst scrapes.

"You're lucky," he says. "No serious injuries. You're not even going to need stitches."

The gurney bobs as he descends to find his sunburned buddy. Like a human prop waiting in the shadows, I listen to the voices on stage.

"So what do you think? She's not hurt. Should we keep her tonight at the station?"

"Yeah, maybe. I can't believe she jumped. She shouldn't be driving, that's for sure. Listen, I've been talking to this lady here—" The low voice dissolves into fuzz, and I catch only a few solid phrases. "Spreading her arms—like she thought she could fly … drugs … teddy bear … jumped … She jumped, right in front of the boy."

"So what do you—"

"We're not equipped … Flagstaff …"

The dark ranger returns with his partner beside him. Unlike my rescuer, the red-skinned blond doesn't try to hide his anger.

"Ma'am, do you realize what you just did?" he demands.

I wince at the loudness of his voice. With my heart beating wildly, I look from side to side but can't escape his hard, red face.

"I just wanted to get my bear," I murmur.

"That was totally irresponsible, what you did! You're lucky to be alive! You endangered your own life! You put others at risk! What about that little boy who saw you jump? What if he goes and tries it?"

My face is searing, and my throat tightens. This guy is talking like some guys fuck. He doesn't care about how I feel—he's just going to slam me until he's done.

"I'm forty-three," I plead, my voice breaking. "I'm forty-three! Don't talk to me like this!"

He shakes his head. "Well, you sure don't act like it."

I rage in the burning left by his blows. How am I supposed to act at forty-three? Should I weigh two hundred pounds? Chop off my hair? Wait on some man and screaming kid? This guy's not mad because they had to haul me out. He's mad because I won't be a slave.

The blond ranger folds his arms and breathes out hard, a dragon with a red-leather face. His partner, who has been studying me, speaks up at last.

"Ma'am," he asks, "have you had anything to drink today?"

"What—alcohol?" I gasp. "No, I don't drink alcohol."

"What about drugs?" he continues. "You do any drugs? Smoke some dope—meth—crack cocaine?"

His list is so ridiculous I have to smile, and again I see a spark that quickly fades.

"We have to ask you this, ma'am," he says. "Especially after what happened. A lot of people come up here to do drugs."

"Well, I didn't," I say, snuffing back tears. "I don't do drugs."

The dark ranger nods skeptically, and they retreat to the stone wall. They frown and gesticulate, but blue haze swallows their words. I am watching a debate without a soundtrack. When they return, they have reached a decision.

"Ma'am," says the dragon, "we're concerned for your safety, and we're going to take you down to Flagstaff where they can help you."

"But I'm not drunk!" I cry. "I'm not on drugs!"

Can they really do this? Capillaries flare on the blond ranger's cheek. If he's mad at me, this is the perfect revenge.

"Not everybody takes the express route down the Grand Canyon," he says. "They just need to ask you a few questions."

"Like what?" I demand.

He uncrosses his thick arms. "Ma'am, if you won't come voluntarily, we can hold you somewhere else."

Something bursts in my stomach. No man has ever talked to me like this before.

"What about my car?" I murmur.

The dragon scratches his ear. "Well, for now it should be okay here. You locked it, right?" Seeing that he has imposed his will, the blond ranger relaxes.

"But I have to be in San Francisco by May thirty-first!"

The red ranger exhales air, not fire. "Oh, that's still a few days away. And your health comes first. Nothing more important than that."

The black-haired ranger climbs in with me, and his partner slams the door and bolts it. I reach for Joey, but with my body strapped down, my fingers stall in midair. With a half smile, the dark man hands him to me. During the two-hour ride, he says little. I rub my scraped cheek against Joey's fur and study the lozenge-shaped bumps on the wall. They lie like bleached licorice pieces, angled but unable to form a pattern. The motor drops in pitch, and I realize we're slowing, letting the lower gears drive us forward. Sometimes we stop, and cries from nearby radios slip through cracks in the metal walls.

"We're almost there," says the quiet ranger. He motions for me to give him Joey.

"What are they going to do to me?"

"Oh, it's all right." He sighs. "They're just gonna check you out."

"How am I going to get back?" His eyes meet mine, but they don't sync.

"Buses," he says. "Every couple of hours. You can take one up tomorrow once you're out."

The red-faced ranger unbolts the door, and I squint at the light streaming in. It is broken by dark silhouettes, all oriented toward me. The rush of voices makes me feel as though I'm being sold at auction.

"Okay, ma'am." The dark man shakes my hand. "We've got to say goodbye to you now."

He hands Joey to a curly-haired nurse, who turns his nose to her breast like I do.

"Goodbye, ma'am. Good luck to you." In the squeeze of the blond ranger's hand, I feel relief.

I am wheeled through thumping double doors and blasted by glowing bars of light on the ceiling. At this time of night, not much is happening in Flagstaff, because I become the focus of the ER. Doesn't anybody get shot around here? When they take my information, I hesitate over next of kin, since my mother's no longer any good. Should I tell them Gonzalo? He wouldn't appreciate a call this late, but he'd probably help me if I needed it.

The nurses check my pulse and blood pressure, which by this time are almost normal.

"What a nice bear!" says the curly-haired nurse. She raises Joey and rubs his nose. She strokes him fondly, picks off a few dry leaves, and sets him down on the doctor's chair.

A good-natured black nurse draws some blood—apparently, they didn't believe me about the drugs. I'm assessing the damage to my purple leggings when the doctor strides up, a muscular man with sunburned skin and wheat-blond hair. Behind gold-rimmed glasses, his blue eyes swirl.

Amid the worry pulsing there, something stops and catches its breath.

"So, Miss McFadden—you fell down the Grand Canyon!"

Behind him, the black nurse splutters. A lightness in his voice tells me he's not American, and I twist my head to read his badge.

"My name is Dr. Fischer," he says with a smile. "Your hands are so cold!" He rubs my right one vigorously between his, icy bacon in a fleshy, warm sandwich.

A sudden flash reveals his badge: "Uwe Fischer." Oh. A German. Shifting blue flecks in his eyes form an ever-changing mosaic.

"So ... Miss McFadden—"

"Carrie."

"Carrie, can you follow my fingers?"

I track them across the ceiling and back. How much pinker they are than that quiet ranger's! This German has been having too much fun in the sun.

"What are you smiling about?" He touches my cheek.

"Oh, nothing—where are you from?"

"Germany." Fischer smiles patiently.

"Where in Germany?"

"Bochum." His mind withdraws as he pictures it.

"How do you say your first name?"

"Oo-vuh."

"Oof?"

"That's all right." He laughs. "Just call me Dr. Fischer. May I ask you a few questions?"

Like the ranger, Fischer checks me systematically, but his main sense is touch. He kneads me, probes me, turns my limbs, and frowns at the oozing cuts. While Fischer explores me, he begins the interrogation that I've known was coming.

"So, Carrie—they say you fell down the Grand Canyon?" The hardness around his lips says he's fighting a laugh.

"Well, not exactly." I smile. "I dropped my bear. I had to go down to get him back."

Fischer flattens Joey's ears with a powerful hand. "That's a very nice bear."

"Yeah, I think so."

Fischer's eyes are shining. "So you're traveling alone?"

"Well, with the bear." I shrug.

"What do you do?" Fischer's gaze is so intense that I falter.

"I'm a writer," I say. "And—and a teacher. I teach in Atlanta. I'm driving cross-country to work on a novel."

"A novel! How wonderful! Listen—can you push your leg against my hands, like this?"

Fischer forms a stirrup of interlaced fingers, and I push as hard as I can. His arms are so strong it doesn't even faze him. From their bulk, I guess he's a weight lifter.

"That's good," he gasps. "You've got some ugly cuts and bruises, but physically you seem all right."

Impulsively, he cups my face in his hands. "But you must understand we're worried about you. Carrie—can you tell me how much you weigh?"

"Oh, about a hundred pounds."

Fischer's lips stir as he calculates in German. "Fünfzig ... ne, fünf und vierzig ... That much? You look very thin to me. Can you tell me what you've had to eat today?"

I try to remember. In my whole life, I've never been able to recall what I eat from one day to the next. "I don't know," I mumble. "Some oatmeal for breakfast … a potato at lunch … I was writing. I can't remember."

"Writing?" Fischer's thick blond brows rise.

"Yeah—when you're really into it, you stop noticing anything else. You hear the characters talk, and you write down what they say."

Fischer jumps. A short, older doctor has crept up behind him. Slightly stooped, he peers at me inquisitively and extends an arm with a burnt forest of hair.

"Hi, I'm Dr. Kyle."

His black eyes inspect me. With my smudged face and tangled hair, I must look dangerous. Kyle lays a thin arm on Fischer's bronzed one and leads him aside. I glance up at the nurses but see only their hair, which gleams in the fluorescent light. In a cool wash of air, the doctors return. Fischer stands behind Kyle, beaming encouragement.

"Okay, Carrie," says Kyle. "I understand you had a little accident today."

"Yeah." I search his dark eyes for warmth.

"Well, I'm a psychiatrist, and I'd like to ask you a few questions." What an ugly voice, all breathy and raspy. Sounds like a dinosaur who just woke up from a seventy-million-year nap.

"Yeah, sure." I brace myself.

Fischer folds his thick arms.

"Carrie, can you tell me why you went down the canyon alone at seven o'clock at night? That's a pretty risky thing to do."

"Yeah, I know," I say. "My bear fell."

Kyle looks down at Joey, whom the curly-haired nurse snatches from his chair. Kyle sits so that his face is right over mine and he can study me closely.

"But you could have left him there. Maybe someone could have gone after him tomorrow."

Kyle's warm, humid breath invades my nose.

"I didn't think about it," I say. "I just had to get him. I doubt if anybody would go down there after a bear anyway—only a person."

"Is the bear like a person to you?"

"Yeah! Well, I mean, he's a bear, but—"

"What's his name?"

"Joey."

Kyle frowns at Joey, then glances at my frozen breasts.

"Oh. That's nice," he says quickly. "So Dr. Fischer tells me you're a professor writing a novel, and you're traveling alone."

What's the deal with this? Doesn't anyone ever travel alone? I squirm and shift my hips.

"Yeah, that's right."

"Carrie, can you tell me how long you've been traveling? Can you tell me what day it is today?"

Fischer's, Kyle's, and the nurses' gazes merge into one searching beam.

"I don't know. The twenty-fifth? The twenty-sixth?"

Kyle blinks, but the force of his eyes doesn't waver.

"How about the day of the week?"

I'm not sure of this either. "Wednesday? Thursday?"

Kyle jots a few words in my chart, like a shop owner taking inventory.

"What about the year? Can you tell me who's president?"

This is too much. "George fucking Bush," I say.

The black nurse splutters. "Oooh, she's oriented."

"Which one?" asks Kyle sharply.

"George W."

Kyle scribbles another line. Fischer squints over Kyle's shoulder to see what he's writing, but Fischer's tense shoulders say he doesn't know.

"Now, you told us that you don't do any drugs—" Kyle's pointed eyes rake me.

"Yeah. I don't do that," I say impatiently. "The blood test will show it."

"Do you think we took blood to check for drugs?" he asks. "Do you have the feeling people are trying to keep track of you?"

"Only the Tenure and Promotion Committee."

Kyle smirks. Fischer looks confused.

"Okay, okay. So you're writing a novel—and you were saying something interesting just as I walked in. I think you were saying that you heard the voices of people talking to you."

I reposition my hips. "Well, no, not literally. I imagine a scene, and then I hear it in my head. I hear them talking, and then I write it down. That's what writing is for me."

"You hear it?" Kyle squints and cocks his head.

"Not with my ears," I explain. "In my head. That's what writing is. Don't you know anyone who writes?"

"Yeah, sure ..." Kyle frowns at his scribbling hand. "Traveling alone can be rough, you know. Are you taking good care of yourself? Do you have some good friends you can talk to?"

"Yeah," I say, "I'm meeting a friend of mine in San Francisco on the thirty-first. It's been going great up to now. I've been talking to my friend Gonzalo in New York, and Clifton in Birmingham."

"That's good. What about family? You have any children? Any family responsibilities?"

Children! The thought of me with children is so bizarre I have to laugh.

"Is that funny?" he asks, regarding me strangely.

"No—no. Family—my mother's in a nursing home. My father's dead. Children?" Another heave of laughter rises.

"Well, you're past forty. Most women your age have children. It's not such an unusual question."

Fischer frowns at Kyle's grizzled head.

"Well, I don't."

"That's okay." Kyle shrugs. "I was just asking. All right, Carrie, that's it for now. We'll keep you here tonight, just to make sure you're okay. These nurses here can help you get checked in. Then we'll decide where to go from there."

"What do you mean?" I prop myself up on one elbow.

"Well, we may need to run a few more tests." Kyle's eyes cloud.

"What tests?" I demand. "I'm okay! I need to get back to my car. I have to be in San Francisco on the thirty-first!"

Kyle's lips twitch. "Well, can't you change that? Your health comes first, you know." His voice is maddeningly soft.

"Isn't that my decision?"

"Yes, of course. Of course. Look, why don't you get some rest? I need to get some too. We can decide this in the morning."

Kyle rises and looks down at me, assessing the girth of my thighs. I wish he would test them the way Fischer did, so I could kick him across the room. Geez, this guy is even worse than that angry red ranger. Quieter, maybe, but deadlier. With his hairy arm on Fischer's, he ushers the bulky doctor into the hall. This time I can hear them—not Kyle, whose words are a level murmur, but Fischer, whose accent bursts loose as his voice rises.

"Oh, come on! Do you know what day it is when you're on vacation? Delussional? No! It's chust her way of talking about writing! You must see that!"

The two nurses lean toward the door.

"No! What—no! She's not isolated. She's going to wisit her friend … Yes, she's underweight. If it was a suicide attempt, why is she so worried about seeing her friend in San Francisco? … No! Not everyone who's different needs— Yeah. Yeah. Okay."

When Fischer returns, he's trying harder to smile. He grips my hands and looks down affectionately.

"I'm in charge tonight," he says. "So we're stuck with each other. Let me know if you need anything …" His blue eyes pulse. "And I'll come around to check on you."

"Honey," asks the black nurse, "would you like to take a shower?"

Once she's promised me Joey will be safe, I consent gratefully. I take my clothes in with me and scrub hair, crotch, toenails, and shirt with odorless green liquid that won't lather. The cheerful nurse shows me where I can sleep: a dark, temporary holding cell.

"This is normally a single," she says. "But for you, we'll make an exception."

In the narrow bed, I clutch Joey on top of me, so that we look like one fat person under a sheet.

"Are you going to let me out of here?" I ask.

"Well, if it was up to me, I would," she says. "And you've got Dr. Feel-Good rooting for you."

My laugh jounces Joey, and the nurse scratches a protruding ear.

"Oh, that's nothing," she says. "You should hear what they call him on the day shift."

She snaps out the light, and I laugh until my voice runs down like a brook in winter. Sleep is the last thing I want to do. From the hallway, light slices the room in brilliant bars. The hospital sounds invade haphazardly, voices calling, gurneys rattling. What does Kyle think is wrong with me? They can't force me to stay in this place, can they?

I wrench awake as something warm grabs my arm. Standing over me is a bulky shape topped with gold.

"Sh-sh." Fischer puts a thick finger to his lips. "Sorry to scare you. It's six o'clock. I'm getting off now, and I was wondering if you need a ride."

"What about the tests?" I ask. Fischer's frown has none of last night's warmth. The athletic doctor looks jittery.

"Oh, I don't think that'll be necessary," he says. "I'm signing you out—if you want."

I sit up and look around for my clothes. "But Dr. Kyle said—"

Fischer grips my shoulders, stilling my protests. "I'm signing you out. Get dressed. I'll be back in five minutes."

Shivering, I pull on my torn leggings, white tank top, and Day of the Dead T-shirt, all of which are still wet. When

Fischer returns, I'm standing there trembling, my nipples like diamonds and Joey tucked under my arm.

"Jesus!" he says. "Is that all you've got to wear?"

"Yeah."

"That's okay. I'll find you something in my car."

Fischer leads me to the garage through a secret passage, guarded by a door that says "No admittance. Staff only." I follow his tense back between scuffed cinder block walls, unnerved by the buzz of fluorescent lights. Fischer's car is a faded red Toyota whose back door opens with a groan. I have to perch Joey on a pile of junk, which smells of sweat, hardened rubber, and hamburger wrappers. From the trunk, Fischer produces a heavy blue sweatshirt.

"Here. Put this on."

He takes a last look at my breasts before I engulf myself in blue cotton.

"Aren't you going to get in trouble for this?" I ask as he starts the motor.

"Yeah." Fischer stares straight ahead.

"What's going on, anyway?"

Fischer looks at me in the sweatshirt, then smiles and shakes his head. "Kyle thinks you're delusional. Hearing voices. He wants to keep you here and start you on antipsychotic drugs."

"Fuck!"

Fischer grins. "I take it you don't agree with his diagnosis either. You sound pretty sane to me."

"No! What the fuck is wrong with him?" I remember that red-faced ranger and his terrible words, "hold you."

Fischer straightens as we approach the exit booth, and I wonder if I should duck.

"He has a problem with women," he murmurs.

"Women?"

"Yeah. He's having the mother of all midlife crises."

"Looks pretty well past midlife to me."

"Well, don't tell him that, or he'll put you on clozapine."

"Fuck!"

I've never known a guy like that, but as I get older, maybe I'll run across more of them. And that ranger—is this the way guys treat you when you age? I wonder what monsters will populate my future.

"Yeah," says Fischer. "It's pretty scary what a guy will do to women when they don't want to fuck him anymore."

"Yeah," I sigh.

"It's just a feeling. But anytime I've ever called him in to consult on a good-looking woman, he wants to medicate her. The guys he just releases—the ones who aren't raving. I keep trying to stop him, but I'm just the visiting resident. This time—this was too much. I couldn't let him do it. He forgot to sign you in, and I saw my chance."

"Wow, he's gonna have your ass in a sling."

"He what?"

"You're going to be in big trouble. They'll send you back to ..."

"Bochum."

"Sounds terrible."

"It is."

We're speeding down a smooth six-lane road lonely for the massage of tires. Behind dusty strip malls, the sun is rising over black mountains.

"I see it this way," says Fischer, squinting at the ragged hills. "I'm a healer. My job is to heal people, right? Holding you here and drugging you won't do you any good. They may send me home, but at least this thing will be out in the open, and you'll be free to get well."

"Yeah." I draw a deep breath and glance over at him. His red face radiates energy.

"There is something wrong with you, but fucking with your neurotransmitters won't fix it. Whatever's the matter with you, it's in San Francisco."

Fischer pulls into a drive-through restaurant. "Don't look so shocked. You're not such a mystery. Anyone who really listened—"

An avalanche of static greets us.

"What do you want?" He grins. "I'm buying you breakfast. Kyle was right about that. You're too thin."

I order a fruit salad and tea, but Fischer asks for a large coffee and three ham-and-egg breakfast sandwiches.

"You're a doctor!" I gasp. "How can you eat that shit?"

"You try running the ER for twelve hours! I'm fucking starving to death!"

Buried in his blue sweatshirt, I jerk with laughter, and my hair catches on the torn seat.

"And you're German. Don't you know fast food is evil?"

"Oh, issh dffnntly evl ..." Fischer devours his first sandwich in four bites. With a bearlike arm, he snatches one of my apple slices.

"Hey!"

"Well, you told me to eat something healthy."

"All right!" I grab one of his warm, round sandwiches and take a big bite. The warm, salty egg and ham make my soul unfold.

As the morning light blooms, we turn north onto 180.

"So how long have you been here?" I ask.

"About six months," he says. "I was supposed to be here a year, but I'm trying to stay longer."

"You like it that much?"

"Oh, yeah." Fischer struggles to express himself. "I feel as though I'm close to ... the source of things here. Just look at that!"

In the awakening woods, pine needles glisten. A pointed mountain rising over the rest glows against the brilliant sky.

"I feel so alive here ... as though I'm part of something. To be close to that, to be worthy of that ... I go hiking up there all the time by myself—just to be alone in that—to breathe it in, to listen to the quiet. You can close your eyes and feel the force of it flow through your skin."

"You ever use sunscreen?"

Fischer turns on me. "Oh, come on, don't laugh at me— I'm trying to say something here!"

"Sorry."

He squints into the rising sun. "I think we're all here—to make the most out of what we've got. To try to do things, create things."

We shoot past a lone house in a vast green meadow, and he takes a big swallow of coffee. I try another bite of delicious, warm ham and egg.

"Me," he reflects, "I like to fix things. I'm a plumber who specializes in human beings, but I'm also a detective."

I recognize a quality in Fischer's voice, not so much the words as the tone. It's like hearing a song you know with words in a different language. The preacher! He sounds like that preacher.

"Just look at that! Isn't that amazing?"

Fischer pulls over to watch the sun rise. Over the pointed mountain, the sky is turning bright blue, and every needle of the pines is visible.

"I've hiked all through here," he says between bites.

He steals more apple and lets me finish his sandwich. As we streak north again, every surface reflects light.

"Unbelievable," he murmurs, shaking his head. "What can you do in life to be worthy of that?"

We ride in silence, and his gaze hardens to a frown. I suspect he's remembering something in Germany.

"So what's in San Francisco?" he asks finally.

"A guy."

"Oh, I knew that. *The* guy—*der Eine*—the one for you?"

"Depends who you ask." I grimace. "His wife doesn't think so."

"Oh." Fischer brushes off marriage as if it were a bug on his arm. "What counts is what he thinks—and you."

A patch of tall grass glistens with dew.

"Well, I haven't seen him in a long time," I say slowly. "But anytime I'm with him, we just—come together. It's like coming home."

"Like coming home." Fischer's voice softens. "That sounds worth risking our asses for … Does he feel the same way?"

I picture Johnny staring at a journal, admiring intricate molecules.

"I think so," I say. "He never says it. He shows it by doing things."

"Yeah. I know that." Hard and confident, Fischer's doctor voice comforts me.

"What about you?" I ask. "You have someone like that?"

"Well, there's a woman in Germany ..." Fischer studies the dips in the road ahead of us.

"Yeah?"

"Yeah. Ute."

"Jesus! Oof and Oot? I would reconsider."

"Yeah." Fischer smiles at the pines. "I am reconsidering. I am definitely reconsidering."

The Toyota rattles over some rough asphalt. Fischer draws a breath and waits until the noise subsides.

"I'd like to read something you wrote," he says. "I bet it's good."

He looks at me as though he were older than I am, but for once, fatherliness doesn't bother me. "Look, I don't know who this guy is, but it sounds like you're right for him. You communicate by doing things too. You just jump."

I frown. "Does writing count as saying something or doing something?"

"For you, doing something. It's what you do. Like me and these mountains, always climbing them. Why bother? In fifty years we'll be dust, they'll still be here, and nobody will ever know that I've been there. Your books will be out of print. But we do it."

"Seems kind of pointless, doesn't it?"

"No!" Fischer's blue eyes blaze. "No! It's beautiful."

I lean back in the seat and realize that my eyes are full of tears. Through a watery film, I study twisted trees against the strengthening light. The right angles of a tan hotel force their way into my Japanese scroll.

"That was fast," murmurs Fischer.

At the entrance booth, a female ranger greets us cheerily. "Howdy, folks! You getting an early start today?" Fischer flashes a year-round pass.

Feeling surreal, I direct him to the lookout that I left just twelve hours ago. There sits Wilma, waiting anxiously, her windows a little misted.

Fischer peers over the stone wall. "Shit! You went down *that*?"

"Yeah. It was my bear. I had to get my bear."

Fischer shakes his head. "And I've put my ass in a—a—"

"Sling."

"In a sling, trying to claim that you're not crazy?"

I retrieve Joey from his throne of maps and clothes and strap him into Wilma's back seat.

Fischer is writing something down. "Here's my number and address," he says, "in case you ever need anything. Now give me your number."

Since we can't find more paper, I write my cell phone number on one of the sandwich wrappers.

"Now c'mere," he orders, and I find myself crushed in a devouring hug. Fischer's blond bristles pierce my cheeks as he kisses them slowly.

"You stay out of Flagstaff," he warns. "You be good."

"Or what?"

"Or I'll come and get you."

Fischer climbs back into his Toyota and rubs his sun-hardened face. "Jesus, I'm tired. You be good," he repeats, shaking his finger.

I follow him all the way down to Valle, which is hard since he thinks 64 is the Autobahn. Just before we part ways, he honks twice, then heads back over his mountains to bed. Feeling itchy, I turn up the air-conditioning as I speed down 64 toward Las Vegas. I scratch my shoulder, and my fingers nest in soft, absorbing blue cotton.

CHAPTER 9

LAS VEGAS

West of Seligman, the land wrinkles into boulder-strewn hills until it looks like a warm, fresh crumb cake. Devil Dog Road sets off cravings for soft cocoa fingers with white cream gooshing from the sides. Despite Fischer's egg sandwich, I must still be hungry. Wilma's clock says 11:23, so he should be home by now. I picture him sleeping perfectly still, his red-brown face mashed into a pillow.

As I roll up 93, the desert changes tint. The soil turns pink against tufts of tawny brush. Bald brown mountains rise, beautiful despite their starkness. The air turns hotter until Wilma's air-conditioning can no longer cool its rage. In the back seat, Fischer's sweatshirt lies heaped beside Joey, looking like another collapsed animal. Even in this desert, mailboxes and sun-blasted trailers flash in the sun as I streak past. Why would anyone live out here, two hours away from anywhere?

Since Oklahoma, I haven't seen a house with a porch or a sloped roof. In the desert, people live in tin-can trailers or prefab houses you can flatten and fold. Dirt roads lead to clusters of trailers that look like they were tossed down in a crap game. Among them lie rusty cars and stacked tires, except where people are using the tires to secure their roofs against the ripping wind. At last, even these settlements dissolve, leaving only dirt, brush, and sky.

As Las Vegas nears, the lanes multiply—four, six, too many to count. The scale of the place stultifies me, billboards two stories high, local roads eight lanes wide. It takes some doing to reach my Run-Rite Inn, since a U-turn is out of the question. I cross the strip and then double back, giggling at the gilded kitsch. I have always wanted to see this place, but now I don't know why. I don't drink. I don't gamble. Yet something has pulled me here.

In my cool, vibrating room, I pull on my blue sheath dress. In it I almost form an hourglass, small on top but so tiny in the middle that the low volume above doesn't matter. How are my legs? I strip off the bandages. None of the red, oozing scrapes run deep. Around my neck I hang the cool Santa Fe turquoise, and I brush my hair until it shines.

My plan to walk the strip fails utterly. The 102-degree air withers my lungs, and after two blocks, I am sucked out. I can cross the vast side streets only on bridges, so I'm forced to enter the casinos. Once I'm in, I can't find my way out. The checkerboard carpets hypnotize me, and the arrows lead me in circles. Instead of windows, I encounter mirrors everywhere. Still, I like the flashes and gurgles, the rattles and shouts when someone wins.

With my stomach sucked in, I parade up and down, but apart from one leering guard, no one is looking. Something is wrong. In this dark, endless space, I'm surrounded by beautiful women. The waitresses wear tight black miniskirts and bulge out of their flapping white blouses. But the young visitors garner the most attention. Laughing gaily, they race by in spike heels and flouncy dresses. Many wear a kind of top I've never seen before, tight over the breasts, then opening to a veil that reveals a white belly in flashes. Three Elvis impersonators pose with plump girls who suck dizzying drinks from purple bongs. I follow three women in red, white, and blue boas, trying to decide which is prettiest.

When the radiant girls disappear into a theater, I face myself in a gleaming mirror. There's no faulting the quiet curves of my dress, and in the restless darkness, the red scrapes on my legs are barely visible. No, the problem is my face, something lowering in its drawn expression. The lips are full, but under my eyes, the gray circles look like ruts left by a tank. A new generation of big-eyed, soft-haired women has emerged, while I have stayed tightened and clenched. I can't remember laughing like the girls who float by in bright, harmonious clouds. Feeling dizzy, I search for food, and words swirl up from my yogurt parfait.

Next morning Justin's eyes meet mine in a flicker. He is cheerful in a rushed, nervous way. He gropes in his pockets and says he's in a hurry, he's sorry about last night, it won't happen again, he didn't mean to disrespect me. His words seem sprayed out rather than spoken, as little pondered as water from a hose.

Mrs. Marshall's movements say that she's restless too. She tries to keep more space between us, and I feel her watching. When we choose our books, she's obsessed with mine, and I can grab a spiral notebook only when she sneezes. I camouflage the hot pages behind a blue history book, but the handwritten words tell me only of student riots in 1969. I push the notebook back and fumble for the right one while Mrs. Marshall's clear eyes sear into me. There it is, 1965–68.

"What's down there?" she asks. "I don't like this book. I want one from down there too."

From the same shelf, I pull out a heavy science book with bright pictures, and she seems content—or is she pretending?

Luckily my copper-bound pages fit cleanly behind the blue history text. Mrs. Marshall smiles at her colorful, candy-like pictures, and I begin to read.

Tighter. When I asked Jimmy why he wanted to do this, he led me over to the mirror. He was right, as always. That biting black cord crisscrossed my breasts and made me look like an X-rated Wonder Woman.

"You see?" he said.

He pulled it tighter, twice around my waist until I could hardly breathe. Then it snaked my wrists, bound my arms, and he mashed my face into the quilt. He took me fast and hard, since when he sees me like that he can't—

"I have to go to the bathroom!"

"Okay, Mrs. Marshall."

I close the notebook inside the blue cover and leave it waiting on the love seat. She won't let me take her hand to lead her, but I hear her soft steps behind me. Strangely, she wants me to stay while she pulls down her pants. I smell something awful.

"Oh no! Mrs. Marshall! Have you—"

She yanks down her panties and laughs as a big piece of shit plops on the floor. I grab some toilet paper and stoop to catch it before she can mash it around. Luckily it leaves only a faint chocolate trace. It warms my hand through the paper. As I try to drop it in the toilet, she stands there and laughs, blocking my way.

"Why didn't you tell me you had to go?" I ask.

"You were reading."

I think about what Raúl would say, vieja asquerosa, gringa de mierda. I pull her pants way down to her ankles, but she won't lift her legs so I can take them off. At least I can reach her underwear now, hot, heavy, and stinking. I twist her panties and empty them into the toilet. She laughs as a chunk glances off the seat.

"¡Que la chingada! Sit down!"

Only by pushing her can I make her sit so I can pull off her shoes, socks, pants, and underwear. She giggles as I rub the panties with toilet paper.

"I need to get you some clean clothes," I say. "Can you wait here for me?"

Mrs. Marshall nods, amused, and I hurry upstairs to her room.

I almost never go up here, where the air feels tight enough to give shocks. If the downstairs is too dark, this room is too bright. Sun streams through the window onto the beige carpet, revealing ancient, shadowed stains. By choice, la vieja has kept the room just as it was when her husband was alive. A white spread lies uneasily on the lumpy double bed. Justin must have made it this morning.

On the white dressers stand more silver-rimmed pictures, Bill and Sandy on their wedding day, Justin as a boy. In her cream-colored dress, Mrs. Marshall beams, chin out, and Bill smiles radiantly at his taller bride. Justin at seven looks like Justin today, round face, dark eyes, anxious smile.

In the top drawer of one dresser I find rolled-up socks; in its twin, a tangle of bras. I pull on the snarl to look under it for panties. ¡Qué pena! Someone with such beautiful bras should take better care of them. The elastic nest rises, and a lacy black bra comes free.

In all my life, I've never seen such a bra. The cups curve enticingly, solid black to the nipples. Above them lies a network of loops, and tiny black bows mark the middle and sides. Downstairs I hear only silence, so I whip off my shirt. I push up on each breast so that it fills the cup. In the mirror, I hardly recognize myself.

Against my skin, the black loops form a tattoo, and flesh bulges deliciously over each cup. I whisk back my hair, and my breasts rise and push out. Like a hungry animal, the bra bites into them, but I love the feeling. I look just like a model in a magazine. If only Raúl could see!

In the mirror, something flickers. Bony hands seize my breasts.

"Give me that! That's mine!"

"¡Ay!"

With pain shooting through me, I pull at her hands, but her fingers are strong.

"You! You!" she screams.

To unhook the bra, I have to let her pinch me full strength. I shout at her as I fumble.

"Stop it! ¡Vieja de mierda!"

The pain burns so badly I'm nearly sick. She is trying to pull off my breasts. At last the hook comes free, and she staggers back, clutching the balled-up bra.

"It's mine!" she yells.

She rubs the loopy cups against her cheek.

"Okay! Okay!" I sniff.

I grab for my shirt and wipe my tears with my wrists. Naked from the waist down, she strokes the bra as if it were a black kitten.

"Let's get you some underwear, Mrs. Marshall," I sigh.

In the next drawer down I find panties.

I blink. That should be enough for now. The words have stopped coming. Outside, darkness has bloomed, but the heat on the strip is still fierce. Instinctively I move toward the sound of water. Before a pink casino, people have gathered to watch brilliant jets squirt to the love theme from *Titanic*. Under gleaming lights, the crowd is so thick I can barely shuffle. Rows of Latino guys are handing out flyers, among them an old woman with a greasy gray braid. Reaching up— since she's well under five feet tall—she thrusts a fuchsia flyer in my face.

"Beautiful Girls Just 4U!" it says.

Her black eyes demand that I take the paper, so I do. Probably she can't read it, not even if it were in Spanish. She must have just come on the last truck from Oaxaca and is living in a trailer outside town. Flyer in hand, I shuffle along with the crowd until I'm so wilted I want to turn off the lights. For dinner, I buy an apple and some Wheat Snacks. When I check my phone, I find that I have three messages, all from Birmingham, Alabama.

9:32: "Hey, Theresa. Just wanted to know what you're up to tonight. Hope your trip's going well. Oh—this is Clifton."

11:09: "Hey, Theresa. It's me again—Clifton. Listen—I just got this great idea I want to tell you about. Please call me if you can."

12:13, just ten minutes ago: "Hey, Theresa. Please call me. I've got such a great idea I wanna tell you 'bout. Great li'l idea. Just gimme a call, hey?"

By the time I reach the Run-Rite Inn, I am smiling broadly.

Before I call Clifton, I kick off my sandals. Something tells me this is an idea I need to hear lying down. For someone so eager to talk, Clifton takes a long time to answer.

"Mmmmph—hwo?"

"Clifton?"

"Oh—oh—mmph—Theresha—" His voice sounds heavy and sticky.

"Are you eating something?" I grin at Joey, who grimaces in disgust.

"Mmmph … Yeah … Oh. God, it's great to hear you. I'm so glad you called." Clifton's voice emerges.

"So what's going on?"

"You called me!" Clifton seems to have swallowed, but something's still not right.

"Yeah?" I glower at Joey, but he's not intimidated.

"No—no—" stammers Clifton. "I mean here—here at home. You called me at home, and Karen answered."

"Yeah. She said you were having breakfast."

I scowl at the ceiling. What are all those dark flecks around the light?

"Yeah," says Clifton. "I took today off. We were gonna do some work around the house. But she got mad. Took the kids up to her parents' place for the weekend. Said if this new bill design is so important, I should spend the weekend on that. They won't be back until Sunday night."

"Wow," I breathe.

I raise one leg and then the other. What are those black spots up there? Mildew? Bugs? If flies crashed into the light, why would they stick up there?

"No, no—I'm glad you called," he murmurs. "I like that you called. What got her was that I gave you our home number. But I didn't, did I? I can't remember …"

"Yeah, you did." I squeeze my bottom as hard as I can and wait for the burn.

"Oh …"

I hear a clunk and some gurgles.

"Oh, shit!"

"Clifton?" What's he doing? Those can't be bugs. They would have fallen.

"Sorry," he grunts. "I just spilled something."

"Oh." I release my bottom and my breath along with it.

"So you wanted to talk to me?" Clifton's voice gains strength.

"Yeah. I like talking to you."

"Me too."

My heart beats toward his next words, but there is only a wash of breath.

"Clifton? What are you doing, anyway?"

"Oh, nothing. Just having some supper."

I imagine him opening the stainless steel vault, eager to swallow anything he sees.

"Like what?"

"Oh, lessee. Some soup. Some leftover chicken. Couple pieces of pizza. Finished the ice cream ... The kids' Twinkies ..."

"Is that all?"

"Yeah," he murmurs sheepishly. "Guess it's kind of a lot, isn't it? Had to unzip my pants an hour ago. Don't know if they're ever gonna fit again."

"So what are you doing now?" I wiggle my hips, still frowning at those scattered flecks. I guess they could be water spots. But why around the light, like puckers around some old lady's mouth?

"Well, right now I'm lying here on the couch, eating my wife's Turtles."

"Ew!"

Clifton laughs deep in his throat. "Wow, you're really not from the South, are you?"

"No."

Joey has gone comatose.

"Turtles are candy—chocolate-covered caramel. Pecans for the head and feet."

He chews in a slow rhythm, and I wait for him to swallow.

"So, Clifton—you have anything to drink with all that? Y'know, just to wash it down with?"

"Mm-hmm. Ran outa beer. Had to switch to bourbon."

"How much beer?"

"Oh, I dunno. All we had in the fridge." He sounds very pleased with himself.

"So you're lying on the couch with your pants unzipped, eating Turtles and drinking bourbon?"

"Yes, ma'am. And reading your book. I finished it, y'know. That's partly why I called. I love it! Especially the sexy parts. I keep reading 'em over and over. God! When she goes into the tool shed with that tall guy! Man, was that sexy! All those tools … How'd you ever come up with that?"

"Oh, I don't know. Just sort of came to me." I swivel my hips in slow circles.

"Well, I'd like to hear more of your ideas. I wanna get to know you real well. Where are you, anyway?"

"Las Vegas," I murmur. "In bed at the Run-Rite Inn."

"Las Vegas! God, that's sexy … I wish I were lying there with you …"

"I'd probably start eating your Turtles."

Clifton laughs, low and deep. "If I were there with you, I'd let you do anything you want … anything …" His voice fades to a breath.

"That's nice. I can think of a lot of things."

"Yeah?" he whispers.

"But first tell me your idea. I want to hear your idea. You called me 'cause you had an idea."

"Oh, yeah! Man! Well, it was your idea, really!"

He prepares himself in a wave of gurgles.

"Well, you said you were a design consultant—working with me on the phone bill. Suppose I had to fly to San Francisco to see your designs? Sign a contract or something?"

Oh, shit. But maybe— "Yeah?" I say.

Another wave of gurgles wets my ear.

"I could see you. Really see you. Spend some time with you, get to know you ..." A serious tinge in his voice tightens my stomach.

"Would that work?" I ask.

"Sure." Clifton's voice rushes out. "I'd just tell everyone I was meeting a designer. And—and we could hang up one of those Do Not Disturb signs—and I could be alone with you for days and days and days. I would take you to all the finest restaurants—and just be real nice to you. And you could be with me, instead of that mean guy who makes you cry ..."

I picture Johnny and me walking up a dark, wet street. I am riding a camera behind us. Johnny wraps his arm around my shoulders and leans toward me because it's so far down to reach.

"Theresa? Oh, God, I've offended you, haven't I? We don't have to— I don't mean—" Clifton's voice quivers.

"No, no." I sigh. "That's okay. I was just thinking ..."

"Thinking maybe ... yes?"

"Thinking what it would be like to be with you, yeah." Clifton can't see me, but I'm nodding.

"Theresa ..." He hesitates. "Know what I like about you? You're so experienced. All those guys ... and you're so ... relaxed about it. I never met a woman like you. You're so sexy— and so casual. All those guys ... Everything you've done with them, I want to do with you. I want to do everything."

I imagine the glow in his eyes and wish I could encircle him. The puffs of his breath come so fast they worry me.

"All that in just a few days?"

"Yeah. I want to do it nonstop."

I remember Clifton's soft, sad tone—when was that, just a few days ago? He's gone from nerd to sex maniac in a week. Am I responsible for this? Seems like in every guy, it's just below the surface, and I manage to bring it out.

"Clifton," I say, "you've got to take it easy."

"No," he breathes. "Not with you. Ever since I saw you, I've had this feeling that I don't want to waste time. My life is going by, and I'm spending it doing … stupid things, when I could be with you."

What would it be like to spend my life with Clifton? I squint at Joey, who has raised his head.

"But you don't even know me," I protest.

"Oh, I'm gonna get to know you. Because—"

"Yeah?" The new force in him exhilarates me.

"Because I think you like me. You keep calling me … called my house … I think you want to be with me."

Relief smooths his voice as though he had coughed a bit of food from his throat.

"Well, I do like talking with you," I say.

"So I'll come to San Francisco, and we'll talk."

"I just don't think—"

Clifton cuts me off. "Please, Theresa. I never wanted anything so bad in my life. I want to be with you—I want to lie down with you. Can't you—can't you give me just a little taste?"

I smile. "You want to know what I'd do if you were here?"

"Yeah …" A whisper. "Please tell me."

"Okay …" I shift my hips and glance toward the mirror but find only a blank silver square. "Well … what I like about guys is that every one's different. I like getting to know you … the kinds of sounds you make, your sensitive spots."

"Oh …"

The bed squeaks as I swivel.

"With you, I think I'd start with a kiss."

"That's nice," he murmurs. "I like kisses."

"Soft and long, just barely touching you with my tongue. Then I'd slide my lips down and explore your neck …"

"Ohhh …"

There's a clunk and a rush of static.

"I unbutton your shirt …"

"Yeah …"

Joey glares.

"Are you nice and furry?"

"Yeah. Mm-hmm."

"Good. I like that." I arch my back. "Now I'm rubbing my face back and forth in your fur, and every now and then I give you a little kiss."

"Mmm." His voice slides into rushing breath.

"Just a kiss, soft and wet, just a touch of my tongue, anywhere, anytime."

"Oh … Oh …"

"And I'm moving my head down slowly … No … no … you're pushing it down."

"Oh, Theresa …"

"And your belly's so big, it takes a very long time …"

I can almost feel it, that mound of living warmth.

"Ohh …"

"But I find you. I find you—"

"Oh! Oh, God! … Oh, shit! The couch!"

"Clifton? Are you okay?"

He's laughing. Of all the guys I've ever known, I don't think I've met one who laughed when—

"Oh, shit! God, that was good ... Whoa—"

"Clifton?"

The room flickers back: purple bedspread, pale dresser, angry bear.

"It's okay. Just tried to stand up. Wasn't such a good idea."

"That's okay," I say. "You can clean up tomorrow."

"Yeah. I better get some sleep."

"That's okay. What happens in Vegas stays in Vegas." I wish I could hug him.

"Yeah. But—" Despite that burst, his urge hasn't died.

"Yeah?"

"I'm comin' out there. To San Francisco. I'm gonna come out there and find you."

"Okay," I whisper.

"Yeah? Really?" He is drowsily ecstatic.

"Yeah."

"Ooh, wow," he moans. "I feel kinda sleepy ..."

"Go to sleep, now, Clifton," I murmur. "Have some nice dreams ..." Maybe he'll think this was one.

"I'll dream of you ... I love you, Theresa ..."

"You're nice, Clifton ... Go to sleep, now ..."

I'm always sad when the phone goes dead, and the loss of Clifton's voice turns my room to a black box. I glance at Joey, but he has gone catatonic, staring straight into the mirror. I slip the phone back into my purse, whose open mouth flashes pink. What is that? Oh, yeah. With my thumb and finger, I pull out the flyer that says "Beautiful Girls Just 4U." Below is a local number, not 1-800- or 1-900- but the lifeline of some small company. Who's at the other end of that line? What women work for these people? Only when a voice jabs my ear do I realize I've punched in the numbers.

"Hello. Beautiful Girls Just 4U."

Oh, shit!

"Hello? You looking for some company tonight?"

"Yeah." I release my breath.

"Ah, a lonely lady." The man's voice flows too smoothly, like a fountain in a desert yard.

"No, no, not lonely. I was just wondering ..."

"That's okay. We like ladies who like ladies. We get 'em all the time. So what kind of lady would you like to meet tonight?"

Shit! I reach for Joey.

"Are you still there, ma'am? Listen, it's okay to be shy. Most people are. This your first time?"

"Mm-hmm." My voice breaks, and my eyes sting.

"Come on, now, ma'am, there's nothing to be ashamed of. You'd be surprised how many people call us, and the ones who don't, they wish they did."

I try to make a sound, but my voice has collapsed.

"Just take your time, ma'am. Tell me your fantasy. If you could have anything you want, what would it be?"

In one frozen frame I see Johnny in his office, his head turned toward the doorway.

"I'm not giving up on you, ma'am. I know we have something for you. Maybe a beautiful blonde lady—"

"A Latina. You have any Latinas?" Was that me?

I would love to talk to one of these Beautiful Girls and follow the turns of her voice.

"We sure do, ma'am," he answers. "We sure do. I'd be glad to send a lovely lady from south of the border."

"Oh, no, I—" Maybe if I just hang up—

"Oh, come on, now, ma'am," he says. "You called us. You know what you want. You're a gutsy lady. Why not go for it? This is Vegas."

"Well—how does it work?" I ask. "What do I …?"

"It's a hundred for her to show up. Anything she does from there, you work out between the two of you. What hotel you staying at?"

"The Run-Rite Inn. On Tropicana." I can't believe I'm saying this. I should just hang up. But probably he has my number.

"Okay," he says. "No problem. She can be there in half an hour. Is this the number you'd like to use?"

Now I can say no. But I wonder what she looks like. "Yeah … uh … This is okay," I mutter.

"She'll call you when she's outside your hotel, okay? Then you can give her your room number."

I hesitate. "How do I …?"

"Cash only. And, ma'am—you're gonna want a whole lot of cash, 'cause you're gonna have a really good time tonight. Okay?"

"Yeah," I sigh.

"Thanks for calling us, ma'am. You have a nice night."

Shit! I press my nose into Joey's soft neck. I can't believe I just did that. How much money do I have? Twenty-seven dollars and thirty-four cents. Well, I'd better go get the cash. These people will kill me if I don't pay. In the blazing light of a convenience store, I withdraw three hundred dollars. That ought to do it. All I want to do is talk, and if she doesn't show, I can spend it slowly. As I push open my door, my purse vibrates and glows. Oh, no! Not already!

"H'lo?"

"Hi. Ju called?" She speaks English words made of Spanish sounds.

"Yeah. I'm in 393."

"Okay. I'll be right up."

I count my breaths along with the bedspread's purple squares. Fifteen. Sixteen. The stairs clang under her heels. Seventeen. She knocks softly.

When I open the door, I breathe spicy perfume, and my eyes dance among reflected lights. Before me stands a sturdy Mexican woman in a halter top of copper sequins. Without her three-inch heels, she'd be shorter than I am, but with them, her eyes are level with mine. She fills her hot pants and flashing top admirably, although she isn't fat. Her bare brown arms look powerful, thick like her legs. She wears her hair in a ponytail that hangs to her waist. Her rounded lips glisten with gloss, and her eyelids shine with copper shadow.

"Hi," she says. "What a nice … animal."

I realize I'm holding Joey on my hip.

"Hola. ¿Cómo te llamas?"

"Maribel." Her pink lips catch the light.

"Pasa, pasa." I smile, waving her in.

Her eyes sweep the mottled bedspread and pale dresser and return to the bear. I hand him to her, and she sits on the bed, cradling Joey's back between her copper breasts.

"¡Qué suavecito!"

"Sí. Lo quiero mucho. Se llama Joey."

Maribel looks me up and down and rubs her chin against Joey's head. I feel like I'm being studied by a troubled totem pole.

"¿Qué te pasó? ¿Algún bato te hizo eso?" She frowns at the red scrapes on my legs.

"No. I fell."

"Oh ... Your first time with a woman?"

Her perfume floats in a cinnamon wave.

"Yeah," I whisper. "How did you know?"

"It's how you—es como te pones. ¿Nerviosa? You don't have to be. I am always happy when it's a woman."

I settle beside her, checking where I put each part of my body so that I won't look nervous.

"Women don't hurt you. They like to talk. Men are different."

"Mm ..." I stroke Joey's shoulder.

Maribel glances at her tiny silver phone. "So this is your first time?" She bites her lip. "Maybe you like me show you some nice things to do?"

I nod, not trusting my voice.

"First you pay, huh? Two hundred dollars."

I lay all six fifties on the dresser and secure them with a half-filled water bottle.

"Good." She smiles.

I can't take my eyes off those shiny pink lips. She sets Joey on the bed, lowers the air-conditioning, and snaps off all the lights but one.

"Ven. Levántate," she whispers and nudges me toward the mirror. "What a beautiful dress! ¡Qué bonito collar! ¡Qué chula estás!" She runs her hands over the indigo curves, caressing the small of my back.

"You want to try it on?"

She laughs. "It is too small. Look."

In the mirror, my body is half the width of hers. She pushes up under her breasts so that the sequins flash. Her reflection runs its hands over my virtual breasts, along my waist, and out over my hips.

"¡Estás chulísima! ¡Y qué bonito pelo!" She strokes her hand over my hair. "Oye—¿tienes un cepillo?"

I give her my brush, and with gentle strokes, she works it through my loose hair. I try to undo her ponytail, but she deflects my hands, and I see it's been lacquered with hair spray. She runs her forefinger all the way around my necklace, then bends to kiss my neck. I writhe. Her hands return to my breasts.

"You like it, eh? You should be with a woman before. I can tell. You are a woman who likes women."

Her hand catches my zipper and creeps down my back. The dress falls softly to the floor.

"Could you take off your top?" I whisper.

With a jingle, a copper heap lands beside my dress, a pirate's treasure next to a blue pool. In the golden light, her brown-tipped breasts look like marzipan garnished with chocolate. Unable to resist, I lean forward to kiss them. They tauten under my lips, and she laughs prettily.

"Ven." She pulls me toward the bed. "Ven." She pushes me down, taking care not to mash Joey. Her lips feel even more delicious than they look, and before she's done, they have visited each part of me.

CHAPTER 10

SANTA MONICA

Scratchy fuzz tickles my belly. Nuzzling fur, I make a low sound. Where ...? Who ...? I don't remember Maribel leaving, but she must have tucked me in next to my bear. I reach for my watch. 10:06! What a scandal! On the dresser, my necklace anchors two dry fifty-dollar bills. My blue dress hangs folded over a chair, rippling in the current from the air conditioner.

Leaving Las Vegas proves easier than entering it: pull out of the lot, keep left, and I'm on I-15 South. In the morning sun, the pastel desert glistens, its yellow grass and green shrubs reaching up. Even the bare, distant mountains glow with the pink of Maribel's lips. I hadn't realized they would feel so much better than a man's—so much softer, wetter, lighter. What would Johnny think if he knew? Probably just one more piece of evidence that I'm crazy. The road shimmers into silvery waves. I wonder what Fischer would say. He grins, shakes his head, and likes me better. And I thought— Well, I guess there's one woman I don't hate. A smile warms the curve of my belly.

How different Maribel is from Teresa! So much a girl, so eager to please. I see Teresa standing, tough, dark, and solid. Maribel's sequins flash through Teresa's image, but they only feed her glow. Teresa's troubled face reflects the desert light, and gleams fly over the hardened sand.

A quick swish jolts me. This highway may look surreal, but it's no place to dream. Cars are leaping between lanes. The state line must be coming soon, since lonely cubes are rising, last-chance casinos in the desert. When I pass the sign "Welcome to California," I thrust my fist in the air and scream. Tears roll down my cheeks, and I squeeze my eyes dry. I am in the same state as Johnny Turner.

I last invaded California four years ago. No conference that time—I flew out for spring break. Of course, I couldn't say I had come to see Johnny. I told him I had a meeting at Berkeley. I reached the med center an hour early and drank green tea in the union. With ten minutes to go, I rode up to his lab. "Go see his secretary," said a student in clipped Indian tones. In Johnny's new warren, his secretary formed the first line of defense. There she sat, a thin, brown-haired woman with a nervous smile. Behind her, a closed door said "John R. Turner."

"Are you Carrie?" she asked.

"Yeah," I answered. "I used to work here. I'm a friend of Johnny's."

The secretary studied me reservedly. "You're the one who wrote that book, right—*The Rainbow Bar*?"

"Yeah, that was me," I murmured.

"I loved that!" she exclaimed. "It was so sad. I read the copy you sent him. We all did. It went all around the lab."

"Even—" I glanced toward the closed door.

"Oh, you know him." She laughed. "He's always so busy. But he was touched that you sent it. He really was."

Her brown eyes shifted guiltily toward her top drawer, and she pulled out a folded note.

"He told me to give you this."

Her eyes burned my face as I read.

"Hi, Carrie," said cavorting letters. "Sorry to miss you. Big mess at Berkeley. Would have loved to see you, but it's something only I can fix. Hope the writing's going well. Catch up with you soon. Johnny."

His signature was a loopy scrawl. I couldn't talk since I didn't want her to see me cry.

"He really was sorry he couldn't see you," she said. "You came all the way from Atlanta?"

"Oh, no, I had a meeting at Berkeley. I just came over because I had free time today."

"Well, maybe you can catch up with him there," she assured me, her dark eyes moist with sympathy.

All the rest of that day I walked—across the park, past the Russian cathedral with its gold ice-cream dome. I trudged all the way out to the Cliff House, where seals yelped and the wind blasted my hair. Then I called Gonzalo and cried for an hour, and he said that Johnny was a gilipollas de mierda.

I blink. Desert signs are warning me that I'm sinking. Six thousand feet. Five thousand. Three thousand. Around me, the cars seem to smell the sea. They charge like parched horses, ignoring the lanes. The radio offers a feast of music, thumping rappers and wailing Mexicans. No preachers, though. I miss the preachers. Like a dusty wind, they stay east of the Rockies. Two thousand feet. One thousand feet. In San Bernardino, I climb last-chance snowcapped mountains. Three lanes multiply into twelve, and slim towers poke through the blue haze.

As I approach downtown, the traffic thickens until Wilma can only creep. She shudders as we pass a line of crushed cars. A distraught woman strokes her red SUV, as though wondering how her only friend has turned to crumpled metal. I glance at Joey, but he's staring down to avoid the traumatic sight. A silver car lies upside down in the median, its confused tires facing the gray sky.

Though it's nearly five, the pace quickens. All the cars are pushing toward the sea. I follow I-10 until it empties onto Santa Monica Boulevard. Once I settle Wilma at the Run-Rite Inn, I vow not to move her until I leave town. After the fire of Las Vegas, the ocean air makes me shiver. I root through my suitcase and choose blue leggings, my Day of the Dead T-shirt, and a lavender jacket. I take the first bus to the pier.

On one side of the bridge, people are filing seaward; on the other, back to their cars. I join the outbound ant trail, stepping down into traffic to pass slow-moving bodies. Far out on the pier, a man sings "Desperado," and a black-haired toddler lurches toward his scuffed open case. In her fists she is holding a crumpled dollar, which she crushes and tautens like an accordion. An Indonesian woman guides her blind daughter, who smiles into a sunny void. Near some Peruvian singers, a man who looks like their cousin fondles his son and bounces him to their chords. The force of life here charges me so intensely I could soar to the horizon in a trail of fire. With blazing steps, I walk until there is nothing before me but blue.

＊ ＊ ＊ ＊

Snick!

Terrible sound.

Snick! Snick!

On the white floor lies a question mark of black hair.

"No!" I scream, but my mother is relentless.

"It has to come off," she says.

Already one side of my head feels lighter, and black tresses lie like murdered crows.

Snick! The scissors take another bite. I grab for them, but I'm tiny, and she's huge.

"It has to come off," she repeats in a deadly voice.

I writhe in her grip, but I can't wrench myself free. She doesn't stop until I look like I'm in the last stages of chemotherapy.

The air conditioner shudders and groans, and I raise my hand to my head. Still there, heavy and smooth. I am slick with sweat, so I flap the sheets to dry myself. God! I haven't had that dream in a while. With my right hand, I gather my hair. I clench it protectively and slide my fist all the way down to the soft, free-floating ends.

Today I would pass Dr. Kyle's test with no trouble. It is Sunday, May 29, and I'll be in San Francisco tomorrow night. Picturing myself on the beach, I pull on my turquoise bikini top and a little skirt that trembles with each move. At the last minute, I add my Santa Fe necklace and am pleased with the result. My eyes sparkle blue and green, and my body glows with energy. After a large tea and some cereal with banana, the sentences boil up. I sit down in a bookstore café with the same relief as if I were settling on a toilet.

I have to decide now what to tell Raúl. I liked it better when I could tell him everything. With his night job, he doesn't get home until late, and with his dinner, he likes to hear stories about la vieja y el gordo. The one about Cathy made him choke on his rice.

"¿Perdió diez mil pesos—así, no más—de un chingadazo?" he spluttered.

"Well, at least she looks good," I said.

"Poor guy." He shook his head. "Must be a real loser if he can't make it with a woman that dumb. They made bets? I would never put money on him." He took a forkful of beans and chewed them thoughtfully. "Pobre gordo. He's got to get some sometime. Maybe we could fix him up with Juana."

Juana got fat when Diego left her, or maybe he left her because she got fat. She has bristles on her chin and works nights cleaning stores, and people always talk about fixing her up.

Last night, I even told Raúl about Mrs. Marshall's black bra and how she raged when I tried it on. He made me show him my breasts to make sure she hadn't hurt them. Even though he was eating, he kissed them to make them better, and we never finished dinner. He said that if that gringa de mierda ever hurt me, he would put her in the cemetery where she belonged. As soon as he could, he would buy me a black bra more beautiful than any she ever owned.

Every night now he wants it, no matter how long he's worked, and he keeps talking about a baby. I think we should wait until we have a house, but he says if you think like that, you put it off until you're forty, like the gringos.

When I told him how we danced, I described it all except the end. In my version, Justin danced with his mother while I washed the dishes. I don't know what Raúl would do if he knew Justin touched me—kill him definitely. Maybe kill us both.

The day after the bra, Mrs. Marshall acts so strange that even Justin notices. When I come in, she creeps behind him and won't say hello.

"Here's Teresa, Mom!" He beams.

"No!"

"Don't you want to stay with Teresa?" He fumbles to button his coat.

Since I've been cooking for them, Justin has gotten even fatter. I haven't told Raúl about that either.

Glaring at me, Mrs. Marshall hisses, "She steals things! She steals!"

Justin smiles apologetically and shakes his head. "I don't know what's gotten into her today. She keeps saying that."

"She steals!"

"Well, Mom, as soon as I get home, I'll check to make sure everything's here. Does that sound okay?"

"No!"

Justin ducks out, still shaking his head.

It is one of the worst days we've ever had. In the book room, she asks to go to the bathroom, but when I take her, nothing comes out. We drift back, and on the bottom shelf I find her science book *with the gumdrop pictures. I take* Indians of North America *and reach for a spiral notebook.*

"I have to go to the bathroom!"

"But you were just there! You didn't have to go!"

"I have to go!" Mrs. Marshall glowers.

I lead her back, pull down her pants, and help her settle before returning to the book room. On my plush chair, I fall into the spring of '65.

Oh, God, which one? Which one? Maybe it's just late. I've been working so hard lately, who knows? Last one started on the 17th, so the midpoint would be the 31st. What was I doing that day? The prep. Always the prep. We're so close to getting the vesicles pure. Bill's been liking it in the mornings now since he's so tired at night. Jimmy never gets tired. Christ, which one? It's pretty—

A puff of damp breath tickles my neck. Mrs. Marshall has shuffled in silently. She's dragging a streamer of troubled white paper, and her pants are wadded around her shins.

"Did it come out this time?" I ask.

"No."

I grasp her bony hand and pull her back to the bathroom. Once I've got her seated, I coil the paper around my wrist. She laughs as she watches, and I wish I could smack her.

"You keep trying," I say. "I'm going to be right outside."

I run back to 1965. No sound floats from the bathroom as I flip through to find my place.

Christ, which one? It's awful, these two guys playing roulette with my eggs. I'm sure I'm not the first woman this has happened to. Probably it's Bill's—if there is an "it" and I'm not just late. All that earnest squeezing seems like the

kind of thing that would make a baby. Most of the stuff I do with Jimmy can't get you pregnant anyway. Sometimes he wants it normal, though, and he can't stand condoms. Says it's like taking a shower in scuba gear.

From the bathroom comes a wet plop. I turn the page.

Good thing about working in a medical center, you can see a doctor fast, just slip out and be back to take down your spin. I even did it twice, once for the test and once for the results.

"Congratulations, Mrs. Marshall!" The obstetrician beamed, warming my hand between both of his. Behind him, the thin nurse looked at me sharply. When I to—

The paper holder rattles.

"Need some help, Mrs. Marshall?"

"No!"

I push open the door and find a coiled white spiral. I tear four sheets off a fresh roll. Probably I should stop leaving paper in the bathroom.

Mrs. Marshall holds the new paper to her nose. "This is dirty!" She tosses it away, and the white squares fall limply to the floor.

I rip off four more sheets and wipe her myself. When I've pulled up her pants and washed both our hands, I lead her back into the book room.

"What's that? You stole that!" She spots the spiral-bound butterfly on my chair.

I snatch the open notebook before she can grab it. "No, no, I was just putting it back."

I sit her down with her science candy and hide the notebook behind the Indians.

When I told Bill, he began to cry. He couldn't say anything, just pressed me close. He clutched me against his shaking chest until he was sure of his voice.

"This is wonderful! Let's go celebrate. Let's celebrate right now!"

Bill ran to the cabinet where we keep plastic glasses to make toasts when people pass their exams. The whole lab stopped work and started drinking champagne, and people drifted in from other groups. When Jimmy came in, his face was white, but he hugged me and shook Bill's hand. With everyone watching, it wasn't—

Boom! The science book falls.

"I don't like this book! I want that one!" Mrs. Marshall aims a drilling finger. I hand her the Indians, and she gazes interestedly at a picture of a Comanche.

It wasn't until the next day that Jimmy got me alone. Gripping my arm, he pulled me into his office.

"Is it his?" he asked.

I looked up at angry black eyes.

"Shit." Jimmy shook his head. "Shit!" He kicked the wall. "You don't know?"

Tears warped my voice, but I was determined to talk. "I hope it's yours. I want to be with you, not him."

"What do you want? You want me to marry you?" asked Jimmy bitterly. "You want to divorce him? Are you nuts? You have any idea what that would involve?"

He studied my wet face and lowered his voice. "So you really don't know? I mean, count the days. You're pretty regular, right?"

Sobs washed away my response.

"Aw, c'mere." *He sighed and wrapped his arms around me. "It's okay. So you really don't know, huh? Too bad we don't look more alike." His chest shook under my cheek. "I'm not ready for a kid, Sandy. I don't want to get married. I'm not ready ..." He glanced toward his desk.*

His warm shirt drank the wetness.

"If we knew it were mine, I'd help you get rid of it. But you told everybody ... Why did you do that? Why didn't you tell me first?"

I couldn't say. Just wasn't thinking, I guess.

Jimmy gave me a tissue and tried to make me laugh.

"Least if it's tall, we can say it takes after you." Jimmy chuckled.

It's easy for him to laugh, easy for him to say he's not ready. He has a choice. I'm the one who's going to get fat and spend my days changing diapers. And who's going to run the prep now?

"I want THAT book!" Mrs. Marshall points—

Brrrp. Brrrp. Brrrp. Doo-doo-doo-DEE-doo!

Oh, fuck. Forgot to—

A leather-skinned blonde woman beside me frowns.

Brrrp. Brrrp. Brr—

"H'lo?"

"Hey, Theresa!"

"Oh, hi, Clifton."

The stringy blonde glares up from her journal. With my left hand, I fold the sheet that my words have invaded like ants. Awkwardly I climb off my stool, seeking solid ground.

"Theresa?" Three anxious tenor notes. I hope that wild night didn't get him in trouble.

"Yeah," I mutter. "I was just somewhere I couldn't talk. I'm out on the street now."

"Oh. Where are you?"

"Santa Monica. Third Street Promenade. I'm heading for the beach."

"Wow, what an amazing life you have! I'm just home trying to clean this place up."

I picture Clifton earnestly studying his vacuum's dials.

"You sound happy, though." I smile. "How did it go yesterday?"

Clifton hesitates. "Oh, yesterday I was pretty sick. Don't think I'm gonna touch bourbon again for a while."

"Gee, I'm sorry."

The sweet burn of popcorn invades my nose, and I glance around for the source.

"Yeah, it was all your fault." Clifton laughs. "No, I'm okay, really. Spent most of yesterday hunting for Turtles. And Twinkies—and bourbon. Had to replace everything. Started feeling better toward the end of the day."

There it is. Pop Heaven: 37 Flavors.

"Theresa," says Clifton, "I'm calling 'cause I've got great news. I bought my ticket. I'm coming to San Francisco on Tuesday ... Theresa?"

"Yeah ..." Oh, shit. Now what? I quicken my pace.

"You don't sound happy. Don't you want me to come?"

"Yeah—yeah," I murmur. "I just didn't think you were going to."

Spirals of copper pull my eyes to a veil top glittering in a shop window.

Today Clifton has no trouble finding his words. "Well, I may have been drunk, but the way I feel about you, I'm dead serious. I meant what I said—didn't you?"

"Yeah …" I frown. "But we should talk about this."

Traffic is blocking the last street between me and the ocean.

"Okay … Okay …" Clifton sighs. "Let's talk. I've got time."

A bus whips past just feet in front of me, creating a suspension of air and grit.

"Clifton? … Well, what about Karen? Have you talked with her about this?"

"She's fine," answers Clifton steadily. "She's forgiven me for that phone call. I just broke a rule, that's all. Everything's okay again now."

Clifton's resolve bothers me. He can't be this calm. "How did she take it when you said you were going to San Francisco?"

"Haven't told her yet." I sense a guilty smile.

"Clifton! You're leaving in two days!"

Finally he breaks, and his angst relieves me. "What are you saying? Don't you want me to come? If you don't, just go ahead and say it!"

I cross to a grassy promenade, which is littered with sprawled-out bodies.

"No—no—I do. It's just—you haven't done this before, have you?"

"No."

Even this early, the Ferris wheel is turning, and insect arms are waving against the gray sky.

"You have to think of everything that could happen," I warn. "I mean, come on. Some woman calls your house. A week later, you take off for San Francisco. If you were her, wouldn't you be suspicious?"

"Yeah, I guess so …" His voice shrugs with his shoulders.

A grizzled man on the grass inspects the underside of my skirt. Clifton hesitates, then regains his confidence.

"Well … there's no proof. I'll just tell her that it's work and she shouldn't worry, and she'll believe me. Besides … who would want to have an affair with me?"

In the hollow behind my pubic bone, I know that Clifton can't do this. If he does, his dense world will explode.

"I doubt if she thinks that," I say. "You have to think about this. When you're back, you'll have all these pictures in your head. How good an actor are you? Can you act the same way as before?"

"I dunno." He chuckles. "Probably. Probably I can do it."

This is no good. I can't let him do this.

"What about the worst-case scenario?" I ask. "Let's say she finds out. What would she do? Would she leave you? If she divorced you, she could get full custody, take the kids. You seem like you like your kids."

"I do!" he cries. "This is crazy! She's not going to find out! Why are you saying these things?"

I head down a cement stairway that reeks of urine and step around a dark, sticky pool.

"It's just that you have to think of everything before you do this," I say. "When there are kids—even if you don't split up—there could be fights. Think what it could do …"

I picture a black-haired girl sitting on a faded porch. Chin on her fists, she stares at her scuffed-up sneakers.

"Why are you telling me this?" demands Clifton. "If you feel this way, why didn't you say so before, as soon as I said I was married? Why have you kept calling me?"

The little girl looks up with frightened eyes.

"Because—because talking on the phone is different from what you're about to do."

At a corn dog joint, a generous sign offers burgers, fries, onion rings, tacos, burritos, and tamales. Clifton's voice returns with the inherent sympathy I heard on the first day.

"Theresa—look. I understand what you're doing. You just don't want me to get hurt, right? Or my family either. You're a good person."

I hesitate, my throat swelling. "I'm just saying, not every guy can do what you want to do—be with one woman and go back to another. It could make you unhappy, keeping that to yourself—and if you melt down, it could hurt a lot of people."

Clifton has the fearlessness of the inexperienced. "I can do it. Theresa—no woman has ever talked to me the way you did the other night. I—I've only been with one other woman besides Karen. And neither one of them— Since the kids came, she's— I can't say this. She's stopped— We don't— Oh, you know what I mean. It's like being dead. I don't want to live like this for the rest of my life. I guess I thought it was okay until I saw you. I have to know what it's like to be with you."

I peel off my sandals and step onto the sand, avoiding pebbles and sharp spikes of wood. I dig with my toes and move toward the water. My voice rises and dips with the waves.

"You're nice, Clifton … I—I'm not such a good person. But you're right. I don't want to hurt you … or your kids."

The horizon blurs.

"Oh, don't cry, Theresa. God, I can't wait to be there to hold you. Where are you now?"

"On the beach." I sniff. "It's so beautiful ... but empty. There's no one here but me ... Oh, wow, look at this seaweed! Looks just like a Purkinje cell."

I laugh through my tears.

"A what?"

"A Purkinje cell. In the brain. A big, fat cell with a whole bunch of dendrites hanging off it. Looks like a round, dark head with a giant 'fro."

Confusion breaks Clifton's focus. "What ... brain cells?"

I breathe the cool, salty air. "Yeah. I used to study science. A long time ago. I worked in this lab in San Francisco."

Clifton's voice darkens. "So that's how you got to know that guy, isn't it? He's a scientist? Is he still working out there?"

"Yeah ..." I move onto firmer sand, where the ground throws me forward with each step.

"Theresa, you've got to promise me something," says Clifton.

"Yeah? Oooh—" An icy wave bubbles over my feet.

Clifton pushes on as though he hadn't heard. "Theresa—promise me you won't see that guy till I get there. Promise me you won't. I have a bad feeling about him."

"He's the nicest guy in the world!"

"No, he's not," he says, and I sense what's coming. Every guy is wrong for me except Clifton Bowles.

"How do you know?" I demand.

"Because anyone who makes you feel that way—he can't be nice. Please promise me. You can still see him. I know that's why you're going out there—but not till I see you face-to-face."

"Okay." I sigh, moved by his quiet force.

"Yeah?" He brightens. "'Cause ... I don't know, maybe he's great looking, maybe he's some genius or something, but I can be good to you. I have this feeling—like you've been hurt. It's that guy, but it's something else too. I want to help. Get to know you ... make you happy. I don't want to just do this and then forget it. If we have a good time ... maybe I could see you in Atlanta. It's only a two-hour drive."

"Wow, you've really thought about this!"

The thought of Clifton planning our lives makes me feel like a soulless object. As if I were some park, some airy place to visit.

"I can't stop thinking about you," he whispers. "I think I love you."

I stare at the line between the ocean and sky. How can it be so sharp when they're both gray?

"Theresa?" he asks. "Are you all right, Theresa? You're not upset—that I said that?"

"No, no ..." I murmur. "It's just so crazy ... You don't even know me."

"I will very soon," he says. "I want to so much. Just tell me now—where are you staying?"

The sand has swallowed my feet.

"The Van Ness Motel," I say. "Six blocks south of Ghirardelli Square."

"Oh, good. Now we're talkin'." He sighs. "It should take me an hour or two to get there, and my flight gets in around noon. You lived there—how long will it take?"

"Better say two hours." I move toward firmer sand.

"Okay. See you at two o'clock, on the thirty-first, at the Van Ness Motel. I'll call you when I get there, and you can tell me your room. Okay?"

"Yeah." I scan the vacant beach ahead of me. What has happened to Venice?

"This is going to be good," he murmurs. "This is going to be so good. You won't regret it. I swear."

"Yeah ..." His clean-cotton embrace warms me.

"Now I better go throw some cold water on myself, so I can get through this afternoon." He chuckles. "Theresa ... since you're so experienced—you know how I can tell Karen?"

I grimace. "I would just tell her straight out, soon as she gets home. And tell it ... like it's already decided, not something negotiable."

"Yeah ..." Clifton hesitates. "This isn't going to be easy ... but it'll be worth it. If it's anything like that taste you gave me the other night ..."

A seagull cries that he's master of the air.

"It'll be better."

"Wow, I don't think cold water's gonna work. I better try the ice machine."

"Okay. Whatever works. See you in San Francisco."

"See you in San Francisco ... I love you, Theresa."

When Clifton's voice vanishes, I feel like a tiny speck. All that sand, all that water, all that sky ... I point my toes and slide a ballerina foot over rubbery brown kelp. A burst of sand fleas scurry for cover. Since I'm approaching Venice, I head onto soft sand, which encrusts my feet like unwanted love. There's no tap to wash them, so I rub them with Kleenex. I wince as sand grinds between my toes.

On the lively street, music pulses in the bikini shops and people with sunglasses sip juice in bright cafés. I sit down at a smoothie bar with gouged wooden counters and plug my ears against the blenders' roar.

"I want THAT book!" Mrs. Marshall points her skinny finger at me like a gun.

I have no choice but to give her the notebook, and for the rest of the day, she grips it like a saint holding on to her faith. I offer her magazines, but as she eyes the pictures, she clutches the notebook until her knuckles look like knobs on a conch. At lunch, she grasps the notebook in one hand and tries to eat with the other. She says she doesn't have to go to the bathroom, but when I take her, she looks relieved. I reach for the notebook.

"No!" she screams. "That's mine!"

"But, Mrs. Marshall, you could get it all dirty."

"No! You want to steal it!"

I pry her fingers loose, and with her free fist, she belts me on the ear. The world rings on a high-pitched note.

"¡Ay! ¡Gringa de mierda! ¡Pues no me eches la culpa si tu pinche diario se llena de mierda!"

The diary remains pure since she calls me back to wipe her and pull up her pants. Late in the day she asks to lie down, so that when Justin comes home, I greet him alone.

"Hey, Teresa. Where's Mom?" His thick blond brows gather with concern.

"She was tired. She wanted to rest."

"Hmmm." He frowns. "She never did that before."

"I thought it was strange, but it's what she wanted."

"Okay. I'd better go check on her."

While Justin is upstairs, I choose lettuce and tomato from the refrigerator.

"Oh, you don't need to do that," he says. "She's asleep. You don't have to stay here. I can fend for myself."

Under my fingers, the lettuce is wet and cool, with hidden drops lurking in its crisp valleys.

"That's okay," I say. "I like to be here. Raúl won't be home until ten. I don't like to be alone."

Bottles clink in the door as Justin pulls a beer from the refrigerator. He settles at the kitchen table and breathes out in a slow sigh. I pour a clear pool of oil into a black pan, and his eyes tickle my neck.

"What are you making there?"

"Enchiladas."

I turn to him and smile. Under the bright light, Justin is red-faced and golden, but his eyes are almost black.

"Why are you looking at me like that?" His round face tightens with amusement.

My skin is searing hot. "Oh, sorry. I didn't mean ..."

"No, no, it's okay. I guess I'm just not used to people looking at me."

Justin takes a big swallow of beer. I run my fingers over the soft tomato and brush it aside in a wet heap. Under my hair, my ear feels swollen and sore. I lean forward to tear off a lettuce leaf, and his eyes pierce like two lights behind a dark curtain.

"So what did you guys do today? You do anything that might have worn her out? I don't like this sleeping. I'm worried about her."

"No, we just read. She was in a bad mood. She got mad when I took her to the bathroom."

Justin shrugs. "Nothing new about that." He gulps his beer and goes for another. "So what are you doing now?" He sidles over to inspect.

"Oh, just making the sauce."

"It has chocolate in it?" He dips in a plump finger and sucks it.

"¡Quita!" I push him back, and he returns to his table, embarrassed.

"I just wish I knew what to do for her," he says. "I don't know what's best. I want her to be happy. At work they keep telling me to put her in a home. So that I can have a social life. They tell me I'm crazy, keeping her here like this." His dark eyes plead for comfort.

"She's happy here with you," I say. "She took care of you; now you take care of her."

"Yeah, that's what I think." Justin sighs. "I just wish they would stop laughing at me. This thing with Cathy—you know they transferred her? To another part of the company—where there's not as much money involved. I'm going to miss her. I kind of liked her." Justin brings his finger back to his lips.

"I'm sorry."

"I just wish I knew what's best for my mom. I don't know how much time she has left. I want her to feel good—at least, as much as she can. She's never been happy."

"That's too bad." Can it be true? Such a beautiful woman, such an easy life. But when I look at Justin, I can believe it. I don't think he's ever been happy either.

"Are you sure she didn't do anything special today?" he asks.

I drop two tortillas in the oil to fry. Cheerful bubbles nibble at the edges.

"Well, she did ask— Does she ever talk to you about a guy named Jimmy?"

Justin frowns. "She never used to, but she has lately. I think he used to work with my father. I never met him."

I look up from the sizzling tortillas and seek Justin's eyes. "You know what happened to him?"

"No. Probably he got another job somewhere. People move around so much in science."

I scoop up the tortillas and replace them with two more. I fill the first with chicken while the others fry.

"Boy, that smells good." Justin smiles with anticipation.

"These people at work—es gente mala," I say. "Bad people. You shouldn't listen to them. Family comes first. It is good you take care of your mother."

Justin's soul seems to open and spread. "I hope you're right," he murmurs. "I just hope I—we—are taking good care of her."

I arrange the tortillas on a plate, angling them like tiles on a roof. I form a bright flower of lettuce and tomato, then cover them with thick, warm sauce.

"Oh, Teresa," sighs Justin. "This is wonderful. But I can't sit here eating while you cook."

"No, it's okay," I say. "This is how we always do it. They'll get cold. You've been working."

Justin shakes his head. "You've been working too. Here, I'll wait. Make some for yourself. I'm not going to eat until you do."

I hurry to fix myself a plate, then turn off the oil on the stove. When I come to the table, Justin is hungrily smelling the sauce, but he hasn't touched his food. His bottle of beer is almost empty.

"Can I get you another beer?"

"Oh, sure ... but—no—you shouldn't do that."

He smiles as I put it in his clean pink hand. Not until I'm sitting does he touch the enchiladas.

"Oh—oh my, this is amazing." Justin is awed by the taste, as though meeting a new love for the first time. "So you think she'd like it if we found this Jimmy? I mean, I could ask at the medical school."

"I don't know," I murmur. The sauce is rich on my tongue, much better than it tastes at home.

Justin's face reddens as he eats. "I can try finding him if you think she'd like it."

"Okay." I nod. I'd like to meet Jimmy.

"Teresa," Justin says with a smile, "thanks for being so nice to her. And to me. It means a lot to both of us."

"Thanks." I flush. "I like to be here."

With his second and third platefuls, Justin is less polite. Since I'm full, he lets me cook while he eats until the chicken and mole are all gone.

"God, that's good," he sighs. "But let me help you clean up." He rises, though I can tell he doesn't want to move.

"Oh, no, that's okay." I smile and reach for his empty plate. Against the blue flowers, the smear of mole reminds me of the bathroom floor.

"No—no," says Justin. "I can't sit here while you work. I feel ashamed."

I rinse the dishes while Justin dries and stows them, but he's used to working alone and keeps bumping me.

"Sorry!" He brushes me as he turns toward the sink. "Teresa—what's wrong with your ear?"

My face burns. "Oh, nothing. I woke up with it this way. Probably I was squashing it while I was asleep."

Justin sets down a plate and lifts my hair with his hands, comparing my ears on both sides.

"No! It's really swollen. Teresa—a pillow couldn't do this." He stands there solidly, his thick hands full of my hair.

"Teresa—put that down. Come over here." He leads me to the table. "Sit down. If Raúl—or someone—is hurting you, there are things you can do. You can go to the police. You could go away somewhere. I—I'll help you. Teresa, I don't want anything bad to happen to you."

"He's not hurting me." I study the taut white threads that hold my jeans together.

"Teresa—first your face, and now your ear?"

"It wasn't him."

I raise my eyes, and he takes my hands. "Please—I don't want you to get hurt. You don't deserve it. Leave him! You could—you could stay here with me until you find another place. You'd be safe with me."

"No—you don't understand!" I clench his hands tighter when I should push them away.

"What don't I understand? Please—let me help you!"

His blond hair shines over his anguished face.

"Raúl and I—" I falter. How can I make him see? "We're not like you. We're good together. I like to be with him. We're different from you."

"I know," he says. "But that doesn't give him the right—"

"He just gets angry if he thinks I don't respect him. If I think of another man. If I talk about him to other people."

Justin's golden brows wrinkle. "But you have a right—"

"A man and a woman must respect each other," I say, marking the beat with our clasped hands. "If they are going to have kids— she mustn't think of another man."

"But does he respect you?" asks Justin.

"Yes." I nod fiercely. "Very much. I mustn't think—"

"Teresa ..." Justin's voice fades. "Are you ..."

"No. Not yet. But soon—maybe."

His dark eyes soften, and I sense he understands. "I bet you'll be a wonderful mother."

"You think so?"

"Mm-hmm." Justin releases my hands. "I'm sorry. I just want to help. I know we're different. But I want to help you."

"I know. You're such a nice person."

Justin shakes his head. "Okay. Let's get back to work here." He pushes himself to his feet. We clean and wipe the dishes in silence, and when we bump each other, we just smile.

"Teresa?" asks Justin. "He doesn't—Raúl doesn't think you're thinking about me, does he? Because—I would hate—"

A knife slips from my grasp into warm suds.

"No, no, not you." I shake my head.

"Oh, good. You didn't tell him—" His lips are so round for a man's.

"No, no. Never."

"Oh, good ... Because I would never ..."

His warm hand brushes my arm. My shoulder. He pulls me close. His lips are soft like a woman's, and this time I don't push him back.

"Teresa ..." He presses me against him and strokes my hair. He doesn't touch me like a man—grabbing, pulling. His body feels so good, so warm and full, that my arms can't push him away.

"Teresa ..." Justin's hand slides over my hair. He kisses me again.

Oh—that felt like a man. I break away.

"Oh—I didn't mean—" Justin's eyes are black with fear.

"I know. But I have to go home now. I don't want there to be things I can't tell him."

Justin nods. "But you know you can stay here. I promise—I won't do anything. We have so much room ..."

"Thanks. But I have to go now."

Justin watches anxiously as I pull on my jacket. "You're sure you're all right?"

"Yes."

"Okay." He smiles weakly. "See you tomorrow?"

"Yes."

"Good night, Teresa. You be careful."

"Yes. Good night."

The rasp of a blender scours away Teresa's footsteps. My eyes stray to "Sarah and Mohammed" chiseled into the wooden counter. I rub my neck and gaze out at the street, wondering what time it must be. Outside the window, a blond boy with Rasta braids pushes an Asian girl, and she pretends to kick his crotch. I finger the bikini bow under my hair but feel no smooth metal. My turquoise necklace is gone.

With my heart thudding, I scan the counter. I lift my word-encrusted sheets. Nothing. I climb off the stool and grope the dusty floor. In my triangles of cloth, I feel naked.

"Did you lose something, ma'am? A contact lens? Can I help you find something?"

Over me stands the greasy teenager who minds the shop. The way he's cocking his head, he must have been studying me for some time.

"Oh—yeah—thanks. My necklace. I can't find my necklace."

"Is it valuable?" He frowns sympathetically. I wonder when his shiny brown curls last saw shampoo.

"Yeah—well, no. Not really. I just like it."

He shoves the stools aside and joins me on the floor. We find crushed brown napkins, thirteen cents, and a gold stud earring.

"Have you been on the beach?" he asks.

"Yeah."

"Oh. Wow. That's gonna be hard."

I am breathing too fast to think. My necklace is lying like some rare, stunned snake, waiting to be snatched and dangled. The silver ring must have snagged in the loops of my bow. Despite the price, the blue band had only one hopeful hook, not a determined clasp.

I stand, and the world turns to gray mush. Something firm grasps my arm. The last thing I remember eating was that cereal, and it must be close to three. Although I've been in a smoothie joint, I never got around to ordering.

"Hey, are you all right?" Over his bumpy nose, the boy's hazel eyes radiate warmth.

"Yeah. Just hungry."

The list of smoothies fills a wall like hieroglyphics on an Egyptian tomb. The letters dance as I read: Mango Madness, Berry Beautiful, River of Raspberry.

"Uh ... can I get a smoothie? I'll take an Orange-utan—a small."

"Okay. Comin' right up."

The mop-haired teenager pours orange juice, ice, and white goop into a blender, which assaults my ears like a cement cutter. My hands shake as I reach for my wallet. Maybe the necklace fell into my purse. I rifle it as though stirring a stew, then empty it onto the counter. No silver. With the boy's eyes warming me, I inspect my clothes. I check both turquoise cups, pull my skirt out in front of me, and jump up and down. Nothing falls.

"Hope you find it. Maybe you'll get lucky." He smiles and hands me a green-striped cup.

The orange goop is so delicious I suck like a famished bug drained by a long flight. By now more people have gathered on the street, and as I scan the sidewalk, each becomes a potential suspect. I try to retrace my steps, but the sand has swallowed them. I search my brain for subliminal memories. When was the last time I felt metal against my neck? Did I sense it slipping? Instead of a stealthy slide, I feel Johnny's grip.

"You know, just because you haven't found an antibody this first round, that's no reason to leave science."

"I know," I say. "That's not the reason."

We're in the black-and-brown Japanese restaurant, but neither of us is eating. On my plate, lonely tempura puffs sit like rocks awaiting the tide. Despite all of Johnny's work, he's giving me his full attention—maybe because I'm a problem he has to solve.

"A lot of this is pure luck, you know. You're smarter than half the people here."

"Thanks." I try to suppress my tears.

Johnny's weary smile tells me I'm a foothill in his range of troubles.

"If there's somethin' else you wanna do—you should do it," he says firmly. "Or do you just not know what you wanna do?"

His black eyes seem sympathetic, but his lips curve with amusement. He pats my arm as a tear slips from my eye.

"It's okay," he says. "It's okay. I know. You don't belong here. Anyone can see that. You just don't know yet where you belong. I know how that feels."

Since I can't talk, Johnny takes my hands and squeezes. "Look at me," he says.

I raise my eyes to meet his, dark and steady.

"What do you wanna do? That's what you've gotta ask yourself. You've got the guts to do anything. You've just gotta find out what you want to do, and do it. That's what counts. Now, what do you want to do?"

"I want to write."

That was the first time I ever said that out loud.

"What—like journalism? A science writer?"

"No." A fierce wind rushes through my chest.

"You mean like novels? Short stories?"

"Yeah."

"Gosh—that's different." Johnny grins and shakes his head. "Can you make a livin' doin' that?"

"That's what my mother says." I sigh. "She wants me to do science. I like science—but not like you do."

"Yeah, I know. We're different. But writing's okay. If you wanna write—that's great."

Johnny pokes a blob of tempura, which wobbles, uneasy in its new spot.

"So you're really leavin', huh?"

"Yeah, in a few weeks."

Johnny sighs. Behind his shadowed frown, I think I see regret. That, and a restless curiosity.

"Wow. So what are you gonna do now?"

"Get a job." I shrug. "Maybe work as a lab tech. Take some creative writing classes at Berkeley. It won't cost much, 'cause I have state residency."

Johnny studies my face and frowns skeptically. "Okay." He nods. "That sounds like a plan. But this isn't goin' over so well back home?"

"No. It shouldn't matter. I mean, I'm twenty-four. But I feel like I killed someone."

"Yeah. I know the feelin'."

With little enthusiasm, Johnny bites into his tempura. He was having more fun nudging it across the plate. He chews slowly, his eyes drifting to the far wall.

"What you're doin' takes guts, you know—knowin' what you want and then doin' it. Probably we're both nuts, but I respect you."

He glances at his watch and eats another piece of tempura. "You know, I should probably be gettin' back."

"Oh." My stomach tightens. "You have a gel running?"

"No, but I told Gina I'd help her with her rotation report. She has good hands, but she's missin' the big picture."

"Yeah. I know what you mean." The tempura monoliths stand solid.

"Hey, you wanna take that with you?"

"Nah, not really. But—I'll see you again, right?"

"Why would you wanna hang out with a guy like me?" Johnny grins. "I mean, now that you've made your decision. I like your company, but don't you want a clean break?"

"No—not with you—not with science either. Not with you—not ever!"

Johnny pauses, reined by an unspoken thought. His eyes seek his slender wrist. "Gee—we'll have to hurry. I told Gina I'd be back by nine."

I race after him, and the street dissolves. My eyes are sweeping brown sand.

The awakening wind makes me shake with cold, and I remember why I don't like smoothies. In my right hand, I can no longer feel the fingers. My breasts have shrunk into tight balls of pain, and the white beach looks like Antarctica. With my toe I raise a heap of kelp, hoping for a blue glow. A few sand fleas scuttle out, and I let it flop. A seagull wheels over the breaking waves, and I imagine turquoise dangling from his beak. Since the long, thin shell is tasteless, he drops it in the ocean and glides off after juicier fare.

At the pier, I head up onto soft, dry sand and try to recall how I came. Here a single footstep could bury a necklace. What a waste. Seventy-five dollars—and I had it less than a week. I picture the sunburned blonde artist who saw blue-green eyes when she chose the stones. Relief washes me when my feet hit gray asphalt. Theft troubles me less than oblivion. If the gleaming snake slid off me here, it must have been snatched hours ago. Still, I can't lift my gaze. Squashed fries mark the turf of the corn dog place, and the foul-smelling steps are bare. On the grassy promenade, the pavement is bleached as though freshly scrubbed and dried.

I cross Ocean Boulevard and turn onto Third Street, where a levee of buildings blocks the wind. Like a blind man's cane, my eyes sweep the ground. I avoid collisions only because I see people's feet. At the bookstore, a woman in purple has settled where I wrote this morning. I creep up behind her and scan the space beneath her sturdy, bent legs.

"May I help you?" She twists her veiled bulk.

"Sorry. I lost my necklace. I was sitting here this morning. I was hoping—maybe it might still be here."

"Oh, you poor thing." She groans as she rises. "Why don't you try Information? Maybe somebody turned it in."

"Yeah." My throat tightens.

Instead of going to Information, I head to Fiction to survey the *M*s. Usually I'm right there next to Carson McCullers, but today I find *X-Girl* by Joan McGuiness, a writer I've never heard of.

I approach the tall man in the central island. "Did anyone find a necklace in here this morning?"

"Can you describe it?" He looks at me with guarded blue eyes.

"Turquoise. Alternating blue and green. Silver base."

He disappears and returns with his hand extended, like a butler. "Is this it?"

On the counter he lays a leather-thong necklace with fluffy brown feathers between blue stones.

"Nope. But thanks for looking. Oh—I wanted to ask about a book too."

"Sure. Author or title?" The slim man frowns into the screen.

"Title. *The Rainbow Bar.*"

His long white fingers find the letters slowly. "By Carrie McFadden?"

"Yeah, I think so."

"Yeah. We don't have it here, but I can order it." His blue eyes search me for a wish to buy.

"Oh, no, that's okay. I'm just passing through. Just wanted to see if it's still in print."

He compresses his lips and opens a new window. "Oh, yeah. That came out in 1998. It'll be around for a few more years. Just try any of our stores. They can get it for you."

"Okay. Thanks." I wander back to Fiction.

As my eyes sweep the shelves, Fischer's voice arises. What was it that he said? "Out of print … we'll all be dust." How long before people forget I ever wrote anything? How long before they forget I ever lived?

A sudden vision pulls me from the store: a blue-and-silver S curve on a beige rug. If the necklace opened because of my bikini bow, maybe it fell before I left the hotel. In fifteen minutes I'm at the Run-Rite Inn, but the pale carpet is empty. Joey hangs his head, depressed. The starched brown spread covers the bed like chocolate over an ice-cream bar. I raise it with a jerk but discover no gleam, only clean, silent darkness.

I call the main desk. "Did anyone find a necklace today?"

"No, sorry," answers a Latino voice.

Phone in hand, I catch myself in the mirror: white skin, scrawny shoulders, tire tracks under the eyes. On my legs, the swollen red scrapes look like drawn-out leeches. In two days I'm going to be with Johnny. Is this what he'll see?

Without the necklace, I have no idea what to wear. I throw off my clothes and try everything I've brought. My blue sheath dress is sexy, but San Francisco is cold, and with a jacket over it, I'll look like a flasher. I pull on the skirt I was wearing today, but my legs seem to have been attacked by a grater. If I cover them with leggings, I can only wear tentlike T-shirts. What's the point of a shape no one sees?

With the contents of my suitcase twisted on the rug, I glance at my watch. 6:14. The stores will close in less than two hours. I pull on my blue leggings and Fischer's sweatshirt, and for the first time all day, I feel warm.

When the bus releases me, I rush into a shop, but the clothes match the ones in Las Vegas. If I wore these low-slung jeans and glittering tops in a lab, they would question my sanity. If I wore them in San Francisco, I would freeze. Behind each bright window are shimmering clones. In those shiny veil tops, I disappear. And—and—they seem made for someone else, someone who doesn't grade stories or feed her mother.

With twenty minutes to go, I try a lingerie store, and here I find something I like. The cups of a lacy black bra hold me like custom-spun webs. My heart stomps a flamenco beat as I buy it. When the stores' chain-link gates rattle down, that's all I have, so the trick will be undressing as fast as possible. With the Run-Rite Inn's heater blowing full blast, I fold the clothes I tossed on the rug.

From the bed, Joey's black eyes follow me reproachfully. "I came all this way," he says, "and you haven't even shown me the Pacific Ocean."

CHAPTER 11

SAN FRANCISCO

glide down to the Pacific Coast Highway in a slow-motion parachute drop. At 5:30 a.m. I gave up sleeping, but my dreams have resumed command. Although it isn't yet seven, parked cars are screening the gray ocean. Through a gap I spot surfers balanced on foamy waves. When the road shrinks to two lanes, I pull to the side, liberate Joey, and dart across to the water. I perch him on my head and order him to look outward, so that fuzzy brown legs frame my view of blue gray merging with awakening sky.

"There it is, man. The Pacific Ocean."

Joey bobs in the wind, deeply pleased. Even at this hour, the waves flash a hundred blues, like those pulsing spots in Fischer's eyes. Some are dull gray; others, bright turquoise, hinting at secret currents below. On the surface, the wind carves rippling furrows, and a surfer drops into the foam. Joey watches anxiously until a pink head appears; then my bear tells me that he wants to go on.

In Malibu the sun gains strength, and the water turns a calmer blue. On the hills to my right, millionaire houses monitor me as I cross their ocean views. In my years in California, I never got used to these bare mounds that display every bump and crack. Why won't any trees grow on these naked hills? How strange to see the earth's bare skin without the cover of leaves.

When I reach Oxnard, the land flattens, and I breathe the familiar scent of farms. But the scale is so much greater here! In the East, you can see the bounds of a farm, the proud silo marking its lands. These fields are endless. On two-story wheels, giant sprinklers stalk brown men picking berries. On the radio, a Mexican singer wails a ballad to a throbbing accordion.

It takes me four hours to reach San Luis Obispo on a road that winds through grassy yellow hills. I stop to buy gas and gnaw some tangy beef jerky. With the sun warming my neck, I head for the ocean. The hills cut clean curves against the sky, but from Morro Beach onward, the coast is shrouded. Gray clouds solid as a Persian cat hover between me and the crashing waves.

On the bright eastern hills, brown cows with white blazes stand watch in the tawny grass. Hugging the cliffs, the road curves in twisted ribbons until I feel like Tom Cruise flying his jet upside down. "Slide area, next 60 miles," warns a sign, and I pass stony heaps that the cliffs have vomited. Clinging life holds the pink soil in place, dark-green bushes and tufts of yellow flowers.

As I push north, the blooming plants shift their colors as though I were tilting a kaleidoscope. Orange poppies flutter among lavender stalks and pools of bright pink succulents. At last the sun scares off the gray cat, revealing blue waves smashing black rocks. Like lava, the fields of glowing flowers cascade down to the surf.

Joey has to see this. I pull to the side, but a fierce wind holds the door closed. Its gusts strike me like a hundred fists slamming me from every side. I perch Joey on the hood to take his picture, but he tumbles from the car, nose down. With a shriek I jump after him, but he's only a little bruised, with grass whiskers stuck to his face. I strap him in gently and refuse to stop again until I reach Monterey.

Since it's four o'clock, I should slice north on 101, but I cling stubbornly to the coast. In Santa Cruz, I creep through suburban clog until the traffic crystalizes in a barren valley. On a grassy stretch with a lone farmhouse and tree, the northbound lane freezes solid. On the slope before me glints a necklace of cars. The southbound lane is perfectly free. What the—

Brrrp. Brrrp. Brrrp. Doo-doo-doo-DEE-doo.

Where did I—

Brrrp. Brr—

"H'lo?"

"Hello, Carrie?"

"Yeah?"

"Oh, Carrie, thank God I got you." The female voice is tight with urgency.

"Louise? Have you been trying to reach me?"

"Yes—over and over ..." Her distant voice wavers.

My eyes sweep the surrounding hills, bald except for a few live oaks.

"Well, I've been in kind of a remote area. How is she? How's she doing?"

"Not well. Carrie ..."

Oh, no. Not now. "Yeah?" I murmur.

Louise draws a deep breath. "Carrie, I think this is her time. You've got to come right now. No matter where you are, no matter what you're doing, if you want to see her again, you need to come right now."

The gray convertible in front of me creeps forward. Hesitating, Wilma follows.

"What's happening?" I press the phone to my ear.

"The doctor needs to put her on a respirator, honey. She can hardly breathe. But ... well, you know, she has that do-not-resuscitate order. You know I respect that—I think when it's your time, it's your time. But ... if you could hear her trying to breathe ..."

I remember that sickening rattle, that loose flapping in her throat.

Louise's voice gains momentum. "She may not make it through the night. You've got to come right now. Where are you?"

Lurking in this brown grass, I feel as though I'm in Kansas. "Just south of San Francisco."

"What is it—about seven thirty your time?"

"Yeah ..."

The necklace of cars slides forward as though a child were pulling its unseen end. Next to the house, a lone blue shirt ripples on the line, its arms reaching out in the wind.

"I'm sure there are lots of flights."

"Yeah ..."

"Carrie—I'm sorry. Whatever happened between you and your mom, I know you love her."

"Nothing happened! I've just been doing things. Writing ..."

Louise seems not to hear. "I know she loved you. She must have been proud of you. Having a daughter who writes ..."

My mother's face shimmers into view, her eyes cold, her jaw set. She has that look she used to get when she was going to make me do something, whether I wanted to or not. That glare used to make me want to smash things until it cooled to remote disgust.

"She didn't like my writing," I say. "She never wanted me to write."

Louise remains immovable. "I can't believe that ... Anyway, it doesn't matter now."

On the gray convertible's Nevada plate, a yellow sun rises over snowy hills. Tendrils of blond hair reach out from the driver's orange scarf.

"Honey, if it's any comfort, your mom's not alone. The ladies from my church, we're taking turns, and we're going to watch with her all night."

My voice breaks. "That's—that's good of you. That's really nice."

"I know you love her, honey. I know you'd be here if you could."

I draw a rough, slow breath, absorbing the letters on the Nevada plate. R—U—

"Louise—mothers and daughters don't always love each other. Sometimes they just wish they weren't there."

"You're upset, honey. I know you don't mean that. You'll feel better once you get here."

I rise over a hill and spot a small, gleaming lake. Do its waters mingle with the ocean?

"You know, when you're face-to-face, all those things you fought over seem so small …"

A flash arcs through my chest. "We didn't fight! We just—"

"I know it's hard. But God wants us to live through things like this—so we can help other people with what we learn."

On the water, the sun creates a rippled path leading relentlessly west.

"So I'll tell the doctor you'll be on the first flight?"

"Yeah. It may take a while. Probably I'll have to change planes."

"In Chicago, maybe?"

The glowing path beckons. "Yeah, or Pittsburgh. I don't know."

"Well, we'll pray for a safe flight, and time to make peace with your mom."

"Okay. Bye, Louise."

"Bye, honey. You have a safe trip."

In the golden light, Joey looks anxious to see the white city. A road sign says "San Francisco, 20 miles," but no house breaks the hills' mossy curves. Grinning surfers lope across the road, and one waves at me goofily. I'm twenty miles outside a city of a million people? When I cut east to 101, two lanes become twenty, and Wilma flashes along at eighty miles an hour. Exhausted, I can make no sense of the signs. Suddenly there are a hundred ways to enter a city that wasn't there ten minutes ago. "San Francisco Airport," says one, and I start to move right.

As I rise around a curve, the Mount Sutro Tower raises its red horns. In the foggy twilight, it stands like a pitchfork with a gray cloud speared on its prongs. I used to watch that tower from Johnny's office. One night its red lights surprised us with their first flash. Johnny started, a red point piercing his forehead like the laser of a sniper's rifle. Tonight the sentinel stands with its arms upraised, daring me to approach its city. I point Wilma toward Mount Sutro and shoot past the airport. I turn off onto Nineteenth Avenue.

Instantly I'm locked in traffic, and the rushing urge in me subsides. As the light fades, I creep north between bleached houses and count the street names' descending letters. Taraval. Noriega. Judah. Irving. I am in Golden Gate Park. When I emerge from greenish black, I turn right on California and roll past two-story houses of beige, cream, pink. A woman in blue leggings wheels a baby, and a man swings a bouquet of purple flowers. Ahead of me, a silent creamsicle bus sips power from overhead lines.

On Van Ness Avenue I cling to the right and watch desperately for my hotel. There it is! A greasy-haired Indian woman welcomes me and tells me to park in the third garage. I pull back onto Van Ness, inch up a forty-five-degree grade, and roll into an underground warren. Sweating and shaking, I guide Wilma back and forth, missing the other cars by inches. Once I have Wilma wedged into a spot, I refuse to move her again. I sprint across the street for Wheat Snacks, and under the covers with Joey, I shake a little less. I don't untangle my hair or brush my teeth, but I turn off the power on my phone.

A vile, pasty scum fills my mouth. The room is so black it must be midnight. When I switch on the light, my watch says 9:12. I claw hair from my neck, where it pulls like a noose. Next to me, Joey is lying nose down, so I set him upright on the pillow.

"What's happening?" he asks.

With my tangled hair and swollen face, I look like a cavewoman whose legs have been mauled by a bear. With ceremonial slowness, I wash myself. I shave my legs and armpits and inspect each bit of flesh that Johnny might see. Under flickering lights, I strap on my black bra and arrange each breast so that no wrinkles mar the curve. I choose my black silk panties, even though they're dirty. Since I've missed breakfast, I crunch through the rest of the Wheat Snacks. Once I've pulled on a T-shirt and soft blue leggings, I head out into the city. I leave the lifeless phone next to Joey on the nightstand.

I don't know where I'm going except that I want to climb. Any street that leads upward, I take, and any that descends, I shun. I reach the summit of a hill so steep that any path leading down is a stairway. In front of me, an old Chinese man bends his knees, his back straight and his arms outstretched. He seems to be listening, so I strain to hear. Far below me, the city is breathing. Traffic moves in murmurs, and seals yelp on distant piers. Red and purple flowers burst silently around me. A magical shaded walkway descends toward Chinatown. I close my eyes and forget everything except the air flowing in and out. With the sun on my face, I breathe with the city.

"What do you want to do?" asks Johnny.

I walk back down the hill and land on Polk Street, where the shops are starting to open. An Asian girl wheels out a rack of Chinese jackets, and I stop to admire the colors. One is pale-blue silk with silver threads that wind in parallel curves. The girl motions for me to try it on, then nods and beckons me into the shop. The shiny cocoon encases me perfectly. Catching the light, the silver lines twist like a Dalí web glistening in a fine rain.

All the way back to my motel, I smile. I throw off my T-shirt and leave it balled on the bed. Under the fitted silk, I wear only the black bra, although the jacket's frog buttons pop open easily. I grab Joey, stuff the phone and T-shirt into my suitcase, and check out.

"But you were staying five days—why didn't you tell me last night?" asks the Indian woman crossly.

"Something's happened. I have to leave town." My voice flows fast yet surprisingly smooth.

By noon I am rolling down Van Ness Avenue. The only problem is, I'm not sure where I'm headed. I know only that Johnny's lab lies in the new Bay Park Research Center. I turn left onto Market, then south onto Third, advancing slowly until I reach the ballpark. The stadium stands like an oversize green cactus on the edge of an industrial desert. Dust dances in swirls, and festering warehouses quiver in the throb of a vast construction site. White cranes bob beside grim steel skeletons. In this wasteland, a new city is rising.

A few sealed glass buildings already house scientists. I follow an arrow that says "Visitor Parking." Wilma sucks down her window, and I smile at a round-faced Filipino guard.

"Good afternoon, ma'am. What brings you to the research center today?"

His cheerful black eyes unnerve me. I haven't come to trash the place, but somehow I'm slipping in under false pretenses.

"Uh … I'm here to visit a friend."

"Oh, that's nice." The young guard smiles at Joey. "So how long do you think you'll be staying?"

"Uh … I'm not sure. A few hours, I guess." My heart thumps as he reaches for a yellow card.

"Okay. Let me give you a ticket." He steps out of his booth to note my license number and suddenly grins like a small boy. "Wow! You drove here all the way from Georgia?" His dark eyes glow with hunger. "That must have been fun."

"Yeah." I smile.

"Okay—enjoy your visit. Just leave this on your dashboard on the driver's side."

I find a spot easily. When I step out into the dust, the wind whips up my hair. Joey nods and tells me to go. I head for the nearest finished building and, with effort, force open the door.

"May I help you?" A blond guard frowns at me dubiously. With my shiny jacket and wild hair, I must look like a windblown geisha.

"Yeah. I'm looking for the Turner lab."

"Oh, okay." He nods. "They're over in the Munson Center for Molecular Research." He glances at the dust swirling beyond the gray glass. "Are you driving?"

"Yeah," I mutter. "But I'm already parked. I'd be glad to walk."

"Okay." He frowns. "But it's not a very nice walk."

"Oh, that's all right."

"Well, you see those cranes over there?"

He points toward three nodding cranes hoisting beams despite the wild wind.

"Yeah," I say. "I see 'em."

"Hm." The blond man's doubtful look returns. "Well, you're gonna have to go around 'em. The Munson Center is right behind them."

I use my full weight to push open the door. From inside the sealed building, the trek looked easy, but out in the wind, it's brutal. With my left hand, I hold my hair in a tight roll and bend my right arm to shield my eyes from the dust. Grit slips between my feet and sandals and grinds away with each step. I keep my mouth closed, but dirt crunches between my teeth. To avoid open trenches, I have to make detours, and the cranes recede as often as they advance. By the time I reach Johnny's building, I am blasted and dazed.

An anxious guard opens the door for me. "Hi! I saw you coming! Wow—you should have driven!"

He's an older man with a prominent belly, and he frowns at me, concerned. With his warm, dark eyes, he looks like that Colombian coffee man who smiles reassuringly beside his donkey.

"Yeah, next time I'll drive."

"So you must have wanted to get here pretty badly." He smiles. "Which lab are you visiting?"

"Turner lab," I murmur and run my hand over my hair.

"Okay." He nods. On his clipboard, he records me carefully. "Who are you coming to see?"

"Johnny—Johnny Turner." As I say his name, my face ignites.

"Mm-hmm. What company are you with?"

"Oh, no company. I'm just a friend."

The gray-haired guard looks up from his writing and scans me warily. Behind his brown eyes, his brain seems to have changed settings. "Oh," he says. "Are you expected?"

"Yeah."

"Your name?"

"Carrie McFadden."

He reaches for his phone. "Yeah, hi, Jeannie, this is Arturo. I have a Carrie McFadden here to see Johnny ... Yeah ... Yeah? Yeah, okay. I'll tell her. Bye, Jeannie."

Arturo's eyes push into mine. "Ma'am? They say you're not expected until four."

"Yeah, that's right." My face smolders. "It's just—I've never been here before, and I wanted to leave plenty of time in case I got lost."

The guard's eyes scan me one last time from forehead to feet. I finger the frog buttons of my jacket—tight braided rolls of silk cord.

"It's twelve thirty," says Arturo.

"Yeah ... Well, I was going to get some food, then do some reading in the library. I used to work here--back on the old campus."

"Oh. Okay." He nods.

Gingerly, he hands me a badge that says "Visitor. Turner lab. 5/31/05."

"You'll need to keep this on you at all times."

I wince as the pin pricks my silk jacket. I search the new-smelling halls for a bathroom, and for the next half hour, I brush my hair, wash my feet, and experiment with my frogs.

If I leave the first three open, black lace can be seen lining the walls of a private pink cave.

In the wide, bright halls of this research labyrinth, I look for signs of life. The labs lie clustered in twos and threes, each entryway leading to a prairie dog den. Outside of each warren hang pictures of groups. The proud, shining faces look so young. Since I have barely eaten, I find the cafeteria by swimming up a gradient of people with paper cups.

In the café, I am tossed by noisy waves of scientists. I take a cup crammed with fruit cubes, a bottle of water, and a nonfat raspberry yogurt. Since I can't find a free table, I settle with a group of students. Some boys in black T-shirts stare at my jacket, but most turn away after a glance. They gossip about their competitors' science as though I were unhearing air.

A few doors down I discover the library, where I feel more at ease. On a gray metal shelf lie the *New York Times* and glinting copies of science journals. The May 26 issue of *Nature* features a fleet of articles on bird flu. The autoradiographs' charcoal bands look familiar, but the printed words are gibberish. I turn a few pages and pause at an article on vesicle fusion. I used to study these sacs of neurotransmitter and the factors that control their release. Has science changed this much? I force myself to read the words, but they might as well be in Turkish. Among the references, I notice Connie and Marty's 1986 paper on vesicle transport, the only source older than 1990.

One frayed sheet of paper remains in my purse, so I sit down and try to write. But picking up Teresa here is like finding a cell phone signal in the Grand Canyon. I glance at my watch—1:23. The thesis defense hasn't even started yet.

The front page of the *Times* tells of a twenty-five-year-old woman who served as police chief in a Mexican town. My mind relaxes as it follows the words, swimming from story to story. When I finish the *Times*, I start the *San Francisco Chronicle*. At 3:45 an alarm erupts in my chest.

Where is Johnny's lab? For security reasons, the building lacks directories. I ask the reference librarian, and she draws me a map. Johnny's group is working right overhead. As I approach his space, my hands turn cold, and I rub them against my thighs. When this fails to warm them, I stick them in my armpits, so that when I reach the door that says "Turner—Lazlo—Zhou," I feel as though I'm in a straitjacket. Next to the narrow entrance hang pictures of young scientists with fearless grins. With his sparrow-brown hair sticking up, Johnny looks just like he did in 1985. I draw a breath and pass through the main portal.

Through a doorway, I spot his brown-haired secretary.

"Hey, Carrie! In here."

Her dark eyes compare me to the memory she recorded of me four years ago.

"Can I get you anything? A glass of water? Johnny's in there with someone. He'll be out in a minute. He knows you're here."

On a scratchy armchair beside her desk, I sip water and try to feel warm. Over the straps of my sandals, my toes are blue petals. I rise to study a photo of a redwood forest and feel a puff of air against my back. I whirl.

Johnny looks smaller than I remember, maybe because his shoulders curl forward slightly. Behind his copper-rimmed glasses, his brown eyes are keen. They flicker with amusement when he sees me, but they stay focused on his guest, a nervous old man. Jeannie's eyes follow Johnny's movements. With his elbow, he nudges the old man forward.

"Yeah. Yeah, sure. Don't worry," Johnny is saying. "He's gonna pass."

"Are you sure …?"

"Yeah. Minh doesn't know what he's talkin' about. It's gonna happen. Okay? See you next week."

With a quick glance at my jacket, the troubled man shuffles out.

"Carrie McFadden!" Johnny grins. "Man, it's been a long time. C'mon in."

He waves me into his office, and I sit on his black leather couch. I try to convince myself Johnny is real, that I'm truly here in this moment. There is something worn and dim about him, while in my memories, he radiates light. As he settles beside me, his steel-gray sleeve brushes my arm, and he withdraws it quickly. The one familiar thing is the energy of his dark eyes, which are studying the cranes at work.

"Isn't this somethin'?" Johnny raises an enormous hand in a gesture that encompasses the whole office.

I leap up to explore. On two walls, bright rows of books frame molecular models. The other two sides, made entirely of glass, look out onto the construction site. Below the cranes, tiny men in yellow hard hats are milling in a massive pit.

"C'mere." Johnny beckons me to the window. "Look at this. That's gonna be the new gym and residence hall. And if you come over here—" He lays a warm hand on my shoulder and pulls me back. "You can see the new hospital … That's gonna be the Genetics Institute. It's almost done."

He handles me familiarly, and I lean against him as I look out. Between the rising buildings, dust devils swirl. The downtown skyscrapers huddle in the distance.

"Wow …" Johnny's quick breaths press my back. He steps away.

"You know, I never would have believed it," he murmurs. "That I'd work in a place like this. Actually, you're one of my witnesses. You know what it looked like before."

"Yeah." I smile at him, and his lips twitch.

"Well, you're lookin' good." He grins good-naturedly. "I love that jacket. Is that silk?" His long fingers dance over my shoulder.

"Yeah, I think so." His black eyes scour me. "You look a little tired, though. Little thinner than I remember. You sure you're okay?"

The force of that stare … "Yeah, I've just been on a long trip—doing all this driving."

"Oh, yeah, right! How was that?"

I look up at him, and my eyes fill with tears.

"Aw, no—no. C'mere. C'mon." His long arms collect me. "Aw, c'mon, now, Carrie. I thought you were doin' so well. You look terrific—and you've got this great book out. Jeannie told me it was wonderful." Johnny strokes my hair, and I press my face into his chest. "C'mon. Let's go sit down. Let's get you a Kleenex."

"I—I'm just so happy to see you," I choke.

"It's real good to see you too." Johnny squeezes my hand. "That over now? You gonna be okay?" In his flickering smile, embarrassment elbows concern.

"Yeah—yeah—I think so. It's just so good …"

"Yeah." Johnny presses my hand again. "We had some good times, didn't we?"

I focus on breathing and wait for my voice to steady.

"The trip has been great," I say finally. "I saw Connie."

"Connie?" Johnny gazes upward.

"Yeah, you know. She used to work with Marty on vesicle transport. Vesicle recognition. She trained me."

With his eyes on his bookshelf, Johnny nods slowly. "Oh, yeah—that was a great paper they did. So what's she doin' now?" His gaze meets mine, sharper than ever.

"Well, she married this guy Bruce ... works on the cytoskeleton."

"Oh, yeah, Bruce Sterling," Johnny says quickly. "He does good science."

"And—well—she's a research assistant there—they're both in Norman—but mainly she takes care of their kid."

Johnny grimaces. "Yeah, she'd do that. She never seemed to be that into it. So they're in Norman?"

He stretches his legs as far as they can go. It's an awesome sight, like a peacock unfurling its tail.

"Yeah. Seems like a pretty nice place. Better than West Texas. Least they have trees."

"You were in West Texas?" Johnny squints at the top shelf. "Yeah—that's right. You took I-40?"

"Yeah. I saw the Turner Ranch."

Johnny's stare turns cold. "You saw the ranch? What the hell were you doin' there?" He pulls in his legs.

"I just saw the sign. I stopped to look at it. That's all."

His eyes drill me, trying to pierce my memory.

"What'd you see?" he demands. "What does it look like? Man, I haven't been there in a while."

"Just a sign swinging in the wind. A road leading to the horizon. I didn't even see any cows."

"Oh, you must have been at the I-40 entrance." He reflects. "The main one's on 70. That was the old road to Dodge."

He tries to smile, but he's white and taut. "You didn't—you didn't go there just to check it out or anything—did you? I mean—so you could tell me?"

"No, no, it was an accident. I just drove by and saw it, that's all."

Johnny gazes at me mistrustfully.

"So tell me what you're working on," I say shakily. "What are you guys doing now?"

Johnny smiles, and his legs ease forward. "Oh, great stuff! It's incredible. I've got Hyun-a, this new Korean postdoc, working with Dave and Nigel on the herpes virus. It's amazing how those things work, how they get into cells. And I've got two modelers and two geneticists seeing how viruses assemble. If it works, we could set up teams to study all kinds of things— enzymes, receptors, membrane proteins—"

He grabs a model from the shelf over our heads. "Just look at this—isn't this cool? The thing just bends, like this." He pushes up from below, and the red pieces open like a tulip in a high-speed film.

"Wow." I smile.

"It's so great—I've got the best people workin' for me. I just wish I could spend more time in the lab."

Deftly, Johnny recreates the closed bud.

"So why don't you?"

"Well, I've gotta run it." He sighs. "Meet people. Write grants. Give talks—and then ..." He looks toward his desk, whose clean surface is broken by framed pictures.

"Oh, yeah," I say. "How's your little boy doing?"

Johnny grins. "Not so little anymore. He's eleven. And he's got a seven-year-old brother. Here."

He walks to his desk, and his big hand hovers. In the photo he chooses, the boys lean against a redwood, stretching their white arms across grooved bark. They have Johnny's dark eyes, but their hair is lighter, their faces longer.

"Wow," I murmur.

"Yeah, they're great." Johnny frowns at his sons. "Tommy's got some readin' problems, though. Some kind of dyslexia. And attention deficit disorder. They say he's terrorizin' the school."

I catch Johnny's eye, and for an instant we're joined. "Gee, where do you think he gets that from?"

"Aw, c'mon!" Johnny blushes and grins. "I was never too good at language stuff, but I worked hard. I got good grades. School's just not made for kids like me and him. I like to build stuff—move around. Who wants to sit still and read?"

I laugh into his eyes. "You haven't changed at all. You look—you sound just like you did in Wilson's lab."

"No, I don't." Johnny's face tightens. "Man, that was twenty years ago!"

"Yeah, you do. You look just the same."

Johnny glances from side to side. "Carrie, do you know what you're saying? Twenty years? If I had a mirror here, I'd make you take a look. Not that— But we've both aged. Shit, twenty years ago we were just startin' to use computers.

We didn't have PCR! We were listenin' to Michael Jackson on LPs!"

"It doesn't feel like that long." I scan Johnny's face, but he has pulled away.

"Well, it is!" he exclaims. "Y'know, sometimes I think there's somethin' wrong with you." His features soften. "Maybe it's just that you don't have kids. You don't, do you? You still alone?"

On his thighs, he spreads his fingers like skinless fans.

"Carrie, I want you to tell me why you came here today. I want you to tell me the truth. You didn't come here to talk science."

"No. My novel—I wanted to work on my novel—" I can find no air to form words.

"Yeah, you said. But you could do that at home—or if you wanted to travel, you could have gone anywhere. Why here?"

When Johnny wants to get to the point, he has the momentum of a high-speed train.

"I—I wanted to see you …"

His eyes push into mine. "Why? Why did you want to see me?"

"Don't you remember what happened twenty years ago tonight?"

Johnny squints at the ceiling. "Let's see … I was workin' on enzymes … There was this one—I couldn't find the active site … No. You're gonna have to tell me. What happened?"

"Well—you know …"

Johnny blushes deep red. "Oh, yeah." He rubs the back of his head. "Gee. Was that the first time? That was pretty nice, wasn't it?"

"Yeah." My face is searing.

"Oh, man." He laughs. "So what are you here for—a reenactment? Like one of those Civil War battles?"

I toss my head. "Well—yeah."

Johnny shakes with laughter. "Man, you are nuts. You're completely nuts. So this was your surprise. I was afraid it was somethin' like this." With effort, he ventures a low, hard tone. "Look—I'm married."

I shrug my shoulders. "That's okay."

His lips twitch, and he's laughing again. "You're the damnedest—you're nuts! You're completely nuts!"

"You were married the last time I saw you."

"Oh, God. That—" His big hands knead his face. "We were havin' some problems. I saw you, and I couldn't resist."

Now I feel like the bullet train. "That's okay. I don't want to marry you."

"Oh, I think you do."

Black anger rises from under his laughter.

"Look. It's a good thing you came here, 'cause we've gotta get this straight. We went out a few times—we had fun— you're a smart, sexy woman, and I had a great time with you, but we have nothing in common."

He studies me, and his lips curve.

"Okay. Okay. So one thing—but what do you do with that? You can't build a life around that."

I sit rigid, unable to breathe.

"Why do you—why do you have to remember everything, make it all mean somethin'?" he protests. "Why can't you just do somethin', enjoy it, then go do somethin' else?"

Johnny lowers his tone. "I hope—I hope this isn't why you've stayed alone." He looks at me, worried.

"It isn't." My voice emerges dull and flat.

Johnny keeps his eyes fixed on mine. "I'm sorry to have to be tellin' you this, but I think it's for the best. I don't want you expectin' things that aren't gonna happen."

I nod. "Sabine—does she have more in common with you?" My voice floats like a puff in an empty chamber.

"Damned if I know." Johnny shakes his head. "Sometimes … But—yeah. She's uncomplicated."

"I'm …" My voice collapses.

"Man!" He laughs. "Protein folding is nothin' compared to you. If I were lookin' for someone for a weekend in Vegas, you'd be it, but not to live with. We're both nuts, but in different ways."

I finger a braided knob on my jacket.

"Uh-oh. What are you doin' there?" Johnny's eyes burn my fingers. "I was just kiddin' before. I don't do stuff like this anymore."

I push the frog through its loop and inhale deeply. The jacket falls open.

"Oh, shit. What's—what's that you've got on there? Shit!"

I lean forward so that Johnny doesn't have far to bend. He pulls me toward him, and his mouth warms mine. His gigantic hand crushes my breast. His lips open, and with a sigh, he holds me. His breathing quickens. Then he pushes me away. He runs his hand over the back of his head.

"No. I am not doin' this. It's not that I don't want to, believe me. It's just a bad idea. We can't do this. Please … could you close that thing back up?"

My icy fingers fumble with the corded knots.

"That's—that's real pretty, that thing …"

He reaches for my silken arm and fondles it wistfully.

"Thanks." I am on my feet.

"Carrie—you're not upset, are you? 'Cause I wouldn't want you goin' out of here upset." Johnny stands, and his legs push him up into remote regions. "Just tell me—where are you goin' right now? You're not goin' to do anything crazy, are you?" His worried eyes look almost fatherly.

"No, I feel pretty sane."

A laugh washes off his look of concern. "How's your book? You makin' any progress? Just tell me—oh, damn it."

Johnny clasps me in a hug so tight I can hardly breathe. When he releases me, he cups my face in his hands. In his eyes, frustration mingles with sadness.

"Really—I really do like you, you know. That's why I'm tellin' you this. I'll always— Just tell me you'll take care of yourself."

"I will," I murmur.

Johnny strides toward the door. "Okay?"

"Okay."

"That's good." He grins guiltily and looks at his watch. "'Cause I've gotta go see the provost in ten minutes."

Trembling, I try to smile. "Bye, Johnny."

I tell Jeannie goodbye too. As I look back, they are bent over her computer, pointing to something on her screen. Blindly, I rush down a stairway and almost throw my badge at Arturo.

"Hey!" he calls as I push open the door.

The wind scours a bald spot in the back of my head, and I claw my hair out of my eyes. No matter how tight I twist it, some wisps dance freely. I close my eyes to a tiny slit. Where was that parking lot? Far to the left, I spot the young guard's booth. I race toward that glass cabin in the dust. Blindly, I wrench open Wilma's trunk and dig in my suitcase. My hand worms its way through cloth until it hits metal. Without zipping the suitcase, I slam the trunk. Joey winces from the jolt. Inside Wilma, I draw a slow breath. My phone turns blue as I roll up to the lone gray booth.

"Hi, ma'am. Did you have a nice visit?" The round-faced kid looks as though he knows something I don't.

"Yeah," I murmur and look toward the exit.

"Great. Could you show me your ticket, please? Okay. That'll be seven dollars."

My fingers shake as they peel apart the bills.

"Are you all right, ma'am?" His smooth brown face beams concern.

"Yeah … yeah … just tired." I sigh. "What's the best way to the airport from here?"

His professional air reemerges.

"Well, I guess I'd go right down Third here. You can get onto 280 from Sixteenth." He frowns at his watch. "But this time of day, I would stay on Third. A few miles down, it feeds into 101." With warm sympathy, he studies my face. "You need to catch a flight? 'Cause the southbound traffic's gonna be bad."

"Yeah—well, not any particular one. I just need to get somewhere as fast as I can."

His dark eyes widen. "Well, okay. I hope you have a safe trip."

By the time I pull onto Third, my phone has bonded with a signal tower. I check my voice mail.

"You have twelve new messages."

In slow motion, a flattened box cartwheels across the road.

10:27 p.m. "Hi, Carrie. I was hoping to catch you someplace you can talk. Your mom's hanging on. She's a brave lady. I just wanted to tell the doctor what flight you'll be on. Guess you must be up in the air by now. Call me before you get on your next flight, okay?"

1:15 a.m. "Carrie? Hi, this is Louise again. Please could you give us a call to let us know where you are? Thanks, honey."

A stooped black man in a flapping coat pushes a shopping cart full of plastic bottles. He points his grizzled beard south, ignoring the collapsed warehouses around him.

1:37 a.m. "Carrie? I—I'm so sorry, honey. Your mom just passed. She-e was a lovely lady. I know you did your best. I—" The message ends in heaving sobs.

Third Street dissolves into a blur, and I wipe my eyes one at a time. My index finger works as a squeegee but wets the wheel under my hands. My mom. My mom is dead, and where the hell am I? She stands frozen at the kitchen window, staring out over running water. From the floor where I'm playing, she's a lonely giant, and I wish she would look down at me. Anytime she does, she finds some wayward growth to be stamped out. I brush my silky sleeve across my eyes. Hers will be closed forever now, unable to accuse me anymore.

5:56 a.m. "Carrie? It's Louise, honey. Did you get my last message? I'm sure you're upset, but you need to call. We need to know what to do about your mom. I guess you haven't done anything like this before, but there are things you need to decide. Please call us. We're looking forward to seeing you. Bye, honey."

9:13 a.m. "Carrie? I thought I'd try you one more time. Your phone must not be working. Okay—I'll try again later."

On the corner of Twenty-Fifth, a brown shack called Eddie's has attracted a family of pickups. Fanned around the entrance, they look like nursing puppies that have crawled up to drink.

12:01 p.m. "Carrie? I hope you're all right, dear. 'Cause if your phone's working and you're getting my messages ... I don't know what to think. Your mom needs you, honey. Whatever you're doing, you'll feel better as soon as you get here."

A rusted steel bridge dares me to cross a brown canal.

1:46 p.m. "Theresa? Hey, it's Clifton. I'm right here outside your hotel. Sorry I'm a little early. You must still be out. I can't wait to see you."

The road penetrates gray landfills and opens into three lanes each way. Seagulls spin like living scraps. Joey nods, enjoying the speed.

2:16 p.m. "Theresa? Just trying again. It's Clifton. Guess you must have got held up somewhere."

2:18 p.m. "Carrie? I'm sorry—I took the liberty of calling Yankee Air and United Express and explained the situation, and they said you weren't on any of their flights today. They can't tell me which one you're on—they're not allowed to do that—but ... but I don't know what to do. I don't know what to think. Please, if you can hear me, for your mom's sake, let us know where you are."

2:45 p.m. "Theresa? This is really strange. I checked at the desk, and they said they didn't have anyone registered under your name. Did you not like the motel or something? Did you go somewhere else? I'm starting to worry. Please—please call me if you get this."

3:52 p.m. "Hi, Theresa. I've got myself a room now, and I'll wait for you here. The Indian lady at the desk has been really nice to me, but I'm worried. Did you have an accident? Please let me know you're okay."

5:07 p.m. "Theresa? I—I had this idea—I don't know—I was talking to the Indian lady, and suddenly I thought you might have used your other name—you know, your pen name. So she checked for me, and she said you had been here, and you had a reservation for five nights, but you checked out. What's going on? You didn't— Please call me."

I roll onto 101 and nose Wilma into creeping traffic. On the phone, I press buttons with slippery fingers.

"Gonzalo?"

"Mala? Hey-hey! I have not heard from you in a while. Where are you?"

My tears overflow. "San Francisco."

"Malísima—you do not sound good. Have you seen your scientist?"

Johnny flashes into being, his fingers spread on the provost's desk.

"Yeah—but—"

"Gilipollas. Has he been mean to you again?"

"No—no! Listen—my mother just died."

The traffic crystallizes.

"¡Mala! ¡Qué pena! Why did you not tell me? When?"

"Just now," I murmur. "I just found out now."

"¡Ay, Mala! This must be very hard for you."

"Yeah ..." I whisper.

A purple-black limousine creeps forward. He must be going to the airport too.

"Mala," says Gonzalo, "you must not be alone for this. Where are you? What are you doing?"

"I'm stuck in traffic trying to reach the San Francisco Airport."

"So you will be flying home? Where do you have to go?"

"Jonesboro, Pennsylvania. Little town near Scranton. She's—she was in a nursing home there."

"So you will go there to arrange the funeral?" I sense Gonzalo calculating, just like Johnny.

"Yeah, I guess so."

In the car to my left, a curly-haired woman bobs her head. With her rhythm as bass, I try to imagine what she's hearing. A fat blond man on my right glares at me.

"Mala," says Gonzalo, "you must not do this alone. I know you like to do things yourself, but you must have someone with you. If you will let me, I will come up."

"No—that's crazy." Gonzalo in Jonesboro, Pennsylvania?

"Yes, Mala. I want to do this. This is going to be very hard for you."

I waver. "Would you really ...?"

"Yes. Tomorrow morning. I will find it on the atlas. I will rent a car."

I smile. Gonzalo isn't known for his sense of direction. "Should take you three or four hours. She's in the Hillcrest Senior Center."

The lanes beside me loosen, and the angry man and nodding woman roll away. In front of me, the eggplant limo stays put. I watch for an opening on the left.

"Okay. Okay, Mala," says Gonzalo. "But you don't know when you will be there?"

"No. I have to find a flight. You're really going to …"

"Mala, I am glad to do this. I am not teaching this semester. I was going to see Silke this weekend, but she will understand."

How can he be so sure? How can he just drop everything?

"Gonzalo—thanks." My voice quivers.

"It will be good to see you. I am just sorry it is such a sad time."

On my left, the string of cars flows, unbroken.

"Mala—I have some people here. I will ask them to help. They will tell me how to go."

The dark limousine floats forward.

"Call me when you know what flight you'll be on. Be careful," he warns. "Be safe."

"Yeah. Thanks. Bye, Gonzalo."

"Ciao, Mala."

I drop the phone into the cup holder and stare out at the bay. Across the water, Oakland lies like a lost blue-gray whale. I picture Gonzalo hurrying to his guests, asking them how to find Pennsylvania. In front of me, a black Porsche trembles with the desire to run.

When I reach the airport, I head for long-term parking. I zip up my suitcase, which with Fischer's sweatshirt has grown so fat it will barely close. I pull Joey from the back and balance him on my hip. From the front, I take the phone but leave the atlas.

"Boop!"

Wilma's doors click shut. I stroke two trembling fingers across her dusty headlight.

In the terminal, I head straight for Yankee Air. A delicate girl with a brown ponytail greets me.

"Good evening, ma'am. What a cute bear! What can I do for you tonight?"

The Lladró girl is just my height, and I look into her pale blue eyes.

"My mo-other just died. I have to get to Scranton."

"Oh, you poor thing!" Her slim fingers attack the keys. She calls to an older woman beside her, "Hey, can we still put people on the 6:45 to Vegas? This lady has an urgent situation."

Her burly, gray-haired colleague calls the gate. "Yeah. But she'll have to hurry."

Ignoring the man at her counter, the older woman turns to me. "May I see your luggage, ma'am? Oh—" She smiles. "You're only allowed one carry-on. You can keep your purse, but you'll have to check the suitcase or the bear."

I hand her my suitcase.

"That's what I would do." The soft-haired girl grins.

With a slight shudder, she returns to business. "Ma'am? You know about our special grievers' fare? You'll need to pay full price now, but when you have … the documents, you can send them in, and we'll refund the difference. I'm putting you on the 6:45 to Vegas, leaving in just a few minutes. That'll get you there at 8:14. From there you can take the 10:50 to

Pittsburgh, arriving at 6:04 tomorrow morning. Then you can take the 8:35 to Scranton. You'll be there at 9:48."

My quivering credit card protests with a few quick flashes.

"Ma'am—since the time's so tight, we'll have someone take you to the gate."

A slim Indonesian man rushes me through security and then through forbidden doors. I follow him down empty gray corridors. Joey's bouncing nose tickles my neck. I remember my flight from that hospital, but how different this young back looks from Fischer's! The shoulders of that wild German doctor stretched ripples across his blue-green shirt. As I approach the gate, a tall stewardess beckons. She stuffs Joey into an overhead bin and orders me to turn off my phone.

Next to me sits a round-bellied man who looks glad I'm staring out the window. His eyes close, and his fingers relax on the armrest. On the tarmac, a black man in headphones drives a luggage cart crammed like a well-filled bookcase. In the oval of glass, black hair frames my white face. My shadowed eyes grow darker, rounder.

"I want to know what happened." That was Teresa's voice.

With my foot, I snag my purse from under the seat and pull out my last sheet of paper. As the jolts of the ground die away, my hand is forming black letters.

Sometimes Justin calls now during the day. He asks me how his mother is, or whether he can bring me something from the market. I never knew such a nice man, one who takes such good care of his mother. He has been careful not to touch me, not even to hug me goodbye.

Neither one of us likes that she's sleeping so much. Every morning Justin coaxes her out of bed and dresses her, and I make her do stand-up things like cooking and dancing. Mostly she wants to lie on the sunporch, even when I turn on La Mega.

Reading is easier now, but I liked it better when she was awake. I keep stopping and watching her chest rise and fall under her blue afghan of woolen stars. Doesn't she need to go to the bathroom? I feel ashamed that I can do nothing for her, but I want to keep reading. Her story holds me like the loops binding those soft, flowery stars together.

Today the sun is so strong that I have to drag our chairs to a shady place. She seems alert, so I give her the science book, and I pick up a notebook, 1968–69. Since Justin was born, she has written mainly about the first miraculous years of his life. He's a sweet baby, eats well and doesn't cry much, but she wishes he wouldn't cling to her so. I start reading.

I just hope we both get through this party alive.

Outside, a blackbird sings on a quivering branch, his pulsing throat driving the notes. Mrs. Marshall is watching the bird too, and I'm glad to see her eyes mark his rhythm.

Bill has gotten more excited about Justin's birthday than he has about science lately. Since he published the prep and I left the lab, he's had much less direction. If it weren't for Jimmy, I'm not sure he would do experiments at all. For some reason, Justin's turning three is a big deal for him, as though he were coming of age with his son. If Bill spent more time with him, he would know how much this party scares him and how hard he's been pretending to like it. Justin is smart— observant—just slow to learn physical things. He cries so much, not because he's angry, but because he's afraid.

I wish Jimmy would take some interest in Justin. When I bring him to the lab, he manages not to be there. I hardly ever see him anymore. I hope—

Mrs. Marshall's eyes have closed. Under her afghan, she is sleeping peacefully. The heavy science book holds her down like a V-shaped paperweight.

—Jimmy comes to this party today. Bill has invited half the medical school. I wanted it to be just for kids, but he needs to show off his son. Oh, well. I guess that's better than a father who doesn't care.

This past week, I've been reading books about party games and buying all kinds of food. We ordered a special airplane cake from the German bakery. Justin loves airplanes, so I designed it with them. They couldn't bake one in the shape of an airplane, but they're improvising a blue-and-white landing pad with a model Pan Am jet on top. We've hired a colored woman, Nancy, to help serve the food. I just wish there were someone to help with the kids. There will be close to thirty of them, and these games need referees—the treasure hunt, the spiderweb, the piñata.

Mrs. Marshall's face twitches like a dog's in a fighting dream. The next part wasn't written until three months later. That's strange. I wonder why.

I think I can write today. I think I can do it. It just means going back there to that day. It's one thing to remember, but another to write. When you write, you look at a memory under a microscope, and you see things you didn't in real time.

Everything was ready. The frosted blue-and-white cake was hidden in the pantry, and we had rigged the sunporch with a web of taut white strings. The shady yard smelled of manure from a brown-and-white pony that Bill rented. In case of rain, we had set up a green-and-white-striped tent. Nancy arranged the shrimp and meatballs on trays, and she looked like she knew what she was doing. Only Justin seemed anxious, but he brightened when he saw the cake. I said it was a secret between us two, and no one should know that he knew.

Around five, people began to appear. I had been nervous, but they entertained themselves. The kids pounded full steam from room to room, and I didn't try to stop them. It felt like a good day for running. Tim Jervis's wife helped me police the spiderweb, where each kid had to follow a string to a prize. There was a lot of pushing and pulling, and we intervened only when Dave Kramer's boy punched the kids caught in his line.

For the piñata, Judy Moraga taught the kids a special song, something about "Da-le, da-le." The bursts of screams attracted Nancy, and she stopped to watch. I think I was supposed to say, "Get back to work," but I can't do things like that. With her brittle hair and sunken eyes, she must have been thirty years older than I am.

The fat, striped bee piñata hovered with a defiant grin on its yellow face. The kids swung at it with a sawed-off broom, violently slashing the air. Judy yanked it up and down so that no one could strike it, and I realized she was saving it for Justin. When his turn came, she left it hanging low until the other kids screamed, "No fair!" Even then he couldn't hit it, just bashed a chair and barely missed Judy. Fred Yu's little girl came up next and whacked the head off the thing as *though she had radar. In the shrieking scramble as candies rained down, Justin got pushed to the side.*

With my mind on the kids, I barely noticed the adults. The men stayed in the yard, drinking and talking science. Once the piñata was smashed, Bill told me I should start serving cake, so Nancy, Judy, and I carried it outside. The kids followed hungrily, and the grown-ups applauded. I rescued the grounded jet from the sticky frosting, and Justin smiled as he licked a blue patch from the wing. It's so hard to make him happy, but I think in that moment he was.

As I handed out slices, I looked around for—

Oh, shit. I've been writing smaller and smaller, but one piece of paper will go only so far. The cabin is sloping downward, and beside me, the fat man is sleeping blissfully. The stewardess orders me to put up my tray, but I'm determined to keep writing. Nothing in my purse will hold pen tracks, and my Bic leaves no marks on the magazine. It writes perfectly, though, on the airsickness bag.

—Jimmy. Justin hovered so close he warmed my leg, and I let him hand people slices. I kept hoping that Jimmy would be next in line, bending way, way down to thank a three-year-old. Once everyone had a piece of cake, I just started asking. Arty Moraga said he had seen Jimmy that morning and he had been planning to come. Harlan told me that Jimmy was still in the lab around midnight last night.

I took pictures of kids grinning on the pony until Bill said we should let Justin open his presents. On a card table under the tent, they stood like a city skyline wrapped in pa—

My hand slips as the plane hits the ground. We creep over the tarmac, and I lose transmission. The fat man wakes up.

"Well, that was quick!" He grins as though I were lying in bed beside him.

When I'm allowed to stand, I rescue Joey, and I bounce him as I check the airport map. The terminals lie like mirrored jacks, and I have to cross from one to the other. Outside, the sinking sun still glows, but the fluorescent lights make it feel like three in the morning. In dark corners, slot machines gurgle and flash like hungry monsters wanting to be fed. In every store I pass, I look for paper, but I can find only printed pages. Since I'm feeling dizzy, I buy a protein bar. I turn Joey's face to my breast to protect him from people's stares. When I reach my gate, I'm the only one there except for a black-haired man collecting trash.

"Is there any paper in there?" I ask.

He stiffens and shakes his shaggy head.

"¿Hay papel? Necesito papel. De cualquier tipo. Soy escritora."

He smiles widely and roots through his cart. With a scarred hand, he extracts a white sheet but frowns at a wrinkled stain. He bends double, digs deeper, and finally comes up beaming. He offers me a stiff bouquet of pink flyers.

"¡Gracias! ¡Muchas gracias!" I smile.

"¿Usted es escritora?" In the shadows of his grin, a gold tooth flashes.

"Sí." I flush as his dark eyes probe me.

"¿Y qué escribe?"

"Una historia de amor."

"Ah!" he sighs and nods his approval. "Quiero leerla cuando la acabe. ¿Usté regresa por aquí? Me llamo Ignacio. Ignacio." He thumps his chest with a loose fist. Leaning closer, he murmurs, "Usted es muy guapa. Regrese por aquí, y pregunte por Ignacio. Saldremos. Yo le enseño Las Vegas."

Still smiling, he pushes his cart to the next gate. I seat Joey beside me, peel the protein bar, and check my dry paper roses. Every single sheet says, "Beautiful Girls Just 4U!"

Mrs. Marshall makes a wet sound in her throat, and I rise to see if she's okay. She screws up her face as though she's hurting, and I take her hand, but she doesn't stir. When her features soften, I return to my chair.

People brought Justin all kinds of gifts, a golden teddy bear, a watercolor paint set, a pebbly terrarium. I was proud to see how he thanked everyone, just as I told him to. The men laughed when he reached up to shake their hands.

As he was tearing blue paper off a big, round package, Harlan called Bill into the house. Justin paused, his little fingers crinkling the wrapping. I didn't think that Bill should have answered the phone, but Harlan said it was urgent. When Bill came back, his face was gray. Justin swallowed and ripped open the package.

"What is it?" I whispered.

"It's bad," muttered Bill. "But I can't tell you here. All these kids—"

"Tell me!"

Justin looked up nervously and rested his chin on a straining soccer ball. Bill slipped off to the men in the yard.

"What a nice ball!" I said. "What else have you got there?"

Justin set the ball down carefully and reached for his next present. Dave Kramer's boy ran off with the ball, and a noisy soccer game began.

By the blue hydrangea, Bill stood talking earnestly with the men. Harlan looked down and shook his head. Trying to smile, Justin examined his next present, a rectangular box that clacked when it shook. I took a tray of drinks from Nancy and walked over to the men.

Bill's voice reached me in pieces. "I can't—so sensitive—she—"

"Sh-sh!" hissed Harlan.

"What happened?" The tray's fluted edges bit my fingers. Dave Kramer glanced at Arty Moraga.

"What's going on? You tell me!"

Bill shook his head. "Sandy, this is not the time—"

"What happened?" I was almost screaming.

Bill covered my mouth with his hand.

"You'd better just tell her, Bill," said Dave.

"Okay. Okay. But you stay calm, you hear? If you ruin this for him—"

"What!"

"Sandy—Jimmy Mellen just died in an accident. That was Joe Lipton—he was on call at the ER. It happened just now. Less than an hour ago. Corner of Clifton and North Decatur. That damned car—and poor Glenda! Jesus! A first-year student! They were on their way over here—"

The tray fell from my hands, and icy juice splashed my feet. A steel arm encircled my back.

"Jesus! Damn it! I told you she couldn't take it!"

"Let's get her in the house!"

"Where's Justin?"

Gripping hands held me upright, but my breath was gone.

"Sandy, I want you to take deep breaths."

"No!" I screamed.

Something soft and warm caught my leg. Justin dodged the men trying to scoop him up. He clutched my thigh as though I were a tree about to be uprooted.

"Mommy! Mommy!"

On the grass—

"My! My!" Mrs. Marshall aims her finger between my eyes.

"My!" Her face twists with rage.

"What's the matter, Mrs. Marshall?"

"My book!" she screams. She lurches forward and falls to the floor. With so little flesh on her bones, she hits the tiles with a sickening crack.

"Mrs. Marshall!"

Her body tightens and trembles. Her face is hideous, her eyes closed, her teeth clenched. White foam bubbles from the corner of her mouth. I race to the phone.

When Justin answers, I have lost the words. "Justin! Your— mother! ¡Se está muriendo! ¡Tuvo un infarto! ¡Ven!"

"Teresa! Teresa! I can't understand! What's wrong?"

I close my eyes and squeeze my brain. "She—very sick! Very bad! You come!"

"Teresa! Don't wait for me! Call 911!"

"You come?"

"Yes! But hang up now! Call 911! They'll take her to Edgewood. I'll meet you there."

I call for an ambulance, but then I have to wait. I run back to Mrs. Marshall. Stiff and twitching, she lies in a puddle, a string of spit dangling from her mouth. I try to take her hand, but her fingers are drawn into tight balls. I throw open the door. This pinche gringo neighborhood! If a poor old lady collapsed like this where I live, a hundred people would be there in two minutes. Outside I hear only the high peeps of birds. No, there it is—like a baby crying. I wave my arms, and a red ambulance roars up the driveway. The driver looks at me sharply.

"¿Qué pasó?"

"¡La pobre señora! ¡La pobre señora!"

Two men run after me to the sunporch and kneel down beside her. Mrs. Marshall has stopped moving, and her body has relaxed.

"¡Estaba temblando! Estaba temblando de todas partes!"

"¡Cálmate!"

While they probe her, I pick up the notebook and science book, which have fallen to the floor. Since they've stopped noticing me, I slip off to the book room. On the cover of the science book, I read, "The Structure of the Human Cell. By William Marshall and James R. Mellen."

"Oye—¿dónde estás?"

I shove the books into their gaps and make sure they're perfectly even with the ones beside them.

"All passengers for Yankee Air flight 640 to Pittsburgh, we are ready to begin our boarding process."

On my lap lie two pink sheets filled with letters. Next to me, Joey waits patiently. I shove the flyers into my purse and grope for my ticket. Boarding group A. I stir the contents to find my phone.

"All passengers in boarding group A, you are welcome to board the aircraft."

I swing Joey onto my hip. When I reach my seat, my phone's window has turned blue.

"I'm sorry, ma'am, you'll have to turn off that phone," says a stewardess.

She lets me strap Joey into the seat beside me, and I pull out an empty pink page.

All the way to the hospital, they batter me with questions. Does she take any medications? Has this happened before? Are you sure she's only sixty-five? At the check-in desk stands Justin, trembling like his mother. He throws his arms around me, and we cry.

CHAPTER 12

JONESBORO, PENNSYLVANIA

When I step out of the jet in Scranton, my lungs fill with sweet, wet air. Even at the airport, honeysuckle rules with its rich, voluptuous scent. The creeping leaves of soft green hills threaten to invade the runways. The reaching tendrils of the Northeast have finally pulled me home.

I follow men in gray suits to the baggage claim and watch dazedly to see what emerges. As my eyes scan the belt, I feel like two people, one who hasn't slept in weeks and another who is just awakening. In Pittsburgh, I walked in unthinking circles. My legs needed to move, but my brain was embalmed in maple syrup. From the grinding belt, the gray men retrieve their bags, and a young mother catches her stroller. Before long, I am the only one left, and the segmented belt shudders and stops. Que la chingada. Except for three pink flyers and an airsickness bag, every page I've written was in that suitcase.

I sink down onto the belt's steel rim, and my fingers seek shelter in my hair. Joey falls silently beside me. My elbows dig my knees, and my chest pushes my belly in slow pulses. Those pages held voices the way a CD encodes an entire symphony. Why didn't I copy them? Just couldn't stop writing, I guess. Couldn't stop moving. In Wilma I always had them on hand, and I never thought I'd be flying. By September, the new novel has to be in my file, and I don't see how I can rewrite it. When you write a story, you live it, and you can't live it over again. At worst, it will come out stilted, and at best, as something new. No. If Teresa's gone, it will mean that she's gone forever.

Footsteps click toward me, but I can't raise my head. Tears flow as I think about Johnny. This time, in everything he said and did, I find no sign that he wants to see me again. He may have wanted to fuck me, but even that would have been a farewell to the parts that he loved best. Enjoy it, he said, then go do something else. Like what? What do I do now?

"I don't know—she seems to be alone," murmurs a female voice.

A man responds. "You say she's been like this for a while?"

"Yes. She might be sick. We ought to do something. We can't just—"

"Ma'am?" A firm hand nudges my arm. "Ma'am? Do you need—"

"Don't call me that!" I cry.

He recoils. Above his Yankee Air uniform, his tanned face is furrowed. The heavyset woman beside him gazes down with pale, worried blue eyes.

"Let's call someone," she pleads. "Look at her! She needs a doctor."

"No! No!" I yell.

With all my remaining strength, I lower my voice. I tuck back my hair and prop up Joey, who has been lying facedown.

"I'm sorry," I say. "I'm okay. Really. I appre— I do need help. Please ..."

I wish I could stop crying. I snuff, and the brown-haired woman hands me a tissue. Her eyes and the man's stay fixed on me. Anxiously, she grips her phone.

"What can we do?" she asks. "Are you sick? Do you need a doctor?"

"No—no—" I clear my nose. "My mo-other died. My mother just died."

She punches three tiny buttons.

"No!" I cry. "No! I'm okay! I had to take this overnight flight. They lost my suitcase. There was something so valuable in it. I have to get to Jonesboro. My mother ..."

The woman nips her call in the bud.

"You poor thing," she says.

With a plump, warm hand, she pulls me to my feet. My face is crushed against her vanilla breast. The Yankee Air man taps me on the shoulder.

"We can help you with that ... miss," he says gingerly. "I'm sorry about your mother. But we can get that bag for you. We can fix that. We can help you rent a car. Jonesboro isn't far."

I don't want to release the woman's soft, warm body, but she pushes me back. I scoop up Joey.

"Just come with us ... miss," says the straight-backed man.

The sweet-smelling woman turns to me, her clear eyes reddening. "Ma'am, if we can be of any help ..." She digs in her purse. "Just give us a call. The Carbondale Bible Church. I'm so sorry." She hands me a tract and hugs me. Her steps recede in a clean rhythm.

"Just come this way, miss." The uniformed man leads me to a counter where a big, dark-haired woman stares at her console. "Terri, would you help this woman, please? She's lost a family member, and her luggage has been delayed."

The burly woman looks curiously at Joey but quickly begins to type. "Sorry to hear that, ma'am. Don't worry. We'll find it. Could you show me your ticket, please?"

Her badge flashes as it catches the light: "Terri Svoboda."

"Okay. Yup. There it is," she mutters. "Looks like it didn't make it onto that Vegas flight. That's where it is now. It's going to take a while for it to get here."

"I understand. It's just—there's something so valuable in it—"

"Don't worry. We'll find it." She glances to make sure the man has gone, then reaches out to pat Joey. "What a nice bear! You know, he looks just like the guys we chased off the runway last night."

"Bears? There were bears on the runway?" I work my fingers into Joey's fur.

"Oh, yeah. Happens all the time."

"Yeah," I recall. "When I was at Penn College, they had to fire off a gun at night to scare the deer off the runway."

"Oh, yeah." Terri's breasts shake as she nods. "Deer—we get a lot of them, but lately it's been bears. My husband, Tim, he works maintenance, and when that last flight comes in from Philly ..."

Our eyes meet, and I sense a hundred stories. Reluctantly, she looks back at her console.

"So where can we reach you?"

"Oh—I don't know yet. I have to get to Jonesboro. Rent a car. Here's my cell phone number."

She types the digits as I recite them.

"Okay. I understand. Well, once you get settled, you can call us here." Terri hands me a card. "They can let you know where your bag is. All right?"

I hold fast to Joey.

"Rental cars are right around the corner. And—and, ma'am—I hope everything goes all right for you. Just give us a call. We'll find that bag."

Outside, the sunlight is thick enough to drink. I close my eyes and tilt my face skyward. Over the roar of traffic, insects are buzzing. My nose welcomes the humid air, which smells of growth even in this sea of cars. Joey perks up, and I realize that I haven't said I'm taking him to sweet-smelling hills where bears live. After all this time, I've brought him home. Gratefully, he kisses my neck.

Compared to Wilma, my rental car is heavy and puffy, so I decide to name her Frieda. Since I don't need a map, I strap Joey in front. The green hills have aroused him, and he raises his nose. The car fills with a familiar voice.

"—morning Sabbath!"

Oh, boy! A preacher! I haven't heard one of them since Oklahoma. This one doesn't pierce like that Arkansas man, but his rhythm commandeers my thoughts. By the time I hit sixty on the service road, he has me mesmerized.

"Now, those of you who were with us last week know that today's topic is sin. I want to talk about sin because a few weeks ago, a woman told me there is no such thing. 'There are no sins,' she said. Just like that. Said it's a medieval concept doing violence to our lives. Now, if she'd read her Bible, she'd know that sin is a shiny, luscious fruit that turns to bitter ash when you taste it."

Sounds like one of those fruit salads in a cup. I curve north onto I-81.

"A sin will deceive you—it will tempt you—it will look like something you want. Its form may be pleasing, but when you embrace it—if you make that mistake—you'll discover its emptiness. For that beautiful form provides no nourishment—far from it. You might even say that it's poison. Now, I ask you—is that relevant to our life today? How many things have you experienced just like that?"

Bold greenery clings to layered gray cliffs. Thick grass thrives beside the road. On the shoulder lie lumps of raw flesh and brown fur. Joey shudders. Shocked by a dead raccoon with a bushy, ringed tail, I almost miss the turnoff for 6 East.

"Now, as the Bible says, he who sins becomes the servant of sin …"

Route 6 curves up over soft hills in three smooth, empty lanes. On Frieda's dashboard, 11:15 becomes 11:16. Johnny must be in his lab. I wonder what happened to Clifton. Steering with one hand, I pull up his last message. One punch of a button kills the preacher.

Boop.

I swerve to avoid a dead opossum, its head crushed, its plump body intact.

Boop.

Gee, I hope he's okay. I should have called him sooner.

"Mmph … uh? Whuh?"

"Clifton, it's me."

"Theresa?"

How strange to hear Clifton in these dense green woods. The leaves hang so close I wonder how his voice slips between them. It reaches me, anxious and a little askew.

"Oh, God ... Thank God," he mutters. "I've been so worried. Where are you? What's going on?"

"I'm in Pennsylvania. My mother just died." The words conjure her, lying granite-still.

"Oh, God ... Theresa—I'm sorry." He sighs. "I knew it had to be something like that."

"What do you mean?"

"Oh, nothing, just—I was pretty upset last night. I thought some bad things. I'm sorry ..."

A dull clunk hits my ear. "Uh!"

"What's the matter? Are you all right?"

"Yeah, just hit my head. I'm okay. What happened to your mother? When did you hear?"

"Oh, yesterday afternoon, right around when you got in. I had to leave right away."

"But why didn't you call me? I would have understood. Losing your mother—that's terrible."

These juicy woods lure me, and I wish that I could stop and wander. If only I could feel those moist leaves brush my skin. Reluctantly I focus on Clifton.

"I'm sorry," I murmur. "I've been flying. My phone has been off. And I've felt ... kind of numb. I haven't been able to talk to anybody."

"You should have called me," says Clifton reproachfully. "You need to talk to someone at a time like this. What happened? You said she was in a home."

"Yeah ..." I falter. "She had pneumonia. It got so bad she couldn't breathe, and she'd left a do-not-resuscitate order."

Last time I saw her, her phlegmy rattle made me feel ashamed of every breath I took.

"Yeah ..." Clifton reflects. "That's a tough choice. But maybe it's for the best. Once you get someone on one of those machines ..."

In a small field, a gray shack lists to one side. How many storms before it collapses?

"So it was sudden?" asks Clifton.

"No ... it came on kind of gradually ... I just didn't realize ..."

The trees pressing in from each side constrict Route 6 to two lanes.

"But—why did you go to San Francisco, then? I mean, if you thought ... if you knew—" Shock clips his voice.

"I guess I didn't believe it." I squirm. "I don't know. I just had to."

Clifton's tone sharpens. "Oh, no. It's not that guy, is it? Were you still going to see him—even ..."

"No. I wanted to keep writing my novel. It was flowing so well. When I see her ..."

One glimpse of my mother's resentful eyes freezes my pen in midmotion.

"Oh ..." Clifton breathes. "You're sure it was that? ... And not ... uh—hold on!"

There is a thud and a lot of static, then something that sounds like coughing.

"Theresa?" Clifton's voice summons me weakly.

"Clifton? Are you okay?"

"Yeah, I'm sorry … I just got sick. I feel better now …"

I picture him retching in that dark hotel.

"What's the matter? Did you eat something bad?"

"No … no … I can't say."

The phone hisses as he settles under the covers.

"Come on. If you're really sick, you should see a doctor."

"No, that's not it." He sighs. "It's—well—I guess I got pretty drunk last night."

"Worse than Las Vegas?"

"Oh, yeah … I haven't been like this since college. I can't remember how I got back here last night. Mrs. Reddy told me this restaurant to go to, and it was pretty good, but the food was so hot. And then—well, it was only eight thirty, and I didn't want to be alone, so I went to this bar …"

The wet woods swallow my laugh. Joey glowers and shakes his head.

"Bourbon again, huh? You really like that stuff?"

"No! I hate it! … I just … Oh, it's so crazy. I shouldn't be telling you things like this when your mother …"

"That's okay. You can tell me."

"Well, I had all these thoughts. I just couldn't stand it. I couldn't bear to be alone with them. First I thought that you had an accident. I kept picturing you by the side of the road—cars passing—and no one knowing who you were."

How strange. In all these miles, I've never thought that I might crash.

"That's—I don't know—that's crazy," I say. "But it's nice you care about me like that."

"I do—I do care." Clifton's voice gains strength. "It was so awful—not knowing. But when Mrs. Reddy told me you had been here and you'd left—I thought …"

"What?"

"Theresa? Can I ask you something? Please tell me the truth. Is Theresa Ramírez your real name? Or is it … that other …"

I stare at the road ahead, a gray path through a parted sea of green.

"What do you think?"

"Oh, come on, for God's sake!" he cries. "I left my kids to see you. At least you can tell me that!"

I feel strangely calm. "Okay. I'll tell you if you tell me what you really thought last night."

"Okay. Okay, it's a deal."

"You first." I grin.

"All right …" He hesitates. "But you understand, I know I was wrong now, right? I know it was your mother, and I'm sorry."

Joey grimaces.

"Okay. Well—I thought the whole thing was a lie. Your name—your meeting me—your having feelings … I thought you planned it from the start."

My stomach tightens. "You thought that?"

"Yeah … I thought … that guy—he's at the center of it. I thought that you loved him and he didn't love you, so you wanted to do the same thing to someone else. As some kind of revenge."

I feel as though someone kicked me in the stomach. "You thought that?"

"Yeah. I'm really sorry. I didn't know about your mother."

"Wow ..." My voice is tinctured breath.

"I'm so sorry. It's just—well—a lot of women have been pretty mean to me, and I've gotten to expect this kind of thing. I mean—before I got married. I just didn't think it would happen again."

I clench my jaw. "Well, it hasn't—that's not it."

"Good ... So will you tell me now?" he pleads. "That's it—that's what I thought—except ... the worst part was ... how much I still wanted to be with you. I kept seeing you with him, and it made me sick."

"I'm sorry," I mutter. "I've just been at airports ... trying to get home ..."

"So will you tell me now? Please?"

"Yeah. It's Carrie."

In the green woods, the leaves crystallize.

"Carrie ... McFadden? Like it says on your book? So why did you—" Clifton sounds more puzzled than angry. "That's crazy. Why did you tell me your name was Theresa?"

"I don't know. Haven't you ever wanted to be someone else?"

"Yeah. All the time." He laughs. "But I never would have thought of ..."

"I just wanted to know what it felt like to be called Theresa. I've always liked that name."

"That's crazy. But ... I guess I like your reason. I could never get away with it."

The trees thin to reveal a farm that's all curves, soft hills and a round silver silo.

"I guess ... I guess I'm trying to live the kind of life where you can do that," I say. "Pick a name, and people just believe you."

"That's hard to do." Clifton laughs.

"Well, it worked for a while."

"Fresh Strawberries," announce blue letters against dull gray wood.

"So now that I know ..." begins Clifton. "I mean, unless your name is really Eunice Lipschitz or something—"

"Hey, that's pretty good!"

"Now that I know ... does that mean you don't want to be with me anymore? Do you need to keep finding guys who don't know you?"

"No ... no ..." I breathe. "I like you ..."

"You mean that?" asks Clifton hopefully.

A wearier strawberry sign leans against a hammer-shaped mailbox.

"Because I understand," he pushes, "about your mother. But I want to see you. I could come to Atlanta when you get back."

I see Clifton's fat finger approaching my bell.

"I don't know ... I don't know about that ..."

"What do you mean? Theresa—oh—oh, yeah—you just said that you liked me."

I feel like I did on that cliff.

"I don't know," I say. "Everything's happening so fast. My mother—I just can't think. I've had my phone turned off.

You're the first person I've called. I've been in places I couldn't use it ... on planes ... the medical center—"

"The medical center? What were you—oh. Oh, no."

"No. It's not—"

I swerve to avoid a plank lying across the road like an abandoned chopstick.

"So you did see him!"

The phone spits static.

"God damn it! What a liar you are!"

"I'm not a liar!"

The world melts, but Clifton won't relent.

"Has anything you've ever told me been true? Did your mother even die?"

"Yeah, she died!" I shout. "If she hadn't died, I'd be with you right now instead of fucking Jonesboro, Pennsylvania!"

The woods have closed in, and I'm not sure where I am.

"Or with him, more likely!" stabs Clifton. "Unless—what, did he dump you? Did he say he didn't want you? Did you lure me here as a consolation prize?"

"No! No!"

I squeeze my eyes so I can see the road, which is plunging downward. A tone emerges in Clifton's voice like a devil from a puff of smoke, new in him but horribly familiar.

"Because if you set this whole thing up on purpose, then—you're more than a liar—a manipulator. If you never felt anything for me—then you're a whore. You've used me like a cold-blooded whore!"

The phone stays pressed to my ear. The woods are a pale green blur.

"I'm not a whore."

Clifton stays on the line, but I can't hear his breath. At last he sighs.

"Oh, God. Theres— Carrie. Whoever you are. I'm sorry. I can't believe I just said that. I never talked to a woman like that before. I barely know myself—the things you've got me doing. After Las Vegas—I was even thinking of leaving my wife for you. To think of you with him—it makes me sick. Why do you want him so much when all he does is hurt you?"

As Clifton eases off, my breathing settles. Frieda's tires thrum against the road.

"I don't know," I say softly. "I don't know if I even do anymore. He was nice to me when I was just learning who I was. He made me feel like I was worth something."

"But anybody could have told you that."

"Well—he had a special way of doing it."

Johnny's long fingers stroke my arm, and my body smiles.

"But he doesn't love you," presses Clifton. "I know that's it. You keep—"

In my core, a tight form unfolds.

"I know." I sigh. "Probably he doesn't. But there's a bond between us. It'll always be there. I feel it when he looks at me—when he touches me ..."

"He touched you? Your mother was dying, and you drove to San Francisco so he could touch you?"

"Yes!"

"My God, what—"

"Yes!" I explode. "Because being with someone you love means more than pretending to love someone you hate!"

"My God ..." Clifton breathes concertedly, as though trying to cool a stoked furnace. "I risked my family to come see you. I was thinking of leaving my wife. Doesn't that mean anything? What do you care about? What in hell is wrong with you?"

"Nothing!" I cry. "There's nothing the matter with me! If I were a guy, everything would be fine! I care about doing things—science—writing! Talking about things that matter—not pretending."

"Not pretending? You've got to be kidding me."

A muddy pool glints in an empty lot. When I was seven, I dove headfirst into a puddle. I loved the feel of my mother's kneading fingers as she washed the mud from my hair.

"Look—Clifton ..." I sigh. "Have you ever thought about getting ... you know ... a professional?"

"What—a therapist? A marriage counselor?"

"No ..."

"Oh, God, no! No!"

I laugh at his self-righteous horror.

"Because you keep talking about feelings, but I think what you really want is sex."

"No! No! I mean—"

Good thing he can't see my grin.

"Your marriage is okay, right?"

"Yeah, I guess so," he mumbles.

"You just want sex—creative sex? Some variety?"

"Any kind."

Clifton and I drift on the same warm wave.

"So why not just—"

"No! You think the only reason I like you is—"

"Yeah." I shift my hips and wiggle my back. If only I could give him what he needs.

"No! I want to be with you because I have feelings for you."

"You sure it's not the other way around?"

"Yeah!"

"But why don't you try it?" I persist. "I mean, you're on your own for a few days. You can afford it …"

"No!" he protests. "I—I wouldn't like it. I don't want to be with a woman I don't care about. How can you even think that?"

"Oh, I guess it's just because I hang out with guys," I say slowly. "A lot of guys tell me they like it."

I fly past a dull building surrounded by dirt. Rusty bulldozers hunger to clear more ground.

"I just don't think I could—" Clifton falters. "You know, even if I did, I'd be thinking of you."

"Even after—"

"Yeah. God knows why, after all you've told me. But it's gotten to be … You know, I think of you when I'm with Karen. I think I will for a while."

"I'm sorry."

"Oh, it's all right. I got myself into this. I should have known … But I really like you. Even now."

A cardinal flashes across the road in a red streak.

"Look." Clifton's voice is warm. "I understand if you don't want to do anything for a while—your mother—that guy—and … and after what I said … But … just keep my number, okay? If you ever want to talk … 'Cause I've really liked talking with you. I don't mean just like in Las Vegas. I've liked all of it. I really like you. It'll be hard … without …"

The woods smear to a wet blur.

"Yeah … I've liked talking with you too."

"So maybe you could call sometime—when you're back in Atlanta? Or I could call you?"

"Yeah."

"I guess I'd better get cleaned up now ... go see some of this city."

I wish I were with Clifton, looking at heaps of scaly crabs and hearing the sea lions yelp. Then I pull away from the ice-cream city.

"Yeah." I sigh. "I've got stuff to do too."

"Theresa ..." he ventures. "What you said before ... do you know ...?"

"Try the Tenderloin." I smile. "But be careful."

"I was only kidding."

"Right. Bye, Clifton."

"Bye, Theresa."

Quiet resumes its reign, and I peer into the passing woods. More and more often, the wall of green is broken by buildings—Frank's Auto Body and Ellie's Salon. Near a Shell station, I stop for the first traffic light in an hour, and a 30 mph sign orders me to slow. Where was that turnoff? Frieda's direction signal ticks dramatically against her dull breath. Joey frowns as we climb a hill and head into open fields. Beside the road, a split rail fence marks the land of an aging white farmhouse. Everything is so defined here, the boundaries so visible. But beyond the fence, it isn't clear to whom the green grass belongs.

I almost miss the nursing home driveway, marked by a lone red mailbox. Set below the road, Hillcrest rests silently, its clean bricks baking in the noonday sun. Insects zoom through the honeysuckle air, but the windows and doors are shut tight.

In the parking lot, only a few cars shade the pristine asphalt, whose crisp white lines look so hopeful. Frieda's motor dies, and I sit and stare at Joey. I rub my face against his fuzzy head.

A stench envelops me when I open the door—steam, breath, and sticky pastiness. A chair-bound veteran displays his medals, his sad eyes begging me to airlift him out.

"Muh!" cries a sallow woman in a wheelchair.

Another smiles mischievously, her chin slick with saliva. She extends wet claws toward my jacket. Out of habit, I glance through my mother's door. "Judy Bunch. Catherine McFadden," says the nameplate. There is no linen on her bed.

From the sunroom comes a resonant male voice, solid ground in this cesspool of women.

"How interesting! By gravity!"

It has a Spanish accent.

"So the coal came down all by itself! That is—"

A young nurse gasps, and Gonzalo breaks off. I look so much like my mother that when I come to visit, the new ones think they're seeing a ghost.

"¡Mala! You have come! We were worried when you did not call!"

Gonzalo parts the crowd of nurses, and I spot Louise, then lose her as he embraces me.

"¡Mala! ¡Malísima! Let me look at you!" Gonzalo releases me and tilts up my chin. "Pobre Mala—this has been very hard for you. You look so tired—so thin. You must get some rest." He strokes my hair.

"You got here early?" I ask, enjoying his gliding touch.

"Yes—very fast. Jerry lent me his car, and Diane told me how to go. I left around eight."

Gonzalo turns to the nurses. "How long have I been here?"

"Since about eleven thirty," answers the youngest, a plump, brown-haired girl with a glowing face.

"These ladies have been telling me the history of Jonesboro. Did you know that it was once a mining center? They rolled coal down from the hills on a gravity railway and shipped it to New York on canals. Laura here wants to show me an old mine tomorrow."

"It's really cool!" beams the bright-faced nurse's aide.

As Gonzalo smiles at Laura, Louise approaches, her face set under its helmet of gray hair.

"We're so glad you're here, honey," she says. "We were just telling your friend how much we're going to miss your mother."

"Yeah, she was really sweet," murmurs Laura.

"Would you like to see her?" asks Louise.

"Yeah, I guess so."

Gonzalo wraps an arm around me, and the group dissolves. "Come—let's go, Mala," he says.

Louise leads us down the basement, where a cool, sickly wind stirs the corridor.

"What's that you're calling her?" asks Louise. "I thought her name was Carrie."

"Oh—Mala—it is just a friendly name."

"Oh." Louise compresses her lips.

I have an eerie feeling I've been here before, and the rubbery squelch of the sealed door transports me. The cold room in Marty Cohen's lab—the dank smell of persistent, unwanted life. On a table with white bench paper lies the thing that was my mother—deformed, twisted, and bloated. Her eyes are closed, but her face isn't peaceful, her jaw clenched and her lips still pursed. Her hands are balled into tight fists, and her knees are bent. In that frigid room, she is completely alone.

Louise's eyes burn me, and Gonzalo squeezes my shoulders. "¡Qué pena!"

"Maybe you'd like to be alone with her for a while," murmurs Louise.

I shake my head. Louise stiffens.

"I think this is enough—no?" asks Gonzalo. "Come. There are things we must do. We should get started."

Louise sends us to the director's office, where an enormous woman hands me papers to sign. She recommends Smolek's Funeral Home, and we push out into the fresh air. In the scorching lot, Gonzalo's car and Frieda eye each other like two customers in an empty restaurant. He laughs when he spots Joey in the front seat.

"Always that bear, eh? ¡Mala!" He squeezes me until his bristles burn my cheek. "Tienes que encontrar a un buen macho—un buen varón."

"I'll take the bear."

Gonzalo shakes his head. "Come. We can use my car. Where are you staying?"

"Oh!" I clap my hand to my mouth. "My suitcase!"

"You forgot your suitcase?"

"No! I don't have a motel. My suitcase—they lost my suitcase—they lost the novel!"

Gonzalo's hand freezes in midair. "Mala! What are you saying?"

"They made me check my suitcase—and everything I've written was in it."

"You didn't make a copy?" Even in the bright light, Gonzalo's eyes are nearly black.

"No. I was writing—moving around so much—"

"Mala!" He captures my hands. "You must always make copies! Always! I think when these gilipollas are not hurting you, you are hurting yourself."

I blink to clear my wet eyes.

"Is it really lost?" he presses.

"No, I don't know. It's just gone. This morning they said it was in Vegas. They gave me a number to call."

"So call them right now!"

I dig in my purse, and the card pops up from a fold in the airsickness bag.

"Call them! Come on!"

Gonzalo keeps his eyes on mine while I talk to a woman from Yankee Air.

"All right, Ms. McFadden ... looks like your bag is in Pittsburgh today. We should be able to get it to you in Scranton by ten tomorrow morning."

"But do you know if it's all right?" I plead. "Has it broken open?"

"No, I can't tell from here whether it's suffered any damage. But there's no reason to worry. Let's hope for the best, and you can get that bag tomorrow. Okay?"

I drop the phone in my purse, and Gonzalo exhales. "They have found it?"

"Yeah. Looks like it'll reach Scranton tomorrow morning."

He nods. "See, Mala, they have found it. That is good."

We climb into his car, which has a musky sweetness. Gonzalo smiles to himself as he guides us up the driveway and onto the road downtown. "How beautiful! Look at that house—that field! Can you imagine living here?"

Restive brown horses toss their heads in the sun, and Gonzalo pulls off to admire them.

"It would not be so bad—growing old in a place like this—do you think?"

"Yeah—if you have to get old."

We coast into town and pull into Smolek's.

"I'm glad you're here." I nuzzle his shoulder.

"Come, Mala. Let's do this. Then we can eat something—yes?"

In the round front room of a white Victorian, Dan Smolek guides us through our choices. He needs to know what religion my mother was, whether she should be buried or cremated, what sort of coffin she would want, and what she would like to wear.

"She wasn't religious," I murmur.

Dan's respectful round face registers no affront. "Oh, that's okay. That's a matter of personal choice. Was she baptized?"

"Yeah. Catherine McFadden? She was Catholic."

His dark eyes warm. "Well, maybe you should speak with Father Marcek."

"Mala—even if she did not believe—sometimes a priest can be nice ..."

Dan nods. "The participation of a priest can make a ceremony more meaningful."

We head for the parish house, but Gonzalo is lured by the town. Three parallel streets cut furrows between lush, protective hills. Sooty brick buildings support nineteenth-century false fronts. On Main Street, a German restaurant and a luncheonette feed people visiting the banks, gas station, and ski shop. North of Main lies the old rail line, beside the trickling, still-viable canal. Gonzalo admires the redbrick Lutheran and Baptist churches. Dramatically, he reads out their sermon topics, posted like the menus of failing restaurants.

"If You Were a Child, Would You Want to Be You When You Grew Up?"

We cross the green to the courthouse, where a bouquet of withered roses graces a Civil War memorial. Gonzalo pronounces the names of the Jonesboro men, half of whom fell at Gettysburg. Beyond Court Street looms another green hill, and the smell of fresh grass overwhelms me. The sun beats our heads, and bees zoom in the clover. The ground is tilting up slightly.

"¡Mala! Mala, are you all right? Come—you must eat something!"

Gonzalo leads me back to Main Street and into the Pace Family Restaurant.

"Just sit anywhere!" calls a broad-hipped girl with a thick brown braid.

Some of the plastic-covered tables are bright pink; others, kelly green with purple stripes. Each has a white vase with two American flags and dusty orange silk flowers. We settle at one with an extra ornament, a cow dressed in a red kerchief, a red gingham shirt, a denim skirt, and red boots. Gonzalo picks it up and ogles it.

"Mooooo."

He orders a Reuben sandwich, since he's never tried one, and I ask for pierogies and chicken soup. The soup looks safe, bloated rice in gray water, but the pierogies come floating in half an inch of butter.

"What is that?" he asks.

"Pierogies."

I drain one on a napkin and create greasy yellow papier-mâché.

"Mala—what are you doing? You need to eat. A little butter will not hurt you."

I move the cup of soup and put the decontaminated pierogi on the saucer. With a fork, I snag some onions and slide them on top.

"Mala—I have been worried about you. It is not good you are not talking. So you saw your scientist? If he has been bad to you, you must tell me."

"Yeah … yeah, I saw him." I lay down my fork.

"So he took time to see you? That is good." Gonzalo nods. He bites into corned beef, sauerkraut, and cheese. "And? Where did he take you this time? A phone booth? An elevator? Ah! I have made you smile. Mala, you have a beautiful smile."

I look down self-consciously and poke the cow. "Just his office."

"And?"

"He told me what he was working on … He showed me this whole new research center they're building."

"Mm-hmm—mm!" Gonzalo loves his sandwich, but he keeps his eyes fixed on me.

"And he—he almost—well, he kissed me—but—"

"Oh, Mala … he said no this time. ¡Qué cabrón! I am sorry."

"I—I opened my jacket—and he made me close it. He—he sent me away. He said I was crazy …"

The words recreate the annihilation, only this time it's more real. Gonzalo disappears behind a shining curtain.

"Oh, Mala …" His strong hand grips mine.

"He wanted to … I know he did. I could feel it … If you could have seen him …"

"I am sure he did."

"And he planned it—that's what's so awful—he planned it. He saw me at four when he had to be somewhere at five. He gave me exactly an hour."

Gonzalo frowns. "Maybe he didn't know himself. From what you tell me, he can do many things in an hour."

The truth is emerging like a baby I have to push out.

"Yeah," I say, "but that's just it. His plan was to fuck me, dump me, or both, but either way, not take more than an hour."

With his mouth still full, Gonzalo chokes on a laugh. "Mala—there is something I like about this man."

"You're bad!" I laugh, wet-faced. I kick at him under the table, but my leg slices empty air.

"Where was he supposed to be at five?"

"Provost."

"Oh." Gonzalo studies my pierogi. "For you, Mala, I would have blown off the provost … Are you going to eat that?"

I hand him my plate.

"No, no! I meant—I want you to eat it. Try a bite. It looks good."

I fill my mouth with warm, salty starch.

"Mala—starving yourself will not help. Did he say he never wants to see you again?"

I scan my hour with Johnny at flash speed and see no sign he wanted anything but closure.

"No. But I don't think he does. He said to take care of myself. He was worried."

"See, Mala. You are right. He does care about you. Maybe just not the way you want."

"'Take care of yourself' is English for 'Fuck off and die.'"

Gonzalo stiffens. "Mala, I am not stupid. You have said he is direct. Probably he meant what he said."

I slump back, unable to fight Gonzalo's logic. In my despair, I find the words that have been hiding. "Well, even if he did, he thinks I'm crazy. Everyone does! I can't stand having all these labels stuck on me … It's like—I'm this soft, organic thing, and these labels are metal cookie cutters smashing me into the shape of other people's thoughts."

"What labels?" Gonzalo's eyes are golden brown.

"Crazy. Whore. Lonely. Selfish. Immature. People try to force them on me so they can explain me away."

Gonzalo sits motionless, absorbing.

"Twenty years—he made such a big deal it's been twenty years since we were together. It doesn't feel like that long. I feel just the same—only people treat me differently."

Gonzalo gazes at me intently. "I think everyone lives with this—these labels. You know what they call me? Don Juan! Can you believe that?"

"No!" I laugh. "At least that's better than what they call me."

"What?"

"Ma'am. 'May I help you, ma'am?' 'Excuse me, ma'am!' It makes me feel so old!"

Gonzalo's smile twists ironically. "Well—we are in our midforties."

"But I don't feel old! I don't want to be old!"

Gonzalo frowns. "Are you worried your scientist will not want you?"

"Him and everyone! Who wants a disgusting old woman?"

"¡Mala! The people who matter—they like you for reasons other than sex. Anyway, I doubt he said no because you are a disgusting old woman. Probably he was afraid his wife would find out. Or that he would hurt you."

The injustice of it starts me crying again. "Hurt me? Hurt me? I drove three thousand miles to see him! I went to see him when my mother—"

"¡Mala! Mala, here, take a napkin. Mala, tranquila … you love him that much?"

His hand closes over mine.

"Mala"—he lifts my hand and shakes it—"it is okay. It is good to love. It is all right, what you feel. Even if he doesn't feel the same way—it can be beautiful to love someone. Just as long as it doesn't hurt you."

"He was saying goodbye! He doesn't—"

"Hi, folks. You ready for some dessert?" The wide-hipped girl is back, smiling radiantly. Ashamed of my red eyes, I stare at the table.

"Oh, yes, what do you have?" Gonzalo grins. "I bet you have some very nice desserts here."

"We sure do. We have twelve kinds of pie."

"Twelve kinds!" He inhales as though she had opened an oven door and he were breathing their blended scent. He orders strawberry rhubarb and lemon meringue and makes me try them both.

"We need to go find that priest," he says.

Younger and more vital than the Protestant churches, the Catholic one clings to a hill north of the tracks. To get there, we cross a rusty steel footbridge, and I shudder as I glimpse the canal far below. A stubbly old man sweeping the front walkway tells us that Father Marcek is in the parish house. From a side door comes a short, slender priest who scans us with intelligent eyes. He invites us to his study, a dark room where books seem to grow from the walls.

"How may I help you?" he asks encouragingly.

"My mo-other just died," I say.

His small black eyes twinge with disappointment. Maybe he was hoping we wanted to marry.

"She was baptized in the church," says Gonzalo.

"Ah … I see. But she was not of this parish?" Father Marcek's eyes dig me until I squirm.

"No," I stammer. "She was at Hillcrest. She used to live in Scranton."

"Ah, yes …" He eyes my silk jacket and my hands that won't keep still.

"She wasn't religious … didn't go to Mass …"

"I see." He frowns. "So she didn't receive the last rites?"

"No."

Father Marcek looks out at the southern hill, whose soft, moist green seems to pulse. "Is your father alive?" he asks.

"I don't know."

"What?" Gonzalo twists in his chair.

Father Marcek's eyes jump back to me. "So you've lost contact with your father. Were your parents married?"

"Yes." I sigh. "He left when I was very small."

The priest's eyes soften, but his gaze still burns. "Do you have any brothers or sisters?"

"No."

"So you're planning this memorial yourself—you and your friend—and you'd like my assistance?"

"Yes."

For the first time, Father Marcek smiles. "The church welcomes you and your mother. Your love for her has brought you back to us."

"Oh, I—"

Gonzalo silences me with a soft gesture.

"I'd be glad to officiate. Can you come back tomorrow? Mr. Kelly will make you an appointment. Right now I need to get ready for six o'clock mass. I hope you'll join us."

"Of course," says Gonzalo.

With old women in kerchiefs, we sit through the evening mass. In action, Father Marcek is impressive. In his pleated white robe, he moves like a representative of God. His quiet voice swells with conviction, and when he raises his arms to bless us, he means it.

For dinner, we drive to a Chinese buffet, and Gonzalo won't let up about my father. As soon as we fill our plates, he starts in again.

"Mala! Why didn't you tell me? Why did you lie?"

"I don't know."

I stare at an oily green broccoli tree, but the force of his gaze draws my eyes.

"Something as important as this! I have known you twenty years! Why did you not tell me?"

Slowly I breathe in and out. Hurt has widened his brown eyes.

"I don't know." I sigh. "It's what my mother told me to say. I've been telling people so long I almost believe it."

"So why did you not say the same thing to Father Marcek? It would have been easy. How would he know?"

"I don't know." I shrug. "He's a priest."

"You lie to your friends, and you tell the truth to a stranger?"

His disappointment tightens my stomach.

Slowly Gonzalo releases his breath. "When did it happen?"

"Oh, when I was just a baby. I never knew him."

"And you tried—"

"No." I shake my head. "My mother didn't want to. That was back before computers and deadbeat dads. He just left, and she never saw him again."

"Mala, that is terrible. We must talk about this some more. Why don't you stay with me tonight? At the Gravity Motel."

Though our plates are half-full, he reaches for the check.

I nod. "Okay. Thanks." This should be interesting.

On the shadowed highway back into town, I ask, "Can we go get my bear?"

"That bear?" asks Gonzalo incredulously. "You want to get that bear?"

"Yeah. He's all alone in a strange car."

From the way Joey's been holding his head, I don't think he likes Frieda's smell.

"Okay, Mala, okay." Gonzalo sighs.

He drives down Main Street and turns up the hill into absorbing blackness.

"So you have written a lot?"

"Yeah." I brighten. "I can feel the story now. I have to flesh it out, but I've got the skeleton. One more scene, and I'll have the framework."

"One more scene! And you have done this in—what, two weeks? When you have been trying for six years?"

"Yeah." I smile.

"So what happened?"

Ptt! A juicy bug splatters on the windshield.

"Well—you know the story of the Chinese warlord and the two artists? There's this Chinese warlord, see, and he wants to find an artist to paint his portrait. So he takes the two best artists in the land, and he gives each one ten years to paint a rooster. When the ten years are up, they both come back, and the first one's carrying the most detailed painting of a rooster you ever saw.

"'This is brilliant,' says the warlord, but then he looks at the second artist, who sits down and paints a rooster in thirty seconds—whoosh, whoosh, whoosh.

"'What is this?' asks the warlord. 'I give you ten years, and you sit down and paint me some crap in thirty seconds? Don't you take this seriously? What have you been doing with yourself?'

"'Oh, I take it very seriously,' says the second artist, 'but it took me ten years to learn how to paint a rooster in thirty seconds.'"

When we reach Hillcrest, I take Joey in my arms, and Gonzalo enfolds us both.

"Oye, Mala," he says. "You say you have just one more scene to write?"

"Well, yeah, of this first draft." I settle Joey on my lap.

"So why don't you write it tomorrow?" he urges.

"Oh, no …" I can't imagine writing in a place like this. I mean, where would I do it?

"Sí, Mala!" he insists. "What time do you have to go and see that priest?"

"At three."

"So you have lots of time …" reflects Gonzalo. "Mala, listen … I was planning on being with you … all the time here, but maybe it would be better if you finish your story. You always say that writing is best."

"Yeah … I don't know … I guess I could try."

I peer out into the passing fields but see only my pale reflected face.

"Sí, Mala. I will leave you alone for a while. That way you can write your scene."

"Okay," I mumble. "Okay, I'll try."

Gonzalo pulls out his phone.

"Hello? Yes, hi, this is Gonzalo … No, I am not kidding … Listen, do you still want to go to that mine tomorrow? … Yes! It will be very cool … So 31 Charter … Oh, 31 Carter … No, do not worry—I will find you … What time is good? Yes— eleven … Yes, I like to sleep too … Sweet dreams … Oh, that is very nice. Maybe I will dream of you too. See you tomorrow! Yes … yes … Bye."

I smother my laugh in Joey's fur.

"You're leaving me alone with a priest while you go down a mine shaft with a sixteen-year-old?"

Gonzalo smiles at the pool of light flowing into the road ahead. "I leave you with your art, Mala—for your art I make this sacrifice. And she seems like a very nice girl."

"Yeah—*girl*. *Girl*. Just check her driver's license before you go down there, okay?"

"Oh, I do not think she has one. She is not old enough."

I extend a lobster claw to pinch his side.

On a dark slope near the Catholic church, the Gravity Motel forms a fungal shelf. Our door opens to reveal brown carpet, a dark-green bedspread, and a small TV. I set Joey on the counter, and he looks skeptically at the bed, one side of which is higher than the other. Four hookless hangers jangle in the draft. While I brush my hair, Gonzalo watches with interest, and he lets me use his toothbrush and toothpaste. He disappears into the bathroom, and I undress and creep under the covers. He emerges in a pair of navy-blue-striped pajamas.

"Ooh, this is nice! Very nice!" Gonzalo fingers the lace of my black bra dangling on the chair.

We decide that if I take the low side of the bed and he takes the high side, it should even out, but we quickly fall into the middle. Gonzalo drapes his arm over me and strokes my hair.

"Try to sleep now, Mala. You look so tired. You must take better care of yourself."

It's so nice, the warm body behind me, his belly filling the small of my back.

"You are a nice woman, Mala." He kisses my hair.

"Mm …" I push my backside into him playfully.

Gonzalo breathes faster, and between my cheeks, he hardens and grows. A warm hand reaches for my breasts.

"Mala ... You are such a nice woman ..."

I arch my back, and he pulls me closer.

Gonzalo raises his head. "Mala."

His lips brush my ear. "Mala, I think we must not do this."

"Mm?" I roll over to face him.

"Mala, it feels very good ... pero tengo que frenarme. I think it is not good for us. See?"

"Mm-hmm." I reach up to stroke his thinning hair.

He bunches the quilt between us until we're separated by six inches of wadding.

"Here, Mala. This will keep you safe. Try to sleep now."

Gently he touches my cheek. Even through the quilt, I can feel his warmth. It stirs a little with each breath he draws. Soft, warm, black, the hiss of air ... I feel as though I'm rising and spinning ...

What? Who shook me?

"Mala! What is wrong?"

"What?" A hand grips my shoulder.

"Mala! You have been crying! What is wrong?"

I don't know where I am, but it feels like the cold room in Marty Cohen's lab.

"She's all alone! She's all alone in there like a dead rat!"

"Mala—you have been dreaming. Come here."

Gonzalo rolls me over so that I'm facing him, but I can't stop shaking. I start to recognize the bed, but the cold room is much more real.

"She's all alone! I left her all alone in there!"

Gonzalo hugs me, trying to squeeze out the fear.

"No, Mala. She was in a place full of people. Always with people, all the time."

"But she felt so alone," I sob. "She was alone, and it was my fault!"

"No, Mala."

Gonzalo pushes me back. A slice of light from the window splits his face.

"Yes!" I cry. "It was my fault he left. She never said so, but that was what she felt."

"Mala, that cannot be true."

He can't imagine a mother who regrets having her child.

"Yes!" I blurt. "She was so old when she had me—old for way back then. She was working as a secretary, and she hated it. She was studying at night—biology, because she wanted to work in a lab. Biology was so exciting, she said, and people were learning things so fast. People were figuring out how genes worked, and here she was typing. Then she met my father, and I guess she liked him so much she took a chance. She always said never take chances. And—and—"

"Mala, ¡tranquila! It was not your fault!"

He pulls me closer as my voice dissolves.

"She lost everything!" I moan. "She had me, and she couldn't study, and I drove him away! She said he hated my crying. He didn't want a baby. If it weren't for me, he'd still be there!"

Gonzalo rocks me and kisses the top of my head. "She said all that?"

"No, not exactly. But she thought it—I could tell by the things she said. From the way she breathed, from the way she pressed her lips together. 'If it weren't for you, he'd still be here.'"

"But she had you—didn't she want you?" His voice loosens as he starts to believe.

"In 1961? What else could she do?"

"So what did she do—how did she manage?"

"Well, she kept on working as a secretary, but she had to stop studying. She had to stay home with me at night. We had no money. We lived in the Spanish neighborhood."

"Ay, Mala," he sighs. "She blamed it all on you?"

"Yeah! She hated me!" I tremble. "She always made me feel ... like I didn't belong with her. I've never felt like I belonged anywhere!"

"Mala, that's crazy!" says Gonzalo. "Of course you belonged with her. How can you think that?"

My mother's image overpowers his voice. She shimmers in the dark like a burnished saint.

"She hated everything," I blurt. "Cooking. Cooking more than anything. She'd make a pot of stew on Sunday to last the week. If I ate too much of it, she'd get so angry. She called me a pig. She hated having me! She wished I would die!"

"But maybe she also liked you a little?" Gonzalo works his fingers through my hair. "And you didn't stay little for long." He squeezes my breast. "Mira, ¡qué chica más grande! Why didn't she go back to school when you got bigger? Didn't she have boyfriends? Why didn't she remarry?"

"Oh, I don't know. That's just the way she was. She built her life on being miserable."

"Ay, Mala. ¡Qué pena! So she was mean to you?"

"No, not mean ... She pushed me to study. Science—medicine—anything but writing. She hated my writing. She told me it was bad."

"Probably she was afraid of what you'd write." Gonzalo laughs. "Or that you'd end up like her."

"Well, I'm not like her! I'm not going to end up like that!"

"Of course not, Mala," he murmurs. "Of course not. When you die, thousands of men will come ... gordos ... flacos ..."

"Pollos ... gilipollas ..."

"All with big bunches of flowers. Father Marcek will not be able to fit them in his church."

"Tantos gordos ... tantos flacos ..." I have stopped shaking.

"See? You are not like her. You do what you want." Gonzalo's pajama top clings to his chest, wet from my tears. "Oye, ¿qué tal el gordo?"

A laugh bubbles out of my belly. "He came to San Francisco ..."

"¡No! ¡Qué mala eres!"

"But I went to see Johnny ..."

"Johnny? This is a name for a grown man?"

I quiver with laughter.

"¿Y qué le pasó al pobre gordo?"

"Se emborrachó ..."

My laugh infects Gonzalo.

"¡Me llamó una puta!"

"¡No! That is not so nice." He frowns. "I would leave this fat man."

"Well, he forgave me for stranding him there." I hesitate. "He wants to see me in Atlanta."

"So you will give him a workout?" Gonzalo smiles.

"What, like you're getting today?"

"Mala ..." He shakes me gently. "I am only learning the local history."

"Yeah? Well, just don't make it. They have guns out here."

Gonzalo presses me close, and we laugh in the darkness. Around the rubber curtain, a frame of gray light glows. Joey emerges as a fuzzy, dark blob and scowls at us suspiciously. In spite of the glimmer, we linger in bed, comparing stories of our recent loves. Gonzalo asks me about my trip, so we don't reach the Pace Family Restaurant until ten.

This morning, it is almost full. A scrub-head and two bickering kids occupy the cow table. We sit near the window, and after some puffy pancakes, Gonzalo heads for the mine. I sit stationed at my sticky green-and-purple table.

Raúl says that he can smell Justin on me. I guess it might be true. Until the doctor came, Justin wouldn't let me go, and lately he's been wearing some sweet cologne. For an hour we sat by the candy machine and stared at the speckled green tiles. Then a tall doctor with a brown beard came out and told us to follow him to an examining room.

"Mr. Marshall?" he said, looking down at Justin. "I'm terribly sorry. Your mother suffered a massive stroke. We did all we could, but the damage was too great. It was probably sudden ... She didn't suffer."

Justin caught a tear on his index finger.

"You knew she had multi-infarct dementia?"

Justin nodded, evading the doctor's brown eyes.

"So I guess you must have known that at any time ... even with her medication ..."

"Yeah ... I just didn't think ..."

"We're never ready for it," said the doctor. "There's never enough time."

Justin's shoulders shook, and I took his hand.

"I'll leave you alone with your mother. Let us know when you're ready."

After that, I couldn't leave him. That's what I keep telling Raúl.

"He has no family! No one. No brothers or sisters, no wife or kids. Both his fathers are dead. Can you imagine?"

Raúl glares at me, his eyes black and hard. "I imagine he saw a chance to screw a woman who felt sorry for him."

"No! If you could have seen him crying! He has no family! How could I leave him alone there with his mother lying dead on the table?"

Raúl folds his thick brown arms. "You didn't see any problem leaving me alone."

"Your mother didn't die!" I shout. "We called to say—"

"We?" Raúl grabs my shirt and yanks me like a fallen branch. His hand slams into my face.

"Stop!" I scream. "You could—"

His rough hands grab my shoulders. "That was for being stupid! Can't you see he's just using you?" He hurls me down on his battered chair. "What am I supposed to think when he brings you home at three—como una puta callejera?"

"I'm sorry! His mother just died! Wouldn't you stay with someone if his mother died?"

Raúl seizes my leg and pulls me down on the rug. I land with a thud, and pain flashes up my back.

"¡Basta! Dios mío! Vas a—"

Raúl glowers at me, but his voice quiets. "He's not your friend. He's your boss. Men and women aren't friends. Look—you're not a bad woman. You're just stupid. There's only one reason a man ever talks to a woman."

Raúl extends a hand and frowns at my cheek, which is starting to swell. He strokes my hair and rests his hand on my shoulder. "So she's dead—la vieja?"

"Yeah. I liked her." I am shaking with sobs.

Raúl nods, smiling as he remembers. "Me too. But him—you don't see him again, you hear? You don't see him." Raúl's eyes are wet and black, and his fingers tighten on my shoulder. He frees me with one last shake.

The next day, when Raúl is at work, I call Justin from the market. I tell him I can't come, and his faint voice says he knows why. I ask him when the funeral will be, but he says there isn't going to be one. His mother left her body to the medical school. ¡Qué barbaridad! That can't have been her idea. He is planning a memorial on Wednesday at noon, and if I come to the house, he can drive me. All right, I say. Raúl will be at work, and even if he finds out, he can't hit me that hard now.

As I walk from the bus stop, I stare up into tall trees until the lacy green circles spin. Justin opens the door, and I look behind him for Mrs. Marshall, forgetting that she's not there. He gazes sadly at my cheek, which is swollen and hot. I let him hold me without pushing him back. His soft embrace is starting to feel natural, almost more natural than Raúl's.

In Justin's new-smelling car, we drive up to Edgewood, and he leads me into a clean white building. Instead of in a church, the memorial is being held in a round hall where famous doctors give lectures. Justin says it makes more sense to do it this way, so the scientists who knew her and Bill can come at lunch. I guess he's right, since the place fills quickly. Everyone wants to talk to Justin, but he keeps me right by his side.

"This is Teresa," he tells everyone. "She took care of my mother."

They stare at me strangely, and I'm not sure if it's my bruised face or my black skirt. No one else is wearing black, and the long-legged gringas are dressed in pants. On a dangling screen, they show pictures of Mrs. Marshall with Bill and Justin. They tell funny stories about her days in the lab. No one mentions the name Jimmy Mellen. The last speaker describes discoveries about nerves using some kind of procedure she developed.

Afterward, Justin wants to walk in a nearby park. I'm wearing my shiny, high-heeled shoes, but I go with him. Slowly, we make our way down a muddy path. Seeing me struggling, Justin offers me his arm.

"It was good of you to come," he says. "You look so nice."

His eyes sweep my pinned-up hair, my black blouse and skirt, my glossy black shoes.

"I thought—for a funeral …" I can't say what I think. These gringos, they have no respect.

"It's okay." He smiles. "These are scientists—doctors—"

"But what about her other friends?" I ask.

Justin gazes down sadly. "Well—she didn't really have any that were just hers. Just friends of my father's. Their families. After he died, she was mostly alone."

"Oh." I can't imagine the pain of living like that. I worry about Justin.

Ancient oaks lead us to a choked brown pond, whose scummy water looks thick enough to slice. Justin sits heavily on a green bench, and I smile to see his belly fighting his gray suit. He pats the slatted wood and invites me to sit beside him. A group of ducks glides toward us in a V, hoping that we'll give them some food.

"You haven't—you haven't gotten yourself in trouble by coming here today, have you?" he asks.

I shake my head. Justin raises his hand to my bruise, and I wince as his fingers brush it.

"Oh! Did I hurt you?"

"No, it's okay."

"Teresa … You can't let him do this to you. It isn't right."

The ducks approach us with beady eyes.

"Did he hit you again? Teresa—let me help you. It doesn't have to have anything to do with me. I guess you must know … you must know how I feel about you …"

I nod and eye three taut ripples across my skirt.

"But it doesn't have to have anything to do with that. I can lend you money … help you go to college, so you can find a good job … I could get you an apartment, someplace where he couldn't find you …"

"You're so nice." I meet his anguished brown eyes. "So kind. I can't understand—"

Justin inhales sharply. "Or if you … Teresa—if you did feel—I—we—"

"No." I shake my head. "I'm married."

Justin's eyes are so different from Raúl's, softer, rounder, deeper.

"But you could get divorced," he says. "If you made a mistake— marriage doesn't have to be forever."

"I am going to have a baby."

"Teresa!" Justin smiles brokenly. "That's good—I mean, you having a baby—but ... if he hurts you ... He might hurt your baby—are you sure you want to raise it with him?"

"Of course," I say. "He's the father." How can a man be so nice and understand so little?

"But I could still help you ..."

"No. You need to find someone like you," I say. "Maybe at work ..."

Justin looks at me desperately. "Teresa—I hate the women at work. They don't care about anything that matters. All they talk about is clothes—TV shows. They say mean things about people ... You're the only woman I like."

"You're nice." I touch his cheek softly, and he kisses me. I let him hold me as long as he wants, but I don't kiss back. Finally he pulls away.

"Maybe now—" I say. "Now that you have more time, you could meet new people. Move out of that big house. Go someplace where young people live."

"Yeah ..." he sighs. "I can't think about that yet. I keep thinking about her—about you."

"When you're ready, then ..."

Justin shifts his weight and meets my eyes with a sudden jolt. "Why does he hit you? How could anyone ...?"

"He was angry," I say slowly. "Men are like that. I came home at three in the morning, and he had to show me ..."

"You didn't tell him?" asks Justin, confused.

"Yes. But he thought it was because of you. And he was right ..."

Justin kisses me again, and this time I kiss him back. He pulls me close and makes a low sound in his throat. With his eyes shut, he releases me slowly.

"Teresa," he pleads, "stay with me! Just stay. Don't go home. Don't go back to him. Come home with me now. Stay with me!" He grips my shoulders.

"No. We are going to have a baby. He only did this because I was with you. When I'm home with the baby, he'll have no reason."

Justin shakes his head, but I rise to my feet. The ducks circle hopefully, their slick bodies cutting grooves in the glassy black water.

"I have to go home now," I say.

"No—Teresa—please—"

Justin reaches for me, but I extend my arms to keep him back. "No."

"Can't I drive you?"

"No. Someone might see."

"Can I call you—or you call me—to make sure you're okay?"

"No! I am going to be fine. I am going to have a baby. We have to respect that."

I start back down the muddy path, and his heavy steps fall dully behind me.

I lay the pen on the sticky table and exhale an endless breath. I have held a universe of air in me, its molecules condensed to save space. Like Justin, I can't accept that I won't see Teresa again. My life has flowed into her solid arms, her bruised face, her matter-of-fact voice. Either one of these men would hold and crush her, whether in a vise or a mudslide. What if this isn't the end, but the beginning? What if her story starts here? In my core, I can feel a strained frame crack, a structure buckling as its beams collapse. I have written a skeleton, all right. Now I need to create life.

Outside the window, the six-year-old from the cow table is bullying his younger brother. He grabs the back of his red sweatshirt and swings him around, avoiding the little one's fists. Their mother runs out of the convenience store and shouts inconsequential threats. When she reaches them, she grabs both by the neck, but the older one twists free.

I climb back to the church, where Father Marcek greets me more energetically than he did last night. It impresses me that the truth doesn't faze him.

"There are lots of ways to tell this story," he says. "How about this? A woman raises her daughter alone, and she grows up to be a professor who writes a best-selling novel."

"But that doesn't—"

The pale priest cuts me off effortlessly. "Those of us who don't have children can't know what it's like to raise them." His soft voice rolls like a train. "You've said your mother was unhappy—you're unhappy. But that can change. Because of her, you're alive. She's given you that chance."

"I feel as though I'm alive in spite of her."

"I know." The priest smiles, and his dark eyes snap. "The feelings of a child for a parent I can understand."

I check the buttons of my jacket—all closed.

"I know you don't believe in the church." His eyes pin me. "But that may change. If it does—we'll always be here. Now—I could do your mother's service on Tuesday at noon. Would that give you enough time?"

Father Marcek has me call Smolek's, and we set the funeral for Tuesday. An ice jam cracks, and the bergs float free. With Father Marcek officiating, my mother will have to be buried, so I walk across town to choose a coffin. There remains the strange problem of how to dress her, an obstacle even Smolek's words can't dissolve. How do you clothe a body that hasn't moved in six years? Sheathing it will be like dressing that cow. Since the heat is fading, I hike out to Hillcrest. Maybe in her closet I'll find the right dress. It's a bigger decision than I realized at first, choosing a garment she'll never take off.

As I trudge up the hill, I study each battered house and wonder what horrors it conceals. Behind each door, accusations ricochet. My sneakers pat the road with a determined beat. I breathe more softly when I reach open fields and the smell of hot grass rises. At this time of day, the world seems to enfold you. Crickets meditate on a high-pitched tone. Distant trees hover over fuzzy fields, and a lone white farmhouse shimmers. From the top of Hillcrest's driveway, I spot Frieda nearly alone on an asphalt sea. I draw one last breath of warm, sweet air and push through the doors into stale stickiness.

By now my mother's name is gone from her door, and her bed is a mosaic of stacked clothes. The closet's folded doors frame Louise's broad back. She starts, and her big hands set the hangers jangling.

"Oh!"

"Oh—hi, Louise."

She turns to reveal a streaming face. "I was just—just packing these things here." She sniffs. "I thought it was one last thing I could do for her."

Louise aligns the sleeves of a maroon robe. She has such strong fingers, such thick wrists.

"Oh—I can do that," I offer. "I need to pick out something anyway. I've just come from Smolek's. We're going to do the service Tuesday. Father Marcek is going to officiate."

Louise nods, and the maroon terry cloth drinks a tear. She's been assembling this rainbow of clothes since my mother arrived, buying them from a traveling vendor. Next to a fuzzy green robe with three plastic cherries lies an indigo gown with embroidered violets.

I pick it up and finger the cloth. "Maybe this one ... She always liked blue ..."

"Honey, you can't bury your mother in a housedress!"

I step back, and the gown opens into a deep blue wave. "But this is pretty—and it's just going—"

"I won't let you bury her in a housedress! I wasn't going—for her sake—but I can't help it. You have no respect! It's outrageous!"

Louise advances on me, her arms tense. "You think I don't know what you were doing in San Francisco? Why you wouldn't come see her when she was struggling for breath? We cried all night—every one of us here—watching her try to hold on so she could see her daughter!"

I toss the blue gown on the bed as something inside me breaks free. "Look—she's been a vegetable for six years! She didn't know whether I was here, or you, or John Paul II! It doesn't make any difference!"

"Oh, yes it does!" Louise's heavy hand twitches. "I know Father Marcek, and I bet on Tuesday he's going to say how wonderful it is that she raised a daughter like you—a professor—a famous writer. Well, I've read your book. We all have here. And I think it's trash. No content—no values—just empty. Like you."

I turn to face her head-on. "How would you know? What do you know about me?"

Louise storms in my face with warm, wet breath. "I know you've left your mother here alone for six years! I know you let her die alone while you were cheating on your boyfriend in San Francisco!"

My lips spread with amusement. "Gonzalo? You think Gonzalo …?"

"What a nice guy like him sees in a woman like you is beyond me." She shakes her head, but her gray curls stay fixed.

"He's not my boyfriend."

Louise raises her brows. Behind her forehead, a frenzied matchmaking dance swirls.

"Look—I don't believe in—" My voice breaks.

Louise leans forward, threatening. I think of all the children she must have terrorized.

"Well, I can see that! What *do* you believe in? Do you believe in anything?"

"Yes," I answer. "I believe in doing things. I believe in doing what you want."

"That's just plain selfishness!"

"No!" I cry. "It's better to live the way you want than to stifle yourself and blame it on someone else!"

Louise's eyes shoot gray hatred, trying to paralyze me. "You think the world could go on if we all lived like you—self-centered—promiscuous—living in sin—"

"There are no sins!" I shout. "Except deceiving yourself."

Louise shakes her head disgustedly.

I seize the indigo gown. "Look, she's wearing this. She always liked blue. I'll finish packing this stuff. You can go."

Exhaling contempt, Louise gazes down. "God help the world if you're our future. She deserved much better than you."

Her sticky steps recede, but I don't watch her go. I knead the plushy cloth between my fingers. Outside, the light has turned golden, and the outlines of the trees have softened. I flip the safety latches and push the window up, and a wave of sweet air rolls in. In the lot, Louise's motor growls. I pull out my phone.

"You have three new messages."

11:10 a.m. "This is Yankee Air calling for Carrie McFadden. We have your bag here at the Scranton Airport. We'll keep holding it until we hear from you. Please let us know what you'd like to do."

5:37 p.m. "Oye, Mala, I have had the most amazing day. Pero estoy hecho polvo. I am so tired, and I need a shower. Let me know where you are, so we can make dinner plans. Laura says there's a great steak place out in Waymart."

5:46 p.m. "Uh ... Carrie? This is Uwe ... uh ... Dr. Fischer. I was cleaning my car today, and I found your number. I wanted to see how you were doing, and ... uh ... I was chust wondering ... do you still have that sweatshirt?"

ACKNOWLEDGMENTS

I would like to thank the many people who helped make *Lacking in Substance* a better novel. I am grateful to Victor Anaya, Jimena Canales, Manuel Montoya, and Edna Suarez Díaz for their advice on Mexican and Mexican American language and culture. I thank Winfield Sale and Victor Faundez for their suggestions about cell biology. *Lacking in Substance* benefited from the critiques of my Emory Creative Writing colleagues, Jim Grimsley, Joseph Skibell, and Lynna Williams, who offered valuable thoughts on the novel's structure and style. I am indebted to the faculty and students of the 2008 Community of Writers at Squaw Valley Fiction Workshop: novelist Cecile Piñeda, poet Al Young, and student writers Robin Caton, Renée Christensen, Matthew Harrison, Joe Heinrich, Lee Kaplan, Eric Kael Kenny, Tana Maurer, Mark Maynard, Regina O'Melveny, Darcy Vebber, and Cynthia Walker. I would like to thank the friends who offered feedback on the story in terms of human psychology as well as writing quality: Christina Brandt, Lorraine Daston, Uljana Feest, Shlomit Finkelstein, Sander Gilman, Jim Goldenring, Diego Luis, Jesse Moskowitz, Jennifer Rohn, and Kelly Wilder. From all of these generous people, I have learned about life as well as writing, if one can ever separate the two.

The lyrics quoted and song titles mentioned in this novel were created by the following artists: Carlos Vives,

"Mi Consentida," EMI Latin/Virgin Records, 1999; Víctor Manuelle, "Tu Volverás," Sony Discos, 1996; Cuco Valoy, "Juliana, Qué Mala Eres," Putumayo World Music, 1995; La Sonora Dinamita, "Abajo las Suegras," Discos Fuentes Edimusica, 1999; and La Banda Gorda, "Aquí Pero Allá," MT & VI Records, 1999.

Finally, I am grateful to the hard-working people at iUniverse who have invested time improving this novel and making it available to readers: Check-In Coordinator Vinnia Alvarez; Editorial Services Associate Courtney Wallace; my superb line editor, Kelsey Adams; and Publishing Services Associate Reed Samuel.

Printed in the United States
By Bookmasters